Jonathan Buckley lives in Greenwich, London.
His first novel, *The Biography of Thomas Lang,*
was published in 1997.

by the same author

The Biography of Thomas Lang

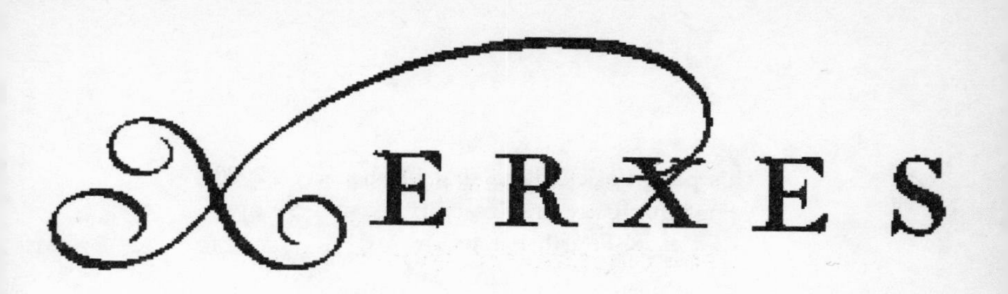

JONATHAN BUCKLEY

FOURTH ESTATE • *London*

This paperback edition first published in 2000
First published in Great Britain in 1999 by
Fourth Estate Limited
6 Salem Road
London W2 4BU
www.4thestate.co.uk

1 3 5 7 9 10 8 6 4 2

A catalogue record for this book is available from the British Library.

ISBN 1–85702–997–6

Typeset by Palimpsest Book Production Limited
Polmont, Stirlingshire
Printed in Great Britain by
Cox and Wyman, Reading

1.

This was the Paradise of Xerxes, here, at the farthest corner of the compound on the landward side, below our map-maker's cartouche.

Within the Paradise stood numerous pavilions, each of them roofed with brass and covered with buckskin on which the night sky was painted. Beside one of them there was a wall of jasper which sprayed a mist of water from fissures too fine to be seen. Elsewhere there were myrtle bushes cropped flat as table-tops and so dense that a man might sit on them; cypress avenues that the sun could never penetrate; fifty flower-beds, each of one colour and each different from all the rest; pavements of waxen porphyry which, when stepped upon, released jets of water perfumed with the essence of jasmine; bowers of lime and quince and pomegranate; a belvedere shaded by a web of gold filaments; fountains of glass and onyx and alabaster; rectangles of grass as soft as silken rugs; cisterns in which swam fish as big as babies, with gills like oyster shells. Crystal pipes, fastened to the branches of the citrus trees, chimed whenever a fruit fell or was plucked; clay flutes, hidden in the vines, made music at the weakest breeze. On one side of the Paradise stood a machine of tiny waterwheels that made a sound like the twittering of canaries. On the opposite side was the garden of the sea, planted with hard-leaved trees and crisp foliage through which the wind rushed with a noise like the falling of surf. Close to the gate of the Paradise, its entrance aligned with the gardens' portal, there was a labyrinth of laurel bushes, tended into the shape of three battling serpents. Somewhere in the vicinity of the labyrinth there was a model of the Paradise, and within that model there was another miniature Paradise, so small that an adult's thumb might cover it.

2.

In a stupor of tedium, August Ettlinger leans against the door of the hut that has become his home, and regards the sap that seeps from the faces of the logs he has hewn. The sticky beads resemble tiny garnets and carnelians, and the rings of the wood might be the rings of a roll of linen. He recalls a white cravat, fastened with a pin into which was set a fat red garnet; it looked like a spot of blood upon the wearer's throat.

Ettlinger presses a forefinger into the buds of sap on the uppermost log, commencing with the innermost. He leaves none intact. With a thumb he presses flat the small gluey stalactites on the underside. Raising his hand to his face he inhales the breezes of his homeland's forests. He strives to hear, against the rustling of the olive leaves, the remembered torrent near the village of Ettal. The corrugated path of the setting sun dissolves into the sea.

He enters his dwelling and passes through the inner door. In the second room is laid the pallet he has made from the crates in which his possessions were brought from the port. He lies down on the layered blankets that serve as his mattress, and lets his hands fall onto the sides of the pallet. The wood is burred with soft splinters, raised by the lethargic scratchings of his fingernails. Brushing his fingertips through the dust of the earthen floor, he stares at the spars and wattle above his head, and sees a Bavarian fresco of Apollo and Daphne. He remembers examining the painting while string music played, and struggles to quell a nostalgia for his former discontent. There is a lyrical quality to the unhappiness that is recalled by the silver of Apollo's lyre, the watery lime of Daphne's hand, the talcum-white of the painted clouds. And from this mood there proceeds the image of Helene von Davringhausen, standing in the garden of her father's house.

The shower had just ceased; the sun emerged clear but heatless, as if cleansed and chilled by the rain. Immense clouds lay on every portion of the horizon; they glared like the glaciers of the Alps, and were riven by crevasses with ice-blue walls. Bright droplets slipped from the leaves of the chestnut tree, which shone as if they were scales of glass. In the dark space underneath the branches, Helene crouched to raise a leaf from the grass, and turned it slowly, thoughtfully, on its stem. Ettlinger approached her and she smiled at him in a way that impressed upon him his irrelevance to whatever it was that occupied her.

This is perhaps not how it was, thinks Ettlinger: it is possible that her smile has acquired this quality only in memory. His hand tightens on the frame of his bed and a splinter pierces his skin. He rises, and returns to the outer room. He crosses to his desk and presses the dot of blood onto a sheet of paper, between the cypress avenues and the flower-beds.

3.

Ettlinger writes on boards of sea-warped pine. Above his makeshift desk is pinned a map created for him by a fisherman of the northern village, a man whose family first charted the bays and estuaries of the island some eight generations ago. The horns and maws of the coast are traced with a line as fine as a thread of black silk, and a wash of sky-blue ink follows the shore, deepening to indigo at the depths. The largest of the villages is marked as twelve blocks of sepia, on one of which stands the church, represented as a pediment and a cross upon a square. The quay is delineated by a sawtoothed indentation on the western side of the village. Of the settlement on the western coast, nothing at all is detailed: a darkening of an entire headland denotes it. Inland, columns of fractured triangles and freely drawn semicircles denote the mountains and foothills, but few accord with the terrain in which Ettlinger now lives. Placed randomly among the hills, minuscule oblongs represent the shepherds' huts. The ruins known as the Tower of Xerxes, or the Phoenician Castle, are shown by a wall of ochre bricks to the north of the plot of land that Ettlinger occupies, whereas in truth it lies to the south.

A picture hangs opposite the desk. It is an engraving of the portrait of Helene von Davringhausen by Karl Lizius, the original of which was last seen in 1848, the year the painting was destroyed, it is assumed, in the fire that gutted the home of Gotthard von Davringhausen, the subject's nephew. The early sun always strikes some part of the picture, and by now the printer's work has in places been bleached to the brink of invisibility. Yet the image has not disappeared. Most evenings, Ettlinger removes the picture from its hook, eases apart the frame to release its glass, and places the yellowing paper upon his desk, securing its margins with his inkpot and some books. With a pencil he makes good the damage the sun has wrought, strengthening the darkness of the hair of Helene von Davringhausen, repairing any break in the embroidery of her Turkish shawl, restoring the tones of her naked shoulder, freshening the points of light in the twisted cord of pearls about her neck, in the pearls of her headdress and in her eyes, where the reflection of the skylight that illuminated the studio of Karl Lizius can be seen.

On the desk lie two reams of paper, an ivory pencil holder, an ink drawing of a glass factory and a copy, closed, of the *Histories* of Herodotus, a gift from Johann Friedrich von Wolgast. Interleaved with its pages are numerous paper fillets, each covered with jottings erased, annotated and embellished so thoroughly and so minutely that even Ettlinger cannot read what is written on many of them. Protruding from the middle of the book, however, is a slip on which he has clearly noted: 'It was two o'clock. Two o'clock precisely.' And on another: 'J. F. von Wolgast – *in memoriam*.'

4.

This rise is where the emperor's poet first addressed us.

We had removed to this place at the approach of a storm from the sea, to watch the downpour engulf the Residence. Called upon to speak, the poet set his face in an expression of fury, an assumed dementia of inspiration. He raised an arm, fluttering his cochineal-dyed cloak, marshalling our gazes in the direction to which they were already turned.

'The river seethes behind the screen of rain,' he began. 'The trees drip like colanders. The herb garden is now all mud; it is a sheet of wet leather. The clouds advance like the shadow of night. Let us give ourselves to memory,' he enjoined us. Though he had not been there, he evoked for us the capital in the week of our departure. He recalled the marketplace, its smells of nutmeg and old meat, and the breezes that carried always the perfume of jasmine. He recalled the ammoniac reek of the animal pens. Enraptured by the beauty of his feelings, he went on talking until the storm expired, wafting sentences as if his voice were a fume, issuing from his mouth in beautiful curlicues.

5.

From the ramp below the Tower of Xerxes he observes the action of the wind. Out at sea, perhaps a mile distant, a battered sail dips towards the water and quickly rises erect again, like the motion of a butterfly's wing as it settles. The sea-surface imparts no sense of the water's motion; its waves resemble lines of salt crystals on a tray of dulled tin. Down the hill, where the track to the ruins emerges on the valley's side, the wind skims a layer from the friable earth; the dust flies up as a curtain that instantly tears apart and vanishes, like steam becoming dry air. A cyclone of dust enwraps the hut in which Ettlinger lives, collapses in a moment, and revives to shroud the walls once more with a coarse-grained mist. The olive tree in his garden flinches before the wind, swells again in the brief abatement, and flinches in another gust. Perfectly white clouds slither swiftly by, then seem to curdle at the horizon, turning to pewter.

Ettlinger ascends to the remnant of the gateway. Its lintel, he now knows, lies overgrown beside a barn in the environs of the western village. Towed there to be carved into a figure of Columbus, it has not been moved or worked on since the emigration, some ninety years past, of the only man then competent to sculpt it. Ettlinger seats himself atop the stump of the spiral staircase behind the larger of the broken jambs, and runs a finger along a fissure of the outer wall. It seems most likely that the crack was created by the levers with which the plunderers prised away the upper steps. One of these stones has become a capstan on the quayside; it was perhaps the one to which the boat that brought him here was tethered. Four more are said to have been built into the foundations of the lighthouse; another, according to the folklore of the port, has become the lintel of the doorway of the harbourmaster's house, where a rosette of plaster, surmounting the date of the harbourmaster's appointment, now masks the stolen stone.

He removes the notebook from his frock coat and checks the ruins against the plan he has sketched. To his left is the triangle of fallen columns, greener than the vegetation in which they lie, and beyond them the remnants of corridors that once converged on a chamber that is now obliterated. Straight ahead, behind the hummock of brick and thorns, are the octagonal foundations and the rectangle of what might have been a bath or a cistern, its lineaments clarified by the grass that has grown since last week's rain. Slightly to the right are the charred and sunken bowls, and farther across is the quadrangle defined by a single course of terracotta blocks, with the rim of what might have been a well-shaft in its centre. Beyond the six aged cypresses, at the farthest extent of the ruins, is the trench containing the skeletons of two horses. Across to the right, in the middle distance, connected to the principal site by a thread of scattered stones, rises the curved ridge of what perhaps was a stadium; the welt of compacted earth extends farther than is shown by Ettlinger's sketch, which he now amends with his ivory-handled pencil.

A lizard the size of Ettlinger's forefinger and striated with sulphurous yellow bands advances by short dashes across the pavement. Venomous snakes are said to breed among the ruins, but he has yet to see one. The wind agitates the moistureless stalks at his feet, and the sound they recall is the swish of stiffened fabric against a polished floor. He makes a note of the sound's character, and rises to walk over to the area adjacent to the drooping cypress trees, where the soil is seeded with smooth pieces of porphyry.

6.

A clock was striking in a room above him. It was precisely two o'clock when August Ettlinger, an hour after arriving at Nymphenburg, climbed the flight of steps on the westward side to admire the gardens. There was nothing in the sky but the sun, and on the brilliant stone of the façade the gilding glistened like a moisture sweated from the building. From the shadows of the banqueting-hall came a voice that explicated loudly the frescoes of the ceiling, where Flora received the homage of her nymphs and Apollo rode his chariot across a buttermilk dawn. From deep inside the hall a flautist expelled long, slow notes that seemed to waver under the heat. A young woman stepped out onto the terrace, and the sunlight through her parasol splashed her face with a pattern of rose petals; she turned to return to the company in the hall; a footman followed close behind, his thumbs tugging the frogging of his coat to loosen its fit. The flute ceased, and a flock of birds rose above the woods to the north; they resembled a paragraph of black script on blue paper.

For several minutes Ettlinger allowed his gaze to move back and forth along the paths and skip between the points of colour that the women's dresses applied to the lawns. Wolfgang von Klostermann hailed him from below; Ettlinger raised the hand that shielded his eyes, saluted the unseen caller, and returned to his survey of the land that stretched out towards the distant church tower of Pipping. He descended to the parterre and paused for a while beside the plinth of Mercury, his palms pressed flat against the hot stone, his thoughts on the work ahead. A path trailed off to the south. He followed it, and at its first bend he saw before him, walking alone, a young woman dressed in aquamarine silk. Her hair, wrought into coils at the crown and the sides of her face, gleamed like oiled slate, and the nape of her neck was crossed by a triple cord of pearls so bright they seemed to be made not of any mineral but of a distillate of the light.

She entered the Amalienburg and disappeared through the guests who thronged the doorway. Having eased a path through them, and failed to find her, Ettlinger perused the room he had come into. Mirrors were set into every wall, and each mirror was framed with silvered stucco and silver-painted carvings. From the cornice hung swags of silver flowers, below silver willows and vines, and nymphs and putti with bodies of silver. Arabesques of silver plaster obscured the walls with a calligraphy of ice. The room took the summer day and imposed upon it the atmosphere of midwinter morning.

A quartet was playing something by Mozart. On the left sat the cellist, a portly young man who played with a genial intensity, to whom the others appeared to look not so much for guidance as for reassurance that all was well with their performance. Beside him sat the viola player, perhaps the cellist's father; a tense and miserable demeanour creased his face, and whenever he raised his eyes from the page it seemed that his mind had attached itself to some new worry, though his musicianship was without fault. The pilot of the ensemble, the first violinist, was the youngest of the four; brisk and combative, he frowned throughout the duration of the piece, jabbing his bow across the strings as if asserting through his music an argument against his colleagues.

The second violinist – a tall man, the tallest of the four – conveyed in his posture a nonchalance quite at odds with the concentration of his partners. His legs were stretched straight in front of him, and were crossed at the ankle, while his upper body swayed slightly, incessantly, as though he sat on the deck of a boat that was rocking on a light swell. Whereas the other three were dressed wholly in black, this man wore a chestnut-coloured linen jacket and a white scarf wrapped tightly as a bandage around his throat. His hair, close-cropped and whiter even than the scarf, was so fine that the mere motion of his body caused it to stir, disclosing a scalp as pink as a new-born mouse. Seeing him from behind, seated, one might have taken him for a man aged sixty or seventy. His face, however, was that of a thirty-year-old. His pellucid, gentian-blue eyes were widely and deeply set beneath eyebrows that were femininely fine and had the colour of caramel. His skin was unblemished and pale as candle-wax, with a flush on the cheeks and the tips of his fingers that gave him the appearance of someone who had just stepped into a warm room on a frosty day. Presented placidly to his audience, his face bespoke youthful frankness and freshness. One feature, however, marred this image: a scar of empurpled flesh, which furrowed his left temple from an inch behind the angle of his eye to the upper cusp of his ear, like a groove gouged by a bloodied thumb across a head modelled in purest gesso.

The quartet concluded, the musicians exchanged a few words with each other. The second violinist, addressing the cellist, smiled, or rather formed an expression that involved a widening of his mouth, and showed teeth that were white and shockingly small, like those of a child. The cellist raised a hand as though to clap it upon the other's back, but stopped the motion an inch or so above the violinist's shoulder, as if his hand had come into contact with a carapace of air. As his three companions withdrew, the white-haired man prepared to perform a solo piece. He was adjusting the tuning when the young woman dressed in aquamarine re-entered from the door by which the three musicians had left. A party of four or five women of middling age detained her. She greeted each one, and detached herself from them as the violinist raised his bow. The music began; she halted behind Ettlinger. He introduced himself.

'Helene von Davringhausen,' the young woman replied, facing the violinist, who was playing some high-spirited Italian item. The composition was nothing but a succession of rapid scales and flurrying little melodies, yet in playing it the white-haired man was utterly changed from the character he had been but five minutes earlier. Whereas he had dispatched the complexities of Mozart with an uninterested facility, the elaborations of this Italian frivolity suffused him with a strange passion. Standing stiff-legged, he jerked his shoulders and arched his back as though resisting the pull of a halter tied about his neck. He mouthed words silently, he grimaced, he assumed the expression of a man indignant. His eyes convulsed shut, as if his scar were causing him intolerable pain. Little screeches came from his fingers as they sped along the strings; a tail of snapped hairs streamed from the bow as he flourished it above the strings. The violin worked at his throat like a feral cat he could not shake off.

Ettlinger looked away and was startled to see himself in the mirror opposite, his head cleft into misaligned quarters by the seams in the glass. At a break in the music he praised the performance of the quartet. Helene von Davringhausen turned towards him. Her eyes, so dark that there was no boundary between pupil and iris, regarded his face as if it were in no way associated with the remark he had just made, but were merely some aspect of the room's decoration. Nonplussed, he sought out his reflection through the bodies of the people then passing to the door, and was emboldened by his own accusing glance. The violinist resumed his spasms and flailings. So quietly that none but his companion might overhear, Ettlinger muttered: 'There is something unseemly in this.'

Helene von Davringhausen again looked at him, but this time her eyes engaged with his, to seek the thoughts that had preceded his utterance, or so it seemed. A slow lowering of her eyelids suggested she had settled upon some provisional judgement of him, but whether favourable or not it was impossible to tell. And then she smiled, and released the loop of satin that kept closed the fan she was carrying, which only now did Ettlinger notice. 'I must assume that this is the first occasion you have been called upon to admire this gentleman's skill?' she said.

'This is the first occasion on which I have found myself in the same room as this gentleman,' he replied. 'He is quite unknown to me.'

Helene von Davringhausen received this comment with a tilt of her head and an expression that might have signified the beginning of wonderment.

'Ought I to know him?' he asked.

She snapped open her fan, and inspected its design,

while asking herself, it appeared, if she were justified in being surprised by his ignorance.

'That is Johann Friedrich von Wolgast,' she replied, and one thing only was clear, and that was that she now intended to leave.

Hoping for elucidation, Ettlinger asked for and received permission to accompany her. Together they crossed the great parterre and strolled along a shaded path to the Pagodenburg lake, but Helene von Davringhausen offered nothing further concerning the violinist, and Ettlinger felt that to pursue the subject would be improper. They talked instead of the Mozart piece, of the extraordinary warmth of the season, of the landscaping of Nymphenburg and the ingenuities of its architecture. She said little more than was necessary to sustain their conversation, but later he would recall every word. As they walked alongside the canal, towards the Cascade, he told her about his work.

'I am building a chapel,' he said. She stopped at the water's edge and folded her arms in a manner he took as an encouragement to tell her all. 'It is a classical temple, a tempietto,' he continued, and told her about the circumstances of the commission and the travails of its gestation, until his attention was distracted by two young men who were watching them from across the canal. Helene von Davringhausen looked over her shoulder at them.

'Ah,' she sighed, 'my brothers.' She tapped Ettlinger's elbow with her fan, and they recommenced their walk towards the Cascade. 'Karl and Maximilian. By their rule I must be escorted wherever I venture.' Her brothers walked in parallel to them, maintaining their surveillance. 'Karl – the nearer – is a father of some five months' standing. He was always predisposed to pomposity, but he has become far worse since the birth of Gotthard. I too am now his child and am the object of his daily solicitude. I love him, as I love Maximilian, of course. But they are both ridiculous,' she concluded, waving to her brothers, both of whom acknowledged her greeting with a bow.

Ettlinger, disconcerted, turned his attention to a gardener who was trimming a tree with a pruning bill. Helene von Davringhausen worked her fan with such vigour that its breeze lifted the curls from her cheek. He glimpsed within the folds of the fabric a woman's naked back, a quiver of arrows, a rock, a dimpled knee. She quickly reversed the fan, looked at the side that had been displayed to him, and reversed it again. 'A pastoral-mythological invention by François Boucher,' she said, as if identifying something she had never seen before. 'I wield the most subtle needle in all Bavaria, I am told,' she went on, and laughed. 'I detest Boucher and his frolicsome girls, but I confess that I take some enjoyment from exposing this scene to my brothers.' She snapped the fan fully open, showing him furious Diana and the prone, pregnant Callisto. 'You are familiar with the tale?' she asked him. He confirmed that he knew it, but she allowed the subject to fall. Looking down the canal, she winced at the glare from the water, which the sun set glowing like a trough of molten metal.

They had come to the Cascade. Karl and Maximilian were approaching, but their sister ignored them for a minute more. Suspiciously, she stared at the palace, as if it were a tower from which her movements were being observed, and raised the furled fan to her right eye like a telescope. Directing it at her brothers, who were now somewhat less than fifty paces distant, she remarked in a singsong voice – 'The amiable boys are upon us, and so our conversation is ended. It has been enjoyable for me. Thank you.' Sternly she turned to him. 'My brothers have been to Rome. They have visited London and have negotiated with merchants in Marseille. And I' – she hesitated, turned about and pointed towards the horizon with her fan like a general indicating an enemy placement – 'and I have been given leave to travel all the way to Augsburg.' She repeated the city's name in a tone that was wearily incredulous. 'You see, the absurdity of it is that my brothers do not suspect how large the world is.' She lifted a dry worm-cast from the grass and rolled it in her palm; raising it to the level of her eyes, she inspected the little ball of soil as though it were the mechanism of a watch. 'Whereas for me the world grows larger every day.' A press of her forefinger pulverised the cast; in a long, steady breath she blew its powder from her hand, and with the last of that breath, murmured: 'My brothers.' The sensual, melancholic exhalation stirred in August Ettlinger something akin to astonishment, a feeling which he was later to recognise as the birth of love.

'And now,' said Helene, 'we must part. I should like you to meet Karl and Maximilian.' The brothers greeted Ettlinger as two defendants might greet an unsuccessful plaintiff some years after his lawsuit against them. Both were handsome and sturdy, and had eyes as powerfully dark as Helene's, but in the manner of both there was something uncertain.

In the case of the elder, his candid interrogation put Ettlinger in mind of an ambitious young officer recently promoted to a rank he suspects might be beyond his capabilities; with Maximilian there was a watchfulness to his gaze that suggested an essentially nervous disposition, an impression exacerbated by his habit of pausing for a second between sentences, as if to anticipate the reception of his utterance before proceeding. For five minutes or so they stood by the Cascade, as the brothers elicited piece by piece a summary of their sister's conversation with this unknown young man. Helene was then escorted by her brothers back along the canal, towards the building in which Ettlinger had met her.

Ettlinger retraced the route by which they had come to the Cascade, pausing at each place where they had paused. He spent some time, alone, at the artificial ruin of the Hermitage, listening to the drowsy sound of the string orchestra then playing on the palace steps. He departed from Nymphenburg having spoken to nobody after his separation from Helene.

A week later he received from Johann Friedrich von Wolgast an invitation to make use of his library. 'I believe you might find it instructive,' Wolgast wrote. 'It is a recreation of mine to give assistance to young scholars.'

7.

This is the seaward wall of the compound, where Cassandane, the emperor's third wife, used to walk. It was said that she had a chamber panelled with silver, where a maidservant once spied her naked, and that she had the girl set ablaze for the offence. She had eyes like malachite, and her hair had the grain of young oak.

One afternoon I saw her stride out towards the turret above the menagerie, then stop suddenly and look up, as if alarmed by a sound. I heard nothing, and I saw nothing in the region of the sky at which she continued to gaze for a minute or more. She was accompanied by her son, the grim and capricious Darius, who was born soon after our arrival, twelve years before. At the celebration of his eleventh birthday, he rode into the arena standing on the backs of two unsaddled horses. From a silk pavilion above the entrance to the arena, his father applauded the boy's prowess and beckoned him forward to receive a sword and sash. He clasped his son by the shoulders, and inspected him with wary deliberation, as though Darius were a fine statue presented to him by an ambassador of a hostile country.

8.

On the Friday of the first week of October in his twenty-sixth year, August Ettlinger approached the house of Johann Friedrich von Wolgast. In the shadow of the Residenz he stopped to extract Wolgast's invitation from his pocket. He recalled the wild spectacle of his playing, and the unfathomable face of Helene von Davringhausen as she stated Wolgast's name. He continued on his way, clenching the folded letter in his hand as a reluctant duellist might clutch his pistol.

A handsome linden obscured the façade of the

house. The building was of the same dimensions as its neighbours and distinguished solely by the peculiarity that, in the early hours of the afternoon, every shutter was closed but for a pair on the upper storey. Ettlinger surmised that this oddity might signify that his invitation had been revoked, and in this notion he found a momentary release from his apprehensiveness. Taking advantage of the respite, he raised the steel door-ring and let it fall. Instantaneously, as if he had been watching through a spyhole, a footman hauled open the heavy door and stood aside for Ettlinger to enter.

Ettlinger placed in the footman's free hand the letter in which he was granted permission to consult Wolgast's library; the footman thanked him and balanced the unopened letter on his open palm, as though its weight were the mark of its authenticity. Requesting Ettlinger to follow, he conducted his master's guest to the foot of a service staircase at the rear of the building, and led him to the first of the upper floors. The air of the staircase smelled faintly of mould and vinegar; patches of plaster had lifted from the wall in papery crusts.

A door opened from the staircase onto a landing that crossed the house and linked with the main stairway, a broad flight of polished stone steps. From the landing a door gave access to Wolgast's library, a room so capacious that Ettlinger could only think that somehow his sense of the building's arrangement had failed him, that he had been taken out of the house he had entered and into an adjoining, far grander one. The library was as large as the church of St Johann-Nepomuk.

Directly in front of him stood a steel armillary sphere supported by a figure of Atlas. Atop its axle was an openwork bronze cast of the Wolgast coat of arms, a black oak tree with a golden phoenix in its upper branches. On each side of the door a spiral staircase of filigree ironwork rose to a horseshoe-shaped gallery which, supported on volutes of cast iron, divided the bookshelves into two tiers. The floor gleamed like the parquet of a ballroom, reflecting the thermal windows that were cut into the walls above the shelves, and the four small square windows that punctuated the lower ranks of books. Grilles of brass wire, set within frames of cherrywood, dressed the dark leather spines with a scintillating veil. The motif of Wolgast's oak and phoenix was everywhere – in medallions on the ceiling, on roundels above the windows, on the massive lock of the library door, on the footman's shoes, on the hand-guard of the épée that hung from a cord behind the door.

'You will find that the tables have been prepared for you,' the footman informed him, his manner now suddenly so softened that he might have been a guardian addressing his orphaned charge. 'Should you require anything, please summon me thus.' He tugged a silk sash that hung beside the door, and with that he withdrew, leaving Ettlinger alone in the silent library.

Tentatively Ettlinger advanced to the centre of the library. On the nearer table had been placed a ream of paper, fat and fresh as a new loaf of bread. To one side of the ream was a case of pencils and pens, rulers of various lengths, a compass, a divider and a set-square; on the other a silver flask filled to its brim with ink, a silver casket of pounce and a pair of white cotton gloves.

Close by, the second table was covered entirely with precious books. Peering at the leather-encased volumes as if they were exotic animals slumbering under glass, he whispered to himself the titles that were embossed in gilt lettering on the bindings. Here was an edition of Alberti, issued in Italy in 1550; here the Aldine edition of Pietro Cataneo's *I quattro primi libri di architettura*; Scamozzi's *L'idea della architettura universale*; Serlio's *Tutti l'opere d'architettura*; Cesariano's 1521 edition of Vitruvius; the first edition, from the house of De'Franceschi, of Palladio's *I quattro libri dell'architettura*. He put on the gloves and, hooking a finger under a corner of each cover, revealed the title pages. The type was so clean and the paper so crisp that he might have been the only one to have opened these books since the day they left the bindery.

Eventually he lifted the Palladio and transferred it to the table at which it was intended he should work. He slowly turned the pages to admire the Villa Foscari, the Villa Pisani, the Palazzo Valmarana, the Palazzo Thiene, the church of Il Redentore, each delineated in its ideal landscape of perfect whiteness. He recited under his breath the names of the towns and villages where these buildings had been raised: Montagnana, Maser, Poiana Maggiore, Piombino Dese – names resonant and ultimate as Avalon, Monsalvat or Thule. He became aware of a pastoral fragrance in the air; wiping a finger across the grain of the table, he found that the wood seemed to have been treated with oil of vetiver.

In the course of the afternoon, Ettlinger jotted some

disjointed notes, copied inelegantly a few elevations and frequently rose from his place to inspect Wolgast's prodigious library. He discovered a case reserved for books on chemistry, another dedicated to German history, a third to theology, flanked by Roman law and cartography. The collection of architectural books appeared to extend from the floor to the upper windows. Ettlinger was contemplating this section when he was startled by the scrape of the latch. Believing that his encounter with Wolgast was now upon him, Ettlinger was paralysed by an upsurge of ambivalent emotion, in which were mixed an unaccountably intense fear of Wolgast and a sense of gratitude so strong that it might make him foolish if he did not compose himself at once. Before he could push back his chair, the footman was standing beside him, a twin-headed candlestick in his hand. Dusk was settling and Ettlinger had not noticed it.

'You must leave now, sir,' said the footman. 'I am to tell you that you are welcome to return on any day you wish, between the hours of noon and six o'clock.'

'And how should I thank my host?' asked Ettlinger.

'However you see fit,' came the reply, 'but it shall not be today.'

The footman led Ettlinger to the street by the way they had entered. On the stairs a pair of lamps had been lit; Ettlinger passed his hand through the lax spirals of black smoke that turned above the sooted bowls. Midway along the ground-floor corridor a light far off to his left caught his attention, and he spied Wolgast through an enfilade of doors, seated, his palms pressed to his brow. His immobility and posture suggested to Ettlinger the image of a man sitting for his own memorial effigy.

9.

This was the green quarry. As the first summer was beginning, a tremor of the earth caused the land to slip here, revealing a cleft of dark green rock. It was an extraordinary stone, mottled like compacted leaves and snow, and very hard. Within days the engineers were at work, drilling cores from the cliff, erecting sawbenches and lathes, diverting a stream to cool the blades. Ten plates of stone were sent to the Residence, where they became a wall of the atrium. They were washed each morning and polished with oiled hides, so that one's reflection moved across the surface of the wall as across a pool of viscous, leaf-clogged water.

Not long after the quarry was opened, the emperor ordered the architect Anysis to oversee a project of the emperor's own devising, an unwalled hall of one hundred columns, ranked in ten lines of ten, all to be fashioned from this marvellous stone. This thicket of columns was to have been built in the lee of the dunes on the western coast, but no more than a quarter of the hall was completed. Faultlines in the quarry made it difficult to cut flawless blocks; the stone blunted the sawblades faster than we could replace them; and the mass of the columns was such that it took a month or more to transport each one to the coast, and several days more to fix it in the soft ground.

Some of the columns are standing, though the wind has wrapped deep collars of sand around their bases. You can still see the lintel into which we carved the motto proposed by Anysis. It reads: 'The proportions of voices are the harmonies of the ear, as the proportions of measurements are the harmonies of the eye. They give pleasure to all, but are understood only by the student of causes.'

10.

The ball at the house of Ernst von Kreisel took place a little over five weeks after the day at Nymphenburg.

Ettlinger had been in Munich but a short time when he first heard mention of the Kreisel mansion, and its appearance in no way fell short of its reputation. The windows of its forecourt façade contained panes of glass that were the size of bed-sheets, and the light that fell from them was produced by Venetian chandeliers that seemed too heavy for any ceiling to bear. The main staircase, so broad and so gentle in its gradient that a carriage could have been driven up it, was covered by a newly-laid carpet of plush red wool, with a running dog pattern in gold along its edges. At the top of each flight, a stair-rod of ivory ran across the base of the riser, and on a mahogany table in the centre of the landing, angled so that anyone ascending was subject to its scrutiny, was placed a bust of Ernst von Kreisel's father, the redoubtable Klaus, to whose theories of strategy Clausewitz himself was said to have confessed his debt. The light on the staircase came not from chandeliers but from flambeaux held by gilded wooden archers; positioned at the turns in the banisters, they raised their torches like an honour guard. The air bore the perfume of jasmine.

When Ettlinger reached the top of the stairs, he

stopped for a moment beside the bust of Klaus von Kreisel, to listen to the music coming from the ballroom. It ceased, and was succeeded by a rustle of many skirts, a sound like sacks of seed emptied onto a floor. Someone called his name from the opposite side of the landing; he turned to see Leopold Meier, seated on a sofa, beckoning him from a small room that appeared to be lined with cases of garish faïence. Meier and Martin von Stein sat side by side underneath a pair of Italian vases that resembled some bizarre ceremonial headgear, like the crowns of Byzantine monarchs. A case of champagne served as Meier's footstool and there were glasses around the legs of the sofa, some empty, most not.

Keeping Meier and Stein company were three boys who were introduced by Stein as nephews of Kreisel – Wilhelm, aged twelve; Willibald, fifteen; and Werner, seventeen. It soon became evident that their presence was tolerated solely because it sanctioned the guests' presumptuous occupation of this room, for neither of Ettlinger's friends paid any attention to the trio of Kreisels, eagerly though the young men followed their bantering.

The bibulous Meier was in sardonic mood. 'The salon will next be in session three weeks hence, or so we hope. We await the word of Wolfgang, who intends to read us the opening canto of his epic.' Meier took a sip of his wine. 'He has assured me it will come to be seen as the *capolavoro* of his apprentice years. He has some fine phrases, and has been good enough to let me sample them.' He drained his glass. '"The lassitude of noon". We shall all be hearing those plangent words at our coming parliament. The only thing that Wolfgang has to decide is the subject to which to append them. The vainglorious Faust has been weighed in the balance and found wanting. When last I spoke to him, he had reduced his choice to three: "The Rout of Publius Quintilius Varus in the Teutoburg Forest", "The Death of Lord Byron at Missolonghi" and "Oberon's Convocation of the Fairies". I favour strongly the first, for I loathe the English and tales of the elfin brethren bore me senseless. To Wolfgang the sprites and pixies are the distillations of our national spirit, but to me they are nothing but ethereal nomads and hobbledehoys.' A smile of mischievous self-satisfaction spread across Meier's face.

'You must earn your superiority, Leopold,' Stein rejoined. 'We can at least be certain that Wolfgang will bring something for us to enjoy. His muse might not share your tastes, but she is regular in her attendance. What can we expect from you? More than another declaration of intent, we hope?'

Meier, blushing, grinned and poured himself more champagne. 'For you, August?' he asked, waving the bottle's neck in Ettlinger's direction. 'Yes, you are quite right Martin,' he continued, as he charged Ettlinger's glass. 'I am a master of the manifesto, but my talents should be exercised by more strenuous genres. I am open to all reasonable suggestions.'

'And what about you, August?' Stein asked. 'How does your project progress?'

'The design has been approved,' he replied. 'There are some finer points to finish, but in essence it is done. I await an estimate of the cost, and my patron's approval of that.'

'Doomed, then,' joked Meier, packing a pinch of tobacco into the bowl of a small meerschaum. 'Martin, have you thought what you might sing for our delight? No more Schubert, I beg of you. Our hearts cannot bear so much woe.'

As Stein responded, Ettlinger heard briefly a voice that might have been that of Helene von Davringhausen; a crescendo of violins superseded it immediately. Ettlinger excused himself, and went to verify what he had heard.

In the ballroom the chairs were arranged in two ranks on two sides of the open floor, flanking the door at one end and the low platform on which the orchestra was seated at the other. At once Ettlinger ascertained that Helene was not among the dancers and neither was she among the spectators occupying the nearer seats. From his place at the door he could not, however, discern the identity of every person seated in the rows close to the walls, and though there was no reason to expect Helene to be present, his failure to find her on his first survey of the ballroom instilled in him a certainty that she would be found among these hidden guests. Ettlinger moved across the ballroom behind the forward seats, his hands joined at his back, greeting with a respectful bow a succession of upturned and unrecognised faces. With every face that was not Helene's his anticipation of contentment faded further, giving way to the notion – as groundless and as deeply felt as his former certainty of success – that her absence was in some way a judgement of his conduct.

A waltz began, and Ettlinger saw Wolgast. On this occasion Wolgast was attired almost completely in black, but extravagantly so. The nap of his clothing flexed the reflected candle-light like the coat of a mole, and the polished leather of his shoes shone like dark water. His white satin cravat, rouched into dandyish folds, was secured by a silver pin, the head of which was a garnet of unusual size and clarity. He was partnering a woman whose face had something Slavic in the broadness of its structure and the paleness of her eyes and complexion, and was made particularly appealing by the expression of ingenuous amusement that seemed never to disappear from her eyes and mouth. Wolgast was talking to her as they danced, and his manner was one of quite incongruous seriousness. He would make a remark, his partner would smilingly reply with a word or two, no more, and Wolgast would quickly and severely scrutinise her face, as if it were a painting of dubious merit.

Wolgast's attitude at the conclusion of the dance was even more remarkable. With a languid extension of his arm he distanced himself from his partner and regarded her with an indiscreet gaze that seemed to focus initially on her neck, then travelled upwards to meet her eyes, whereupon there flitted across his face an expression such as one might have seen if only now had the chandeliers been lit to show him the woman with whom he had been dancing. He released her hand with a gesture of punctilious gallantry and the young woman turned her back on him. At this moment, Wolgast's volatile spirit underwent another alteration, for across his face there passed a look that could be described only as one of distraught contempt, a look that was erased in the second of its appearance, as if the presence of his fellow guests, having lapsed for an instant from Wolgast's consciousness, had once again been impressed upon him.

Ettlinger watched Wolgast approach a family who stood between the rows at the far end of the ballroom. The father greeted him and stepped out of his place beside his wife to present his sons and daughter to Wolgast, or so it appeared. There was now a torpid precision in Wolgast's movements and manner which, with the dullness that had settled on his eyes, reminded Ettlinger of the stupefied courtesy he had observed in the behaviour of the bereaved.

Unsettled and intending to depart, Ettlinger returned to his friends. Clamping his jaw in his hands, he simulated the symptoms of an acute neuralgia. Meier prescribed champagne, to no avail. Ettlinger apologised for his being so abruptly indisposed, and promised to attend the forthcoming meeting of Wolfgang von Klostermann's salon.

He passed the entrance to the ballroom and was about to ask for his coat to be brought when he came upon Stein's brother, Clemens, who insisted that he make the acquaintance of the young woman next to whom he was standing. Having effected the introduction, Clemens von Stein hurried away, leaving Ettlinger and Pierangela Maddalena Cempini at the head of the stairs. Pierangela Maddalena was born in Verona, Ettlinger learned as soon as Clemens had departed, and she was born on the first day of the century – the first minute, her lamented mother told her. 'Have you ever visited my city?' she asked.

'No, I have not, I regret to say,' Ettlinger replied. His admission prompted Pierangela Maddalena to purse her lips in sympathy. Her mother's family, she told him, could be traced back beyond the time of Dante, who had once been in the employ of 'the famous Scaligers of Verona'. These ancient forebears were fervent Ghibellines, and so it could be said that Pierangela Maddalena Cempini had the German spirit in her blood. The taciturnity of her audience did not deter her from providing him with a synopsis of her family's fortunes in the centuries that had passed since the lifetime of Dante, and Ettlinger could not muster the will to intervene. Her narrative slipped by him as if it were the life story of her favourite pet that she was relating. At last she arrived at the present, with her arrival in Munich six months previously in the wake of her father, an amateur historian with time on his hands.

'So I came to this strange place,' she was saying when Wolgast passed in front of them, talking to the woman with whom he had been dancing.

Without hesitating in his descent of the stairs, Wolgast turned to look up at Ettlinger and Pierangela Maddalena Cempini and, as he returned his attention to his own companion, his lips momentarily formed a smirk – at whose appearance or behaviour, it was impossible to tell.

'Might you know who that young woman is?' Ettlinger asked.

'I think I do,' Pierangela Maddalena Cempini replied. 'I believe her name is Josepha Heldt. She is some magistrate's daughter. I was told she is a musician, though what she plays I forget. And who is that ugly man?' she in turn asked.

'That is Johann Friedrich von Wolgast,' he replied, and in the next instant he realised that he had repeated the words Helene had spoken to him in the Amalienburg. This coincidence so diverted him that he did not hear what he was being asked.

'Who is Johann Friedrich von Wolgast?' repeated Pierangela Maddalena Cempini.

'I'm afraid I know nothing but his name,' Ettlinger replied, and was gratified to see that his response instantaneously convinced Pierangela Maddalena Cempini that he was a bore who should be abandoned as soon as possible. He soon furnished her with an opportunity to seek more stimulating company. A minute later he left the Kreisel house, wondering what answer he would have received had he pursued that question with Helene von Davringhausen.

11.

Here is where Tigranes lived. This was his herb garden, and this the trough in which he would bleach the linens that were the emblem of the esteem in which for a time he was held.

His elevation came about through an accident that befell the emperor's nephew, the son of Bardiya, at a festival on the anniversary of our landing. Two dancers, in mock combat, brought their wooden swords together with great force; a splinter from one of the blades flew into the ring of spectators on the edge of the stage; it struck the emperor's nephew, piercing the tissue above his left eye. He was carried to a windowless room and there he remained, unconscious, the splinter still in place, while the physicians pondered.

Fearful of the consequences of failure, the physicians did

nothing but pray that their inactivity would suffice. It did not. On the third day the boy's skin grew grey, and he lay lifeless against the bolsters, his mouth ajar. Still not one of the physicians could bring himself to act, though they knew that all would suffer in some way if they allowed the emperor's nephew to die.

On the third night the boy's breathing became deep and irregular, and the physicians withdrew to confer. They left Tigranes, an apprentice to one of their number, to sit on watch. While they were out of the room, the emperor's nephew, seeming still to sleep, slid his hand across the bedding to touch the shoulder of his attendant. Terror-struck, Tigranes took the boy's hand. The dying boy returned his grip with far greater strength and pulled Tigranes towards him, until their faces almost touched. The good eye opened and stared vehemently at Tigranes, who could only think that he had been taken for the cause of the injury. Yet the boy then smiled as he rolled his head to place his cheek against their hands. His fingers tightened. Tigranes, not thinking what he was doing, raised his free hand to take hold of the splinter. Swiftly, as if taking a quill from a pot of ink, Tigranes extracted it from the cap of pus that covered the injured eye. The boy fell back, but there was no issue of blood. Tigranes cradled the boy's head, and washed the wound before the physicians returned.

The emperor's nephew lived, and Tigranes was installed in one of the finest suites in the Residence. For a year the name of Tigranes continued to thrive on the memory of the miraculous recovery, a memory sustained not by the author of the event but by the emperor's nephew, whose prowess in archery was born with the destruction of his eye. Every morning, in the forecourt of the Residence, the boy fired arrows into targets no bigger than his wound.

Then came the day on which Cassandane, while gathering poppies from the field beyond the stadium, disturbed a snake that lay basking amid the stems and was poisoned by its bite.

The guidance of the physicians at first prevailed. A poultice was placed upon the wound, and seemed to arrest its decay for a while. To cause vomiting and expel the venom, thirty berries of wild sesame were ground into a potion; when she worsened, a more virulent tincture of pear and garlic was prepared, and blood was let from her arm. Still Cassandane worsened. She was placed on a couch on the roof of the emperor's chambers to let the balm of the sun do its work, but her arm now swelled to the thickness of her waist. To assuage her fever, an elixir was compounded of sumach, purslane seed and pomegranate juice. Her body was smeared with mercury paste, oil of mastic, black hellebore, galbanum, orris root, asafetida and horse fat. We immersed her in water so cold it made our hands turn grey as we settled her into the pool. On the fifth day her skin blackened and split like a seed pod, revealing flesh that had turned the colour of mustard. Tigranes was at last summoned to sit with Cassandane, for the corruption of her body was such that his agency was the only possible means of reversing it. Cassandane died that night.

It was to no avail that Tigranes argued it to be the grossest impiety to impute to any man the power to summon the aid of the divine powers at any time he chose. Cassandane's hair was cut from her head by the physicians, and was brought to the emperor. He made from it a rope, with which the physicians and Tigranes were hanged in the hour in which the body of Cassandane was placed on her catafalque.

12.

Martin von Stein began the evening, accompanying himself at Klostermann's new piano. The song he chose was a Schubert setting of a poem by Mayrhofer, the announcement of which was greeted by Meier with a groan. Meier poured himself a glass of brandy and passed one to Ettlinger, who was seated beside him on Klostermann's divan. 'You may need this,' said Meier, and he set his face into an expression of humble concentration.

Stein's song could not have better suited the quality of his tenor, the timbre of which was always suggestive of fortitude and wistfulness combined. By the second verse they were all listening intently, even Meier, whose facetiousness had, it appeared, been annulled by the veracity of Stein's performance. Stein sang the song twice, at the request of Ettlinger, for whom a poignant congruity had arisen between the atmosphere of Schubert's music and his memories of Nymphenburg.

'Enough,' said Meier at the final note, rising from the divan. 'Do not exhaust our goodwill.' He handed a glass to Stein. '"I can find no happiness on earth"? Not one of us past thirty, but Martin would make hopeless cases of us all. I, for one, must decline membership of your brotherhood of valetudinarians.'

Annoyed by Meier's goading, Stein closed the piano and sullenly declined to complete the modest programme he had planned. Klostermann, sorting the pages of his manuscript on the arm of his chair, sipped a beaker of water in readiness for his recital. Then, having explained his choice of subject, he began his reading of the completed portion of "Hermann, or The Rout of Varus in the Teutoburg Forest". The phrase that Meier had told them to expect in fact did not appear in either of the five-hundred-line cantos, but in all other respects the poem was much as Ettlinger had anticipated for the past half-year – thoroughly earnest, sporadically felicitous and heroically prolix. Scenes of decadence, ostentation and cruelty filled the first canto, in which Klostermann dealt with the career of Varus in Africa and the Levant. Intimations of imminent reversal became frequent as the posting to Germany loomed, and with the second part the pace quickened, reaching its sustained climax with the summer of AD9. The catastrophe was heralded by a glut of tenebrous and crepuscular adjectives, strewn about the poem as thickly as the Teutoburg battlefield was soon to be strewn with bodies. The brave Hermann was raised before them as a veritable Green Man of the forests, and his wily manoeuvres wound about the legions of Varus as tightly as ivy around a rotten stump. Flocks of German javelins obscured the sun; fasces and Roman eagles were swallowed in the mire as the invaders blundered into ineluctable swamps; breastplates lay covered by shattered branches of oak. The fragment broke off at the close of the battle's second day. Overweening Varus faced his ruin and the triumph of 'the pitiless north'.

Meier, inebriated well before the thousandth line was

gained, approved of what he had heard. 'Evocative,' he judged it. 'I endeavoured to maintain my scepticism, but I could not. Like the hapless Varus I was disarmed.'

Stein commended Klostermann's efforts with no qualification and shook his hand. He then turned to Meier: 'Now, Leopold, will you break your cover, or has your courage failed?'

Raising an appeasing hand, Meier fortified himself with one last gulp of brandy. He took his manuscript from under the divan, removed a small portfolio from his satchel and squared the pages within its cover. He squinted at his handwriting, seeming to reconsider the merits of proceeding, and then, planting his fingertips on the uppermost sheet, explained that what he was about to read was a draft of an allegory set in the north of England. There were parallels with Dante's *Inferno*, he continued. 'A tour of nine factories, a parade of the avaricious, the violent and the fraudulent . . .'

'The exegesis can come later,' Stein interjected. 'Please – the text.'

Turning to the third or fourth page, Meier read his description of the foundry owner, the reincarnation of Charon, a man 'with eyes of burning coal' who turned the ring on his finger as he assigned the tasks to his benighted employees. With a disgruntled fidget, Meier forsook the ogre in favour of a second individual from the company of the damned – Geryon's equivalent, a smiling manufacturer who swindled his suppliers and loaned money at interest to his own family. From there Meier skipped back and forth through his poem, alighting briefly on a miscellany of malign personalities, until, downhearted, he closed his manuscript in mid-sentence.

The ingenuity of the allegory was praised by Klostermann, who courteously contrived to devise half a dozen ways of paraphrasing a single observation – that Meier evidently knew his Dante intimately. Stein, eschewing all tact, objected to the 'lurid and pedantic details' with which he had peppered his creation, and impugned Meier's geography: 'I believe you will find that the route from Manchester to Leeds, far from resembling your continuous vale of factories and suffering humanity, in fact encompasses some of the nation's most entrancing countryside.' In conclusion, Stein said, it appeared that the writer was less familiar with the terrain of England than the venerable Florentine had been with the pits of hell. Meier bowed in acceptance of the criticism, his right hand pressed over his heart; he would not meet Stein's gaze.

Ettlinger had nothing to say, for he had not so much listened to the reading as overheard parts of it, his attention having promptly been stolen from the poem by the portfolio within which Meier held its pages. The portfolio itself was nothing but a rectangle of thick card, folded along its shorter axis and threaded with a black ribbon, but stuck to its front was a picture that Ettlinger found engrossing. It was an ink drawing of a valley with a forge in its depths, partly obscured by an enormous beech in the foreground. Streaks and spots of watercolour enhanced the image: a wash of grey cloud above the forge, a spill of yolky yellow on the horizon, a dab of infernal scarlet in the luxuriant, silvered greenery of the beech's leaves.

'That scene,' he asked Meier, 'did you draw it?'

Meier held the portfolio at arm's length in front of him, and gave the picture an appreciative inspection. 'No,' he answered. 'I have no hidden talents.' Slipping out the manuscript, he passed the portfolio to Ettlinger. 'It was given to me by Maximilian von Davringhausen.'

'You know Maximilian?' asked Ettlinger.

'Oh yes,' replied Stein. 'Not well, but we know him.'

'It was made by his sister,' continued Meier, as though Stein had not uttered a word.

'Perhaps we might invite him again?' Klostermann suggested.

'Perhaps we might invite his sister?' added Meier, reviving his spirits with a lubricious grin.

Ettlinger was both embarrassed and angered, and further embarrassed by his anger, but none of his companions appeared to notice his blushing. He requested Stein to bring their evening to an harmonious ending, and Stein obliged with one of Schubert's settings of Goethe.

'A silent peace descends upon me, I know not how,' his song concluded. Meier sat through it with his face frozen in a rictus of simulated happiness.

13.

Here, on the grassy plain of the southern headland, was the great equestrian field, where we gathered on the anniversary of the defeat at Urmia.

The field was bisected by a broad trench that represented

the defile in which our infantry, pursuing what they took to be a vanguard in flight, were entrapped and swept away by the mercenary horsemen. The ceremony commenced at noon. In one broad front at the southern end of the field the horsemen waited, as the infantry began its march from the gate. Caparisons of velvet, in gold and vermilion, draped the horses' backs, and their cruppers, shaved into patterns of diamonds and bands, gleamed brightly in the high sun. The footsoldiers, clad in white, advanced with their heads lowered and arms held straight by their sides, as if encumbered by invisible cords. On each side, a single rush blade, stiffened with saline, was the only weapon carried.

In the base of the trench, the lines of the infantry meshed with the lines of the cavalry. Moving at walking pace, the horses brushed against the shoulders of the walking men as gently as courtly dancers. No hand was raised, and no animal broke from its plotted course. Rank by rank the footsoldiers raised their arms, sank to their knees and toppled forward, and the horses swayed slowly up the slope and out onto the upper part of the field, where they turned to repeat their pass through the defile. The infantrymen opened their mouths to declaim the curse the emperor's poet had written for them. From the emperor's podium the sound seemed not to come from their bodies but rather to be uttered by the air on their behalf, and the movements of the battle appeared as the motion of the tides.

14.

On his second visit to Wolgast's library, two weeks

after the first, Ettlinger found the tables in exactly the state he had left them in, and he was left to continue his studies undistracted until six o'clock, when the same footman escorted him to the street door by the same route as they had taken on the first visit. This time, however, there was no sighting of Wolgast, for every door on the lower corridor was closed.

A week later Ettlinger returned to the library, and again it appeared that nothing had been disturbed since he had risen from his chair: the volume of Palladio sat upon the Vitruvius at exactly the same angle; the casket of pounce still occupied the wedge of space between the untouched ream and the treatise of Leon Battista Alberti. But things had been added to the tables' array. A block of wove paper had been left by the pens, along with lozenges of watercolours in a ceramic tray, two jars of water, a sheaf of brushes and a cotton rag. Underneath the compass and rulers an unsealed envelope had been inserted; on it was written Ettlinger's name.

The envelope contained a tiny brass key and a piece of paper on which was written a message in a script so tangled with flourishes and dashes that it was several minutes before Ettlinger could be certain of the text. 'I am appreciative of the respect with which you have conducted yourself,' it began. 'I had been led to expect nothing different of you – and, after all, such respect is the entitlement of these treasures – you are – I feel – a young man in whom trust can be placed. In acknowledgment of this, I herewith enclose the key to my kingdom of paper – it fits the lock of every case. I ask you to observe the hours that I have prescribed for you – and of course I must insist that no book ever be removed from here. Within these constraints – which are not, I think, exigent – you are free to make what use of my library you wish.'

That afternoon Ettlinger explored Wolgast's collection. In one bookcase he found several other translations of Vitruvius, editions of Palladio in various languages, and a plenitude of obscure Italians. The adjacent case contained priceless editions of all the great French treatises, from Philibert de l'Orme's *Architecture* to Laugier's *Essai*. Close by there was a shelf of English books, where pristine examples of Gibbs, Ware and Chambers were filed. Wolgast even owned a manuscript by Lord Burlington. Most thrilling, however, was an album of sumptuous French watercolours. Ettlinger marvelled at the Roman forum as depicted by Auguste-Jean-Marie Guénepin, where every moulding of the triumphal arches was defined by shadows as crisp as those thrown onto the sheet that Ettlinger held open. Inspired by a spirit of emulation, he gave the last two hours to watercolour copies and departed dissatisfied with himself.

The following day Ettlinger arrived at the library at the earliest permissible time, and immersed himself straight away in a study for the elevation of his temple. He was replacing a book in the section devoted to Athenian antiquities when the footman entered, bearing a summons from Wolgast, who asked him to bring his portfolio.

Wolgast was seated at a bureau in a sweltering little chamber on the same storey as the library, beside a window that streamed with droplets of water. Seeming not to hear Ettlinger and the footman enter, he slowly creased and sealed the letter he had been writing. A high collar and foulard formed a plinth for his head, which he held motionless while his hands completed their business. Ettlinger noticed that Wolgast had applied some oil to his hair, which was teased into a fringe of tiny waves at his temple, and that the skin of his cheek had a granular appearance, as though dusted with powder. His jacket was tailored from a black velvet that had a layer of crimson worked deep in the material, so that when his arm stretched to return the ink-pot to its niche, the action made flashes of red appear in the folds of the fabric, like a glow from fanned embers.

Saying nothing, Wolgast rose and pointed to a stool tucked under a small square table set opposite the tile-oven. He lifted the chair from the bureau, placed it on the other side of the table and sat down again. Wolgast prolonged the silence, crossing his arms as if he were contemplating how he might broach a delicate subject. He directed his gaze at the empty table-top; to diminish his discomfort, Ettlinger did the same. To anyone standing at the door they would have resembled a pair of chess players contemplating their moves on a phantom board. A catch in Wolgast's breath made Ettlinger look up, but Wolgast's impassive face remained downturned. Ettlinger scrutinised the figure seated across the table – the marmoreal ridge of the nose; the hands, so white that at first glance one might think they were clad in gloves; the scar now less inflamed than it had appeared at Nymphenburg. He looked closely at the flesh in the trough of the scar and noted that it was cross-hatched with scratches, like the first formations of a skin of ice.

At last Wolgast spoke, in a voice like the murmur a solitary reader might make over a letter that brings saddening news.

'Tell me, have these days been profitable?'

'More than I can say, sir,' Ettlinger replied.

'And what have you been reading?' asked Wolgast, his manner brightening.

In answer Ettlinger opened the notebook in which he had recorded all the books he had consulted in Wolgast's library, and began to recite the list.

Wolgast took the notebook from him, examined the page and closed the book. His gaze fell upon Ettlinger. Slowly the pale lashes were lowered over the beautiful blank blue eyes, as if operated by clockwork, and were as slowly raised again.

'So you have compiled an inventory,' said Wolgast. 'It is to be hoped that this does not represent the total yield of your hours in my house.' He put an index finger to his lower lip. 'No, I know that there is more than this,' he continued and placed both hands palm upwards on the table to receive whatever Ettlinger had to offer.

Ettlinger untied his portfolio and extracted from it, one by one, the sheets of watercolours and pencil drawings. Wolgast twisted in his chair to angle the paper into the window's weakening light. He made no comment as he scanned the sheets in regular succession, putting down a drawing with his left hand as he picked up the next with his right. Ettlinger watched the pendulum motion of his eyes, which appeared to be enacting a parody of the act of reading.

But Wolgast was reading, and with close attention. 'I would make just one criticism,' he said when he had finished, patting the papers into a neat pile. 'What you have shown me bespeaks a far from common skill, but I must draw your attention to a misapprehension.' Wolgast withdrew a watercolour of the Parthenon. 'This is very fine, very uplifting, very chaste. But it is a mistake.' His voice now acquired a tone both paternal and pedagogical. 'The obsession with hygiene was a Roman invention, you know. Gaudiness and bawdiness are as much of the essence of ancient Greece as are geometry and Plato. This spiritual whiteness is but a trick of time.' With his fingertips he pushed the sheets towards Ettlinger. 'Perhaps, nonetheless, your policy is the right one. We must write our own histories if we are to write our own futures.' Wolgast paused, his lips slightly apart, as if about to phrase another, similar thought, but suddenly his mouth contracted and tensed, as though at a bitter taste, and the subject was gone.

'I have taken an interest in you,' he resumed. 'I am happy for you to continue your studies here. Perhaps I might see the inauguration of your temple,' he concluded, and smiled tepidly – not, it seemed, at Ettlinger, but at some corollary of his own remark.

Wolgast extended his hand. Ettlinger took it and recoiled inwardly, for it was like taking a claw of warmed wood.

15.

The shadow of Ettlinger's body lies in the sand like a plate of battered black iron. He scans the shadeless strand between the cliffs and the sea and scowls against the light off the water, a light so intense that it seems as if spheres of mercury are trembling in the space between his eyes and the sea. Yet again he recalls the light reflected by the canal at Nymphenburg and tries to revive the sense of immanence that the recollection of it has often brought. He remembers only the sight of the canal by which he walked with Helene that afternoon, and feels nothing but the discomfort of staring into the glare.

He makes blinkers of his hands and looks across the bay. A fishing boat, anchored in the mouth of the estuary, vibrates like a fly on a spider's web. A flock of gulls billows from the sea surface, sprays outward, falls back and settles again in the very same place, with a faint rustle of feathers. Ettlinger stoops to take a scoop of hot sand into the funnel of his hand, and lets it flow away through the loop of his curled little finger. A strengthless gust, a mere pulse of air, widens the stream as it flows to the ground. He commits to memory the words for the shape that it makes: a horse's tail of sand.

Ettlinger removes his shoes and digs his bare feet into the ground until they find a seam of cooler sand. In a moment the coolness has gone. He removes his shirt; the fabric comes off his skin with the sound of a sheet of paper lifted from a printer's stone. He strips naked and lowers himself onto the sand. It sears the skin along his spine and across his shoulders, but almost at once the temperature of his body establishes a balance with what it lies upon. The boundary of his flesh dissolves in the sand.

Sweat stings his eyelids and makes a crystalline haze of the sky. Ettlinger closes his eyes. The air smells of washed stone floors and rotted wood. The sound of the waves is the voice of a calmly relentless chorus, insisting that he remember everything that brought him here. He sees the face of Wolgast on the windowsill of the library, blowing droplets of water onto the glass. As if glimpsed in a hurrying crowd, the figures appear and vanish. Helene's lips form a kissing mouth and blow dust from her hand; her eyes survey snow-covered fields from the bench of an inn; the shadow of Wolgast, thrown by a torch's flame, flits across a cellar wall; a frightened young woman walks by, her eyes downcast; Maximilian von Davringhausen surreptitiously throws an admiring glance at Wolgast; a sundered head lolls on a table in Wolgast's sanctuary; a soft arch of painted flesh fills the entire field of his vision. Multifarious as the thin little waves that crimp themselves onto the glossy foreshore, they rush into his mind and collapse. The pursuit of meaning within them seems as pointless to Ettlinger as listening for a music in the never-ending whispering of the water.

The sound of the sea is the same as the hush of the dune grasses at the caress of the rising breeze. A coolness moves over his body like a skein of trailing silk, and then the heat lays its blanket on him, weighing him down into sleep. He dreams that he stands in a room that is a bare and perfect cube, with a ceiling he could touch if he stretched to his greatest reach. The room has no windows and no lamps, and yet is filled with the sort of light that would fill a green canvas tent when the sun is at its zenith. Though he does not enter the room, all at once Johann Friedrich von Wolgast is in it. Ettlinger stands with his back pressed flat to the wall. Wolgast places a hand on each side of Ettlinger's head and stiffens his arms, caging Ettlinger against the wall. Wolgast is so angry that every part of his body quivers like a kettle of boiling water; the whites of his furious eyes are crackled with zigzags of blood vessels. Wolgast's voice, however, is sweet and insinuating. With the voice of a blackmailer he hints at his knowledge of an offence that Ettlinger is indeed certain has been committed, but by Wolgast himself. Ettlinger tries to reply but cannot, for a membrane, thin as a mayfly's wing, has grown across his lips. Wolgast extends a finger and prods the elastic skin; he smiles as if his action has confirmed something.

Ettlinger awakes in bewilderment, choking. His skin is wet and scalded. He stands up, half-clad in a coat of sand, and runs down the beach. He runs on, his shins splitting the water, his thighs churning it, until it drags him to a stop. A sudden current, flowing obliquely to the shore, buckles his legs. He succumbs to it and sinks to his knees. In his throat there is a bitterness of brine; the back of his scalp seethes upon contact with the water. He leaps up and flings himself forward, breasting the gentle swells, then ducks his head and dives under. In an instant his body feels brittle and hollow, as if he had been transformed into a vessel of glass. He draws his arms to his sides and tumbles slowly, through thick silence. Couched on the soft sand of the shallows, curled amid shells and ribbons of weed, he lies motionless for as long as his breath allows. Gasping into the sea, he rises in the roaring turbulence of his breath, breaking into the blinding sunlight with the violence of a new-born.

Bracing his legs against the current, he regards the empty sea and the threadbare scrub on the parched earth, all of it colourless in the hot light. Over the horizon is another parched hill on which his hut is cracking in the heat. He looks down at his legs; under the water they are pallid as a dead man's. A shoal of tiny brown fish swerves in a single body around his waist. The gulls lift from the sea like a sheet of white cotton whipped from a table-top.

He hears Helene's voice again, saying, 'I did not make a mistake,' but with a voice that is emotionless, as if her imagined self were but quoting the woman of whom she is the ghost. Conscious that grief is within him, yet at this moment disengaged from it, Ettlinger wipes the salt water from his face, wiping the edges of his palms like strigils across his skin. He imagines himself as the bronze figure of a weeping man, the centrepiece of a fountain in a courtyard of the Residence of Xerxes.

16.

This is the place where we saw the first signs of the end.

A squalling wind battled with the sails all morning, turning from seaward to landward within the space of a minute. It cracked the ropes against the mast and flung gobbets of salt water onto the quay. When it ceased, the sea lapsed into drab placidity, and for the rest of the daylight hours the sun seemed constantly to be gathering the clouds about itself. As it declined towards the horizon so the caravans of cloud moved with the sun down the sky, keeping us in shadow until the final episode of sunset, when briefly the half-disc appeared unmasked on the lip of the gelid sea.

We intended to begin fishing at dusk among the islets of this estuary, where the river of the Valley of the Sun, swollen by its lowland tributaries, obliterates itself in the ocean. For three days it had rained in the mountains, and the rising waters had raked the vegetation from their banks. Uprooted trees and vast knots of grass drifted through the channels of the estuary, churning on the surface of the rust-tinged water. Though the catch would be plentiful, we were obliged to sail on, for our net would have tangled on the debris of the rivers. We rounded the headland and crossed the wide-mouthed bay to the north, edging between the twinned stacks we knew as the Portals before casting our net. When not a glimmer of light remained we dropped anchor and pulled in the paltry catch. We ate together, assigned watches, and made our beds on the open deck.

At the fifth hour of the night I was roused from my sleep. The man who had woken me was pointing across the water, where low in the sky could be seen the flickering of what seemed to be a large star. Our companions were summoned, and soon we distinguished that it was not a single point but rather a crescent, a wavering curve of gold that was both thickening and rising infinitesimally as we watched. We raised the anchor, unfurled the canvas and began to sail towards the line of light. Within an hour it became plain we were approaching a fire that was advancing up a hillside on the mainland. The sun was rising when we anchored but the air was hot and was filled with the roar from the burning land and the spit and crack of the trees.

Smoke drifted across the shallows, mixing the smells of resin and ash with the stink of the seawrack that lay like old nets on the margin of the water. Nothing green remained. On the flank of the hill, the grass had become a silver fur marked with the greasy black scribbles of roots and saplings. A ball of smoke was snarled on the branches of a charcoal bush, like a tuft of grey fleece on a thorn.

We walked round the foot of the hill, and as we crested a ridge we noticed a solitary cedar just below the line of the fire's limit. It was a fine tree, with russet bark and boughs that curved like upturned hands. Metal objects sparkled amid its foliage, and as we drew closer we saw that shields and short scabbards had been tied to the branches. All around the trunk the weapons had been arranged, all of them bronze and polished as if to impress us with their gleam. I detached one of the shields from the cord by which it hung: its boss was chased with the representation of a horseman, on whose arm was fastened a shield of the selfsame shape. On the scabbards were images of footsoldiers brandishing daggers, engraved as childish stick-men with circles for heads and circular eyes. I reached for one, and as I did so a splash of blood appeared on my arm.

I looked up into the shadows of the cedar. A man was crucified in the midst of the upper branches, each hand and each foot transfixed by a dagger. I climbed up to him. Around his neck hung a shield; runnels of blood streamed out from underneath it. I lifted the shield and the heart flopped out of the open chest.

We laid the body under the cedar's cover. He was like no man we had ever seen. Shorter than the shortest of us and almost completely covered with coarse flaxen hair, he resembled a beast that went on four legs more than he resembled a man. A collar of muscle spread over his shoulders like the muscles of a fighting dog; his forearms were as broad as his calves; each thigh was almost as thick as his waist. We stood over him for a while, and none of us spoke. In a silence of foreboding we withdrew a distance from the inexplicable body. The sacrificed man lay on his back under the cedar's boughs, his stiffened arms upraised, as if imploring to be restored to the place where we had found him.

17.

In mid-November, shortly after Ettlinger's first conversation with Wolgast, a costumed party was held at the house of Konrad von Laun, a cousin of Wolfgang von Klostermann. The invitation enjoined every guest to attend in the person of some figure of the Renaissance period. Ettlinger, reluctant to make himself appear foolish in the manner prescribed by the host, maintained his resistance in the face of Klostermann's entreaties, until informed that Martin von Stein had prevailed upon Maximilian von Davringhausen – and through him his sister – to accompany them.

On the evening of the ball, it was as an approximate twin to Albrecht Dürer – in striped black and white cap, with his hair ringleted for the occasion and an immature beard adorning his jaw – that Wolfgang von Klostermann mounted his carriage and set off to collect his entourage. Leopold Meier, the first to be collected, wore an outfit not dissimilar from Klostermann's, but sufficiently modified to identify him as the impersonator of Oswolt Krel, a subject chosen by Klostermann partly on the basis of a slight resemblance about the nose, but chiefly because the Swabian merchant was once imprisoned for a misjudged carnival prank. For Stein a double dissembling had been ordained: dressed as Lukas Paumgartner in the guise of Saint Eustace, he wore scarlet stockings and bore both a heavy sword and a banner depicting the stag with the crucifix between its antlers. Ettlinger, on whom Klostermann had endeavoured to impose the alias of Dürer's Saint John, instead boarded the carriage as the gloomy madrigalist Don Carlo Gesualdo, the Prince of Venosa. The character had been proposed by Stein, who had secured Ettlinger's assent by pointing out that, as none of them had any notion of the appearance of the historical Gesualdo, the wearing of a plain penitential garb and the application of artificial shadows around the eyes would suffice for the creation of the pretended man.

Maximilian von Davringhausen, swaddled in a fur cape, wearing a broad black hat and carrying a wooden pomegranate in one hand, attended in the likeness of his royal namesake, as depicted by Dürer. He arrived in his own carriage with Helene, who, spurning the meagre disguises devised by Klostermann on her behalf, came dressed as Queen Elizabeth of England. A ruff of coarse starched linen encircled her neck and a tight string of pearls was woven into her hair, which she had stiffened and worked into a style resembling the shape of the suit of clubs in a pack of playing cards. She had coated her skin with some substance that gave her face the pallor of flour.

Disinclined in principle to find any diversion in the masquerade, Ettlinger detached himself from his companions as soon as he could. Sullenly watchful, he patrolled the gallery of rooms on the garden side, turning aside, whenever engagement with a fellow guest appeared imminent, to cast an eye over one of the landscapes that covered the walls. His host seemed to possess an illimitable passion for the flatlands of Holland and the vagaries of its coastal waters. Down the entire length of one room a succession of barges and sloops were painted in various situations of distress between seas and skies of various profundities of grey; opposite, countless elephantine clouds traipsed above plains on which were always to be seen at least one windmill, half a dozen cows and a broad, sluggish river. In a closet off the ballroom he discovered a portrait of a huntsman, a vividly incompetent work in which he found it quite easy to feign absorption for a while, until he noticed the reflection of his own face in the glaze, framed by the hood of his risible costume.

Ettlinger stepped out of the small room into the path of a young man with features that, while not unpleasant, were somewhat fox-like, owing to the combination of small mouth, small eyes and long, sharp nose. He was dressed in a particoloured tabard and carried a terracotta flagon. 'You have nothing to drink, sir?' he asked, and hurried away without waiting for a reply. He returned with a cumbrous earthenware goblet, into which, raising the heavy flagon far above its lip, he dextrously poured Ettlinger's wine. Ettlinger thanked him, then looked around to ascertain where he might be least at risk of disturbance. For a few minutes he found safety on a balcony, from which he had a view of an avenue of stone sphinxes receding into shadow. A gun dog of some species loped across the grass and paused beside a sphinx to look up at him. He then heard the voice of Helene, laughing.

She stood in the doorway, accepting the tributes of two young men who stood side by side and bowed to her in what Ettlinger assumed they took to be the Elizabethan mode. His face must have made manifest his distaste at Helene's delight in these theatricals, for the moment she saw him her face took on an expression of impatience and she waved her sycophants away.

'The monk of the sorrowful countenance,' she said with mock compassion. 'What might be the source of today's ill-temper?' she asked, and there could be heard in her voice an undertone of disappointment in him, or perhaps anger. She smacked her stomacher with her fan, the very one she had been carrying at Nymphenburg.

'I find it impossible to play the part,' Ettlinger replied, an apology that seemed to do nothing to make her less displeased with him. 'But I suppose that my inability puts me in character despite myself. Being discontent at my performance makes my performance successful,' he said, taking some confidence from his witticism, laborious though it was.

'But who are you?' asked Helene.

'Gesualdo of Venosa,' said Ettlinger. 'I murdered my wife and her lover, killing them both with the same blow.' Helene feigned horror at his confession. 'But this calamity brought out the best in me,' Ettlinger continued, 'for in my later years I composed some very strange music. So Martin tells me, and I have no reason to doubt his authority.'

Helene raised the tip of the fan to her cheek and looked at him quizzically, a response that Ettlinger tried to interpret as an indication that something about his appearance or his speech had not been badly done. He commended her appearance, remarking particularly on the ruff, a complicated decoration which she wore with an ease he thought remarkable in view of its impracticality. She received the compliment as though it were a naive answer to a question she had put to him.

Thus finding that neither jesting nor flattery were to her liking, and recalling her frankness at their previous meeting, Ettlinger ceased to dissemble. 'You will, I hope, excuse my lack of adaptability,' he recommenced, 'but I cannot bring myself to participate in this.'

'Then I must ask why you have bothered yourself to attend?' she asked. It was indubitably the case that she did not know the answer to this question.

Ettlinger was spared the test of devising a plausible response by the entry of Konrad Breitbach, his head crowned with a triple tiara and his obesity encompassed by a cope on which was embroidered the device of the Medici. 'Leo X,' whispered Helene.

Behind Breitbach came the broken-nosed and imperfectly barbered Johann Wilke, who had donned a paint-spattered smock to become Michelangelo, followed by Ernst von Kreisel, who was armoured with a shining breastplate. 'Would you care to guess?' asked Ettlinger, venturing a smile which, to his delight, was reciprocated.

'I should not,' Helene replied. 'But he does look handsome, as even you must admit.' She rested the tip of her tongue against the edge of her upper teeth, an action that nonplussed Ettlinger, as if the sight of it were an indelicacy he himself had committed.

With a nod he indicated Pierangela Maddalena Cempini, who had paused in the farther doorway, almost certainly conscious that the plasterwork of the moulding set off her appearance as splendidly as a picture frame. 'Now, as whom is that fine young woman dressed?' he asked. 'Raphael's beautiful mistress, La Fornarina? Or one of the Sistine sibyls?'

'Or Veronica Franco,' Helene proposed, pausing to enjoy his look of incomprehension. 'A courtesan-turned-poetess, admired by Montaigne,' she explained. 'It doesn't matter anyway. She is gorgeous and perhaps in her antiquated garb she will inspire someone to paint her, whereas La Cempini herself might not,' she said, giving Ettlinger a furtive smile.

'You know her too?' Ettlinger asked.

'We all know her, August,' she chided. 'And do not try to lure me into uncharitable talk. Pierangela has many talents, and she finds it agreeable to pretend, as do I. You think it childish, whereas I find it of interest. True, some of these people are just playing, like children. Unlike you, I think there is nothing wrong in that.' Helene touched the fan to her lips and made a little cough, a gesture that had about it something both demure and epicene, as though she were savouring the aftertaste of a splendid wine. 'Others,' she continued, 'are playing seriously, and are fully aware of what they are doing. Wolfgang von Klostermann, for one, is giving himself airs and I find them amusing. In his homeland he is unappreciated, Dürer tells me, but really it is Wolfgang speaking. He says he may leave for Italy, where they know how to treat their artists.'

Ettlinger was about to tell her of Wolfgang's preparations for the evening when Johann Friedrich von Wolgast walked by, dressed in the white habit of a Dominican, with a rosary and crucifix tucked into his narrow leather belt, and a Bible in one hand. He had put a dark dye in his hair, an embellishment that had the effect of making sinister the blue of his eyes. As Wolgast passed in front of Ernst von Kreisel he shook his free hand at him in what Ettlinger at first took to be authentic rage.

'I have it,' said Helene, who was also watching what had quickly changed from an altercation into a robust embrace. 'He is Savonarola, the bane of the Medici and of the modern world.' On the spot where Pierangela Maddalena Cempini had been standing, Wolgast stopped to talk to a young man dressed in black, whose cunning gait and surreptitious gaze were, Helene ventured, affected in homage to Machiavelli, whose double he was intended to be.

An onrush of listlessness swept over Ettlinger, for he took as a criticism of his own timorousness the swaggering manner in which Wolgast conducted himself in his disguise. It seemed to him imperative that he at once disengage Helene's attention from Wolgast. 'Wolfgang can be very inventive,' he began. 'To understand quite how inventive, you would have to attend a meeting of what we like to regard as his salon.' Helene turned to look at him, perhaps because Wolgast was now moving away into the adjoining room.

'Yes, August, I know all about it,' she said, placing a

finger on the cuff of his left sleeve. 'Wolfgang himself has invited me and Maximilian to join you.'

'And you have accepted the invitation?'

'I have not rejected it,' replied Helene artfully. 'It would not be appropriate – ' and at this word their conversation was broken by a scream from beneath the room in which they were talking.

Klostermann, somewhere towards the front of the house, called out for his cousin, a cry taken up by Kreisel. Laun sprinted into the gallery, seized Kreisel by the elbow and hurried him out onto the balcony and thence down into the garden. Meier and Ettlinger hastened in pursuit, leaping down the flight of steps and stumbling onto the damp grass, where Klostermann was standing. Ettlinger strained his eyes into the darkness of the garden, but saw neither Laun nor Kreisel, nor any trace of their steps. Behind them, under the balcony, a door was ajar. Klostermann heard from within the cellar the sound of a crate hitting the ground. They went running through the unlit vault, colliding with crates of wine and racks of vegetables, taking blows from the hams that hung from the ceiling. A light flared in the depths of the cellar, stamping the forms of two arches onto the gloom, the inner one crisply defined, the outer a penumbral shape. The silhouette of a man appeared in the inner arch, a flash of yellow on the armoured torso disclosing him as Kreisel. A sheet flapped in the place into which Kreisel was looking, and its shadow rippled across the cracked tiles of the cellar.

Ettlinger, Meier and Klostermann were at once at Kreisel's side. Laun stood in the furthest recess of the storeroom amid stacked barrels and bundled staves, a lantern raised in his right hand; Wolgast, walking away from Laun, was pushing a young man before him. It was the one who had poured Ettlinger's wine, and he had a flush on his skin as if he had drunk too much. Behind them, her hands covering her face and her dress dishevelled, stood a girl of perhaps sixteen – one of the kitchen staff, it appeared, from the stains on her knuckles.

At Kreisel's demand for some account of what had happened the girl's breathing became louder and more fractured as she strove to prevent herself from wailing. Wolgast tightened his grip on the back of the young man's neck.

'You do not need an explanation, Ernst,' said Wolgast. 'You have seen all that it is necessary to see,' he stated. Passing between Klostermann and Ettlinger as if they were merely the posts of a gate, he marched the assailant out into the garden. The girl followed, weeping; as she walked under Meier's gaze, her fingers parted and she looked up at him in a way that implied, as Meier later told his friends, that the worst was still before her. Like jurists processing into a courtroom they trod in Wolgast's footsteps, then watched him disappear with his charges into the darkness of the avenue of sphinxes. In the instant of their disappearance, Ettlinger noticed, Wolgast had a hand on the shoulder of each of the young people, as if he were not the nemesis of one and the salvation of the other but instead the guardian of both.

The group that had run to the rescue now returned to the gallery and was soon dispersed as people pressed for a report of what they had seen. Ettlinger, unsure that he knew what he had witnessed, stayed close to Klostermann, allowing him to deflect the questions with a tact and imprecision that Ettlinger could not but envy. 'A transgression committed unwittingly,' Klostermann surmised. In reply to another enquirer he suspected 'the curse of Bacchus'; to a third he blamed the 'misguided application of an affection that had long become unreciprocated'. Helene had already left with her brother.

When Wolgast entered the room, some fifteen minutes later, Ettlinger was in fitful conversation with Ernst von Kreisel, whose reiterated indignation at the assault required, and indeed permitted, no response other than sombre concurrence. Bowing to Ettlinger, Wolgast hooked a hand round Kreisel's forearm to ease him towards the windows that opened onto the balcony. Ettlinger overheard one phrase from Wolgast – 'in a suitable manner' – and saw Kreisel look at Wolgast in a way that seemed to convey that he knew Wolgast's meaning. The two men crossed the threshold, and through the panes Ettlinger watched Wolgast perform a mime that could have been nothing else but a recapitulation of the events that had preceded the arrival of Kreisel and the rest. Wolgast's brow buckled with wrath; his hands sprang open, extended traps towards Kreisel's face; he grasped the breast of his tunic, as if he intended to rend the fabric; he shivered and let his arms lie limply at his side. And then Wolgast broke into laughter, exposing his childlike teeth and widening his eyes. His eyes looked as white as bone under the lamplight.

Stein appeared soundlessly at Ettlinger's side. The sight of his absurd banner and scarlet stockings provoked from Ettlinger a sigh of annoyance, though it was not with Stein in particular that he was exasperated. 'I'm sorry,' Ettlinger began, but Stein himself seemed shamed by their frivolous apparel, and held the banner away from his body as though it were an object tainted with contagion. At Stein's suggestion they retrieved Klostermann and Meier, who needed no persuasion to return to their carriage. The journey back to Munich elapsed in silence, except that Meier three times requested that Stein sing to them and Stein three times refused, though the request was sincere.

18.

Here is where we built the apparatus to measure and mark the divisions of our days.

At the heart of this mighty instrument was a bell-tower of such a circumference that twenty men linked hand to hand could barely encompass it. Arrayed in an arc one hundred paces from the base of the tower were ten boulders. When the shadow of the tower touched one of these stones, a sound was spread across the land from the summit of the tower.

For some three months after the tower's inauguration, the new hour was announced by a machine of vast pipes and bellows: blown once with the onset of the first hour, twice with the next, three times with the succeeding hour, the pipes produced a noise that reached the Residence like the far-off roar of a slaughterhouse. At the emperor's command, the pipes and bellows were replaced by a shaft of hollowed cedar on which the signature of the time was beaten. Within a month this was replaced by three discordant whistles, a device in turn succeeded one month later by a huge iron bell. In the course of the year we heard the hours as the boom of a horsehide drum, the crack of a small cannon, the crash of an immense cymbal, a descending scale struck from tubes of bronze, a human cry.

For a while the first hour of the day was announced by a single cry; six cries heralded the sixth hour, eight cries the eighth. Eventually these monotonous exclamations became melodies, and with the passage of time the melodies grew more elaborate, though always the briefest was the first after dawn and the longest the last before nightfall.

The emperor commissioned from his musicians a piece of music woven from these emblems in sound. The flutes played a sequence of notes derived from the melody of the fifth hour; they embellished it, and were joined by a single horn that blazoned a tune we at once associated with the sunrise; into their medley cascaded a rivulet of harp notes, in which we could recognise some aspect of another hour's theme. The lassitude of noon was mingled with mid-morning's evanescent promise, with the satiety of the late afternoon, with the pathos of the last hour before the nameless hours of the night. The music conjured an imaginary day in which the moods of the different hours cancelled, refined and intensified each other in their co-existence.

The emperor often commanded that this music should be played, and the bell-tower of the southern headland was in time left to crumble.

19.

The first session of the Klostermann circle that Helene

attended was the next one, in the last week of November, not long after the costumed ball.

Meier was talking as Ettlinger entered. Sitting cross-legged on an Ottoman rug, pensively stroking the coppery whiskers of his beard into a Mephistophelean point, he was expatiating on the subject of someone's great-grandfather, once an astrologer at the court of the French king. He tasted his brandy and praised the ingenuity of the charlatan, with his 'hermetic paraphernalia, his mixture of mathematics and gaseous ambiguity'. Meier slid a finger round the lip of the glass. 'For several months the man prospered, protected by the gullibility of his audience and the vatic mist in which he wrapped his prognostications. Then one day, pressed by a hostile minister to judge the advisability of a naval expedition, he stood on the harbour wall, looked out upon the tranquil sea, and foretold that for the coming month the ocean would be as calm as a tub of butter. And the next day the fleet foundered amid waves that were as high as the clifftops and the wizard vanished into thin air.' Meier chuckled and proffered his empty glass to Klostermann. 'The grandson, in atonement for his forebear's stupidity, has become a maker of timepieces of the most extraordinary accuracy. My parents have acquired an example of his craft, and I must say that I find it more impressive than any painting,' he asserted, directing the remark towards Stein, who reclined in an armchair in the opposite corner of the room, studying a page of manuscript that Klostermann had handed to him. 'Its workings are so fine, so intricate, so infallible. I tell you, they make me ashamed to be made of flesh,' he asserted, sliding a hand over his bow-fronted belly.

'Yes,' responded Stein doubtfully, and at this moment Maximilian and Helene von Davringhausen entered the room.

'I bring a neophyte,' announced Maximilian, bowing to each of them in turn.

Helene nodded, and the fur of her collar bent against her cheeks, to which the cold air had applied blushes as pretty as a marionette's. With a shrug and a twist of her body she slipped her coat onto Maximilian's arm, and shook hands with first Klostermann, then Stein, Ettlinger and lastly Meier, whose face reddened instantly at the touch of her hand. Ettlinger could detect no partiality to her greeting.

Stein indicated that she should take the place that had been his.

'I have heard that you sing well, Martin,' Helene said to him, and the gracious familiarity with which she addressed his friend gave Ettlinger a pinch of jealousy. 'Will you sing for us this afternoon?'

'Indeed he shall,' Meier interrupted, folding his legs as he settled again on the Ottoman rug. 'But please,' he said to Stein, 'no more Schubert. Let his music remain an esoteric doctrine.'

'Of which I am a follower,' said Helene, giving Stein a smile of solidarity.

'I always sing,' Stein confirmed, 'and Leopold always reveals to us the pettiness of his soul. He is a consummate critic.'

'I thank you,' Meier responded and raised his glass as for a toast – 'To our sybarite of desolation,' he declaimed.

The sniping continued, to the amusement, it appeared, of Helene, who seemed moreover to have expected just such a situation. While Stein and Meier argued, Maximilian, seated on a dining-chair beside her, stroked the back of her hand; she returned Ettlinger's dismayed smile, then looked to Klostermann, whose face expressed embarrassment and rising impatience.

'Enough, enough,' Klostermann at last declared. 'We have a guest.' Having effected a truce and sealed it with a bottle of Moselle, he read the company a lyric he had composed as a respite from his ordeal in the Teutoburg forest. Telling of two friends who part forever amid the ruins of the Roman forum, the poem restored the harmony of the group, casting its sweetly regretful mood over them all. Each praised the poem briefly, and a conversation ensued that comprised more silence than speech, until Helene announced that her brother had a story for them.

'A little ghost story,' she revealed. 'Recited from memory, in the best folkloric style.'

Maximilian accepted a replenishment of his glass from Meier, cleared his throat and began his tale. 'It is the story of a young man of whom great things were expected. A keen and intelligent student, he was destined to become a famous lawyer, or a doctor, or a great writer, even. But then came the day of his father's decease and the reception of his inheritance. Suddenly rich, he abandoned his studies and set about squandering his patrimony and his time in the company of actresses and other disreputables. Three years flowed by in dissipation.

'One evening this young man – Richard was his name – went to the opera house in the company of a courtesan whose favours he had been enjoying for some time, at ruinous expense. They took possession of a box and had champagne brought to them. The opera scarcely engaged their attention beyond its overture. The courtesan made herself comfortable on the floor of the box and fell asleep.

'Half drunk, Richard looked around the theatre. In the box directly opposite him sat a handsome, flirtatious woman whose immodest dress he found diverting for a while; in the adjacent box a notorious drunkard caroused with a trio of male companions; above them, a much-decorated soldier sat beside a woman who was perhaps his daughter, or perhaps not.

'Richard scanned the stalls, where the patrons appeared to have a more serious intent. He was soon intrigued by two gentlemen who trained their opera-glasses on the stage as purposefully as hunters. One of them was silver-haired and flaunted a florid moustache; the other had thin red hair just like Richard's father's, and had a score open on his lap, which he consulted now and then, as his father had been wont to do. The first act ended, and both men lowered their glasses. The red-haired man turned. Richard, deeply troubled by the resemblance to his parent, took his opera-glasses from the courtesan's bag and peered through them at the two men. As if at a kick, his breath left him in a moment. There was no question of mere resemblance – the red-haired man seated in the stalls was his father. Though he was three years dead, his father was sitting in the midst of the living audience, talking to a living man, surrounded by the living. Richard watched the silver-haired man whisper to his father; his manner was that of a confidant. He watched his father's reaction to the performance, and saw him rise from his seat as those around him rose to applaud the singers. The people in the stalls moved towards the exit for the interval, and Richard's father left with them.

'Richard bolted down the stairs, pushing people aside in his haste. Like a man deranged he rushed back and forth across the lobby until at last he saw the back of the red-haired man, addressing the one beside whom he had been seated. Richard dashed towards him and grabbed his arm. It was not his father, nor did this man's face in any way look like his father's. And in that moment Richard knew with absolute certainty that he was damned.'

As Maximilian drained his glass to signal that his story was finished, Klostermann applauded him briefly and was joined by Stein and Ettlinger. 'Bravo, yes,' added Meier, pressing a hand into the small of his back and grimacing. 'Hamlet transplanted from the stage to the stalls. Unlike Martin I am no gourmet of the uncanny, but I liked it. I did indeed.'

'I too have brought something,' said Helene, sensing, it seemed to Ettlinger, that Stein had bridled at Meier's jibe, and was about to resume their bickering. She placed a hand palm upward on her brother's knee, and he withdrew from an inside pocket a leather wallet, from which he extracted a piece of stiff paper the size of a tarot card. 'My donation to you, Wolfgang, in your capacity as this society's *primus inter pares*. Maximilian assured me it would be acceptable.'

Klostermann inspected the gift, pronounced it delightful, and held it out so the others might see it. The picture was a fastidiously detailed watercolour of a seascape. A harbour in the foreground was populated by a host of tiny figures, one of whom, a woman in flowing robes, watched the activity of the docks from a throne set on the farthest point of a wharf.

'Dido in Carthage,' Helene elucidated.

'Where's Aeneas?' asked Meier, squinting at the picture from a distance of a finger's length.

'He's not there,' she retorted. 'This is Dido, queen of the Phoenicians, the first people to plough the seas. An allegory even my father can comprehend.'

Chastised, Meier turned his attention to Ettlinger. 'Anything from you today, August?' he asked. 'Or are you as barren as myself?'

'I am glad to say that I have nothing,' replied Ettlinger. 'My sketches would look clumsy today,' and he took the picture from Klostermann's hand. His eyes did not read the image, for what was depicted on the paper was but a secondary feature of the object that Helene had presented. Seeing nothing but the feathery brushstrokes she had made, Ettlinger rested the picture on his fingertips.

'Do you ever read at these meetings?' Helene asked him.

He returned the picture to Klostermann as he replied, averting his eyes from hers – 'Never. Sometimes I bring drawings. Nothing like this. Of buildings.'

'One building,' Meier corrected.

'Perhaps one day you should write something,' suggested Klostermann. 'Be bold. Follow Maximilian's example.'

'I'll give you a theme for your literary endeavour,'

said Meier – '"The Classical Column is the Member of Satan."'

Maximilian rubbed his hands down his thighs as if in nervous anticipation of something. 'I must be honest with you,' he said. 'I read the story, but I did not devise it. The tale is Johann Friedrich von Wolgast's.'

'You know Wolgast?' asked Ettlinger, obscurely confounded by the admission.

'Leopold and I, independently of each other, conversed with him at the Kreisels' house. He made a deep impression upon us both. A learned and unconventional man.'

'A singular man,' Meier concurred, and winked at Ettlinger.

'Will you sing for us now, Martin?' Helene requested, and Stein duly sang the song about the King of Thule. As he sang, Ettlinger, feigning an aesthetic transport, glanced repeatedly at Helene through half-closed lids. Her eyes seemed to seek some point of focus in the room, betraying perhaps that she was moved by the song, or, on the contrary, that she was bored by the entertainment. When the song was finished Helene and her brother departed, and there was no clue as to her thoughts in the manner of her farewell. She shook hands briskly with them in precisely the order in which she had greeted them, smiling at each warmly, equally.

20.

This was the office of the bestiarist, a timid and tremulous man whose face was fretted perpetually by worry over the precariousness of his tenure.

He was the chronicler or creator of a host of creatures: the animal with its eyes in its mouth; the goat covered with scales instead of hair; the lizard with a gland under its brain which, when the head is cut off, hardens and becomes a jewel; the dog that lives underground, and can be heard at night howling for the light; the snake with flesh that turns to blood in the instant its skin is removed; the white-feathered bird whose body is so cold that rain falling upon its plumage turns to snow; the animal that has skin too tight for its muscles, which are constantly bursting through its bristly hide; the bird that crumbles into ashes if ever the sun ceases to shine upon it, and is thus condemned to perpetual migration; the cow whose eyes are mirrors; the fish that eats wood so voraciously that if a boat sails into a shoal of them it is as though the vessel had hit a reef; the monkey that never leaves the tree in which it was born; the black-legged deer that will drink only flowing water, and can easily be trapped by springs and waterfalls; the lizard that from its third year diminishes in size until it becomes so small that nobody can be sure if the animal ever dies.

The bestiarist was required to explicate the significance of the things he reported. 'What does the creature hunt?' the emperor might enquire, or 'What does its behaviour signify?' From time to time one of the emperor's favourites would hear that he had been granted a patent to bear a particular beast as his heraldic device. Just as there was no greater honour than to receive such a patent, so there was no greater disgrace than to be deprived of it. Such was the consequence of failure to honour the principle embodied by one's emblematic creature. Gaumata, whose emblem briefly was the mirror-eyed cow, prevaricated when asked for his opinion of a design for the emperor's tomb, and in so doing he lapsed from the frankness prescribed by the badge he wore. For this transgression he was stripped of his device and consigned to a menial role in the upkeep of the Paradise. Ardashir, whose device was the animal that rends its own skin, was required by his emblem to sacrifice all other considerations to the exercise of his strength and valour, and so was disgraced on the day of the first siege of the Residence, when he was absent from the place of greatest danger. In the second siege he was compelled to carry his undecorated shield at the main gate, where he was killed.

21.

Ettlinger's reverie – a delicious, steady effervescence of the mind in which were blended visions of the fateful afternoon at Nymphenburg, fragments of the declaration of love he would one day make, and imaginings of the circumstances in which he might make it – was ended by the noise of hail on his window. His eyes regained their focus. The ink had crystallised on the nib of his pen, which rested on a pear-shaped blot to the right of the phrase: 'This solution is to be preferred for the following reasons.' Able neither to recall immediately the points he had been about to marshal nor to muster any desire to excavate them from his memory, Ettlinger moved his papers aside and leaned back in his chair. The fire was low; the damp logs were whispering steam under their iron-grey smoke.

He crossed to the window and looked out. Pellets of hail lay on the sill and blades of frosted mud receded to the corner of the street. A gust of wind raised fringes of snow from the gables of the houses and blew the white dusting from the road. Stepping off the pavement directly below Ettlinger's room, a man placed his foot gingerly between the rails of hardened earth.

The hailstones crunched against the underside of the frame as Ettlinger pushed the window open. He swallowed the air, which filled his mouth and flowed through his throat like a draught of spring water. The cold set his skin tingling and the burden of the morning's wasted work was obliterated in the chill atmosphere. An invigoration of his whole being seemed to be portended. As he gazed out at the empty street Ettlinger thought of himself as a wayfarer looking upon a mountain stream he has to cross to reach his destination. He would walk and return to his work, and his work would proceed fruitfully.

He walked westward, towards the sun, which lay on the sky as a dead lily might lie on the surface of a frozen pond. There were no people on the streets and no thoughts of any substance in his mind, but this nullity did not concern him. On the contrary, he felt himself to be in a condition akin to the state of emptiness that mystics seek as the means to enlightenment. For an hour he walked, to the very limits of the city, where the prospect of the infinite forest raised the assurance that his labours would be successful. The wind had subsided. He turned back towards his home, anticipating an evening in which his plans for the temple would reach their definitive form.

He was no more than five minutes from his door when he took a side-street down which he had never walked before, and came upon Wolgast. With his hands in the pockets of his coat, Wolgast was standing in the middle of the street, facing a door he seemed to be scrutinising as if uncertain of what might lie behind it. The sight of Wolgast took Ettlinger aback. For some reason, he was surprised in the way one might be surprised upon encountering a creature out of its habitat. There was something untoward in the very fact of Wolgast's standing alone in the open air.

Clad in a coat of fine black wool, Wolgast stood as still as a column of basalt, but he nonetheless knew Ettlinger was watching him. 'Good day to you, August,' he called, before turning his head. 'What mission brings you out of doors on this inclement afternoon?'

'No mission, sir,' replied Ettlinger, failing to make his reply not sound apologetic. 'A break from my studies, nothing more.'

Making no response, Wolgast considered for a few seconds the tondo of splintered ice at his feet. 'I have a social obligation to honour,' he remarked, seemingly resentful either of Ettlinger's presence or of the duty by which he was bound. He advanced to within arm's length of the door, and turned to Ettlinger once more. 'I am to visit an old friend of mine, whose home this is.' He paused, as a schoolteacher might pause after the preamble to his lesson. 'This friend goes by the name of Abbadon. This is, of course, a self-appointed title. His baptismal name is Siegmund – Siegmund Michael Mölck – but were one to address him thus he might well not respond. On some days he would take it as an insult. On others he would be thrown into perplexity. He has not answered to the name his parents bestowed upon him for a decade.'

Extending his left hand, Wolgast invited Ettlinger to stand beside him. 'Your presence, I promise you, would be appreciated by my friend, in whose life variety is rare. Would you care to accompany me?' The insinuation in his voice, that Ettlinger might lack the character for whatever it was that Wolgast was about to do, compelled acceptance of the invitation. Wolgast wrapped a hand about the bell-chain and rang it thrice.

The doorman greeted Wolgast with familiar deference, and led the visitors across a paved courtyard and through a low archway, to the side of which a door decorated with patterns of black nail-heads opened onto an anteroom. The crudely plastered walls had been painted hastily and recently with pallid blue distemper; the only piece of furniture was a wide, low chair of bare oak, placed below the room's one picture, an unlabelled portrait, dating probably from the middle years of the previous century, of a seated gentleman wearing a wig which more than doubled the diameter of his head. There were no windows to the exterior, but a square glazed hatch opened onto the adjoining room beside the connecting door. Through this hatch Ettlinger saw the doorman talking to a man who was seated in a hidden corner of the room. Beyond the doorman was a tapestry of what appeared to be the battle of Jericho, and a flaking depiction of the Transfiguration, framed in a rectangle of writhing gilt. Wolgast gestured that Ettlinger should be seated and took up his station with his back against the inner door, his hands locked at his waist, his eyes closed.

For perhaps ten minutes they waited, in silence, before the doorman emerged and stood back to make way for them.

'Abbadon,' said Wolgast, bowing to the figure who sat on the edge of a threadbare *chaise longue* at the far end of the room.

Abbadon stood, drawing together the lapels of his crimson velvet cloak. He reciprocated the bow and adjusted the fit of the high wig he was wearing, a frayed and mouse-coloured hairpiece from the same period as the portrait in the anteroom.

'May I present August Ettlinger? My young colleague is an architect,' Wolgast continued. Abbadon gave Wolgast a kindly but puzzled smile, as though he were a well-intentioned foreigner addressing him in a language of which he knew nothing.

Slowly Abbadon reseated himself on the *chaise longue*. 'Please,' he said, indicating the two chairs that had been positioned before the fireplace, in which twigs and sawn branches were piled criss-crossed. His voice was urgent, but his gaze flitted away from them as if tracking the flight of a butterfly.

'Is there anything you require that has not been provided?' asked Wolgast. Abbadon appeared not to hear. He lifted from the floor a folded ribbon of black paper and opened it between his outstretched hands. He grinned at Wolgast over the chain of silhouette heads. 'The shadow of a man is his truest measure,' he said, intoning the phrase as one would a folk motto. 'A face in which there is nothing accidental.' There were twenty identical profiles in the chain, perhaps more.

'Who?' asked Wolgast, touching one of the silhouettes with a forefinger.

Abbadon gave them both a sly look, and pointed towards the anteroom. He rummaged in a pocket and brought out a pair of silver scissors, with which he snipped three profiles from the chain. Kneeling on the *chaise longue,* he pressed them onto the rime that covered the window. Wolgast knelt beside him, and placed a hand upon his arm in a way that suggested the solicitousness of a devoted son for his ailing parent. Abbadon looked at the hand as if it were a garment he could not recall putting on.

The silhouettes slid askew on a dribble of meltwater; Abbadon adjusted them, then let them peel from the glass. He pressed a hand against the window, removed it, and peered out through the palm-print. 'Shall we sit beneath my tree?' he asked, directing the question to Ettlinger.

'That would not be wise,' Wolgast answered, laying the ruined silhouettes on his chair. 'It is so cold in here. Let us light a fire instead,' he suggested, searching for a taper amid the slews of paper beside the hearth. Panic flared in Abbadon's eyes. He pulled away the wood that had been set in the fireplace and scattered the paper across the floor with a flurry of kicks. He clutched Wolgast by the forearm. 'Courtesy is due!' Abbadon shouted, and then quietly insisted: 'We must obey the rule. I have awaited you.'

Wolgast's dissuasions were futile. Abbadon took a thin cambric gown from a hook on the back of the door, draped it over his shoulders and, standing to attention, requested his guests to follow him. He led them to a small garden at the rear of the building, abutting his quarters. An untended lawn occupied most of the garden's area; brown tracks of matted grass had been trodden across it, and in places fresher blades stood upright, clogged with phlegmy balls of ice.

At the centre of the garden a skeletal mulberry tree overhung a rectangular brick-lined pit. Abbadon sat on one side of the parapet, and pointed to the places where Wolgast and Ettlinger should sit. 'We must observe closely, for all things signify,' he informed Ettlinger, stirring with his foot a frost-stiffened pulp of rotting leaves. He uncovered a snail and lifted it towards Wolgast on a platform of leaf. 'Give me the words for this, Johann,' Abbadon beseeched him, and from the alacrity of Wolgast's response it appeared that this exchange had happened before.

'I doubt there could be anything more touching than the viscid movement of the snail,' said Wolgast in a subdued, sacramental tone. He extended a finger to the edge of the proffered leaf. 'What could be more discreet, more humble, than the retraction of its soft horns?'

Abbadon looked intently at Wolgast as he spoke, and Ettlinger saw tears swelling on his eyelids. 'Thank you,' said Abbadon, as he deposited the leaf and snail on Wolgast's hand. Crouching at Ettlinger's feet he rooted about in the mulch till he found a second snail, then knelt to coax it onto a fingertip. He transferred it to Ettlinger's hand. 'Can you feel?' he asked, turning to Wolgast as if this were a cue.

'The tender rasp of its foot,' Wolgast murmured, again as if following a practised form of words.

At this Abbadon seemed smitten by the thought of

something he had nearly forgotten to disclose. 'In the night,' he told Ettlinger, 'I sit by the window and I hear these creatures moving through the grass. They are louder than the foxes. Perhaps this is a sign of the last days.'

Wolgast attempted to distract Abbadon from the idea that had struck him, a notion that made him gape at the ground, astounded. 'Abbadon, my colleague is building a temple,' he began, but his speech was broken by Abbadon's interjection.

'I often hear a voice and I think it is my mother's and I think it is of me she speaks,' Abbadon told them. 'She calls me her little golden man and wants to know why it is I cannot look upon the sun. But nobody can look upon the sun. What time of day is it?'

'Three o'clock,' Wolgast answered, at which Abbadon smiled as though an inexperienced tradesman had tried to dupe him.

'Oh, no. No, no. Later. Far later,' insisted Abbadon. He took from his breeches a tiny folding sundial, opened it, turned it in his hand, then hurled it across the garden. 'Johann, why are you here?' he demanded, but the question seemed to be put to the air, for Abbadon smiled to himself, doffed his wig and let his long, sparse grey hair fall over his shoulders. He twisted his hair into a cord and curled it in his palms, holding it close to his chest, as if it were a leveret he was cradling.

Wolgast motioned to Ettlinger that they would soon be taking their leave and at that moment there appeared at the gate by which they had entered the garden a figure whose head was draped in black crêpe. He raised an arm in their direction, a gesture that prompted Abbadon to stand and salute him; Wolgast rose in unison, indicating to Ettlinger that he too should stand. 'He cannot speak,' Wolgast explained. 'He has no jaw. A French artilleryman took it from him. He writes all day, but nobody can read what he writes, except his signature, which he puts on the paper like a monk tracing the first word of his breviary.'

Abbadon nodded his concurrence. 'Yes, that is true. What Johann says is true,' he told Ettlinger. 'What Johann says is true.'

A guardian took the masked figure by his arm and guided him back towards the house, whereupon Abbadon became as agitated as an infant removed from the arms of its mother.

'The emperor, dear Johann!' he cried. 'When will he come, do you think? When shall the emperor come?' He turned to address Ettlinger, his eyes widening to show pupils as wide as they could grow. Making a hinge of his hands, he stared into his palms. 'There are seven kings; five are fallen, one is, and the other is not yet come!' he shouted, glaring at Ettlinger. His attention leapt back to Wolgast, the sight of whose face seemed suddenly to placate him.

'His head and his hairs were white like wool, as white as snow; and his eyes were as a flame of fire,' muttered Abbadon, and with his left hand he took the index finger of his right and positioned it in Wolgast's scar, as if placing a pen in the groove of a carrying case. Leaning forward, he kissed Wolgast on the cheek, then fell back with a look of horror in his eyes, as if seeing some dire vision in the branches above Wolgast's head. Wolgast clasped Abbadon close to him and placed a hand over his eyes. Though Abbadon resisted, Wolgast held him firmly, and Abbadon was soothed by his embrace. But the instant Wolgast released him the madman began a catechism with himself, his voice rising from an exultant cry to a scream of delirium.

'The first foundation was jasper,' he began. 'The second, sapphire. The third, a chalcedony. The fourth, an emerald. The fifth, sardonyx; the sixth, sardius. The seventh, chrysolite; the eighth, beryl; the ninth, a topaz. The tenth, a chrysoprasus, the eleventh, a jacinth, the twelfth, an amethyst.' At the name of the amethyst he fell into silence and a moroseness overcame him like that which follows a night of intoxication.

He did not react to the doorman's hand on his back, and meekly turned with the pull of his arm. At the entrance to the anteroom Abbadon held out his cupped hands as if to give something held there to a person he saw standing before him, between Ettlinger and Wolgast. 'Here, take this. Our father is not yet home, so I must look after you.' There were tears again in Abbadon's eyes. Wolgast touched Abbadon's chin and kissed him lightly on his brow, closing his eyes as he did so; he resembled a child receiving the host at its first communion.

Ettlinger and Wolgast crossed the courtyard, and were about to open the street door when a triumpant howl from Abbadon made them look back. 'For the former things are cast away!' he roared, and stood rigid in the doorway, his fists clenched against his thighs, his head thrown back. His mouth opened as if to scream, but he made no sound.

This man, Wolgast told Ettlinger as they parted, was a cousin of Karl, Maximilian and Helene von Davringhausen. 'The Davringhausens pay for his lodging and his attendants, but they never speak of him except within the family,' he said. 'And it is perhaps best that they do so, I think you will agree.' Thereby did Wolgast oblige Ettlinger to dissemble with Helene, placing a taint upon Ettlinger's friendship with her, destroying the equality of their relationship by the introduction of advantage.

In the spring, a little more than four months after the encounter with Abbadon, Ettlinger was shown the family tree that Helene had drawn as a Christmas gift for her mother. It was displayed behind glass, next to a portrait of her maternal grandmother, Elisabeth. Lacy strokes of damson-coloured ink, like the fronds of an aquatic fern, linked name to name back through ten generations. With an ironic smile Helene set her handiwork on a table for Ettlinger's inspection. 'The patriarchs of the Davringhausen dynasty have long displayed an overdeveloped sense of continuity,' she said. 'The family tree is a notion they take too literally. Look at the names: it's a little orchard, popping the same few kinds of fruit with each season. For the men we have Ferdinand, Heinrich, Matthias, Karl, Maximilian, Gottfried, Theodor, Gerhard and Johann – not many names for all these boys. Gotthard is the first novelty for five generations, and the women are worse. Helene – six of us in seven generations. A flock of Marias, too many Elisabeths to number. Look at this line, the Spiering branch: Elisabeth, Elisabeth, Elisabeth, every one of them swaddled in a name that was ready for her before she was conceived.' She shook her head with a look of wry sorrow, as at the recollection of something squandered. 'A few Katarinas, a company of Carlottas. Otherwise we have a solitary Hildegard – the fault of a whimsical great-grandmother and her pliant spouse – and a single Magdalena, of whom no one speaks.' She uttered the phrase without the slightest discomposure.

Ettlinger read the names of the offspring of her father's sister and brother; there was no Siegmund Mölck among them. 'Did you do the same for your mother's family?' he asked.

'No,' Helene replied, with what he heard as a firmness slightly in excess of what was necessary.

He felt shame at his question, and a resurgent admiration of Helene, but an admiration which was in some way compromised by his having to leave its explanation unspoken. Later that afternoon, Ettlinger lied to her about a commission he might soon receive for an interior in the street in which Siegmund Mölck was kept. She said that she did not know that part of the city, and he found that he was disconcerted at the perfection of her pretence, even though he too was being false.

When he saw her for the first time after the death of Abbadon, such was his obtuseness that the absence of distress in her eyes caused him a pang of anger, and the sense of his own unreasonableness could not entirely expunge the fact of his having been for an instant displeased with her. The erasure of his dissatisfaction had, as it were, left a mark that was a blemish on his love for her. And when, at the end, he discovered the truth, it was not even possible for him to make amends for an injustice of which she would never have been aware.

22.

Here was the forge. It was constructed two hours' walk downstream from the Residence, beyond the orchards, because the emperor could not endure the noise of the hammers.

The smiths made door bosses, medallions, manacles, statuettes and blades. They made brooches that looked like interwoven cords, bronze harps, griddles incised with the likeness of a boar or deer, couches too fragile to be of use but worked with such finesse that a woodcarver could not have turned a more nimble piece. They made the reliquaries that were kept in the octagonal room beneath the emperor's chambers. We knew the forms of some of these: there were goblets with sealed lids, figurines with hollow bodies, columns with capitals that could be opened by a hidden catch, tabernacles, calyxes, censers, ewers, candlesticks and crowns set with jewels. One such crown, a coronet of tin, preserved the tongue of the emperor's brother, the treacherous Bardiya. In the centre of the room, on a plinth of rock-crystal, there was a gilded bronze head of Xerxes himself, but the largest of the reliquaries was the one in the form of the towers of Urmia. This piece, so perfect in its representation, was revealed to us in a room hung with gauzes and cunningly lit, so that in looking upon it from the distance of the chamber's door we felt ourselves to be looking upon the real Urmia from the hill to the south of the city, from which we had cast our final glances at its walls. Each of the bronze towers housed a fragment of stone from the corresponding tower of the lost city.

With their splenetic complexions and lashless eyes, their faces tight as inflated bladders, the smiths looked unlike any of the other craftsmen, and they lived and worked at a place that had its own climate. When snow fell, none of it settled on the forge, nor on the ground encircling the walls, to a breadth of five paces. In the spring, the earth around the building flowered before any other part of the island, and a girdle of crocuses would surround the forge.

Once, soon after the turn of the year, I was sent to the forge to collect a pair of spurs for Amestris. The earth was still hard but the air was mild, and a stalk of smoke was spreading slowly above the forge, making so pleasing a sight that I settled for a while on the frozen bank, a short distance upstream, with no thought but to watch the melding of the smoke and sky. I had been seated but a moment when in the doorway two men appeared, carrying pincers as long as their arms, by which they clamped a piece of red-hot metal. They bore it to the millrace, and as they paused by the water's edge, and the incandescence of the iron began to fade, I saw that what they carried was a bust of Xerxes, its hair flying and teeth bared. The smiths set the bust in the water, and the millrace hissed at its touch, swathing the men in steam. Stiff-armed, like executors of a sacrifice, they held the iron under the boiling surface, then dragged their creation back to the forge, pulling it along the ground as if it were a lifeless animal.

Rejected by the emperor, the bust was soon installed between the inner and outer arches of the main gate, on a ledge that was perpetually in shadow and littered with the twigs of birds' nests. A wreath of iron convolvulus had been brazed onto its neck and the lips had been hammered flat; lettering embossed in the base identified the subject as Bardiya, the hated brother of Xerxes.

23.

At the very end of the year the antagonism between Meier and Stein came to a head with an argument near the Hofgarten, at three o'clock in the morning, it was said. Rumour had it that Stein's objection to Meier's intemperance was the cause of the dispute, that blows were traded, even that there were threats of a duel, but nobody knew for certain what had occurred – nobody, that is, except the protagonists and Wolfgang von Klostermann, through whose mediation a reconciliation was achieved in the first week of January. The trio then proposed that, to celebrate their renewed concord and the dawning of the new year, the Klostermann salon should hold its next session in the Steuermann inn, on the road to Andechs, and that two sleighs should be hired for the occasion.

Ettlinger assented readily, as did Maximilian and Helene von Davringhausen, and by the time the designated day came round, one week later, it had acquired an additional significance. It was to be the first session at which Johann Friedrich von Wolgast would be present. He was not, however, present when they assembled at the stables, having left a note on Ettlinger's desk the previous day, informing him that he would meet them at the inn at noon.

The prospect of the sleigh-ride seemed to have put everyone in good spirits. Stein and Meier greeted each other with a cordial handshake, Helene kissed each of the four friends on the cheek, and her brother had a fraternal embrace for all. Klostermann, the master of ceremonies, clapped his gloves together and announced that they must depart for Steuermann's forthwith, at which command Meier leaped onto the seat beside Helene, and Stein sprang into Ettlinger's sleigh. Once Maximilian had taken up his post on his sister's bench, Klostermann jumped up to join the other pair. He let out a hunter's cry as he cracked the reins, and one behind the other the sleighs slipped out of the yard and onto the street.

Accompanied by the sportive jangle of bells they sped between the head-high snowdrifts, calling back and forth to each other in their exhilaration. Meier, the pilot of the Davringhausens' sleigh, kept standing to doff his cap to passers-by until held down in his seat by Maximilian; Klostermann, in response, wielded the whip to put distance between himself and the others, and looked back over his shoulder to yell a taunt at his pursuers. Once they were among the open fields, however, their prankishness elapsed and each fell quiet, as if the silent white land had imposed a mood of meditation on the party. Klostermann removed the garland of bells and Meier did the same. The hushing of the runners on the snow was the only sound, and even that became an irksome distraction, like chattering in church. Three times Klostermann brought them to a halt and stood to survey the sepulchral landscape that extended all around them, under a roof of snow-charged sky. No one questioned him or spoke a word, for it seemed they all shared the same wish. After each stop they sat enclosed profoundly in their thoughts, their eyes on some point in the midst of the whiteness, as if they were being vouchsafed some vision of things beyond the world. Close to their destination, however, Ettlinger did once glance back at the other sleigh. He saw Maximilian and Meier in whispered conversation, and Helene facing the opposite way, not so much regarding the scene as reviewing it, as a visiting dignitary might review an honour guard.

Shortly before noon they arrived at the inn. Hidden in the base of a dell to the side of the road, it sat in the centre of a dish of virgin snow and bore on its thatch a casque of snow that looked as dense as stone. The aroma of cooked meats assailed them as they opened the door onto a room that had but a single occupant – a wolfhound, sprawled on the flagstones in front of the fire over which the spit was mounted. The heat of the fire was so fierce that they were obliged to take a table by the window, where it was, nonetheless, so warm that the glass was completely clear. The innkeeper, a beery, profusely bearded and muscular man whose gratitude for their presence made him almost lachrymose, swiftly brought them platters of beef and glazed potatoes, and a bowl of hot wine, which Klostermann volunteered to distribute.

As he waited for his portion, Ettlinger realised that he had deduced too much from the conversation he had witnessed between Meier and Maximilian von Davringhausen. The latter, sitting back against the wall with his arms braced against the table's edge, was in dour humour, and the cause was clear. Meier was conducting an overt and inept flirtation with Helene, every moment of which was warily observed by her brother. When Helene smiled Meier smiled too, making sure to catch her eye as he did so. Whatever Helene said he commended with a significant look; when Helene removed her gloves and pressed them flat on the seat beside her, Meier allowed his gaze to dwell on the gloves as if their position were a clandestine message meant solely for him. It was not long, however, before he received his rebuff. Refilling her glass, he tilted the ladle in such a way as to bring his hand into contact with the fur of her cuff. Helene looked at his hand and then lingeringly regarded his face with perfect blankness, a rejection so absolute and refined that it intensified Ettlinger's affection to such an extent that he could foresee himself following Meier's maladroit example.

Her indifference was feline and superb, but in the next moment it seemed to Ettlinger that it encompassed not just Meier but everyone present, himself not exempted. She turned to look through the window at the countryside around the inn. The sky was the colour of the moon and the fields as bright as quartz; a solitary crow was perched on the blunt summit of a snow-cased hedgerow. Ettlinger was captivated by the intensity with which she inspected what she saw. She stared out at the scene as if impelled by a need to commit it all to memory, or by the fear that at any moment it might cease to exist. And in her almost avaricious gaze Ettlinger saw the possibility of his success. He allowed himself to imagine that he might one day make something, cause something to be made, that might command such attention from her.

When Klostermann suggested that they begin, Ettlinger, convinced that he would risk irreparable failure by exposing anything provisional to Helene's scrutiny, decided to leave unshown the sketches he had brought. 'My contribution must be held over until another time,' he said. 'I think Wolfgang's poem is rather better suited to this setting,' he continued, and it appeared that Helene approved his deference to the founder of their group.

So Klostermann read them more of his Teutoburg epic, retailing the flight of the defeated Varus and his suicide in the camp beside the Rhine. He read it with unaccustomed verve, slamming a fist on the table with each blow of misfortune, raising an arm to invoke the valour of the ancient tribes. Applause was given at the final couplet, by the innkeeper as well as the friends, and then Helene asked if that was where he intended to end his tale, or were the Romans to be allowed their revenge? Was Germanicus to have his day?

'I think, like Varus, I can go no farther,' Klostermann replied. 'I shall rewrite and rewrite, but the story ends here.'

Meier, citing 'my famous concept of the cult of the fragment', suggested that he write a few more stanzas, then leave his work unfinished, 'as if its author had been cut down in his prime. Or simply become too inspired to continue.' Expiring under the intoxication of his lofty thoughts, Meier wiped a tremulous finger across his brow.

Klostermann thanked him for his advice, and promised to give it some thought. 'Very little thought,' he added, and raised his glass in a toast to the new year and their friendship.

Meier persisted, in a manner that suggested he had drunk more wine than Ettlinger had seen him consume. He noted the omission from the poem of the barbaric woodland altars, the tortures and the sacrifices recorded in the ancient chronicles. 'Where are the trees dedicated to Thor, the heads nailed to branches?' he demanded. 'You have kitted out our barbaric ancestors in the uniform of the officer class.'

Rising to his feet, Maximilian announced that he had another story for them.

'Another ghost story?' asked Klostermann, whose face conveyed his thankfulness for the intervention.

'Perhaps,' replied Maximilian. 'Certainly a strange little tale, again with none of the customary trappings of the supernatural. No mists, no night-time shadows, no ancestral ruins.'

'Another of which you are not the author?' asked Meier, insouciantly dividing his cut of beef.

'Wolgast is again the author,' Maximilian confirmed, and glanced irritably at his sister, as though he held her responsible for Meier's conduct. 'Shall I begin?' he asked, addressing Klostermann, and received a bow of permission.

'Very well. Our story concerns a simple tailor, and it takes place one late afternoon, on the seashore of the island on which he lives. The sun is blazing; his day's work has been finished ahead of time; he can rest for an hour. Making a pillow of his shirt, he lies down on the sand.'

'Perverse,' mumbled Meier through a mouthful of meat. 'A tale of the tropics on a day like this.'

'A small red boat comes into view,' continued Maximilian, pretending to have heard nothing. 'As it draws nearer, the man on the shore sees that the rower is a friend of his. The rower stands in the prow of his vessel to lift his net; the man on the shore hails him. They shout a few words to each other across the water.

'From a cleft in the dunes a group of men and women descend onto the beach. They settle in the shade of a pine tree, not far from where the tailor lies. He listens to their talk for a while, but before long the heat lulls him to sleep. When he awakes he sees that yet more people have appeared on the strand. Three young men are standing thigh-deep in the water, looking out at the boat; ten paces from them is a group of young women, paddling in the shallows. The tailor dozes, and the voices of the people on the beach follow him into his dreams. He dreams of a shipwreck. On the waterlogged deck, people discuss calmly what they will do after their deaths. The sea in his dream rises to dissolve the ship, like the tide washing over a hummock of sand. Gulls call across the water, but softly, as if in mourning.

'When the tailor awakes again, a woman who might be the mother of one of the young people is sitting a short distance out of the shadow of the pine. She addresses our tailor in the manner of someone who knows him, but he cannot recall ever having seen her before. She asks him how his son is faring in the city. They talk about the boy's apprenticeship to the goldsmith; the woman's nephew is also an apprentice, to a carpenter in a neighbouring street.

'At length the tailor rises. It is time to return home, for his wife will soon be back from the market. The woman wishes him and his son well. Two or three of the young men bid him farewell too, and an older man raises a hand to salute him as he tramps through the soft sand. On the crest of the dunes the tailor turns to look for the fisherman's boat, and is just able to make it out against the dazzle of the sea. He waves an arm slowly but cannot tell if he has been seen.

'"No, I did not see you leave," says his friend the following day. He asks what it was that had so agitated the tailor, for he had seemed to be a man with worries on his mind.

'"I have no worries," the other replies. He relates his conversation with the woman, recounting the things she had told him about his son's life in the city.

'His companion listens, but is unable to understand what is being said. For in all the time that he was casting his net and drawing in his catches, his friend had been quite alone on the beach.'

Maximilian sat down quickly and attacked his food, as if to forestall any discussion of the story, and indeed very little was said about it. Meier expressed his lack of enthusiasm with a single twitch of an eyebrow, for which Ettlinger endeavoured to compensate with a few words of approval, echoed by Stein with something less than conviction.

'Does Wolgast have many such tales?' Stein asked.

'We shall soon find out,' said Klostermann.

They passed another two hours at the inn, an interval during which a hunting party came in, soaked to the thighs and bearing empty bags, followed ten minutes later by a newly-married couple and their parents, who insisted on buying a bowl of wine for their fellow guests. It was a most convivial afternoon, but eventually they acknowledged that Wolgast was not going to join them, and thus it was in an atmosphere tinged with disappointment that they returned to the sleighs.

Meier offered an arm to assist Helene into the nearer sleigh. 'Next time perhaps I shall surprise everyone,' he said, as she put a hand on his wrist.

'I thank you, Leopold,' said Helene, and then, more quietly: 'You will one day make an accomplished suitor, but I think that you have practised on me long enough for one day.' As she was speaking, her brother pushed Ettlinger forward to take the place that Meier coveted.

'I think he has decided he needs a muse, and I am to be she,' commented Helene to Ettlinger as Maximilian set the sleigh moving. She fluffed her collar around her face and turned away to view the snowbound land, which now was greying in the early dusk. For several minutes her attention was fixed on the passing scenery so determinedly that Ettlinger did not feel in the least bit slighted. Her pleasure in it was manifestly immense, and provoked in Ettlinger both admiration and an urge to make some reckless declaration to her, an urge he knew he must resist. In his mind he rehearsed a dozen things he might say to her, but he had said nothing when Maximilian, seeming suddenly to take offence at being ignored, wondered aloud if they were too cold to be sociable.

At this Helene reminded him that there was such a thing as sociable silence, a remark to which Ettlinger momentarily attached greater significance than he knew was warranted.

'And you?' Maximilian demanded.

'Perfectly content,' Ettlinger assured him. In the

corner of his eye he saw Helene look at him, he thought, but he kept his gaze on the horizon.

'And so am I,' said Maximilian. 'I prefer this weather. I like it cold. It makes you feel – ' and he clenched his fists on the reins and made the tendons of his neck stand out. 'With the snow, and so many trees bare, everything looks as if it's there because it's been placed there. Like the branches have been inked against the sky, and the hedges laid down where they make the best effect.'

'Almost poetry,' Helene teased, pushing her hands deeper into the opposite sleeves.

'There is no law against men of business being poets as well,' Maximilian cheerily protested. 'Fine feelings are not the prerogative of ladies of leisure.'

Helene's expression modulated fleetingly from mischievous amusement into a look of exasperation that Ettlinger was perhaps not meant to see.

'Anyway, Helene, it was only last week you told us all at breakfast that the snow made you want to stroke the hills, which I must say I find sillier. Remember?'

'I do, but I am sure it is of no interest to our friend,' said Helene. 'What is your favoured season?' she asked Ettlinger, raising her voice to deter her brother from speaking.

'The autumn,' Ettlinger told her, a statement he realised might be true, but was made largely because he suspected that Helene would like him to prefer the melancholy season. 'I like the sense of harmony it brings, the sense of all things being drawn to an ending, of a great cadence of nature.'

'So now I should say that my choice is the spring, the season of revival,' she replied, giving Ettlinger a little bow as a sign that he should take her sparring lightly. 'But in fact this is my favourite time. I love the way the wind moulds the snow. I love the fact that its contours are always changing. Will that do, dear brother? Will you later quote me in circumstances that might embarrass me?'

'Of course,' said Maximilian, and at that instant a rabbit burst out from a bank of snow, an irruption as startling as the snap of a trap. Helene laughed and pressed a hand to her chest, and Maximilian laughed with her. Ettlinger, however, following its zigzag run across the field, thought of Abbadon's grey hair coiled in the madman's hands. He remembered the tears in Abbadon's eyes and looked at Helene, and saw the water that the wind had brought to her eyes. Wanting to take her hand, he kept himself from disgrace by affecting absorption in the progress of the winter sunset until they entered the outskirts of Munich.

'This is what I like best of all,' Maximilian confided as they approached the Theresienwiese. 'Whatever the season, whatever the distance I have travelled, I always have this feeling that the city is taking me back in. A sense of homecoming.'

'I know exactly what you mean,' said Ettlinger, with too much ardour.

Helene said nothing, but Ettlinger believed he saw her make a wry inflection of her lips.

At the stables a letter was handed to Klostermann. 'An apology from Wolgast,' he announced. 'Urgent business. He apologises at length. Next time he will not fail us, he says.'

'Let us hope not,' said Maximilian.

'Heaven forfend,' agreed Helene sarcastically, and

then she shook hands with Stein, Klostermann and Ettlinger, who turned to the task of waking Meier and escorting him back to his rooms.

24.

This is where the women's bath was built. Constructed of brick, it took the form of a sunken hall, with a long rectangular pool at its centre. The water flowed into the pool through a conduit laid from the ice houses across this courtyard, where the heated stones raised its temperature to a pleasant coolness. This courtyard was where the women would dry themselves. A slatted cedar platform kept their feet from the terracotta pavement, for in summer it would blister skin in the second of contact. Some days the emperor would sit in this courtyard and gaze at the marks the women's feet made, watching the footprints contract and form islands on the warmed wood, as if he were looking upon portraits of his lovers.

A colonnade ran along the two long sides of the pool. Set back from each arch of the colonnades was a small chamber, its door bearing the image of the woman to whom that chamber was dedicated. They kept their oils here, and their braids and sandals. All were depicted life-size, seated upon a bench which appeared to run continuously along the wall, linking door to door. All sat in the same posture – knees together, left hand upon left knee, torso and head turned to face the door by which the bath was connected to the courtyard above.

The eyes of Laodice, who died before we came here, were painted shut; the same was done with the eyes of those who did not follow us, and of those who died here.

Cassandane was one of these; the door of her chamber was sealed with a cord of her hair, thickened with beeswax.

Today, in a certain house in the capital, one may inspect a fragment that shows the mouth and nose of Amestris. She mastered four languages as a girl, and excelled at a sport that involved throwing an iron ball from the back of a galloping horse. In a different country is preserved a panel showing the left breast of Cassandane, and a strip of wood decorated with the thigh of Amestris's sister, whose chamber adjoined that of Amestris.

In a third country one can see a panel of wood on which is painted the right forearm and hand of Artaÿnte, who could compose a song in the time it took to sing it, and whose face was the most beautiful of all. Her skin was of an extraordinary pallor, and so delicate that the veins on her temples showed in faint blue lines, as if a feather dipped in watered ink had brushed her there. Her chamber was at the far end of the pool.

25.

It was the last week of January when Wolgast at last joined Klostermann and the others.

The day after the expedition to the Steuermann inn the snow began falling again, and it fell every day for two weeks with barely a pause, laying upon the city a covering so thick that gullies had to be dug every morning along the main streets and across the squares. Floes heaped with bales of snow clogged the Isar, and a man was killed when a boulder of compacted snow slipped from the roof of the Frauenkirche. Then one morning, it was a Wednesday, Ettlinger battered open the door of his house and stepped into sunlight so white he had to close his eyes. That afternoon he received a note from Klostermann – if the following day was clear, he would go out at midday to the inn midway along the road to Schleissheim, and he would be pleased if his friends could meet him there.

The next morning Ettlinger squinted through the bouquets of ice that covered his window and saw a city of the sort that puppet shows take place in. The sky was cloudless, the sun as clean as a berry, and every roof shone as if tiled with silver. In a state of elation he dressed and went out into the street, where two gangs of children were hurling fusillades of snow across the road. The people he saw seemed to share his delight, looking about them as if the radiance of the day had now been revealed as the purpose of the preceding weeks' bad weather. No one passed without an exchange of greetings. Nothing could have been more auspicious.

He went to a café to warm himself before his walk, and at ten o'clock set off in the direction of Schleissheim, shuffling along pavements that were plated with ice after the thaw of the previous day and the freeze of the night. Little less than an hour into his journey he was overtaken by Klostermann's sleigh. 'Aboard!' Klostermann commanded. 'Astonishing, what?' he exclaimed, gesturing at the sky as Ettlinger climbed up. His expression was that of a man who had just been given an unmerited reward.

A short distance further along the road they came upon two figures, arm in arm, their heads enveloped in a single cloud of breath, both clad in dark blue serge coats hemmed with snow. 'Could it be?' said

Klostermann, and a minute later Stein and Meier were crammed onto the seat, the former full of praise for the providence of the Almighty, the latter displaying ruefully his violet fingernails.

'Insensate. Defunct. Utterly without feeling,' moaned Meier as he fumbled for his flask of Cognac. Back and forth the flask went, as they sped towards the inn. A raucous hilarity prevailed. They told tales of their families and made anecdotes out of mere moments of the season's festivities. An inebriated uncle had upbraided Meier for his wastrel's ways; Klostermann's cousin, a girl of twelve, had told him they were destined to marry, and said it in such a way that it sounded like a curse.

And yet, even though he laughed no less heartily than the others, the more loudly they joked the stronger grew Ettlinger's suspicion that they were making too much of their merriment. A shadow lay on his mind, and the shadow deepened with their arrival at the inn. While the four were stamping the snow from their boots, the sleigh of Helene and Maximilian von Davringhausen came into the yard. Maximilian slapped Klostermann on the back as if they were brothers rather than friends, and hailed him as their intrepid poet. His sister's manner, however, was the very reverse of his, for the familiarity with which she greeted all of them alike was a cool familiarity, indicative of nothing more than that they had met before on more than one occasion.

Wolgast was already there, seated in a corner of the room in a high-backed chair, across which a bearskin coat was draped. As they filed towards him between the benches, led by Klostermann, Wolgast rose to welcome them one by one, and courteously remained standing until all were seated. Raising his arms in an embracing gesture, he asked what they would like to drink and ordered brandy for all, as none demurred at his suggestion. Ettlinger, taking the chair next to Wolgast, the place Wolgast had clearly reserved for him, observed Maximilian staring at the scar with something very like reverence.

Yet the preliminaries to Wolgast's performance were lacklustre, as if Wolgast's lordly presence had constrained them with an awareness of their youth. Klostermann began the proceedings by reading from his Teutoburg poem a revised version of an episode they had heard before. The advance of Varus into the forest had been improved, thought Stein, by reducing the amount of speechmaking. Meier, though, had reservations: 'It is one thing to make us feel how out of place the Romans were in the thickets of the Teutoburg,' he commented, 'but quite another to imply that the very trees spoke the language of the Germans.'

Klostermann took the criticism well, and concurred that his revision had lost vivacity while gaining too heavy a load of didacticism. He would put it aside for a month or two, he said, perhaps to work on another poem he had begun to contemplate. 'A sort of Walhalla of poets from Homer to the present,' he explained, but said no more about the project, a reticence that seemed indicative of the weakness of his commitment to it, rather than of a reluctance to discuss something as yet unformed.

Stein, having gained the assent of the inn's other patrons, sang a folk song which drew the warmest praise from Meier, who then admitted he had nothing to bring to the day's session. Subsiding into a tone of complaint, Meier reported that a crisis was upon him. 'My family insist that I abandon my life for a career,' he went on. 'I fear I cannot much longer withstand my father's admonitions. The time has arrived, he says, for me to devote myself to the practice of the law, having spent too many years in its study.' The lament continued, and even though Meier succeeded in talking himself back into a more sardonic role, Ettlinger knew that the group's dissolution would happen before long. 'My pen will still be at your service, Wolfgang, of course,' said Meier. 'We shall all support the reputation of our poet,' he insisted, in a declaration of loyalty that was seconded by everyone but seemed to present to Klostermann a burdensome vision of his future.

Seeing Klostermann thus cast into a state of mind not unlike that of Meier, Ettlinger decided that he would show the drawing he had brought. It was a pencil drawing, heightened with patches of water-colour, of the Acropolis as it might have looked in the reign of Pericles. 'A most plausible Mediterranean sun,' commented Meier, as the rest craned their necks over the view.

Helene had as yet said nothing, and she said nothing now, although there was in the set of her mouth a sign, perhaps, that her evaluation of Ettlinger had been in some degree enhanced. 'Should any of you want it, I make a present of it,' said Ettlinger, making his offer as Helene's hand touched the paper.

'Mine!' bidded Maximilian. 'I mean, ours!' he shouted, grinning at his sister.

'Of course,' replied Ettlinger. He applied himself to rolling the drawing carefully, in order that his chagrin might not be apparent.

Wolgast, having listened to their conversation in the manner of a benign despot weighing the merits of his potential heirs, now at last intervened. 'Allow me to bring some lightness into your academy. With your permission I shall extemporise a comic tale, a little comedy in two scenes.'

Klostermann made a gesture of respectful compliance. Clapping his hands on his thighs, Maximilian leaned forward eagerly towards Wolgast, his face suffused with gratitude. Helene, Ettlinger noticed, was scanning the rafters in an attitude of wistful boredom, though it was impossible to say whether the cause was her brother or the prospect of Wolgast's tale.

Wolgast asked them to imagine a Florentine palazzo, 'a building that was once as splendid a dwelling as any in the city, but is now in its senescence. The scene is set in our time, let us say last year. Picture please a throng of gentlemen in a spacious salon of the upper floor – the *piano nobile* as it is styled in those parts. I would have you hear a hubbub of Italian chatter, and the irritant sniffing of English snuff-takers. See the cracked terracotta tiles that cover the floor. They are painted with a fleur-de-lys pattern, and used to be glazed like pastries; three centuries of footfalls have worn away the gloss, which now survives in patches so small you could mistake them for drops of water. See threadbare tapestries on the walls, depicting the abandonment of Dido, the birth of Venus, the death of Actaeon. There are a few lopsided chairs; an ancient bow-legged dog sleeps under one of them.

'An auction is to take place. In a corner of this room there stands an easel. It supports a painting of Saint Sebastian. His pliant and hairless young body is bequilled with more than the customary allocation of arrows. It is a colourful – some would say too colourful – work, executed with pigments as bright as children's eyes. It is not a painting of the very highest order. There is an awkwardness to the drawing of the martyr that might, for some connoisseurs, vitiate its quality. It is probable that the picture is the product of a maestro's workshop rather than of the master's own hand. But what is important is that it is some three hundred and fifty years old and thus of a value that is not to be contested.

'A pleasant, plump and oafish young Englishman, let us call him Lord Chester, is impressed by the picture's pedigree. He is on his way back home from a tour of the peninsula, an experience that has not noticeably improved his sensibility and has yielded no cultural souvenirs, unless the Neapolitan disease be one.' Placing a hand to his mouth, Wolgast forced a prim cough.

'In all his time in Italy our Lord Chester has been offered nothing but a few indecipherable Roman gravestones and a batch of drawings at an absurdly high price – the sort of price for which one would expect to get something finished and durable. However, he has heard that the Saint Sebastian might be obtained at a more reasonable cost, and something in its spasmodic contortions appeals to him. He sees in this painting the making of his reputation.

'The auction commences. Lord Chester tenders a bid a little way short of the rumoured valuation.

An ancient Italian grandee promptly exceeds it – so promptly, indeed, one might think him offended by Lord Chester's niggardliness. As if adding his voice to the reproof of the English pennypincher, a compatriot of the grandee – a green-eyed young gentleman with a twirled little flaxen moustache and a heart-shaped mole on his right cheek – supersedes the second offer. Disconcerted that his acquisition of the painting is to be a more troublesome business than he had expected, Lord Chester trumps them by a small proportion. This provokes an instantaneous response from his rivals. Up and up the bidding goes, pushing the price beyond the sum the Englishman had envisaged as the maximum he might have to countenance. Before long he has undertaken to pay three times what he can afford without discomfort, but his first rival, seeming content that honour has been satisfied, has at last retired from the contest.

'The other, however, will not easily be bested. Cavaliere Gianluca Raffaele Contarini is the epitome of an Italian type that Lord Chester has come to despise. Effete, complacent, untrustworthy, he casts his haughty look upon Lord Chester as if the foreigner were an illiterate peasant endeavouring to impress his masters by passing his gaze across the pages of a book.' Wolgast preened himself and pinched the tips of his imaginary moustaches, impersonating with glee the supercilious aristocrat.

'Cavaliere Gianluca Raffaele Contarini would rather wear sackcloth than give way to Lord Chester, and Lord Chester would rather ruin himself than be beaten by Cavaliere Gianluca Raffaele Contarini. And so the painting of Saint Sebastian becomes a mere ancillary to the auction. The sale has become a joust with promissory notes for weapons.

The men trade expensive blows until finally, with the desperation of a duellist risking all on a mighty lunge that will leave his flank exposed if it fails to hit the mark, the bold Contarini hurls at Chester a bid that is half as big again as the previous one. Grievously wounded, Lord Chester blenches; he places a hand on his purse as if to take its pulse; he looks to Saint Sebastian as though imploring an image of his monarch for guidance. Heroically, with no thought of the consequence, he summons the resources to deliver the *coup de grâce* – an additional two guineas. Aghast, Contarini regards the jubilant and repugnant face of Lord Chester; he turns on his heels and runs headlong from the room into the teeming streets of Florence. Saint Sebastian is bound for the English capital.

'A month later, having scrimped his way across Italy and France to preserve as much of his remaining allowance as he can, Lord Chester is in his bedroom in London, avidly gazing at his investment. He inspects every inch of it. He marvels once again at the foliage of the distant mountain – so many varieties of green in so small a space! The minuscule petals of the flowers around the base of Sebastian's stake – the artist must have painted them with a brush made of a single hair! And the astonishing figures in the background, bellowing and brawling beneath the city gate – some of them are so tiny that his thumbnail would accommodate three of them! He takes a magnifying lens to admire these spectators. He inspects them more closely than he has ever done before, the tip of his nose nudging the surface of his beloved picture.

'Then with a cry he staggers back, pressing a fist against his chest. He shrieks like a woman startled by an intruder. He tears his hair and weeps. What has he seen? What is it in his picture that has driven him to such extremity, and in the merest blink of an eye?

'It is this. Beneath the boughs of a mulberry tree, beside the river that flows in and out of the picture on its right-hand side, stand two men, neither of them bigger than a ladybird. Under the glass their features are revealed to have been painted with a preternatural fidelity to detail. Few artists would be able to match it on any scale. And the character in the middle, smiling out of the picture at the man whose breath flows over him, is a green-eyed young gentleman with a twirled flaxen moustache and a heart-shaped mole on his right cheek.'

Signalling the closure of his plot, Wolgast rested his hands on the table, then shrugged his shoulders to prompt a response.

Meier and Klostermann were enthusiastic, as were Stein and Maximilian. 'It is astonishing,' Maximilian asserted, with an obsequious fervour which Wolgast at once deflected.

'My tale was not spun out of the air. Planning is the thing, isn't it, August?' he said to Ettlinger. 'Planning and research.'

Unnerved at being directly addressed, Ettlinger made no reply.

'I think August might not approve,' remarked Wolgast to Klostermann.

'Not at all, not at all,' said Ettlinger. 'I thought you were about to say more.'

'As I trust you are,' said Maximilian. 'We must hear you admit to some spontaneity.'

'Very little,' Wolgast replied. 'My story is but a little piece of clockwork that strikes a nice note.'

'Johann Friedrich is right, I think,' said Helene, setting her empty glass on the table as though to show that her interest in their talk was now depleted. 'What he has shown is but a talent for combination.'

'I thank you,' Wolgast responded with a modesty that bespoke huge vanity, narrowing his eyes in a glance that Ettlinger found improper. Its implication seemed to be that Helene had said something that only she and Wolgast could understand, but whatever the meaning he had intended, she appeared not to be a willing recipient. She waited for Meier to finish refilling her glass, then trained on Wolgast's eyes a deliberated look that began as an imperious questioning and ended as a dismissal. Nobody could be more magnificent or more desirable, Ettlinger told himself.

A toast to Wolgast, 'our honoured guest', was proposed by Klostermann, but no sooner had it been drunk than Wolgast took a fob watch from his waistcoat and announced that he would now have to leave them to their own company. 'I have enjoyed myself,' he said, 'and, I hope, have given some enjoyment. Persevere, young man,' he adjured Klostermann, and shook his hand.

'This must not be the last time,' said Klostermann, at which Wolgast bowed as though taking the request as an order.

Wolgast donned his enormous coat, which made of him an incongruously clumsy figure. 'Shall I be seeing you tomorrow?' he asked Ettlinger. There was a strange intonation to the question, an intonation that suggested something had occurred in the course of the afternoon that required discussion between them. The next time they met in the library of Wolgast's house, however, no mention of the gathering was made.

An enervated, almost disconsolate atmosphere descended over them once Wolgast had gone. There was some perfunctory talk of his story. Meier drank more than his share of brandy, and instead of becoming expansive and combative, as was his custom, became drowsy and disgruntled. Before long Ettlinger took his leave, reasoning that nothing would be lost on this occasion were he to depart before Helene. This interpretation seemed an error as soon as he announced that he was returning to his lodgings, for the farewell that Helene gave him was little more than the look one might bestow on someone who was leaving the room for a few minutes only. Eventually, towards the end of his walk, he contrived to recast her casualness to his advantage. He should take encouragement from her ease in his company, he told himself, and he had almost persuaded himself that this was true when it occurred to him that no sleigh had passed him, and that perhaps the conversation of Helene and her brother, and Stein and Meier and Klostermann, had revived in the absence of Wolgast and Wolgast's acolyte.

26.

Here, five hundred paces to the south of the Residence,

in the flank of this scarp, is where the silent room was made.

We began by excavating a hole in the rock. The debris was piled in the mouth of the cave to seal it against the sounds of the valley, while a tunnel was bored under the compound's walls to connect the silent room to the emperor's suites. A door of oak insulated the room from the tunnel.

When the emperor reported that the silence of the room was not perfect, that he had been able to hear inside it the braying of a donkey somewhere in the valley, we set about lining the cell with wood. We used thick timbers and pitch was poured over the walls to close the seams. Still the emperor was not satisfied: after less than an hour, his sense of hearing, hunting the silence as one's eyes at night search out the areas of weaker darkness, had detected the screech of an owl.

Heavy fleeces, clotted with grease, were nailed to the timbers. Over these were laid plates of metal, screwed firmly into the wood, and from spikes protruding from these plates were hung mattresses of thick grey felt. The floor was padded with felt; the roof was swagged with rolls of it.

When this work was done I entered the room. For the first few minutes it seemed that nothing could ever be heard there. The space was filled with a silence as heavy as the material that covered the room. But then a noise emerged that was like the beating of a slack-skinned drum, and behind this noise arose another like water forced through pipes in bursts of pressure. These noises had no source that I could find, for whichever way I turned they remained unchanged. They became like the thrumming of hoof-beats and grew so loud that I tried to shout over it. My throat and skull vibrated, but my voice vanished into the walls, giving way instantly to what now I realised was the crashing of my own blood.

The tunnel from the room to the emperor's suites was closed with rubble, and a small circular hole was drilled through the roof of the silent room. Through this hole certain miscreants were lowered by a rope, which then was severed.

27.

In the doorway of Johann Friedrich von Wolgast's residence a man of about fifty years of age appeared. Pausing on the threshold, he adjusted the collar of his coat and the fingertips of his kidskin gloves, smacked his hands together and faced the avenue with the gaze of a man in the moment before a military honour is pinned upon his chest. He passed Ettlinger with not the slightest deflection of his eyes, and mounted the step of the awaiting carriage. He was followed by two servants in livery, each carrying an object the size of a jeroboam, wrapped in muslin. Holding their burdens before them, they cautiously boarded and took their seats opposite their employer. One fussed at his muslin, as if at the nightdress of a sickly child; the other folded his arms about the object on his knee, and closed his eyes briefly. Their master turned his rubicund face to each, his pursed lips demanding assurance that all was in order. Satisfied, he slipped a finger inside his shirt collar and waggled his head from side to side, working the finger around his neck. 'On!' he commanded, in a voice that was choked to the pitch of a girl's. Ettlinger watched the carriage drive away; from the faces of the three men one might have thought they were bearing explosive charges through the streets of Munich.

Wolgast was watching Ettlinger. 'Three days hence,' he said, holding the door open for him, 'Eberhard will be back on his estate, where only his pigs will be pleased to see him. His wife, her whelping done, now passes her days looking out at the pastures and the pigpens and recalling her brilliant days in Bremen, when it seemed she might one day sail with her husband to somewhere that was not Bremen.' They ascended the staircase, side by side. 'But ungallant Eberhard, with his triple-darned stockings and his unlimited money, saw off the romantic suitors, and now she has for company none but their son, an obese grotesque who imagines, in the more thoughtful episodes of his blunt existence, that one day he shall inherit the wealth his father has garnered through husbandry, frugality and usury.'

Wolgast led Ettlinger past the library and into a room from which two other doors gave egress. 'What the son does not know is that Eberhard, the hypocrite, is consuming that wealth at a rate few libertines could match,' Wolgast resumed. He pulled open the door on their left and swept aside the curtain that was then revealed. 'For Eberhard has a vice. He fancies himself to be a connoisseur.' Bowing, Wolgast gestured Ettlinger towards the cabinets and pedestals disposed in a line along the centre of the narrow room, like a host ushering a more distinguished guest towards other guests of similar distinction. So Johann Friedrich von Wolgast introduced his gallery of antiquities, which never again was Ettlinger permitted to view.

Lifting a ruby-tinted bell-jar from its seating, Wolgast revealed a cushion to which were attached ancient adornments of incised and pock-marked bronze, and buckles with enamel inlays in shades of mauve and green. 'This is Visigothic, this Byzantine and this Carolingian,' he explained. 'See here, the name of Agilulf, the Lombard king.' In the adjacent case three rows of coins were held in place by blue-headed pins. 'A penny from the reign of the English king Richard I,' said Wolgast, indicating the largest. 'This one bears the head of Witigis, the Ostrogoth lord of Italy. Here is a likeness of Pericles,' he said, positioning in his palm a small and uneven disc of gold. He raised his hand, so that Ettlinger might more closely inspect the bulbous profile of Pericles, below which a garland of Greek characters, cropped by the press, spelled out the first five letters of the Athenian's name.

Wolgast unlatched the door of a cherrywood cabinet, rattling its thin panel of glass. It threw back reflections that were mottled and misshapen, as if the glass were not a solid substance but rather an arrested flow of water. Exquisite ivory carvings were extracted one by one: a mirror-back showing the Dormition of the Virgin; a casket panel packed with tiny crusaders scaling ladders that stood clear of the body of the ivory, their rungs as slim as daisy stems; a family of standing figures the size of tulip-heads – 'Mary Magdalene, Saint Luke at his easel, Saint Lawrence and his grill, Saint Lucy and her plate of eyes, King David, his fleshly little Bathsheba, all of them thirteenth-century.' In another cabinet were displayed reliquaries from Cluny, Hildesheim and Limoges, their crystals set into marbled stone and framed with motifs in beaten copper. There were illuminated Gospels from Monte Cassino and Benevento, their margins teeming with four-winged angels, prophets, falconers, musicians and snakes in citric colours. Wolgast showed Ettlinger his collection of Sienese book-bindings, his maiolica bowls from Orvieto, Gubbio and Florence, all of them smothered in bright blue and orange nymphs and satyrs.

'My most valued possession I keep in holy isolation,' he announced, and guided Ettlinger lightly by his elbow towards the farthest window. There, in an alcove cut into the embrasure, was set a bust of Marcus Aurelius. 'I can see you are moved,' Wolgast remarked. 'One cannot but be moved when brought suddenly, anachronistically, into the presence of the noblest of the Romans. It is a privilege to be the object of that unillusioned gaze. And perhaps, too, one can detect in the expression of the Stoic prince a hint of the misery he was caused by his offspring, the worthless Commodus.' Shoulder to shoulder Ettlinger and Wolgast stood, as if awaiting permission to take their leave of the dead emperor. 'Note the precision with which the artist has simulated the curls of his beard,' said Wolgast. 'It is, I think, a superb passage of work, and I am certain the artist knew it would become yet finer as the dust of the centuries accumulated in the grooves of the stone.' He conducted Ettlinger away from the window, back towards the door by which they had entered. With a sigh he continued. 'Aurelius will remain here for a month longer, and then he is to be acquired by Ernst von Kreisel, whose vacuous mistress, *la bella* Cempini, you found so charming at Kreisel's ball. He will acquire it for an immense sum of money. To offer it to him at a lesser price might awaken a suspicion that he is being defrauded.'

He stopped in front of a low shelf of miscellaneous pieces that previously he had passed without remark. With a thumb Wolgast stroked his scar, ruminating. At length he took up a dull brown object that resembled a large flake of brick. 'A clay tablet, dating from the reign of Nebuchadnezzar. These marks are cuneiform writing.' The thumb that had been tracing his scar brushed back and forth over the clay, caressingly. 'It looks meaningless, does it not?' Wolgast asked. 'As indeed it is, for I made it, and I know nothing more of the languages of Babylon than does my cook.' He replaced the clay tablet and lifted a pair of primitive limestone figurines; they had over-large heads and stumps for legs and arms, and Wolgast smiled at them as a child might smile at a favourite doll. 'These come from the island of Rhodes. They are tribal effigies made perhaps a thousand years before the coming of Christ, but in fact made two or three years before the coming of Wolgast. I acquired them from a farmer named Demetrios, who chisels them by the dozen in his idle moments. And this' – he pointed to a rectangle of vellum pressed in a picture frame above the shelf – 'is a map of Europe drawn in York in the last years of the fourteenth century; or rather, created in Jena in the last years of the eighteenth. My ivories were fabricated by a cabal of craftsmen who live in the region of the Ardennes; they are devout and skilled men. In the Jura live the craftsmen who age my jewels and coins; using barrels of acidic soil and vats of horse's urine and bad wine, they give the pieces the patina of centuries in the space of mere weeks.'

Wolgast took Ettlinger back to the library, carrying from the gallery a ledger which he opened on the lectern. Within were drawings of all the objects Wolgast had sold, each annotated with its factitious provenance. 'All these I have released to enable Eberhard and his fellow fools to maintain their delusion. This hoard of Roman vases went to Kreisel; Eberhard believes this to be a Dürer engraving and this a gold stater from the period of Alexander; another expert acquired these onyx cameos, which my archives prove were cut in ancient Syracuse and later came into the possession of the great Lorenzo de'Medici. They shall not lose their value, for my documents give them an authenticity more convincing than many a genuine relic's.'

Wolgast pressed his hands to his face, and his lips parted as if in astonishment at his own deviousness. Yet his eyes belonged to a different face, the face of a man asleep though talking. From his waistcoat pocket he tugged a little velvet purse. 'With this money I shall buy for your use the Barbaro translation and commentary on Vitruvius.' He lowered his head. 'It is beautiful,' he added in a whisper, as if he were repeating something just said by someone who had left the room. Still his eyes were those of a man asleep.

28.

Two hours from his dwelling, Ettlinger emerges from

the long, parched gully, and the crescent of white houses by the harbour comes into view. Motivated only by the gradient of the hill, he walks down the track, his thoughts given over to nothing more than picking a path through the sharp-edged stones. His shadow is like a bucketful of tar dashed over the hot white earth. Sour curds of saliva lie on his tongue.

An eagle takes off from the ridge on his landward side, and flies on rigid wings towards the town, sliding across the sky like a stick across a frozen lake. Ettlinger feels his muscles weaken under the burden of the exertions he has made and has yet to make. The mountains flex in the heat. The shimmerings of the sea seem a portent of something moving towards a conclusion. He is perhaps losing his reason. A muted scream of seagulls rises from the town; he can see a spume of plumage above the harbour wall. He can hear voices, two at least, and the banging of planks on cobbles. He has the notion that something depends on his distinguishing the individual parts of this weave of sounds. That is a dog's bark, or another blow of wood on cobblestones. That is a child calling to its friends in one of the alleyways. He scrapes a foot through a pool of fine scree. In a spasm of panic, he sees his hut in the distance and has no recollection of his voyage to the island. A moment later he realises that the hut on the hill is not his.

Ettlinger sits on a tussock of broad leaves and opens his book. The right-hand page is defaced down its margin with a streak of green ink, Wolgast's mark. He reads the first of the paragraphs thus selected by Wolgast. Looking up from the page, he imagines the figure of Xerxes, the king of Persia, son of Darius, grandson of Hystaspes. Seated on a marble throne that has been set on a rise above the Hellespont, the king reviews his fleet and army. His uncle, Artabanus, stands beside him. The sails of Xerxes' navy fill the strait; his platoons cover completely the beaches and the plain of Abydos. He looks upon the forces with which he will destroy Athens, and praises the valour of his expedition. But as soon as he has spoken, tears flow from his eyes.

Ettlinger reads again what Artabanus says: 'My lord, I am troubled by the contradiction between what you do now and what you did just a moment ago. Then you said you were a fortunate man, and now you weep.'

Replacing the book in his pocket, Ettlinger hears, as if uttered by Johann Friedrich von Wolgast, the reply made by Xerxes: 'I was lost in thought, and it came into my mind how pitiful is the brevity of life, for of all these men there is not one who will be living one hundred years from today.'

Ettlinger repeats aloud the words of Xerxes. In full voice he repeats them many times, and with each repetition a little more of his will is returned to him, as if the text were an exercise by which a toxin is expelled from his lungs. He resumes his descent to the harbour. He crosses the narrow, waterless courses of three streams, then turns to walk along the bank of a fourth, a tributary of the river that bisects the town. Having rinsed his hands and washed his face in its water, he follows the river through the lemon orchards, where the ceaseless frenzy of the cicadas agitates his spirits pleasurably. He passes below the church of St George and down the steps of the port's main street.

On the waterfront a gang of five men are loading barrels of salted fish onto the bed of a cart. A bare-footed boy, laughing, presses his forehead against the muzzle of the sleepy mule. A fisherman sits on the edge of the quay, his feet resting on the prow of his boat, and scrapes fish-scales from a board with a long-bladed knife. He is perhaps seventy or eighty years old and his hair is as white as Wolgast's, and cropped so short that his sunburned scalp shows through it like the crust of a loaf under a dust of flour. Ettlinger assigns the old man's features to Artabanus, and walks on towards the tavern at the base of the sea wall.

He admires the crisply moulded rosette of plaster on the lintel of the harbourmaster's house and stops for a while to read the scenes carved into the barrel lids that hang on the wall of the cooper's shop next door. On the lid inscribed with the date 1816 is depicted a shipwreck; eight arms and four heads can be seen amid the waves that spread out from the tiny hull. Huge babies flank a company of townsfolk on the lid dated 1809, commemorating, it would appear, the birth of twin giants. Eight years earlier, a storm threw a boat out of the harbour and onto the quayside. In 1791 something happened that has now been lost to the action of the sea air on the wood.

There is an unoccupied table outside the tavern, with a single chair beside it. Ettlinger peels a piece of paper from the seat; it seems to be part of a bill of lading, and has what might be an eye drawn in charcoal on the reverse. Waiting to be served, he gazes at the sea and his mind loses its engagement in the annihilating rhythm of the wavelets that slap the stone. Dislocated memories – of a foggy street-corner that he could not find again, of wet brown applecores in a square of brilliant sunlight, of Martin von Stein so moved by his own singing that he cannot complete his song – appear in his mind, unarrestingly, like raindrops spreading on damp sand, and peter away.

A woman carries a table out onto the quayside, and sets it on the other side of the door. She goes back inside and reappears with a stack of chairs, which are promptly taken by four men who follow her from the tavern's front room. She has a small waist and broad, flat hips; her hair is very long and black, with here and there a single grey hair. After serving her other customers she comes over to Ettlinger, who conveys a request for water; she brings him a jug, and a bowl of plump green grapes. He plucks one, tastes it, and commends its sweetness, in German; she takes one too, smiles in agreement, and leaves him. Ettlinger takes another grape between his teeth and snips away a little dome of flesh to reveal the ragged, glutinous interior of the fruit. The sun sags onto the horizon of the mountains across the gulf, and as soon as it has gone a beacon appears on the far shore, close to the level of the water. The single point of light, shining out over the oily purple sea, stirs an insipid wistfulness for his life before he knew Wolgast.

Ettlinger hears the woman talking quietly to the men, in a voice that is a pattering of soft plosives and sibilants. He moves his chair a few inches so that he can observe the group more easily. She has a beguiling manner of speaking, leaving her mouth slightly open at the close of each phrase, as if in a silent gasp. On the flyleaf of his book Ettlinger sketches the bay, and puts in the foreground a standing woman, a woman with long black hair. He turns the book sideways and draws quick portraits of the four drinkers.

The woman stands beside Ettlinger to light the lantern beside the door, humming quietly a tune that sounds like a children's round. She looks over his shoulder at his sketches, then walks to the quayside and peers down at the mud-coloured fish that lurk among the fringe of weeds. When she returns he asks her for a jug of wine like the one the others are sharing. He judges that she is perhaps a decade older than he. She says something to him, and when she speaks he notices shallow grooves on her cheeks and little tucks at the edges of her lips. When she steps into the tavern the light from the lantern briefly falls on her face in such a way that the flesh of her cheek seems suddenly to slip underneath the skin, as if prefiguring her appearance many years on. These fleeting marks of time he finds alluring, as much as the mettle of her fig-dark eyes, which are the eyes of someone who can no longer be delighted by anything but whose curiosity is tireless.

Positioning the wine jug in the centre of the table, she leaves a finger hooked in its handle as Ettlinger takes hold of it. In that moment it strikes Ettlinger that he is in a place where he is not accountable to his peers, nor indeed to himself, for he took leave of himself back in Germany. He asks if he might eat here. She brings him a dish of tomatoes and bright green leaves and brittle fried fish, and as she sets the plate down he touches the back of her hand with the back of his. He pours her a glass of wine, which she takes to the doorway, where she stands for a long time. Brushing her forearms as the evening cools, she makes perfunctory remarks to the men and looks out over the boats at anchor. She holds her head tilted to one side, as if unsure what to make of whatever it is she is seeing.

Ettlinger takes a room above the tavern for the night. There she shows him the ring on her finger, then crosses her arms across her breasts and closes her eyes to signify her widowhood – not to elicit his compassion, it seems, but simply to set aside the past before they embrace. If she could have understood him, he wonders, would he have invented a history for himself? He lets the question go, but when he puts his arms around her slumbering body, he finds himself gripping her as if her flesh might offer asylum from memory.

In the middle of the night he awakens. She is lying with her back pressed to his chest, looking out of the window. She wipes a finger across her cheek, and by the light of the moon Ettlinger sees that it is wet. Perhaps her husband came from the village on the other side of the gulf, where still a single beacon shines across the pleated sea. Circling back into his dreams, he imagines her talking about a market in that village, about the things that can be bought there: herbs, fragranced papers, candles that burn with the smell of oranges. She talks to him of the superstitions of the villagers on the other side of the water. They say that the heart of the island is inhabited by dog people and monstrous children born of the couplings of lions and women. They believe that diamonds are nourished by the dew and that they propagate like plants. They believe that in the east there is a measureless well which is perfumed with peppers, and that if a man drinks from it three times in every ten years he shall live to be five hundred years old.

She rolls over and places a hand on his waist; she sighs as if she has decided to confess something to him; she is asleep. Ettlinger, his mind roaming on the borders of sleep, sees himself in the court of Xerxes. His hand is brimming with diamonds, with gems that are like fragments of springwater struck by the never-setting sun.

29.

The first week of March brought a foretaste of spring in mornings so clear the Alps seemed to rise in the suburbs, followed by afternoons of balmy sunlight and immobile clouds. On what turned out to be the penultimate day of this brief, displaced season, Ettlinger received an invitation to visit the estate of his patron, Anton Erwin Herterich, in order to inspect the place on which his temple was to be built. Wolgast, seeing the letter on Ettlinger's desk, asked if he might accompany him to the vicinity of the site, and so it was that, on the following morning, Ettlinger rode in Wolgast's phaeton to meet his patron.

Throughout the hour of the journey Wolgast interrogated Ettlinger about the history of his building. He wanted to know the circumstances of the commission, how Anton Erwin Herterich had come to see the studies that Ettlinger had drafted as a student, how Ettlinger had arrived at his design – in short, he wished to hear Ettlinger's account of every detail of his work, even those about which he had already heard. Flattered by such unwonted attention, Ettlinger responded volubly, and praised at length the resources of Wolgast's library, under the influence of which his work had progressed in directions he could not have foreseen. 'And now, under the influence of the book of nature, it may change again,' commented Wolgast, resorting to a more characteristic, elusive tone for the first time that day.

They were crossing an unkempt countryside, a terrain littered with stands of miscellaneous trees and rumpled by an assortment of low hills, like the foundations for a landscape in which nature had lost interest. The carriage entered the cover of a copse of birch on the crest of a rise. Emerging into the sunlight, they saw before them an expanse of flatter land, with here and there a graffito of hedges. The road curved slackly across the undulations of the plain, like a gigantic rope dropped from the sky. 'A piece of fine architecture would not go amiss,' commented Wolgast, looking around with jocular distaste. 'Who would have thought Bavaria had anything so drab to show?'

'I see a more picturesque passage,' Ettlinger bantered, pointing to the west, where, far beyond a pair of zinc-coloured lakes, rose a ridge covered by a forest so dense it resembled a vast pad of moss. Past the next hummock the view improved further. Beside the road stood a long-abandoned farmhouse. One gable had slumped to the earth and its roof-beam had fallen, and tiles were mixed with grass in what had once been the yard. To the side of the ruin flowed a stream, in which feeding fishes dabbed the surface in such numbers it was as if a private rain were falling on the water.

'We must be near to the place of your rendezvous,' suggested Wolgast. Ettlinger unfolded his map, and no sooner had he determined where they were than Wolgast tapped him on the shoulder with the handle of his whip. 'Your master, I assume,' he said, indicating a figure clad in a scarlet waistcoat and black breeches, standing near the summit of a hill to their left. The man was waving both arms at them like a semaphorist, and shouting repeatedly a word that was probably Ettlinger's name. At the point where the road most closely approached the base of the hill Wolgast brought the phaeton to a halt. 'I shall return for you in two hours,' he said as Ettlinger stepped down. 'Should you require longer, I shall wait longer. I can amuse myself.'

The sententious prose of his letters had given a misleading image of Anton Erwin Herterich. Far from being the gouty patriarch whom Ettlinger had envisaged, he was a young man – approximately the same age as Ettlinger – and possessed the ebullience and guilelessness of an even younger one. Every sentence was punctuated with an exclamation mark, and every few seconds he would clutch Ettlinger's wrist in demonstration of his enthusiasm for the scheme on which they had together embarked. He was at the very least delighted, often astounded, by each of Ettlinger's schemes and utterances. 'Extraordinary!' he exclaimed at a sketch of the Tower of the Winds, combing his soft fair hair with a rake of his fingers. Ettlinger described the topography of Athens, as he understood it, and placed the structures of its golden age within that imaginary domain. 'More, please! I must know more!' cried Anton Erwin Herterich, and his stark green eyes bulged in amazement. He untied a hamper of cheeses, roast ham and chilled wine from his saddle, and spread their repast on the grass. Ettlinger and his patron sat together on the creaking wicker basket, and admired the view from the site as they ate. Then Anton Erwin Herterich, smiling as if he were bringing news that would gladden his companion, gradually revealed that he had undergone a change of heart.

'Last week my father invited several guests to supper. One of them was Caspar Nette. Do you know of him?'

Ettlinger admitted that he did not.

'A most unique man. An excellent priest, a true shepherd to his flock. A scholar, moreover, like yourself, and something of a visionary too. In the course of our supper he said something that impressed me tremendously. "The Italians have abolished God from our churches," he said, "and put History in His place." Provoking that, don't you agree? And true?'

Sensing that his employer was only now nearing the point of this meeting, Ettlinger took a sip of wine in silent annoyance. A squirt of smoke rose from behind a hedgerow close to the road, and then from somewhere below came the report of a shot, a sound like a clap of two lengths of wood.

'Nette was quite inspirational,' Herterich continued, his eyes becoming vague with fond admiration. 'When we think of our great churches we tend to think of towering vaults and traceries and all that sort of thing. But we are mistaken to do so, he told us. These things are incidental. "Light is the essential substance," he said. "It is light that ties Man to God and to His creation." This is the message of our cathedrals, according to Nette, and I can see that he is right.'

'I agree,' Ettlinger responded.

'Yes,' said Herterich after a pause, a little irked by Ettlinger's terseness. 'But what I mean to say is that I have come to see that those are the precedents we should be following. Those are our exemplary buildings.'

'And there, with respect, I do not agree,' Ettlinger emphatically asserted. 'The circular temple, the most ancient of forms, is I believe the most eloquent and admirable. There is no more appropriate symbol of the perfect, the limitless and the omnipresent.'

'But the Greeks and the Romans were not Christians,' said Herterich testily, realising that his enthusiasm had no persuasive power. 'Neither were they of this soil, the German soil, as our cathedrals are.' He stooped to gather the bottle and the remnants of the food. The interview was reaching its end. 'To have proceeded with the project as we have hitherto conceived it would be an error. I am certain of that, and I hope that you will come to share my conviction.' From a pocket he withdrew a small leather pouch. 'I should like you to design something more in keeping with Nette's ideas. I have jotted down some of my thoughts on the matter. You can read them here,' he said, extracting from the purse a tightly folded piece of paper. 'I look forward to seeing what you make of them. And this, I hope, you will consider a reasonable wage for the efforts you have made on my behalf,' he concluded. He spilled some coins into his palm, tilted them back into the mouth of the purse, and passed the purse to Ettlinger.

As Herterich rode off, Ettlinger sullenly counted his fee. It was a generous amount of money, but his urge was to fling it away. He contemplated the patch of tamped grass around his boots, so deeply vexed that he was unaware that Wolgast was approaching until he called out to him – 'A spot made for philosophy, Ettlinger.' Wolgast held aloft a brace of widgeon, then threw the birds to the ground by Ettlinger's feet and turned his face into the breeze from the plain. 'You seem to be listening to the maundering of the wind.'

'My lord has decided that the masons of the thirteenth century were wiser than the architects of Athens,' Ettlinger informed him.

'You are dismissed?' asked Wolgast with a lilt of disbelief.

'I am to continue to do my good work, but to do it differently. Herterich no longer wants orders in the classical style. Now he wants arches pointed like the glades of the German forests. He wants a miniature Köln Cathedral, because that is the German way,' Ettlinger feebly joked. 'I am to do something in the truly German style – the style of Zaragoza, of Chartres, of Winchester.'

'You have my sympathy,' said Wolgast, 'but I am not altogether surprised. I have heard a few things concerning the younger Herterich.'

'Things that I should have known?'

'Things that were of no relevance until today, and mere hearsay.'

'Hearsay might satisfy me,' Ettlinger replied.

'It is said that he is an honest young man. I am sure he will pay you well.'

Ettlinger dangled the purse in front of his face. 'He has paid me well already,' he muttered. 'What else?'

'He is full of good intentions, but has a weather vane for a backbone. He has opinions the way other men have head colds – they descend upon him, inconvenience him for a while, and then are gone, leaving no trace.'

'But a trace is what I must leave.'

'And so you shall,' Wolgast assured him. 'Do not concern yourself with Herterich's reputation, such as it is. I suspect he is not a worthy patron for you, but then neither was Nero for the great Seneca. He might nonetheless be the occasion you require. You have principles enough for both of you.' He laughed loudly, but the fixity of his eyes made his gaiety seem a forgery. 'I remember when you came into that hideous room in which I was playing,' he continued, sawing a violin bow in the air and jerking his head from side to side. 'I struck the postures of a man possessed by the daemon of music. That displeased you, and I liked you for that. I thought you were a man who might be worth befriending. Such is my vanity.' He placed an open hand upon his breast. 'Friendship is so often self-flattery, don't you think?' he asked brightly.

Bemused by Wolgast, Ettlinger could not reply.

Wolgast bowed and retrieved the birds as he did so. 'It would be best for me if we departed now,' he said, slinging them over his back. 'This evening I must attend a performance of *La Clemenza di Tito.* A boring opera, but interludes of boredom are necessary for the health of the soul, I believe. Like fasting. Why has nobody dramatised the clemency of Alexander?' Wolgast asked himself aloud. 'A far more dramatic subject, with plentiful opportunities for battle scenes and disputations. The mother of Darius committed suicide upon the death of Alexander, the conqueror of her son. Do you think you might show such devotion to my memory?' he asked mildly, adding quickly – 'There is no need to answer. Shall we leave?'

'I should prefer to walk back, if you do not mind,' Ettlinger replied. 'There are things I must clarify.' Wolgast did not try to dissuade him, which Ettlinger took as a compliment. During the four hours of his walk, the ambiguous interest that Wolgast appeared to have taken in him occupied his thoughts rather more than did the vacillation of Anton Erwin Herterich.

30.

This is where the emperor's divan was set, at the junction of four blind corridors burrowed through the earth on which the Residence rested. The walls and floor and ceiling of these corridors were clad with a blond stone so finely grained that the masons could dress it into surfaces as regular and smooth as a drumhead. The mortar that bound them was mixed with powder ground from the same stone, and spread in a layer no thicker than a kerchief of cotton. Blocks and mortar were filed and polished into a condition of absolute identity. One could no more discern where the stone blocks met than one could distinguish the water poured into a half-filled glass from the water with which it mingled.

Doors gave entrance to this cruciform room at the end of each of its limbs; these were hung with sheets of the same blond stone, affixed with such precision that the walls seemed to be an unbroken surface. Yet so expertly were they balanced on their pivots that the pressure of a single finger sufficed to open these doors onto the chambers that riddled the underfloor of the Residence. There was no difference between day and night here, for there was no means for the light of the outside world to penetrate. Oil burned constantly in channels cut high in the walls and screened from view in such a way that the flicker of the flames was turned into what seemed a milky emanation of the ceiling.

It was reported that at night the music of flutes and pipes came through the doors, and sometimes shrieks and cries. One of the slaughtermen of the emperor's kitchen asserted that the engineers who had fashioned the doors had also set hidden alcoves in the walls. A wound that appeared on the cheek of Artabanus was said to have been inflicted during the rites that were held in the cruciform corridors.

Once, when I knew the final days were upon us, learning that the emperor had left the Residence on a night-hunt, I crept into the subterranean chamber and occupied the emperor's divan. In the perpetual half-light of the corridors, the divan and my body cast a shadow as pale as the form of a tree seen through the dawn's mist, a shadow the same colour as the silk of the divan. On the floor at my feet, and all around, were pale marks like faint maps of our land, perhaps the traces of cleansings. I sat on the divan and surveyed the four points of the corridors' compass. The walls seemed to meet no end, instead dissolving into an air that had the colour of stone. I heard the blurred tumults of the Residence: commands relayed in the emperor's kitchens; orders given in the offices of the chamberlain; clatterings in the storerooms and armouries. Overhead, the passage of a cart across the atrium made the dull reverberation of a far-off rockfall. At my back, a shouted summons came through the walls like the caw of a rook from a distant copse.

I reclined on the emperor's divan and closed my eyes. The patter of feet through adjacent chambers became the footfalls of ghosts hastening from me towards the invisible doors. All around me were voices and sounds, as if I had become the object of a speaking memory that was not my own. On the threshold of sleep, my body became a vapour, at one with the fog of mingled voices, but sentient with what was perhaps the melancholy of Xerxes.

31.

Exactly one week after his meeting with Herterich, Ettlinger returned to Wolgast's library to continue his studies. On the following day, in the early twilight, he was sketching an angle of the Parthenon when he heard his name called from some distant part of the house – or rather, a sound irrupted into the silence of the library, and a moment later he realised that the sound was his name. He tapped his nib on the rim of the ink-well, and placed the pen across the sheet of paper. Again his name was called, just his name, 'Ettlinger', and not with a tone of summons, but as if someone were loudly rehearsing its pronunciation. He rose, and at the door paused, becoming conscious of a vaporous anxiety. Booming from the corridor of the upper floor, Wolgast's voice reverberated in the great stairwell.

Ettlinger now ascended to the upper floor for the first time. Led by one last repetition of his name, he passed a quartet of closed doors and a quartet of dark walnut chests, each carved with a different heraldic beast in deep relief: a unicorn, a rampant lion, a doe, a wolfhound. At the corridor's head a fifth door stood open, disclosing a plaster wall daubed by the sallow light of an oil lantern.

Inside the room was Wolgast, his palms resting on the chest of a young man who lay on the table before him, naked. Wolgast's head was bowed, as if in prayer. His hair, the enamelled surface of the table and the young man's skin were all of the same hue, the colour of soured milk. Behind Wolgast, in a corner of the room, hung a skeleton which was held together with twists of wire and ligaments of dusty mauve fabric.

'My sanctum, August,' said Wolgast flatly, looking up. His voice was like that of an exhausted man surrendering something he had no wish to keep. His gaze wandered purposelessly around the place that Ettlinger occupied, as if Ettlinger were nothing but a pattern in smoke. Contracting, his hands rose onto their fingertips, pushing dimples into the corpse's flesh. His mouth opened, then closed, and he inhaled deeply, almost lasciviously, as if at a bower of blossoms. The breath gave him sufficient animation to utter a single sentence: 'You have allowed me to see the site of your true work, and now perhaps I might reciprocate the honour?' The weary cadence of his voice suggested he required no response; his face assumed an expression of such superiority and torment that none was possible.

His hands palpated the cheeks of the cadaver, stroking the beard along its nap. The eyes were closed and the face was marked by a thin line, maroon and no wider than woollen yarn, which emerged from the corpse's hair at the centre of its brow, ran along the ridge of the nose, across the lips and disappeared into the beard. 'Allow me to commence,' Wolgast announced as if to an audience of fifty, and as he did so he took hold of the cadaver's temples and pulled apart the two halves of its head, which had been cleft from crown to throat as cleanly as a ball of wood sawn in two. With the sound of a foot placed lightly in mud the halves came back together, and by a turn of his wrist Wolgast slid the features back into alignment.

'Don't look so aghast, Ettlinger. There is nothing untoward in what you see,' he said. 'In an earlier life I was a physician, but I allowed my expertise to lapse, for reasons that need not trouble you. Such errancy is far from rare in the priestly callings. Now former colleagues allow me to continue my researches . . .' and his voice trailed away, his face becoming that of a man listening to a friend who has long ceased to amuse him. He eased the placid face apart and shut it again sharply, with a clack of bone on bone, then eased the head back onto its pillow. As he reached for a knife from the mantel, Wolgast stopped his movement to turn and smile at Ettlinger. His smile was that of a kindly parent obliged to deny his child some indulgence. 'No, Ettlinger. On consideration, it is best that you leave,' he said, and he reached over the torso to encircle with his right hand the wrist of the corpse's nearer arm. Lifting the dead limb, he flapped its hand at Ettlinger. 'Go, my poor boy. We can receive you at some later date, perhaps.'

Having uttered not one word, Ettlinger withdrew, and on regaining the street found it necessary to recollect his route home before hurrying away.

32.

This was the house of Lichas, the maker of portraits.

In the pictures of Lichas, whether painted on metal or fabric or stone, the flesh was transfigured and exalted. Skin in the portraits of Lichas was not the covering of the mundane body but a substance of perfect uniformity, blemishless, vitrified. The contours of a face depicted by Lichas seemed to be formed not by conformity to any underlying bone; rather they assumed the ideal forms of blown and moulded glass, and their convexities gathered the light in a suffusive brilliance, like a perfect, opalescent vase. Preternatural clarity was the arresting feature of his portraits: eyes were discs of unmixed pigment; shadows were as crisp as the black and grey patternings of a heron's plumage; brows were superfine brocades. In his likeness of Cassandane, her oaken curls touched her green velvet collar at boundaries as sharp as a map's.

For his own amusement Lichas often painted things that had no life. These inert objects he would juxtapose in ways conceived to demonstrate his proficiency in emulating the diverse textures of the world. I recall one that placed in conjunction, on a shelf of chipped sandstone, a ring of nacreous fish, two pomegranates, a pair of brass salvers, four heads of corn. In another picture one could admire a cube of mottled marble, an incompletely flayed marten, a crystal vessel of olive oil and a husk of snakeskin, all arrayed on a scarlet carpet. The emperor himself praised highly a swirl of ochre sand on which were arranged a calf's foot, a wig, knives of various sizes, a sheaf of paint-clogged brushes, a mildewed map. The faces that Lichas painted appeared at most viewings to be no more expressive than these dead assemblies. Indeed, I once looked upon a row of his pictures and failed to discern at first glance that in the midst of the fox pelts, the flagons and the weapons was the image of one of my companions.

Lichas once invited us to regard his portrait of Artabanus. We looked at the fleshy eyelids; they were like garlic cloves. The fingernails were ovals of coral; the mouth was no longer an instrument of speech but rather a seal. 'This is not the living Artabanus,' said Lichas. 'It is the totality of him. It is the index of the man in the form of his flesh.' He held a lantern close to the picture, like a gaoler rousing his prisoner. 'Look at those eyes. Are they not the eyes of a bellicose man, and is there not something belligerent about the set of the mouth? But if I were to say to you that this is the portrait of a man for whom the contemplative life is the one most to be desired, would you not, on looking at these eyes, agree that the artist has succeeded in portraying him truly? Then again, can you not see the imprint of terror in this face?' he asked, and it seemed, in that fugitive moment, that we could.

For Lichas, however, his drawings, not his paintings, were the essence of his art. 'Our scholars discern in the world of number the workings of a finer world, a higher world, the one true and lasting world,' he once said to us. 'I find evidence of this higher world as well. But for me all things are informed by a principle whose pure form is not a number but a line. The calf and thigh of a sower, the breast of a girl, the conjunction of two bodies, the articulation of a finger – all reveal the eternal principle through this fluid, switching line. This line is the music of the stars,' he told us, unconcerned by our incomprehension. He showed us a drawing of Cassandane: 'Here the sweep of the arm is what is important. The drapery is as articulate as the smile.'

Lichas drew in our presence, on a hemisphere of stone, a portrait of Ardashir that showed his subject's features as if reflected in his shield. The face bulged like a bubble behind the pillowy right hand. We watched the artist at work, his hand moving as if of its own volition, his eyes fixed on the portrait's eyes as his hand drew the slope of his shoulders. 'What spirit guides him?' I wondered, appalled. I looked at his face and watched the expressions move over it like the shadows of clouds blown across the fields by a hurricane.

33.

What proved to be the last meeting of Klostermann's circle was held in April at his lodgings, the place where the salon had been inaugurated.

Helene and Maximilian were drinking coffee when Ettlinger and Stein arrived; next was Meier, who was not completely sober; Wolgast was the last, and he was dressed in a most bizarre fashion. His dark violet velvet waistcoat and breeches were cut in a style that had been fashionable some twenty years earlier, and were tightly embroidered with small flowers – peonies they appeared to be. His pumps, polished to an ebony shine, were topped with silver buckles that resembled large metallic moths. Freshly powdered, his hair was bright as a nimbus. In his right hand he carried a knapsack-sized case which was covered with red Moroccan leather.

Heedless of the effect his entrance had made, Wolgast set the case under the table. 'For later,' he said, smiling with pretended boyishness. At once taking charge, he sat on the edge of Klostermann's divan and asked who had chosen to begin the session.

Perhaps thinking, as Ettlinger did, that an effort would be required from the start to prevent Wolgast's presence from acting upon them as it had before, Stein volunteered to provide what he described as 'a cheerful prelude'. He had recently discovered a small cycle of folk songs, five in all, recounting the adventures of a young swain and his beloved, a skittish shepherdess who turns out to be a fairy but elects to become a mortal. 'Appropriate songs for springtime,' he said, and so they proved to be. Swaying his stalk-like body as he sang, Stein imparted to his friends a spirit that was joyful and amorous, yet carried a delicate vein of regret for the transience of earthly things.

Helene led the applause and then took from her brother two sheets of paper, one rolled inside the other. Peeling the roll open, she displayed the upper sheet, holding it between her outstretched hands. The picture was worked in lines of ink so thin and closely spaced that Ettlinger thought at first it was an engraving. The scene it depicted, she explained, was a Bohemian glassworks. 'This man is called a slitter and he is cutting a cylinder of glass,' she explained.

'And here it is unfurled to form a pane. This is called broad glass. Whereas this,' she continued, transposing the sheets, 'is a furnace for making mirrored glass by the Venetian method.'

Bemused by the processes shown in the second picture, as he had been by the first, Ettlinger looked to Helene for explication. She affected to believe that his incomprehension was feigned, and turned to inspect the faces of Meier, Stein and Klostermann in turn. Similarly at a loss, they murmured their admiration for Helene's penwork. Wolgast, meanwhile, sat forward on the divan, his chin on his thumbs, as though making some deduction from what he saw.

Helene turned to her brother and, addressing them all through him, declared that it had long been her desire to travel to Venice. 'One day I shall go there. Alone, perhaps. I might offend my family by marrying a glass-blower from the island of Murano,' she jested, 'instead of an ailing nobleman from a family half as old as the earth.'

'You are too clever,' countered Maximilian, and his sister pinched his cheeks.

Ettlinger, to whom it was not clear what precisely Maximilian had meant, now presented to the group his watercolour of the Arch of Constantine, as seen at dawn in autumn. He watched Helene appraising it with an expert eye, and heard little of what the others said. 'As before, whoever would like it may have it,' Ettlinger told them. With two quick nods Helene indicated first her drawings and then his picture, and thus like habituated traders they concluded their deal swiftly and without speaking. The exchange made

Ettlinger as happy as he had been since the afternoon at Nymphenburg.

It was next the turn of Klostermann, who again recited a revised episode of his epic. This time the suicide of Varus was revisited, in verses that accentuated the flawed nobility of the Roman – or so it seemed from the lines to which Ettlinger attended. 'He is almost tragic,' confirmed Stein as Klostermann laid his pages down. Stein looked to Meier, seeming to elicit the criticism that it had always been Meier's function to provide.

'I once adumbrated a story,' Meier duly remarked. 'A story about two sculptors. They are rivals, naturally. Each is allotted one large piece of marble. The first cuts his block into fragments, and proceeds to carve them into exquisite miniatures, a project that will occupy him for the rest of his days. The other, a man of more grandiose ambition, assaults the block entire and hews from it one massive masterpiece. Or near-masterpiece, for he is never quite content that it matches the grandeur of his conception. Year after year he makes the tiniest of alterations to his intimidating creation. Even his admirers cannot fail to notice that his work wears the dust of two decades.' Fatigued, Meier reclined into the cushions; his rumpled collar rose to his ears and the bristles of his beard bent upwards over his lips. 'A parable, but I forget how it ended. And what I thought it was about.'

'Well,' said Helene decisively, 'I have heard it said that haste makes nothing durable.' She turned first to her brother and then to Ettlinger, offering each the same smile, which seemed at the same time to request their approval and reject it.

'And, drudge though I may be, I know what I believe in,' replied Klostermann. 'I have a goal that I am limping towards, in company with my posthumous legions.' His self-mockery imperfectly masked his displeasure.

'I accept your point, Wolfgang,' said Meier, flopping a hand on the arm of his chair. 'Forgive me. One last shout from the drowning man, before the ocean of the law closes over him.' With watery eyes he regarded the ceiling. Rousing himself momentarily, he adopted the expression of a cynical sage. 'But you are right. I am purposeless. This is not a failing, however. To be single-minded is to be false. I have been as often surprised by myself as by other people. We believe we are as certain of our selves as we are of the shape of our bodies. How else could we live? But I would suggest to you that our hearts, our souls, our whatever term you choose, are not cores of crystal. They are caves lit once in a while by a single flame.' Meier held up a hand and focused on his middle finger. 'I am sorry. The drink has disconnected me.'

Wolgast laughed, but making a noise that was more a grunt than a laugh. 'Commendable sophistry,' he said to Meier, then asked if he might have some more of Klostermann's fine coffee. 'My throat is dry, and my contribution today will be a lengthy one.' While Helene filled the tiny cups, Wolgast rose from the divan, took up his ground in the centre of the room, and delivered his preamble.

'I have written for you an old-fashioned Italian comedy, a farce in the spirit of Pietro Aretino, first among journalists, scourge of princes and confidant of the great. It is not quite a story – more an inflated synopsis for a play. I call it *The Wager*.' He produced from his pocket a bunch of tattered pages and a pair of ivory-rimmed spectacles with lenses that were faintly tinted blue. 'Failing sight, a curse of age,' Wolgast explained, settling the spectacles on his nose, but Ettlinger had never been aware of their necessity and was never to see them afterwards. The spectacles made Wolgast look almost clownish, and yet the solemnity with which they were worn made Ettlinger feel that the absurdity was somehow transferred to Wolgast's audience, that in some way he and his friends were the objects of a satire. Ettlinger's discomfort only increased during Wolgast's reading, for the recitation was delivered in voices so mannered, and accompanied by grimaces and flailings so buffoonish, that frequently he could not watch it.

'The action is set in Vicenza,' Wolgast began, with a grandiloquent motion of his right arm. 'It is the sixteenth century, and our hero is one Alessandro Riccio, a retired merchant. Alessandro Riccio is a man whose business acumen was once so great that his fortune is now immeasurable. He owns a large farm and a huge house in the city of his birth, and in the latter he keeps his collection of works of art. Nowadays his financial affairs are managed by his sons, and he spends much of his time in the rooms of his collection, in particular the closet that contains a series of bronze plaques by the illustrious Valerio Belli, depicting the Passion of Our Lord. He spends long afternoons alone with these treasures, a custom that has led to a rumour that Riccio, now in his sixtieth year, is beginning to lose his wits.

'One afternoon, two brothers, Lattanzio and Giacomo,

arrive in the city.' Evoking his new characters with a vulpine crouch and a flickering of his eyes, Wolgast turned to the second page. 'Tricksters both, they travel from province to province sustaining themselves by larceny. Naturally enough, their first port of call is a tavern, where they hope to ascertain what opportunities this place might afford. It is not long before they hear the name of Riccio, and as the wine flows numerous witnesses attest to both the extreme wealth and the approaching senility of the old man. Lattanzio and Giacomo formulate a plan: posing as a nobleman and his uneducated cousin they will gain an invitation to Riccio's house and deceive him into believing that they would like to purchase a part of his collection, for an irresistibly large sum. Having become familiar with the house and the merchant's habits, they can bring about the theft they intend.

'A man is dispatched to Riccio with a letter, asking the old man whether it would be an inconvenience for him to entertain, for one evening, a gentleman who has a great desire to inspect his celebrated collection. A courteous invitation comes back in the hand of the hired messenger, and that very evening Lattanzio and his brother find themselves at the table of Riccio.

'The merchant is affable and the meal lasts many hours. When it is over, the visitors are taken to a suite of rooms in the vault below the dining chamber, where they are shown the celebrated reliefs. Giacomo, playing the dolt, has no difficulty in playing his part. Like his brother he looks upon these works of art in the same way he would regard a warehouse stacked with cloth. Thus, when he is shown one of the finest pieces by Valerio Belli all he sees is the moneybag by which it was gained and into which it can be converted. Lattanzio, the counterfeit nobleman, is in a less natural position, but he does his best, and by a judicious sprinkling of exclamations of delight he manages to convey the impression that he is a man of great discernment but few words. He makes great use of a gesture that involves rubbing his chin and looking admiringly at his host, suggesting that their spiritual affinity lies too deep for words.' Wolgast stroked his chin; slowly he straightened his back and the strokes became slower, showing that a pivotal moment had come.

'However, Lattanzio's mind is not really on his task, owing to an incident that happened while they were eating. Now, while it is true that this young man's heart is ruled by Avarice for three-quarters of his waking life, that particular passion is only the second-in-command in the fortress of his being. Avarice is the deputy to Lust, a governor who is frequently slumbrous but, when roused, possessed of the most savage energy. It remains to be said that although Lattanzio is expert in the dissimulation of his pecuniary appetite, he still is utterly incapable of camouflaging his priapic weakness. So it was then, that when Riccio excused himself for a moment in order to rise and embrace a strikingly beautiful woman who had appeared at the doorway, Lattanzio's gaze followed him, but failed to follow him back. His attention was riveted in like manner when the woman came into the room shortly afterwards; this time his host commented:

'"I am fortunate in having her."' Wolgast produced a voice that was querulous and reedy.

'To which Lattanzio replied, "You are indeed, sir. You are indeed. Long may you keep her."' This voice was a libidinous baritone.

'So, down in the vault, Lattanzio might well be thinking about his future visits to the Riccio house, but now he is contemplating using his time for a purpose quite different from the original one. The second stage of the brothers' operation is concluded when they elicit from Riccio, thanks to the effusiveness of Lattanzio's final compliments, an invitation to return in two days' time.

'In the following scene Giacomo and Lattanzio discuss their strategy. The civilised brother will request permission to study the old man's collection in private, while the other, who has seen quite enough of these dreary objects, will keep their owner amused in another part of the house. This is as intended, but with the difference that because Lattanzio will be both plotting the robbery and pressing the young wife for an assignation, it is now more important than ever that Giacomo keep the husband well away from the scene of the action. It should, Lattanzio estimates, take three more visits to accomplish the seduction and the theft; Giacomo is to be compensated for the self-denial required of him by receiving two-thirds of the proceeds. Both are well pleased with Vicenza.

'It is now two weeks later, and the duped husband is preparing to receive the brothers for the fourth time. He is setting some food upon the table, and also an empty casket and a pack of cards. The guests arrive and after a few minutes of small talk Lattanzio leaves for the vault and the works of Valerio Belli, while Giacomo prepares to eat with the husband.' Wolgast paused to smack his glutton's lips, and raised his eyebrows teasingly.

'We move to the bedchamber of the attractive young woman, where the persistence of Lattanzio is about to be rewarded. As the sheets are turned back by the maidservant, a woman of middle years who has been acting as the lovers' pander, a deal of flirtatious nonsense ensues.

'"I shall make you sing like a nightingale," the ruffian breathes, as he begins to undress.

'"And I shall make you growl like a dog," she brazenly replies.

'"Oh no, I am a lion," he responds, "especially in the heat of love."

'"Oh but, sir, I am sister to the sorceress Armida. If I so desire, I shall turn you into a dog," she insists.

'With a flurry of lewd looks, they embrace. The maidservant leaves.

'Back in the dining-room, things are starting to go badly for Giacomo. The old man has suddenly become very tired and is eager to retire to his wife's bed. Giacomo suggests a number of ways in which they could pass the time enjoyably in this room, but neither conversation nor wine has the power to detain Riccio. Then Giacomo espies the pack of cards and suggests a game.

'"For money?" asks Riccio.

'"If you wish," Giacomo replies.

'The old man cheats on every hand, but what can Giacomo do? If he accuses his host, his game is over and Lattanzio's game is up. So he plays on, losing his money, his rings, his medal, his sword. In desperation he stakes his horse on a hand; the maidservant, who has entered the room at this late stage of the gambling, passes behind Giacomo's chair, signals to her master, and Giacomo loses. He stakes his brother's horse; the maidservant passes behind Riccio's chair and slips a card into his pocket. Giacomo is destitute and, worse, his host is taking his leave.

'"But sir," pleads Giacomo, "please give me one last chance to redeem my possessions, I beg of you."' Wolgast shook his praying hands in Klostermann's face; his mouth wobbled weepingly.

'Says the old man – "Surely a young nobleman such as yourself will scarcely miss these baubles?"

'Giacomo is caught off-guard, but he quickly recovers. "The money I do not need, but these objects are of a certain significance to me. My rings I can never replace. At least give me one chance to recover them, sir."

'Riccio is pensive, but after a while replies: "I will make a wager with you, young man; and should you win I shall absolve you of your debt and add some money of my own to your possessions. Should you lose, I keep all of this. Do you agree?"

'"I do," says Giacomo.

'The old man asks the maidservant to act as witness to the contract, and to fetch a quantity of gold coins from an adjoining room. The coins are poured, along with Riccio's earlier winnings, into the casket.

'"This is the wager. I have for some time now suspected that other men see horns on my head. If you can, within the week, provide me with proof that I am cuckolded, you shall be the winner of our bet."

'"You are staking this on your wife's fidelity?" asks Giacomo, barely able to believe his luck.

'"I am, and with a heavy heart."

'Giacomo instantly clears his conscience. If he refuses to take up the wager he will have broken his word and lost his possessions, and his brother will be discovered anyway. If he agrees to it he will have kept his word and he and Lattanzio will gain ample compensation for the humiliation that will follow.

'"You shall have your proof this very minute," Giacomo tells his host, and leads him out of the room, in the direction of the connubial chamber.

'Inside this chamber, Lattanzio's triumph is upon him. He takes the lady in his arms and is about to remove her gown when suddenly she sits upright.

'"Someone's coming!" she cries. "Take this," she says, flinging a fur around him. "Hide there!" – and she pushes him towards a curtained alcove to the side of the bed. No sooner has the curtain covered him and the lady composed herself than the door flies open and in stride Giacomo and Riccio.

'Open-mouthed, Giacomo stares at the bed's solitary occupant. The husband, a cannier individual, looks for hiding places. He notices a bulge near the foot of the curtain.

'"What is behind there, madam?" he asks.

'"It is only my dog, Annibale."

'"Your dog Annibale?"' Wolgast shrieked, hysterical with incredulity.

'"Yes. Look," says the wife. And, sure enough, at the place to which she is pointing, a tuft of fur protrudes from the curtain's hem.

'"Why doesn't he move?" Riccio demands.

'"He is asleep, sir."

'"Well, wake him, then. I should very much like to see your faithful dog Annibale."

'She takes up the sword that is lying on the floor and prods the form behind the curtain. Just as a growl is heard, the maidservant enters, and is thrown into confusion by the scene before her.

'"I am most sorry for breaking in like this, sir," she says, "but should I lock the rooms downstairs, as the other gentleman seems to have finished down there, sir?"

'"He is waiting for us in the dining-room?" asks Riccio.

'"No, sir," she replies. "I have just come from there, sir. That's why I came here. I thought he was with you, sir."

'"Madam," says Riccio, turning to the young woman, "I find this matter puzzling, and I believe you may be able to help me in my perplexity. One of my guests has vanished, leaving behind his sword – that is, unless I am much mistaken, his sword that you are holding, madam. This hasty departure is strange enough, but then you compound the mystery by using the selfsame weapon to goad an animal that to my certain knowledge ceased to breathe God's air some two months ago. An explanation would be appreciated."

'The poor sinful woman nearly swoons away. She looks at her accuser and weakly draws back the curtain to reveal Lattanzio, swathed in fur but shivering nonetheless. The villain is ordered to dress and join Riccio in the dining-room. The maidservant gives Lattanzio a dirty look and takes the casket out with her.

'In the final scene Lattanzio and Giacomo stand dejectedly before Riccio, who roundly condemns their treachery and banishes them from his house. But Giacomo has not forgotten his wager with the husband, and defiantly he reminds his adversary of it.

'"I am sorry, young man, but your hopes are to be dashed," says Riccio.

'"What!" exclaims Giacomo. "You accuse us of treachery and then you break your own promise? This lady here can attest to our wager," he says, indicating the maidservant.

'"Sir, I promised you your goods and my money if you could prove my wife's dishonesty. I must tell you, sir," and here he takes the hand of the guilty woman, "that this lady is not my wife. My wife is at your side," he says, and the maidservant curtseys to the two brothers. "This young woman is my daughter, of whose talents I am immensely proud." He goes on to explain to the dumbstruck young men that their intentions had been clear from their very first visit and that they had fallen victims to a plan which was guaranteed to deprive them of their belongings and preserve the chastity of the two ladies. Surely they cannot fail to applaud the cleverness of the plot?

'And with that the crestfallen pair are ejected, penniless and horseless, into the night.'

Wolgast bowed low and twirled his hands to the side as if flourishing a cape. Meier rose, shook his hand, yelled 'Your dog Annibale!' and slumped back into his chair. The others applauded, Klostermann most robustly, Helene it seemed more out of obligation than appreciation.

'Perhaps we might perform it one day,' suggested

Wolgast. 'On a makeshift stage under an oak tree. I see myself in the senior role, naturally. August as Lattanzio perhaps, Helene as the daughter. You must have friends who can play the part of the audience?' He bent down to open his case, dropped the spectacles into it, and removed three bottles of champagne.

While glasses were brought and the bottles uncorked and emptied, a debate ensued between Klostermann and Meier on the subject of folk theatre, a discussion mediated dispassionately by Wolgast but conducted with some heat by the other two, for whose passion, it seemed to Ettlinger, the explanation was not so much their subject as the unspoken assumption that the future would hold few more such occasions for argument. It was clear that Maximilian had been provoked by the idea of his sister's playing a part in Wolgast's farce, but he stayed silent, perhaps because the very idea of taking issue with Wolgast on any matter caused some confusion in his mind. Ettlinger said little, for his thoughts were occupied by Helene, who also contributed nothing, but seemed mildly amused by something that was not what was happening in the room in which she sat.

Wolgast, noticing the direction of Ettlinger's attention, remarked: 'I fear August requires a higher purpose than entertainment.'

Raising his hands in surrender, Ettlinger modestly accepted the accusation, but Meier nonetheless continued on Wolgast's behalf: 'He has yet to understand that there is no higher purpose than entertainment.'

'Nicely put, young fellow,' said Wolgast. Meier blushed and pursed his lips complacently, unaware that the praise meant nothing. 'My characters serve no function other than to keep me company,' Wolgast went on, as if still reading from a page. 'The story is just a house to stay in for a while, a pleasure pavilion. A metaphor you might approve, August,' he concluded, and as he smiled at Ettlinger the tone of his gaze seemed to acquire a sincere warmth.

Looking at Wolgast's milky hands, Ettlinger saw them clap together the moist halves of the dead man's head.

Wolgast was addressing him again. 'Here, here,' he said, pushing the pages into his hands. 'I appoint you as my literary executor. Whether I live or die is for you to decide.' Ettlinger looked at the manuscript. He could read scarcely a word of it. The pages were covered with short chains of illegible writing, separated by dashes and exclamation marks, punctuated here and there with a word in lucid script: 'faster' in one place, 'a bit of dialogue' in another, 'a game of cards?' elsewhere.

'I can stay no longer,' Wolgast apologised, as from his bag he extracted a fourth bottle of champagne. Within a minute he had gone, walking out of the room with a strangely creeping gait that prompted in Ettlinger's mind the figure of a saboteur.

The instant the door closed, Ettlinger sensed a restlessness in both Stein and Klostermann, and he knew that they were going to question him about Wolgast. The realisation made him panic, as though he were about to be arraigned for a misdemeanour of which he was innocent. He pretended to recall some business he had intended to discuss with Wolgast, and gathered up his coat.

'I almost forgot,' Helene exclaimed at the moment

his hand touched the handle of the door. 'Two weeks from tomorrow is our nephew's birthday. Our parents will be celebrating, and we are permitted to invite a few friends. You are invited.' She accepted her glass from Maximilian, and held it by its stem close to her lips. She looked at Ettlinger over the gilded rim of the glass. 'You, not you both,' she said.

In the street, Ettlinger repeated her words under his breath, adding insistence to its final phrase. He held the drawings she had given him like a general's baton of office. A horseless dray was tethered to a tree; a baker's boy, shouldering a tray of loaves, was crossing the road; Wolgast, he was relieved to find, was nowhere to be seen.

34.

This was the house of the scholars of the mysteries.

This chamber was set aside for adepts of the weather, who found auguries in the patterns of the clouds, in the qualities of rainwater or in the colour of the sea. Adjacent to this was a room devoted to the laws and meanings of colour; here one learned such fundamentals as the Five Principals of Whiteness – jasmine, ivory, sandalwood, the moon and water. In this room the numerologists pursued their studies, tabulating primes and perfect numbers. Along this corridor were the offices of the interpreters of dreams: to the left were those who maintained that what we dream are allegories of the present; to the right those who contended that in sleep we see forevisions of our afterlife.

The highest part of the house, and the largest room, was

reserved for the alchemists and their affiliates. At its centre was a furnace, its flue hidden within a pendentive of the dome, from the centre of which was suspended an egg as large as a man's head. Beneath this egg stood a circular bench, its surface covered by alembics, mortars, boxes of powders, glass jars clouded milky-blue like cataracted eyes, and flasks of glutinous liquids more brightly hued than anything in nature. Drawings were pinned to every wall: a bow-legged beast with concentric circles for eyes was labelled as the green lion; misproportioned men held banners on which were blazoned epigrams on the subject of Mercury, or Salt, or the Rebirth. Charts of the heavens adorned parts of the chamber: to some were appended the ranks of the upper world; on others were drawn chords between the trajectories of the planets, bearing the labels of musical intervals.

Papers littered the bench and the floor of the alchemists' chamber. Conspicuous among them was the particoloured manuscript of a treatise, forever incomplete, on the nature of the soul, the labour of the youngest of the alchemists, a youth with fervid eyes that were always focused on a point in space an arm's length from his face. Under his supervision the scholars once presented a masque for the emperor. In the first tableau, I was allotted the role of the Hermaphrodite. I wore a close-fitting costume of saturated goatskin and lay in a coffin-like box, with scarlet satin crinkled around my body to look like coals. To one side, level with my face, sticks of incense burned slowly, dropping little cylinders of dust onto the platter. A commentary, narrated by a senior member of the fraternity, purported to explain the allegory. 'He exists for this moment of revelation,' he intoned. 'Like a tree blasted by lightning, his very nature is transformed. He becomes his own angel.' Above the stage, a scroll proclaimed the hierophantic text: 'Man is the perfection and end of all the creatures in the world.'

A month before the fall of the Residence, the head of the house gathered his acolytes. 'I can feel Death beginning to take possession of my body,' he told them. 'He has taken the strength of my limbs, and my flesh feels as heavy as earth. Let me pass my last days under the sky, that my spirit might become familiar with its new home.' He was placed on a pallet on the roof of the house, and there, awaiting his end, he attained the serenity for which his work had prepared him. All day he lay silently under the clouds, watching their passage contentedly, as if their configurations were confirmation of all that he had learned. At night he slept for only an hour at a time, for the patterns of the stars absorbed him more completely than his books had ever done.

Like the final flare of a dying fire, his senses acquired new brightness. He could hear the susurrations of the wind as it flowed along the grassy flanks of the Valley of the Sun. He could hear the rustling of owls' wings in the forest at night, and the shrews and field mice sniffling through roots. As an ordinary man might choose to direct his gaze at one detail of a landscape, so he could choose which sounds to bring to the foreground of his hearing from the multitudinous sounds he heard. At will he could make the tumultuous noise of the cascade to the north of the Residence obscure the waters of all the other rivers and streams within the compass of his hearing. At other times he might choose the surgings of the spring to the south, or the voice of the old river beyond the cascade, which dragged at the boughs of the weeping willows and made them sigh. At night he composed himself for sleep by listening to the breathing of the inhabitants of the Residence as they slept. He called this sound 'the deep-lying music of humanity'.

These were his last words, spoken to his pupils and friends as they retired to their chambers for the night. In the morning, as on each of the mornings of that last week, they gathered to discuss his achievements. When they went up to wake him they fell back from the door in horror, for his eyes were fixed wide and his mouth was open as if locked in a scream, and his arms were raised to the clouds like the trunks of withered bushes.

35.

In the course of the morning a fog had leached from the sky to fill every crevice of the city. Flowing thickly into the streets and alleyways, it had risen to cover the rooftops and drown the trees. Every windowpane of Wolgast's library was a solid plane of grey, as if a wadding of raw wool had been hung outside the glass.

With a millstone's roar a cart rolled slowly past the house, grinding a track through the fog. Ettlinger tapped the tip of his pencil on the table in rhythm with the horse's hooves. He dotted the blunted point across his sketch for the Gothic temple, tapping in time to the receding hoofbeats, darkening randomly the stipple of the foliage around the temple's base. For two barren hours he had sat in the library, dull-witted, fog-brained. It was as if the ideas of the previous week lay beneath a greyness through which nothing had the strength to push but memories of other days in

Wolgast's house. Ettlinger looked down at the vague reflection of his face in the table's veneer, and saw again the cleft head of the corpse on the enamel table. He looked away and heard his name pronounced by the toneless voice of the absent Wolgast. He wiped a palm across the wood; the vernal perfume of vetiver dispelled his torpor for an instant, and in that instant, conscious that he might founder into a more miserable condition if he did not move, he pushed his body out of the chair. Urgent as one who has a score to settle, but with no purpose other than motion in mind, he seized his coat and rang for Wolgast's footservant. He would be back at his place in one hour, he told him, and in speaking the words he felt that he had pronounced an ultimatum to his malingering spirits.

The obligations of study were forgotten as soon as he stepped into the featureless city. He walked through the obscure streets and felt that any manner of thought might crystallise out of the air as he walked. The inscrutable place that the fog had made of Munich was replete with potentialities, and he could not fail to return to the library in a state of inspiration. He breathed deeply, in preparation to receive whatever the morning might offer.

But his thoughts turned soon to Helene von Davringhausen. What came to him was not her face, nor her voice, but rather the memory of her languorous discontent, which impressed itself upon him not as a disposition but as an ineradicable quality of her being. Her detachment was an attribute, Ettlinger told himself, just as virginity was an attribute of Artemis or cunning of Hermes. He recalled their conversation by the canal in the garden of Nymphenburg, the way she had entwined her arms while he spoke, and now it seemed to him that her attentiveness was nothing more than civility, that his words had fallen around her like flowers strewn over a statue.

A couple came out of the fog and passed close by him; the young woman had her hand upon her escort's arm as if it were a tiller by which she was steering them through the murk. Ettlinger tried to imagine how it might be if Helene were now to appear suddenly, as this couple had done. Perhaps in this strange setting, liberated from society in the very heart of the city, they might converse more truthfully, attain a new understanding. He tried to picture her standing before him, closeted with him in the open air, inviting him silently to find the words with which they would be transformed, but he could not make the apparition happen. Instead he saw her as perhaps she was at that very moment, at home in a part of the city that was far from where he stood, with her brothers around her, and all of them scoffing at his impertinence.

Ettlinger began to cross the river, but stopped a few steps onto the bridge to peer over the parapet. A mallard flew overhead and dived down to the water, dissolving from sight in seconds as it veered away. He gripped the cold stone of the bridge, and leaned out over the invisible and soundless river. Below him might have been a chasm as deep as an Alpine ravine.

Gaining the other bank, he gauged the direction of Marienplatz and strode across the empty road. He traversed the pavement of the square, where somewhere perhaps five or six other people were walking. Their feet ticked in varied rhythms on the flagstones, conjuring in Ettlinger's mind the notion that he was moving within a vast mechanism, but a mechanism without form, like a cloud with a clock-work engine. The idea amused him, and he paused in the middle of the square to enjoy his amusement. As if to complement the leavening of his temper, the aroma of marzipan came to him from the nearby bakery. Thenceforward, though he had not been thinking of her at that moment, whenever Ettlinger smelled the perfume of marzipan he was always to be reminded of the image of Helene von Davringhausen walking out from a doorway in a foggy street, an image that grew more potent as the years passed. It became so potent, indeed, that more than once he would recount it to himself as something he had seen.

He walked on into an adjoining street, where he became aware of the drone of many voices in consort emanating from a place in front of him. The voices uttered short and monotonous phrases in regular succession, then fell silent, then spoke again in a short-breathed monotone. An outcrop of boulders against the wall on his right side he recognised as the façade of the church of St Johann-Nepomuk. He eased open the door. A little bell was ringing; the flames of six tall candles were visible on the altar; everyone was kneeling in prayer, but in front of him there was one raised face, the face of a young woman he knew he should be able to recollect precisely. Her cheekbones were unusually broad and she had slanted grey eyes which seemed to widen with delight as she looked at the stuccoed garlands and seraphs along the walls, then at the corkscrew columns above the altar.

Ettlinger remembered her name: she was Josepha Heldt, the magistrate's daughter. He watched her gaze up at the ceiling and smile, as if the scene depicted in its fresco were real, as if the toppling steeple were held in place by a magical force.

The congregation rose; some of the worshippers left their seats and advanced to the altar. Josepha Heldt now glanced behind her; Ettlinger followed the line of her sight, but could not tell what it was she was looking at. He took a step backwards towards the door, and saw that the person who had remained on his knees, on the floor behind the back pew, was Wolgast. He was wearing a suit of black silk, with a stiff collar and buttons of nacre, an outfit that gave him the appearance of a decadent prelate. A small Bible or prayer book was pressed between his palms, and his eyes were clenched as if he were endeavouring to wring tears from them, or prevent tears from falling. Abashed, Ettlinger reached for the handle of the door and tugged at it. The hinge made a squawking noise, a disturbance to none it seemed but Wolgast, who lowered his hands and turned his head with the histrionic deliberation of one who has been provoked beyond appeasement. His stare slowly measured the floor from the place where he knelt to the feet of the offender; there it halted and became, in the instant before rising to Ettlinger's face, perfectly uninterested. The expression that Wolgast presented to him was at once familiar and frigid; it was the expression of someone greeting a person he had arranged to meet some time before but no longer wished to talk to. Ettlinger bowed awkwardly; Wolgast signified with an actorly mime of his hands that he should leave and return in a short while.

When Ettlinger came back, a quarter of an hour later, the candles were being extinguished on the altar and the pews were almost empty. Wolgast, who had not moved from the place he had been occupying when Ettlinger noticed him, came over with his right hand outstretched in affable greeting.

'You have me at a disadvantage, August,' he said. 'It is a rare experience for me,' he added ruefully. Ettlinger started to apologise for his intrusion, but Wolgast continued as if he had not heard him. 'I confess that I am a church-goer,' he laughed, but his raillery could not disguise his embarrassment. 'Your attendance is in a secular capacity, I assume?'

Ettlinger shrugged. 'It was more a matter of getting out of the fog than anything else,' he replied, but again Wolgast was not listening to him.

'To be truthful I should say that I like the music as much as I like the liturgy, and I most like the language of the church when it is most musical.' He patted the pocket in which his book was now tucked; the gilded edges of its pages shone in the pouch of black silk. 'Mad John I find irresistible – "And I saw as it were a sea of glass mingled with fire: and them that had gotten the victory over the beast, and over his image, and over his mark, and over the number of his name, stand on the sea of glass, having the harps of God." Who could resist such lunacy?' Wolgast paused as if repeating the quotation in silence, and then challenged genially: 'I suspect that you are not a man for whom music is important, August.' He continued before Ettlinger could form a reply – 'No, you are not a musical man. But I am. The organist here has a great gift, and he has a passion for Bach. I also like Bach; I envy Bach and I do not understand him. Bach's God is so reasonable. He is a gentleman forever prepared to indulge us in discussions about His inexhaustible goodness.'

Wolgast crossed his arms in preparation to judge the quality of Ettlinger's response, but was immediately distracted by the slam of a door. Josepha Heldt was emerging from the sacristy, accompanied by the sacristan, a stoopingly unctuous man in a badly patched cassock, who placed a sheet of paper in her hand and then slipped back into his room with the air of one who is well satisfied with his social subtleties. Having folded the sheet twice over, Josepha Heldt deposited it in the purse that hung from her wrist, and clipped the purse shut conclusively.

'There is a better critic of musicians than I,' commented Wolgast, beckoning her to come over. She approached without looking at Wolgast, and did not look at him until he said to her, in a tone that made it seem he was resuming a conversation she had left a few minutes earlier: 'I was praising your musical discernment to my friend Ettlinger.'

Josepha Heldt smiled blandly at Ettlinger, and nodded as at a remark that is too obvious for a response to be required.

'You have met my friend Ettlinger?' Wolgast prompted.

'Seen but not met,' she replied. She gave her hand, clasping Ettlinger's strongly, as if thereby to decide how she was to take him. A quick wrinkling of her brow seemed to imply a suspicion that he and Wolgast were complicit in an affair of which she would not approve.

'I was saying that the organist plays well. Or, I should say, his playing gives me enjoyment,' continued Wolgast. 'Does he play well?'

'He plays well,' Josepha Heldt concurred without feeling. 'He plays well but he has a weakness for expression. He tends to think the music is about himself.'

'An egotism inaudible to all but experts such as you,' joked Wolgast drily, a retort that provoked a momentary glare of disproportionate anger.

'You are a teacher?' Ettlinger asked, but received no reply. Josepha Heldt was looking at the book in Wolgast's pocket, and seemed to be puzzling over its presence there.

'Ettlinger is an aspiring architect,' Wolgast informed her. 'I think he is here today to learn from the mistakes of the past.'

'Well, I should not express it quite in that way,' Ettlinger began, but his utterance was cut short by Josepha Heldt.

'So I am the only one of us who is not abusing this place,' she said, smiling curtly at Ettlinger, and in this way signalling her readiness to leave.

'A precipitate conclusion and an unjust one,' protested Wolgast amiably, and he bowed low to her in farewell and kissed her hand, a gesture that brought to Ettlinger's mind his perplexing behaviour at the Kreisel ball.

'Johann Friedrich, your type of gentleman expired with Louis XIV,' Josepha Heldt sternly admonished. She shook Ettlinger's hand again.

'My type, madam?' Wolgast replied jestingly, but she was already at the door. 'I offended her modesty,' he explained to Ettlinger. 'She would rather remain underestimated. On a few occasions I have persuaded her to play some Beethoven for me, the desperate last sonatas. It is extraordinarily touching, to hear the music of that barbarian performed by Josepha. She is superbly serene when she plays. There is the whiff of the convent in her disdain for herself.'

Wolgast, his eyes unfocused, placed a forefinger across his parted lips, and seemed to be browsing towards a distant memory. 'I have become incoherent. Perhaps I might love her.' He turned gradually through a full circle, scanning the walls as if trying to locate something he had just remembered was hidden there somewhere, smothered by the decoration.

'The problem is, August, that I don't think God would be seen in a place like this, do you? I think He'd be insulted by the fittings.' Sneering, he waved an arm to encompass the gilded cherubs and statuary, the tumescent altarpieces and nebulous paintings. 'A devotional boudoir rather than a church,' he stated. 'Yet it does seem to command the devotion of an intriguing kind of woman. Punctiliously correct in the niceties of worship and prayer, and deliciously vain. Not Josepha – she is not of any kind. I mean women who have their rosaries made of the rarest woods by the finest craftsmen. Bibles with chamois bindings. Attractive, I often find them.'

'Piety is too often the perfume of the soul,' Ettlinger proposed, aping unconsciously the style of Wolgast.

'Yes. Yes, very good,' said Wolgast, regarding him with a look of surprise and approbation.

Wolgast preceded Ettlinger out of the church. On the pavement outside stood a corpulent middle-aged man and a somewhat younger woman, who together were assisting twin boys, perhaps nine or ten years old, into a carriage. Dressed identically in dark blue coats with collars of black fur, the boys had the same inadequately barbered hair and uncertainly boastful face. Wolgast leaned against the wall, with one foot resting on the artificial rocks of the church façade, and held Ettlinger back by his elbow. 'Wait,' he whispered. 'A client of mine.'

They watched the family board the carriage. The mother spread a tartan rug over the laps of her sons; the father exchanged a covert acknowledgement with Wolgast, and tapped the driver's shoulder. 'I sell him ivories,' Wolgast went on. 'Table-top Madonnas holding tiny Christs. Reliquary caskets with scenes from the lives of the Apostles. Fourteenth-century French he prefers. Very hard to come by.' As the carriage creaked into motion and trundled into the fog, Wolgast cocked his head to one side, as if pondering a fine point in his estimation of the occupants. 'Unless one has influential friends, or gifted accomplices.' The carriage was engulfed, and Wolgast led Ettlinger in a stroll down the street, away from Marienplatz.

'That man has become hugely wealthy through the possession of two talents,' he recommenced, the pitch of his voice suggesting a forensic summary of superabundant evidence. 'The first is his innate flair for metallurgy. He has no diplomas or degrees. In fact, he is barely educated. But he has a feeling for minerals that is mystical. Like a dowser with water, he detects the location of a seam by a twitch in his muscles. His blood tells him the depth of it. And he understands metals the way a peasant cook understands vegetables and offal. He doesn't think about what he does. He just throws the ingredients together and the result is an alloy that is perfect for the task in hand.' Wolgast sighed in wonderment at what he was relating. 'His other talent is his absolute lack of scruples. He has no more principles than the guns his factories make. Compassion is an emotion quite foreign to him. The men who work for him toil until they die. Generally that is not long, as his factories are more dangerous than the front line of an infantry battalion. It is rumoured that his foundries armed both sides at Austerlitz. In his favour I should say that he is said to be a loyal husband. And he is not complacent. He attends this church every Sunday to thank God – the founder and chairman of creation – for a prosperity he knows might be gone tomorrow. Shall we continue?' asked Wolgast, as they turned a corner into a tributary street. 'I am in the mood for a walk,' he remarked, stroking his forehead along the hairline, as if considering the significance of this disposition. 'It is apparent to me that you have reached some sort of impasse with your work. Perhaps if you accompany me for an hour you might walk free of the strait you are in. Only ideas won by walking have any merit.'

'Not impasse,' replied Ettlinger quietly. 'Hiatus, I should like to think.'

'Whichever you prefer,' said Wolgast. He rubbed his palms together quickly, rekindling his thoughts. 'On the other hand,' he exclaimed, 'the wife of our miner and smelter possesses a brilliant mind. She speaks Latin better than she speaks German, and she speaks German like a poet. Great tracts of the *Aeneid* she knows by heart, and her tongue is as sharp as Martial's. Splendid paintings the miner has in his home, all of them chosen by her. Never mind the boy Klostermann and his band. Enthusiasts they might be, and not without aptitudes, but that woman would show them how to run a salon. She should have been our country's Madame de Staël, but her brilliance is vitiated by the demands of her uxurious husband and her own weakness for costly carpets and the latest fashions. She has bartered her soul for upholstery,' Wolgast lamented with a smile, shaking his head in heavy disbelief. 'Yet it would seem they are happy children. Yes,' he concluded, 'they are contented little heirs.'

For a minute or so they walked in silence, Ettlinger falling in with Wolgast's stride, Wolgast smiling at the fog as if they were enjoying a sunny afternoon beside the Isar. Side by side they waited on the pavement for a rattling cart to loom into view and pass from sight, then crossed together to a junction Ettlinger did not at once know. 'I should think you were a happy child. Were you?' asked Wolgast suddenly, surprising Ettlinger so greatly with the intensity of his question that Ettlinger missed the moment to answer. At that very moment they were passed by a carriage occupied by Josepha Heldt and a man whom Ettlinger did not see clearly.

'I was not,' continued Wolgast, glancing at the carriage indifferently, as if its occupants were both strangers to him. 'I was a guilty child. My grandfather was a pastor, an unflinchingly censorious man. Thanks to him I knew the Commandments before I could write the letters of my name. I never heard him say anything nor saw him do anything from which one might have inferred a love of God, or a love of his family or of his congregation, or of anything else. Whenever I picture him I see a smiling face, but it is a grin like a sliver of cheese rind.' Wolgast twitched his face into a simulation of his grandfather's acetic rictus.

'The corruption of the soul was for my grandfather an unfailing source of acrid delight. Even new-born babies were soaked in sin. They were created through it, he would explain, pressing a forefinger onto an apposite quotation in one of his books. The howling of babies was the mark of their infantile gluttony and pride. I knew this to be nonsense from the day I began to think, and yet I was constantly oppressed by something that I could describe only as guilt. I felt myself to be guilty, and the older I grew the guiltier I became. At night I would lie awake and ransack my memory, but I would find nothing commensurate with my gloom.'

Wolgast paused and stared blankly into the fog. 'I might glimpse a face that momentarily seemed to have the aura of a clue, but then it would be gone, like a fish under the reflections of a stream. For years I observed this nightly ritual, dredging my memory, awake alone in the sleeping house, my eyes trained on the flame of a candle that would burn away before I fell asleep. I recall the night before my tenth birthday. The wind was making the shutters clatter against the wall, and somebody was bawling a carol in a field nearby. Imagining myself on my deathbed, I envisaged a moment when the secret would be revealed, my secret crime: it would be like the blackened, roasted corpse of a lizard found on the soil after a scrubland fire. I made a hood of the blanket and knelt on my bed to open the window. I remember my eyes smarting in the freezing air, and the drunken singer, and the crystals of the snow on the sill that looked like blue pollen under the light of the moon. The notion came to me that perhaps I was guilty of something I had dreamed of doing, and had forgotten when I awoke. Perhaps, I speculated, people were sometimes given an intuition of their lives as finished things, as objects viewed from the vantage of eternity, and I was feeling remorse for something I had not yet done? I complimented myself for the sophistication of my thought, and self-satisfaction went some way to assuage my feelings of guilt. Some way,' he repeated, almost wistfully.

'But with time it changed?' Ettlinger ventured.

'Oh yes, with time it changed,' Wolgast replied, and smiled at Ettlinger's remark with the affectionate condescension of one congratulating a clever child. 'Now I know I'm guilty,' he stated, with no more emotion than he would have given to a statement of his height. He looked at Ettlinger and laughed once, abruptly, perhaps because Ettlinger did not. 'I am talking too much,' he went on. 'Churches invite us to indulge our appetite for confession. I suspect that they may create that appetite. I have often thought that what we take to be effects are, on the contrary, causes. And vice versa, of course,' he added, smacking a palm against the pocketed book.

They had arrived at a crossroads. Two discordant bells were ringing from the same tower somewhere to their left, perhaps on the next block. Wolgast halted and sniffed the air as if taking his bearings from its scent. 'Not far from here there is a shop that sells fine papers and inks and writer's implements,' he explained. 'Jonas Rupprecht's. I am going there now, to collect some ink he has mixed for me. Though the shop will be closed, Jonas will be at work. He is a cultured heathen, interested in the word of God only insofar as he might admire the font in which it is printed. His shop is this way. Would you accompany me? I should like to purchase an example of Rupprecht's craftsmanship for you. You deserve a tribute; you have been a patient audience.'

Following him across the avenue, Ettlinger was surprised that he had never before noticed how strange was Wolgast's posture as he walked. There was no suppleness in his torso, which he carried so upright and so steady it was as though his head were a monstrance balanced atop his body. His arms swung through exactly the same arc with each step, stopping just short of the point to which a relaxed movement would have brought them. His stride was long and stiff-legged, and his feet struck the ground in a manner that was precise and strong, as if he were walking a perilous high track that was absolutely straight and no wider than his shoulders. It was difficult to match the character implied by Wolgast's exaggeratedly rigid gait with the confidentiality of his monologue, and this discrepancy increased the unease instilled in Ettlinger by those confidences, and by the promise of the gift for a reason that was plainly fanciful. Ettlinger could think of but one explanation for Wolgast's intimacy and generosity, and that was that they were a form of apology for having subjected him to the sights of the anatomy room. It was an explanation with which he could not content himself, and from the sardonic smile with which Wolgast turned it seemed more probable that his speech had been a joke, or a tactic to some end that Ettlinger could not guess.

'Hurry up, August,' chided Wolgast. 'We are walking into a better day,' he declaimed, pointing to the aureole of sunlight that was forming in the heights of the fog.

As if emboldened by the appearance of the sun, Ettlinger asked directly – 'Is St Johann the church you commonly attend?'

'Good God, no,' replied Wolgast. 'There is no church I commonly attend. And if there were, it would not be that one. It makes me feel like a man entombed inside another's mind. Worse still, the mind of someone banal and childish. I would rather spend my time in a nomad's pavilion. You detest it, too, I hope?'

'I can admire its ingenuities, but it is not to my taste.'

'Few buildings are to my taste,' Wolgast rejoined, in mock triumph. 'As places to inhabit they too often fail. Or rather, I tend to find them wanting. Often I am already bored with my own thoughts by the time I utter them, so how could anything made of stone or brick keep me in a tolerable humour? My library, my room of paper, is usually accommodating to me, whatever my temper. But few places else.'

Ettlinger's face expressed a tepid protest, but before he could say anything Wolgast resumed, one hand raised placatingly – 'Let me say that I understand the attractiveness and the rewards of your discipline.

Architecture is a noble calling. It requires scholarship, art and imagination. Courage as well – the courage of the despot. For what other art turns its audience into its subjects? But I am reluctant to be such a subject. I must be master.'

'There is a balance to be attained,' Ettlinger interposed, but again Wolgast disregarded him.

'For me Bonaparte was most enviable,' said Wolgast, 'not when he was conquering the nations of Europe, but when he was defeated and in his last exile. Without a second thought I would exchange this place for an island on which I could live in my absolute state, on a piece of land that would become part of my being. To possess a dwelling that was the image of my soul.' So Wolgast tenderly invoked the tyrant's banishment, and then he said, as if he had overheard the words that Ettlinger was speaking silently to himself, 'I am an arrant egoist, August,' and he placed a hand lightly, affectionately, on Ettlinger's forearm, a gesture which Ettlinger found as startling as a blow might have been. 'That is why I enjoy days such as this. The fog remakes the city into something dreamlike, a landscape of myself,' Wolgast mused, savouring his own phrases, then added, 'I should like you to design a house for me.'

Ettlinger looked at Wolgast and smiled to exempt himself from the hypothetical task.

'No, I should like you to design a house for me,' Wolgast reiterated with emphasis. 'It must be a house of infinite flexibility, a house as various as the weather, as multifarious as thought itself,' he said, adopting a bantering tone which he dropped with the next phrase. 'I am in earnest. I am giving you a commission. I have land. Last year I bought some fields on a hill above Starnbergersee. They are surrounded by as much woodland as is necessary to sustain the illusion that there is no one else on the face of the earth. This woodland is mine as well. I shall pay you for your design, of course. We shall agree a price, and it shall not be meagre. Do you consent?'

'I do, indeed I do, of course,' Ettlinger stammered in his elation and confusion.

'What I want, I think,' said Wolgast, 'is something austere and yet satisfying to the senses. A charterhouse for a solitary monk, a monk with too great an attachment to the world. I should like it to be both a residence and a monument, and to that end I instruct you to conceive something that is not too well built, for I envisage a ruin as my memorial. I foresee joists protruding like broken masts, walls at all angles in the swaying weeds. So perhaps you might make it of baked mud and rubble, straw and chippings. But finish the surfaces well. For as long as I live it must appear a thing of importance and good taste.' Wolgast stopped at the road's edge, arrested it seemed by the sight of a carriage that was turning into a side-street some fifty paces distant, between two buildings that looked, in the disintegrating mist, like wash drawings on coarsely woven paper. As if agitated by what he saw, he began kneading the fist of his right hand in the cupped fingers of his left. 'How soon could you begin?' he asked, stepping off the pavement.

'I could make some sketches for you within the month,' Ettlinger replied. 'In your library there exists a plan I have long wanted to use. It is among the books you prepared for me on the first day I came to your library, and I have often returned to it. Only this morning I was studying it.'

'Continue. I am intrigued,' Wolgast cajoled, still stroking his fist.

'It is a building, a villa, by Palladio, but it is one that remained on the page, in the abstract.'

'Describe it for me, please,' requested Wolgast.

'The main façade has a long colonnade. In fact, it is almost nothing but a colonnade.'

'The elevating monotone of classicism,' said Wolgast quietly, as if addressing the remark to himself. He pressed a thumb to his temple, puckering the skin above the scar, then remarked, supplying his own rebuttal – 'But all Latin sounds the same to one who does not speak it. Please, do continue,' he said. 'You talk, August. I shall not interrupt you. I am wearied by my own voice.'

'Well, the colonnade has what appear to be pavilions at each end, or perhaps large dovecotes. In fact, these blocks are the end walls of the blocks that contain the living quarters, which run at right-angles to the colonnade. A corridor runs parallel to the main façade, connecting the ends of the two wings and thereby enclosing the courtyard, which is a perfect square. A small pediment, placed centrally, provides the focal point of the colonnade, but whereas the pediment in most other villas marks the principal room of the house, this one surmounts nothing more than an empty space, a point of transition between the courtyard and the meadows.'

Wolgast nodded at the pavement approvingly, encouraging Ettlinger to go on.

'Palladio's book states that each room of the living

quarters was to be dedicated to a particular virtue, and decorated accordingly. His intention, he wrote, was "to accommodate his guests in the room representing the virtue to which they would appear to have most inclined their soul".'

'An impractical scheme,' commented Wolgast, grimacing, 'and one we should not try to emulate.'

'I agree,' said Ettlinger. 'We should avoid anachronisms, however charming they might be. But I think we could adapt what I take to be the villa's chief conceit – the idea of the house as a structure that rests upon the landscape and augments it. It is, if you like, a tactful building, a thing that also rests upon the landscape of the mind and in some way modifies it. The villa should persuade by virtue of its correctness and grace. It should instruct by giving pleasure.'

'An idea I find appealing,' responded Wolgast, in a voice that was doubtful. 'Do go on.'

'I have little more to say,' said Ettlinger. 'Tomorrow I could show you the book. Perhaps I could write a fuller proposal tonight? I am more loquacious with my pen.'

'Such reticence,' Wolgast commented. His tone was ironic, but his derision seemed to be directed at someone other than Ettlinger. 'But yes, do write a proposal.' Wolgast made a barrier of his arm to stop Ettlinger in mid-stride. 'And, fittingly, behold the lair of Rupprecht,' he announced.

Before Ettlinger could distinguish the premises he was indicating, Wolgast had opened a plain wooden door and stepped into the shop, closing the door behind him. Ettlinger looked in through each of the small barred windows that flanked the door; the glass was so dirty that he could see nothing but a single row of porcelain jars and Wolgast's white hair, swaying slightly in the darkness of the room.

A few minutes later Wolgast emerged, holding in one hand a transparent flask that was three-quarters filled with emerald ink. 'It never fades,' he remarked, swilling the liquid so that it coated the glass completely, 'and it is soothing on the eye.' He held the flask aloft for a moment, and regarded the ink against the backdrop of the sky, like a jeweller admiring a stone against a flame. 'And for you,' he said, reaching into his pocket and taking from behind the book a twist of black tissue paper. He placed the flask on the ground and unfurled the tissue, disclosing an ivory pencil-holder. 'A Rupprecht speciality. With this you shall draw your plans. We shall discuss it further tomorrow, perhaps. I have other business now.'

With that, Wolgast posted the holder into a pocket of Ettlinger's coat, pressed his hands onto Ettlinger's shoulders as if to secure him to the spot, and strode across the road, omitting to make any farewell.

The buildings opposite stood between Ettlinger and the sun, but they cast no shadow in the hazy light. There was no sign of any activity behind their windows; there was nobody but Ettlinger on the street. Every stone looked damp and new, as if the houses had been deposited by the retreating fog. Ettlinger realised that he had been too absorbed in Wolgast's narration to attend to the turns they had made through the city, and did not know where he now was standing.

36.

This sequence of rooms and enclosures was the menagerie.

In these small chambers, abutting the bedrooms of the imperial family, were kept the animals maintained for the amusement of the emperor's wives. This one, open to the sky, was the home of the sloth; it slept all day, slinging its body like a hammock from the rafters. Next to it, behind a grille of iron, lived the mandrill, a dog-faced monkey with chisel teeth and blue-chevroned snout. In this rectangle lived the scaly pangolin, which when frightened would curl itself up to make its body a nautilus shell. Artaÿnte kept a lyre-bird, a crested lizard and a porcupine, but her favourite was her tamarin monkey, an homunculus with a fidgeting mouth, a plume of white hair and feverish eyes. Cassandane's pets were a squirrel that had been taught to fetch a chalcedony from her casket of jewels, and a silken-coated black bear that had been trained to strum a harp.

Other keepers were in charge of the animals that were set against each other in fights for the emperor's amusement. This area was a pasture for the aurochs, which were pitted against lions and leopards. This circle was split by palisades into two halves, one containing the wolves, the other the boars they would later fight. Other antagonists were housed around the periphery: snakes and mongooses, scorpions and rats, dogs and wild cats. There was a pack of dogs reared to eat the flesh of their own kind.

The menagerie was supervised by the son of the emperor's equerry. He was a fearless and gigantic young man, whose features, when one addressed him, buckled in distress at the violation of the wordless world in which he lived. His strength was formidable and his movements were so clumsy that when he walked it seemed as if his limbs were in conflict with his will and with each other. His hands, however, were so supple, fine and pale that they might have been grafted from a different body. For hours at a time he would sit with an animal that would have savaged any other intruder, caressing its fur as a woman might fondle her lover's hair.

No man was familiar with him except his father, and it was his father who, in the first hour of light one winter morning, found his body in the panther's cage. A skin of frost lay over him, making pink the wounds that striped his torso from collar-bone to groin. His arms and legs were half-devoured, one bicep now concave, one frost-coloured shinbone exposed. His head was almost severed, flipped aside like the hinged lid of a bottle. The panther reclined beside him, panting steam into his clotted hair, and did not move when the equerry raised the axe over its neck.

During the preparations for the burial, ashes were discovered in the mouth of the equerry's son, and a chip of bronze was found deep in the gash that cut into his liver. The conspiracy was quickly revealed. The dead man's wife, whose fearfulness initially had been hidden by her grief, confessed that her husband had been approached by a man who had designs on the life of the emperor. The instigator of the plot, she said, was Bardiya, the emperor's brother.

In taking flight on the very day of the woman's statement, Bardiya confirmed that her words were true. He was captured in the cellar of a house on the harbourside. At the emperor's command no harm was done to his brother on his arrest, and neither was any admission of guilt demanded of him. Without addressing even one word to him, the soldiers placed manacles on his wrist and conducted him out onto the quay. Seated in the carriage that had always been reserved for him, Bardiya was brought back to the Residence, escorted by a foot-patrol bearing the emperor's standard on one side and Bardiya's on the other. Nobody spoke to him. When the traitor arrived at the Residence every room was shuttered, and every courtyard empty. The fountains of the gardens had been silenced. The birds in the aviaries called across the lifeless palace as the carriage of Bardiya, the failed tyrannicide, passed through the main gate.

Only the chamberlain emerged to meet the escort and their captive. After the briefest of exchanges, the carriage was turned about and driven back through the gate. Bardiya was taken to the silent room and imprisoned with the remains of those who had perished there. But Bardiya was not to die as they had died. Every morning food was lowered into his cell by a warder whose face he never saw and voice he never heard. For many weeks he heard nothing but the din of his own blood, magnified to such a pitch by the silence of that room that the bones of his skull would have felt like a drumskin, bending with every blow of his heart.

When at last Bardiya was released he was no longer sane. For a day he was left at liberty. At the slightest sound he flinched, and he walked as though he were treading spikes. His lips nibbled at the air incessantly. He kneaded the flesh of his cheeks. On the following day the men who had comprised his escort came for him again. He was brought to the atrium of the Residence, where he was seated beside his brother for the unveiling of a statue of the equerry's son.

The emperor had ordered that the corpse of Bardiya's victim should be made whole again, and that the sculptors should make a statue of the reconstituted body, omitting no mark of its mutilation. A sheet of silk was pulled from the marble colossus, exposing the welted and fissured skin of the dismembered man. The emperor clapped his hands in approval of the sculptors' faithful creation, and spoke to Bardiya for the first and only time after his arrest. 'What you did I have undone, as you can see. And now I shall exceed your handiwork. I will make you a man incapable of dissembling.'

Bardiya's tongue was excised. A stylus was inserted into his mouth and worked under the flesh; incisions were made around his eyes; and the result of these operations was that Bardiya could no longer smile nor frown nor in any way move the skin of his face. A suture was sewn along his lips, sealing his mouth but for a narrow aperture through which a basin of gruel was fed to him, twice a day, through an iron pipette.

The cage in which the body of the equerry's son had been found was installed in the atrium. It became Bardiya's prison. He was shackled to the floor by his ankles and chained to the bars by his wrists, but a chair was placed for him in the centre of the cage, a gilded chair of well-planed cedar, and padded comfortably with cushions of scarlet plush. The bars on two sides were draped with thick purple velvets. A large terracotta lamp, decorated with imps that clung to its underside, was suspended from the bars of its ceiling. Thus it was that the treacherous Bardiya was caged amid the trappings that surrounded him in the portrait that Lichas had painted of him, and as much attention was now given to Bardiya's appearance as the artist had given to his image. Every morning his hair was washed, trimmed and oiled. His jaw was shaved so closely his skin gleamed like paint. His eyebrows were plucked by the women who attended the emperor's wives; it was their task also to clip and polish every nail of his hands and feet.

After a month in the atrium, Bardiya was moved regularly around the Residence. He might be placed underneath an arch of the stadium one week, and the next be planted next to the well in the courtyard of the stables, or in the corridor used by the comic actors. Sometimes the emperor himself would pass a few minutes at the cage, looking at the portrait he had fashioned from his brother's flesh, through which the eyes of Bardiya stared at him in loathing and despair.

37.

When Ettlinger awoke, his first perception was of a noise that sounded like wooden tiles being stacked in the street. He raised himself on his elbows, and saw the water spilling from the cracked gutter above his window. For perhaps as long as an hour he lay in his bed, revisiting and reappraising memories of the months that had passed since the conversation in the gardens of Nymphenburg, watching the intermittent sunlight swell in the shaft of water. He recalled the brazen sun on the Nymphenburg canal and the sigh that had issued from Helene's lips as she blew the dust from her palm.

The rain drenched the city throughout the morning. Ettlinger tried to work, but the incessant clacking of the falling water so increased the tension of his expectancy that he could make no sense of the pages before him. He paced the room, accused himself of posturing, sat down at his desk, traced a meaningless line on a scrap of discarded paper, paced the room again. When the strokes of eleven o'clock rang out, he was dismayed not to hear a twelfth.

Two hours later, when Klostermann and Stein arrived to collect him, it appeared that the rain was beginning to abate. The apex of a dilute rainbow spanned the clouds, and for a few minutes there was but an irregular and light patter on the carriage's canopy. Very soon, however, the drumming on the canvas loudly recommenced. 'Let the summer begin,' mumbled Klostermann, who like Stein seemed out of sorts, as if both were resentful of the insistent din. Neither of them said much as they drove, and Ettlinger was not inclined to fill the pauses in their talk. Enjoying the rush of the mild damp air, he gave himself up to the recollection of the words Helene had spoken when last he had taken his leave of her. Though conscious that his hopes and indeed his memories were perhaps founded on nothing more substantial than his wishes, he allowed himself to believe that the day might come on which he would hurry as a lover past these very buildings. He imagined how the streets would then appear transformed, their vistas narrowing to the distant point of focus, like the painted scenery on a theatre's raked stage.

The guests were crowded into a blue and white striped marquee that had been erected in the garden. The infant Gotthard von Davringhausen slept in a cot in the centre of the marquee, under a little bower of pink and yellow roses woven on wires bent over his pillow. Helene and Maximilian greeted the three friends and were then led off by Gotthard's parents to welcome the occupants of a pretentious carriage that had just come to a halt outside the garden wall. A few minutes later Maximilian returned alone, and proceeded to introduce Ettlinger, Klostermann and Stein to an irascible old man whose kinship with the Davringhausens was of so complicated a lineage that all three became lost in its convolutions. In a slow voice the old man repeated the list of marriages, as if elucidating a basic principle of mathematics to a group of recalcitrant pupils. He was but the first of a succession of people whose names Ettlinger found he had forgotten as soon as they finished talking to him.

At some point the trio became separated. Glancing over the shoulder of the Davringhausen half-cousin who, having ascertained that he knew almost nothing about the religious history of the Netherlands, was endeavouring to inculcate a sympathetic excitement at the subject, Ettlinger observed Klostermann holding court handsomely to a gaggle of Davringhausen girls, the tallest of whom was a full head shorter than Klostermann. Stein stood close by, lending his support to Klostermann's authority and contriving in his manner to mingle sagacity with flirtatiousness. Ettlinger's companion excused himself and departed in search of a more attentive audience.

The rain had stopped. Ettlinger stooped under the flap of the marquee and walked across the sopping grass. The air was cooler now, as if a chill were coming off the glacial clouds. Brilliant droplets were cascading from the leaves of the chestnut tree, and in the shadows around its trunk Helene was crouching to pick up a leaf. She turned it gently on its stem. Ettlinger approached her and she smiled at him as she emerged from under the branches.

'I cannot bear any more of this,' she said. 'So many people – it's worse than the Day of Judgement.' She looked askance at the marquee and laughed. The two pendant pearls of her earrings quivered against her hair.

'You have a large family,' said Ettlinger, following the direction of her gaze.

'A clan is what I call it. Most of them could be imposters for all I know,' she replied, and then shuddered. 'What of your family?'

Ettlinger hesitated for a moment, realising that they were continuing a conversation they had begun more than half a year earlier, at Nymphenburg, and that this was the first intimate question she had ever asked him. 'I have none,' he said.

'None at all?' she asked.

'None at all,' he stated plainly. 'My parents are both dead. There are no brothers or sisters, no uncles or aunts. Nobody, as far as I know.'

'That is unfortunate,' said Helene in a murmur. She directed her sombre eyes towards him. 'How long ago? Your parents, I mean.'

'Many years. Ten years. More,' replied Ettlinger. Voices grew louder as people left the marquee to wander about the garden. 'I fear that intruders will shortly be with us,' he said, then added – 'as before.' To his gratification she understood his reference immediately.

Helene took a pace backwards to hide herself behind him, and peered round his arm. 'Your friends are taking care of the brothers.' He looked in the direction she was pointing, and saw Karl and Maximilian talking to Stein on a path down which Klostermann was walking, with four wine glasses in his hands. 'I shall flee to my quarters,' she said. 'Do you wish to remain here? I am going to read, but your presence won't distract me.'

Ettlinger followed her along the curving garden wall and round to a side door of the house. He was thrilled that he had been granted something he had wanted ever since that afternoon at Nymphenburg, yet wary also, for there was in Helene's peremptory beckoning a suggestion that he was being put to a test.

'This floor of this wing is reserved for me,' she called back to him as they ascended the staircase. 'My family's concession to eccentricity,' she said, and disappeared down the corridor of the uppermost storey.

At an angle of the stairs Ettlinger placed his hand on a teak finial and felt a sting of anxiety, an anxiety that sprang, he knew a moment later, not from where he was but from an unconscious memory of the staircase in Wolgast's house.

The corridor was a gallery, glazed along one side with windows that overlooked the garden. At the far end, partly obscured by bars of dusty sunlight, stood a suit of armour, grasping a mace in one hand and a pikestaff in the other. Two doors opened onto the gallery, and from the nearer came the sound of a chair being dragged on a bare floor. When he entered the room Ettlinger saw Helene stepping onto the seat in front of a wall of books. His picture of the Acropolis was propped between two lower shelves.

'Could you take this?' she said, passing down a heavy volume. He went to place the book on the thin-legged table by which he stood, but then noticed that a sprawl of papers covered the surface. He read the words embossed in gold on the front of the book: *Dictionnaire Raisonné des Sciences, des Arts et des Métiers*.

'Can't find it. Can't find it. Never mind,' Helene muttered to herself. 'Just move them aside,' she told him, running a hand across the spines. 'Or the floor will do.'

Ettlinger swept the sheets together, set the book down, and picked the loose papers up. Most of the sides he could see were blank, but in the midst of them was a drawing of a church in a wooded valley. 'Are these yours?' he asked.

'Of course,' Helene replied, slotting a book back firmly into its place.

'I mean, did you make them?'

'That is what I thought you meant,' she said, giving him an impatient glance. She was behaving as freely as she would have behaved with Maximilian, thought Ettlinger, and the thought gave him a passing sensation of contentment.

'May I see them?' he asked.

'Why ever not?' She pressed a hand on his shoulder as she stepped off the chair.

Ettlinger leafed through the pictures. There were drawings in pencil of pastoral scenes in the style of Claude, and portraits of herself and Maximilian, and studies in ink of mills and workshops and factories, each as precise as the pair she had given him at Klostermann's house. It was indisputable that her skill was greater than his. He congratulated himself that her attractiveness was augmented by her superiority.

'These are fine,' he commented. 'These are very fine.'

'I copy things, that's all,' Helene replied briskly, and gave him a look that accused him of condescension. She opened the book on the sconce to consult its table of contents.

'Sometimes I feel that I am but a copyist myself,' replied Ettlinger, and instantly regretted his blatancy.

Her rejoinder was prompt and, to Ettlinger's relief, disinterested. 'Some forms of copying are more elevated than others. The copies that you are talking about are copies in the sense that children are copies. Our society depends upon them.' She was now back at the shelves, hands on hips, surveying her books as if checking that all were present and well-ordered. 'Please, busy yourself,' she said. 'There is nothing here I would wish to keep from anyone.'

Ettlinger went across to the window, where he leaned on the sill so that he might observe Helene discreetly while studying her drawings. Frowning doubtfully, she turned rapidly the pages of an illustrated book.

'Certain of your interests are unusual,' commented Ettlinger, holding up an image of some inscrutable industrial process.

'Unnatural, in my father's opinion. Maximilian thinks I am calculatedly whimsical. I think they both have a sentimental yearning for the Garden of Eden. I prefer the modern world, even though I am but a bystander.'

'They are wrong,' Ettlinger insisted, with a greater urgency than he intended.

Helene looked at him, unable to decide how she should take his compliment. In her eyes he detected an inchoate affection.

'What is happening in this scene?' he asked, turning an ink drawing towards her. Excused by the neutrality of his question, he returned her look boldly.

'The paper-making machine of Nicholas-Louis Robert, the first in France,' Helene replied, in the tone of a confident examinee. She took the sheets from him, and the movement of her arm brought to him a fragrance of lemon. From the bottom of the pile she extracted another picture, which was partitioned into several parts. 'This belongs with it,' she said. 'Here is the stamping mill in which the rags are macerated.' The fingernail of her index finger, as perfect as an almond, touched the page above the image of a vat. 'Here the men are laying the pulp across the mould. Here the coucher is laying the sheets between felt to dry them. This one is taking the ream to the press.' Her eyes were lustrous with pleasure, but her pleasure came, it seemed to Ettlinger, not from explicating what she had drawn but rather in understanding it.

'A particular interest?' enquired Ettlinger.

'One of many, but one of the earliest. For years my parents have tried to persuade me that girls should read polite novels. I am not interested in novels, polite or otherwise. But how they are made, that is a different matter. My father used to dine with the editor of some journal. I asked him once, when I was small, to take me to the printers. This, I was made to understand, was most uncouth. But now I know how it is done, from the rag pile to the bookshop.' She jerked her head in an exaggeration of boastfulness, and handed the drawings back to him; on top was a beautiful picture of a composing stick, its type spelling the name 'Helene Katarina von Davringhausen'.

'One of many,' Ettlinger repeated with an inquisitive air.

'Very many. You admire these earrings?' she asked brusquely, and presented a coquettish profile to him. Fearing that he was blushing, Ettlinger nodded. 'So do I, but in a different way,' she continued. She went over to the cabinet that stood opposite the bookshelves and from its lowest drawer removed a portfolio of garishly mottled card. Untying its ribbon, she carried it to Ettlinger. 'My fashion and jewellery collection,' she announced, balancing it like a tray on the fingertips of one hand. Helene stood beside him and opened the portfolio, letting Ettlinger take one wing of it. 'You wouldn't want to see these,' she said, impatiently flicking past a dozen pages. 'Not unless you find naivety beguiling. You don't, do you? I don't. Certainly not my own.' She slapped her palm down on a small, square sheet. 'This is better. Do you know what they are doing?'

Ettlinger looked at a room in which six young women were working. The two on the left appeared to be paring berries; the pair on the right, seated on opposite sides of a cradle on which a bowl of berries rested, were sucking or blowing on pipes of some sort. He scratched his head, enjoying his ignorance.

'They are fabricating pearls. Artificial pearls. Over here is a girl scraping a fish called, in France, an *ablette*. Its scales are boiled to produce *essence d'Orient*, a dye which makes these glass beads opalescent. Here they are blowing the extract into the hollow beads; here the beads are being filled with wax. Here they are making holes to thread the pearls,' she explained with a pert smile, making fun of her recondite knowledge. She turned to the following picture. 'A plumassier's workshop. Here they are thinning and frizzing a heron's plume.'

Suddenly she seemed tired of what she was doing, as if it were a chore she had imposed upon herself. She closed the portfolio with a grimace of irritation. 'I have scores of these. Myriad crafts and trades: baker, potter, saddler, soapmaker, ropemaker. With each new object of study my parents' despair increases. They would seem to believe that the usage of my mind is a blight upon my womb. A medieval notion. The female body has but a finite and meagre allocation of energies, and to expend it in thought is to sacrifice one's fecundity. And now that Karl has sired an heir, my foolishness is even more flagrant. What would you do in such a situation, August?' she asked.

Ettlinger started, not so much at the question as at hearing her speak his name.

'I don't know,' he began. Helene's face was turned to the window, but her gaze went no farther than the glass; it seemed that his advice might be of some importance to her. But before Ettlinger could say anything more, he heard rapid footsteps in the gallery, and Maximilian bounded into the room. To Ettlinger's surprise, to his disappointment even, Maximilian appeared to find nothing untoward in what he saw.

'Helene, your absence has been noted,' her brother tentatively warned.

'I am obliged to you, Maximilian,' she responded. She left the room without so much as a glance for Ettlinger, and waited in the corridor, her eyes downcast, for them to join her.

'You don't know who all these people are, do you?' Maximilian asked Ettlinger as they descended the stairs, with Helene leading. 'Neither does Helene, you know. She has an amazing memory, but she is very careful about how she uses it. And of course, she lacks my affability,' he laughed, rectifying the untidiness of his cuff. An idea then quite visibly occurred to him. 'Helene,' he said in an ingratiating lilt, 'why not show August the family tree? She made it herself,' he whispered to Ettlinger. 'Extraordinary thing for a child to do.'

So, while Maximilian fussed at something in a corner of the room, and miscellaneous relatives came and went, Ettlinger and Helene stood below the portrait of grandmother Elisabeth, looking at the names recorded by Helene in damson-coloured ink. And while Helene talked wittily about her forebears, there fell between them Ettlinger's memory of mad Abbadon; and behind the figure of Abbadon, as a mountain might loom over foothills as one rows across a lake, rose the incomprehensible figure of Wolgast.

38.

Ettlinger's teeth crack against each other like the jaws of a jabbering puppet. He swings his legs out of the bed, and the ache flows thickly in his muscles and his joints like cold honey, then settles in his thighs and calves. Dust glues itself to the soles of his feet; tines of cold iron comb his scalp. He stands, and for the second he remains upright it is as if the husk of his body alone has risen, detaching itself from his nerves and their freight of pain. He takes the earthenware jug from the stool beside his bed and tips it against his mouth. The water scores his throat like a knife-stroke.

Beside the jug, on the seat of the stool, are his copy of Herodotus, his two manuscripts, the picture of Helene and a piece of mirrored glass. He holds the glass at arm's length above his face, and looks up at features indistinguishable from those of the morning, and of the previous day. His eyes feel as if they are striving to burst from his face, yet they regard him with insolent calmness.

He brings the mirror closer, so close that he sees his whole face set within the pupil of the reflected eye. He peers into his own dilated pupil, in which are displayed the walls and his face as if they were observed from the back of a skull. The bulkhead of his nose obscures a corner of the room. There is a tangle of ruby filaments in the cornea of his left eye, above the iris; in the right eye is a blood vessel attached to a blurred substance like a smear of crabmeat. Ettlinger tilts the mirror to direct the sunlight across an eye, and watches the pupil flinch. The band of light illuminates a strip of blue-green iris, like a torch directed into clear, shallow water.

He imagines, in the Residence of Xerxes, a room overlooking the courtyard in which the children of the Residence play. At the centre of the room a fountain of mercury sprinkles beads of the liquid metal into a bowl of beaten copper. The mercury coalesces to form a single convulsive mirror, which Xerxes shatters repeatedly with a stab of a finger.

Ettlinger lies down and gathers his nightshirt and blankets about him. Swaddled like a mummy, he invites sleep to come, but his eagerness for sleep repels it. Conceding that he is condemned to wakefulness, he permits himself the indulgence of imagining his own demise. He takes a momentary pleasure in the prospect of dying in a place where none who knew him might visit his resting place. But no sooner has he conjured the affecting image of the exile's unmarked grave than the image appals him, for suddenly he knows that the only fitting place for the conclusion of his life's story is the place where the material of that story was created. Completion necessitates a return to Germany, he tells himself, though aware of the hyperbole of his thinking.

39.

This is where Artabanus supervised the creation of the emperor's texts.

The pages made to his instructions were the most exalted specimens of the calligrapher's art, and the papers he used were milled by men who had made a life's study of their discipline. A description of the Paradise was written in which the script was so thickly laced with vine tendrils and leaves that the lettering was visible only as much as the soil of a summer vineyard is visible. An account of our exile was adorned with tiny landscapes, portraits, battle scenes and hunts; they filled the cusps and enclosures of the words, choked the margins and spaces like blooms of weed on the surfaces of untended canals. A scandalous biography was written on pages of thick vellum which then were bound into a book so stout that it could not be opened except by tearing the book to pieces. For other stories Artabanus devised pen-strokes so florid that nobody could read the words they made. The edict condemning the sister of Amestris had no apparent text, for its sentences were the paper's watermark.

The creations in which Artabanus took the greatest pride were the fragmentary inscriptions. Every week a rectangular wafer of blank bronze was made at the forge, its size such that it would just cover a man's palm and closed fingers. In this building, using a point that scratched a line scarcely thicker than an eyelash, an apprentice would inscribe the words dictated by Artabanus. More than one hundred of them were scattered over the island, buried at places known to nobody but Artabanus. Skeletons were buried with some of them; their bones were riveted together and dressed in a cape of gold cloth, into which might be wrapped a small silver boat or a leather helmet, a flagon or a knife of patterned iron.

Only two of the inscriptions have been recovered since the emperor's death.

I

Xerxes affected

a sudden devotion

poetry and the gaiety

of the

cruelty, whimsicality and

though a public virtue at odds

the sea

cast into the sea, or in a vessel with a prow of

'Oh the far trees

the horizons

his delicate eyes

fantasies in stone, and tombs

whereas in the third year, the warehouses being empty from the drought three weeks, and found with blades of grass between her teeth, curled like a foetus

II

a wooden amphitheatre no taller than a man; there was a bath full of lizards, a cage of dyed mice, a pool of fresh water

'an amethyst with the clarity of air, the solidity of earth, the reflectiveness of water, the splendour of fire. Yet its perfection fills me with a sadness like the

of exquisite glassware: a drinking vessel that seemed to be made of cracked ice, another with a stem so delicate it would crack if the bowl were but half-filled with wine

the thirteen modes of address were explained to the ambassadors and Xerxes received them cordially

throne of jasper, beside him Cassandane

her crown of lyre-bird feathers

the naming of the rivers and hills. The emperor had a chair set upon a small platform in the stern. There he sat until landfall, his head

our course we turned his chair, so that he always faced the mountains. We brought his meals to the chair, where he ate alone, dismembering his food

terror, so much so that nothing more than the creak of a window's shutter

40.

Ettlinger and Wolgast left their carriage in the village and walked up the hill that separated the cottages from the chapel in which the wedding was to take place. The groom was Anton Gustav Schmied, a member of the cadet branch of the von Kreisel family; his betrothed, Marianne Hannelore von Nordau, was a remote cousin of Helene, Karl and Maximilian von Davringhausen. It was a union 'that satisfied the requirements both of the dynasts and of the romanticists', Wolgast commented, as they toiled up the slippery gradient at the top of the ascent. 'The genealogical niceties have been explained to me, but I cannot bring them readily to mind,' he said, shifting from one forearm to the other the purple moiré frockcoat he was to wear for the ceremony. 'I imagine that you are no more interested in the bloodlines than am I,' he continued, to which Ettlinger, short of breath, agreed.

They sat in the shade of a vast oak that rose just below the brow of the hill, and drank from the flask of water that Ettlinger had packed with his sketchbooks and pencils. From that vantage they could see the west front of the chapel, and most of the path that descended between rows of gravestones to the little thatched gate in the churchyard wall. To their left a track of worn grass diverged from the village road and vanished behind a screen of hawthorn; to the right another track, superimposed by the branches of an apple orchard, ran down the riverbank to join the miniature pier at which the wedding guests were already disembarking.

Four young men, standing in a perfect lozenge formation midway between the water and the gate, were watching the proceedings at the pier. Pushing aside the skirt of a weeping willow, a bald-headed, black-clad cleric bent low to offer his assistance to an elderly man, who braced himself with both hands against the gunwales of the rowing boat that had brought him. The rower, a broad-shouldered boy in a crimson jacket, dug his oars into the riverbed to steady the boat. A man and woman of middle age, with a child between them, huddled close to the pier, awaiting the landing of the elderly man. Safely lifted from the prow, he hobbled to join them, stabbing the ground with a brass-collared stick; the quartet turned to follow the path to the chapel, preceded by the four young men, who turned at exactly the same moment, as if in planned unison.

Upstream, an arm's length clear of the willow's leaves, another oarsman held his boat against the current with small alternate strokes to right and left.

Downstream of the pier, out in the middle of the river, the oars of a score of similar vessels jostled the water, breaking the light into quivering pieces, so that it appeared that hundreds of silver fish were frisking on the surface. In the prow of a boat in the heart of the flotilla sat the bride, adorned by a headdress which, from where Ettlinger and Wolgast sat, resembled a colossal white carnation. A huge bouquet of white blooms hung from a peg on the stern, where her father sat, looking from side to side and smiling his approval, as though the abundant foliage of the riverside and meadows had been fabricated at his request. The foremost vessels parted, allowing the bride's to dock before them; the varnished hull slipped into the dark, unruffled water beside the pier, where thick drifts of riverweed opened and closed around it like lips.

As the first of the other boats manoeuvred to dock, Wolgast and Ettlinger saw a second flotilla rounding the penultimate bend of the river, bringing the party of the groom. Close to the apex of the final bend, a man stood up in each of the four leading boats and raised a trumpet to his lips. A fanfare bleated across the fields, raising a flight of mallards from the cover of some nearby rushes. Startled guests in the churchyard and on the pier looked in the direction of the sound, but they could not see what Wolgast and Ettlinger were seeing. A young man standing by the churchyard gate threw his arms wide and echoed the rising notes of the trumpets in a piercing falsetto addressed to the sky. A cheer from the groom's companions responded across the water.

'The fleet of Aeneas announces his arrival at Carthage,'

commented Wolgast drily, yet his face betrayed some admiration for the flamboyance with which the event was being conducted. He reclined on the grass, linked his hands behind his head, and looked up into the branches of the oak as if idly seeking something to interest him there. 'Our groom is a perfect fool, a pure fool. He understands one thing and one thing only – how to breed horses. He doesn't understand how he came to fall in love with his Marianne, and he doesn't understand how she came to fall in love with him. I find it perplexing, too, but infinitely touching as well. You should see them gazing into each other's eyes – two mirrors with a candle set between them. I have never seen lovers so simple and so inviolable. They are children of nature, leaping into marriage like infants throwing themselves into a snowdrift. Anton Gustav and Marianne will be enduringly happy, I am sure. When they come out of the church they'll see before them the names of the married dead – the Glöckners over there, the Windelbands beside them, the Lankheits on the other side. And the newlyweds will not be downhearted. On the contrary. They'll see the epitaphs as certificates of salvation. They too will go hand in hand to their salvation. Yes, Anton Gustav and Marianne will be happy. They are capable of nothing else.'

Down by the pier, Anton Gustav Schmied slung his arms about the shoulders of two of the trumpeters, and steered them towards the church. The elderly man, supported by the couple who had escorted him from the pier, stooped to read an inscription beside the churchyard gate. Ettlinger removed a sheaf of pencils from his bag, impatient to begin and wishing that Wolgast would leave him.

Wolgast sat up, and passed a hand across his face, seeming to spread over his features an expression of stern superciliousness. 'Allow me to sketch some of the guests for you,' he said. 'I find it more agreeable to describe them than to converse with them. Let us begin with the admirable Kreisels, the ones whose friendship you might do well to cultivate. That Kreisel' – he pointed out a man in a dove-grey outfit, standing apart from the others underneath a statue of the Baptist – 'is Otto, a much respected jurist and an expert on Roman law. That is his wife, and that his daughter. You will never hear an ill word spoken of any of them. Over there is Hilmar von Kreisel, a botanist of encyclopaedic knowledge and entrancing modesty. He is also the closest friend of that Nordau, Christian, on whose estate some rare species have thrived, thanks to Hilmar's expertise. I believe it is through their friendship that this match came about. Christian is in some way related to the superb woman standing on the threshold. She is a Pole with a name that nobody can pronounce, a circumstance she takes to be symbolic. She has a voice that would make you marvel, but she sings only folk songs of her homeland, and refuses to tell any German what she is singing about.'

Unfurling his coat, Wolgast took from a pocket a small brass telescope that extended from a cylinder no longer than his middle finger. He opened it and quickly scanned the company below, pausing when he came to the church door. 'Hilmar is rumoured to be besotted by her, as many indeed are.' He passed the telescope to Ettlinger, slapping it into his palm.

'If you look to her left – the diminutive figure, that is Günther, a tangential Kreisel, and once an eminent mathematician.' In the centre of the glass slouched a dishevelled little man, whose smile seemed that of someone who is among people for whom he feels affection, and who knows he is liked by them in turn. 'Günther was a brilliant boy, a Mozart among calculators. On the eve of his twenty-fourth birthday he was offered a professorship in Zürich. He took the position, became famous for the abstruseness, energy and eloquence of his lectures, and spent years refining a theory that only six other people would be able to comprehend. At thirty-two he finally published his treatise, and he resigned his chair the next month. Nobody knows why. He retreated to the villa he had bought beside some secluded Swiss lake, and there became old almost overnight, as if he were now paying for his precocity by ageing ten years in every twelve months. He claims to no longer give any thought to mathematics, other than to calculate the yields from his dairy herd. I find that impossible to believe, but it might be true.'

Ettlinger saw two children, a boy and girl, both of six or seven years of age, present themselves to the retired mathematician. Standing hand in hand, they looked up at him as if his face were a notice on a door. Günther smiled at them and motioned them to come closer. They took a step, and Günther took a step and bent to embrace them with frank affection, pressing their bodies to his chest. The boy kissed his left cheek and the girl his right, and through the telescope Ettlinger saw Günther's mouth form the words 'Thank you both'. Had he not been informed by Wolgast, Ettlinger would never have thought this man in any way remarkable. He might indeed have taken him for a farmer from a province in which there was no society. Another guest passed Günther, patted his arm and passed on without talking to him, as if he thought Günther as simple as the children.

'Note the gesticulating greybeard standing astride the gravestone,' Wolgast resumed. 'That is Magnus Thielemann, another peripheral relative, and the most tedious human I have ever met.' Ettlinger swung the lens so that it filled with the face of Magnus Thielemann. Deep within the clearing of his copious beard his lips moved in gobbling motions, and his eyes kept widening into circles, as if registering successive shocks of pleasure. 'Magnus is an engineer, a master of hydraulics. He is an expert at draining swamps, cutting canals, drilling wells. He is employed in that capacity by the king, but the king's work does not satisfy his mania. He must talk of sluices and dams to everyone he meets. The words he is uttering at the moment he has uttered a thousand times before.'

'He looks as if he is surprised by what he's hearing himself say,' Ettlinger observed, watching the popping eyes and the ceaselessly twitching mouth.

'Indeed. He does that to prevent a crisis. He has become a fanatic because he knows that there is nothing to him but his subject.'

The note of satisfaction in Wolgast's voice, a note compounded with malice and regret, made Ettlinger lower the glass and look at him.

'I have just seen Klaus von Kreisel,' said Wolgast,

ignoring Ettlinger's attention. He directed Ettlinger's gaze towards a bow-bellied man with emaciated arms and legs who was pressing his brow in uncontainable merriment. 'He might serve as a lesson to your friend Klostermann. Klaus has always fancied himself the Virgil of our age. At seventeen he financed the printing of an interminable ode in couplets, extolling the immutable spirit of Freedom or some such grandiosity. But he is no poet, and never has been. He is an antiquarian drone, a bloodless archaeologist of language, a hoarder of pedantries and a veritable cistern of jealous humours. Should you make your way in the world of the Kreisels, avoid him at all costs. The unfortunate gentleman whose remarks he is affecting to find so amusing is the bride's uncle, Waldemar, who, you can be certain, is at the moment wondering what he has done to provoke such hilarity. Waldemar has been a stranger to levity since his wife died giving birth to their son, a child who survived but one month. Waldemar is always pleasant and always gloomy. I know of no man so steady in his temper. Suffering has become the ballast of his soul.' Through the lens Ettlinger watched the widower extricate himself from the conversation and walk towards the church door, clutching his Bible like a prisoner carrying his weekly allowance of bread back to his cell.

Ettlinger trained the telescope on the poet. In the wavering space of the lens, detached from his companions by a rim of darkness, he resembled a doll moving jerkily against a paper backdrop. Ettlinger repeated silently the words with which Wolgast had condemned Klaus von Kreisel, and for a moment he had the sensation that the telescope, shrinking the scene to a face at the end of a barrel, was showing him a projection of Wolgast's mind. He saw Klaus von Kreisel greet Maximilian von Davringhausen. He saw their hands unite and their faces express with absolute sincerity their gladness at their meeting, and he felt a sudden pity for the writer, both for the failure that he may have suffered, and for the calumny that Wolgast may have inflicted on him.

He scanned to the left and the circle of the telescope alighted upon Karl von Davringhausen, and then upon his wife. Next to her stood Helene, whose right hand was curved inside the crook of her sister-in-law's elbow as they listened to the men. Helene lowered her face so that her mouth was covered by the hair of her brother's wife, and she whispered something to her. Karl's wife made a nod so slight that only Ettlinger and Helene could have seen it, then turned to raise a finger in a gesture that urged her to silence. Ettlinger put the telescope down, embarrassed by Helene's discourtesy and by the discourtesy of his intrusion. Aware that Wolgast was turning his attention back to the wedding party, and had been observing him, he formed his hands into a visor and tilted his head as if to inspect some detail of the church. Displaced from the centre of his vision, Karl, his wife and his sister became figures in a frieze, exemplars of sibling and conjugal harmony, like an illustration in a children's book of moral instruction.

'Now I cannot conceive by whose invitation that person is present. The character with the excessive neckwear, patting the hair on the nape of his neck.' Ettlinger saw the cravat of scarlet satin, which spilled from under the collar of a butter-coloured jacket that swelled like a pigeon's breast, but he did not raise the spyglass to his eye. 'That one, as you might deduce from the attire, is an artist. A painter, a portraitist of some skill. He makes a not inconsiderable amount of money, I hear. Men of questionable character hire him to cleanse their reputations by painting their faces.' Wolgast chuckled, and placed his forefingers on the bridge of his nose like pincers. Abruptly, without looking at Ettlinger, he asked – 'Is there one of the guests who interests you?'

'Not in particular,' Ettlinger replied, busying himself with the contents of his satchel. 'But I confess I find it hard not to envy a successful artist.' He opened his sketchbook at a drawing of the monastery at Andechs.

'You've set yourself on the wrong pursuit if it's money you want,' said Wolgast, taking up the telescope from the tussock on which Ettlinger had left it.

'It is not his income I envy. It is the fact that he has something to his name. He has made things that will be admired after he has gone.'

Wolgast, surveying the distant ox-bow lakes through the glass, made a quiet snorting noise.

'Whatever one might think of his work,' persisted Ettlinger, 'he has achieved an immortality of sorts.'

'There are no sorts of immortality,' Wolgast corrected him. 'There is immortality, which is a property of the heavens, and then there are illusions of immortality, which are properties of the imagination. I doubt that the persistence of his fame is of much consolation to the remains of Vitruvius.' A breeze brought with it a perfume of roses. Wolgast breathed it in noisily, and his eyelids flickered like those of a man inebriated. He eased himself back, settling his elbows in the grass to prop himself as he reclined. 'Are you in love, August?' he asked, in a voice quite free of ridicule. He might have been asking him where he was born.

Ettlinger looped his arms about his knees and focused his gaze on the chapel's spire. 'No, I am not,' he stated, copying the neutrality of Wolgast's tone.

Wolgast collapsed the telescope and tossed it to Ettlinger. 'A gift,' he said, then prevented any thanks with the question – 'And have you been?'

'I have not.'

'You should take no notice of my rudeness about Anton Gustav and his girl,' said Wolgast, and paused – in order, it seemed, that Ettlinger might modify his previous reply in the light of this instruction. Ettlinger said nothing, but conveyed by an inclination of his head an inquisitiveness that was not entirely feigned. 'This is not to say that I do not find Anton Gustav foolish,' Wolgast continued. 'I do, as I find so many of his clan. But I envy him also. This envy is no more significant than I believe your envy of our painter to be, but it nonetheless is real. It is a clammy little fog that will pass swiftly over me.' He squinted at Ettlinger, perhaps considering what would best satisfy the curiosity he had deliberately piqued.

'I have been as happy as Anton Gustav and Marianne are now. Or rather, since that cannot be known for certain, I should say that I have been happy in the same manner. Once I loved a young woman and I was happy. But happiness could not make me content. Happiness made me conscious, constantly, that time was rushing away without respite, that every experience was instantly a memory, that there is no substance to the present. My life I felt to be a succession of sensations streaming off from me. That is why I have come to prefer solitude, and work. The slow time of study. But you must not regard me as a person to be emulated. I think you have a weakness for mentors, and you must not make me one. You should at least sample the happiness of love.' Wolgast fingered the skin of his throat and smiled to himself. There was a pensive contentment to this smile, and yet it seemed to Ettlinger that Wolgast's thoughts were of the speech he had just made, and not of any episode in his earlier life.

'Certain of my friends have told me the same thing,' replied Ettlinger, 'and I do not doubt the wisdom of their advice. But I cannot create love from thin air. It is something beyond one's control.'

'Ah, but it is not,' said Wolgast. 'Love can be conjured into existence as easily as enmity. The will is all.' He raised his eyebrows at Ettlinger, inviting him to be astonished at what he had said. Moving crabwise with his heels and elbows, he shifted into a spill of sunlight under the outer branches of the oak. He looked up at the azure sky through the sparse cover of the leaves, and Ettlinger saw his eyes, in the shadow of his hand, withdraw in an instant from what they were directed at.

'"We love to contemplate blue, not because it advances to us, but because it draws us after it,"' Wolgast recited. 'And now I shall assuage my yearning in the house of God,' he piously intoned, rising to his feet. 'My homesickness knows no end.' He took up his coat, scooping it from the ground as if it were a rag littering the floor of his library. Striding into the full light, he drilled his arms into the sleeves and shrugged the shoulders into a comfortable fit.

Most of the guests had entered the building; Ettlinger heard the melody of a Bach choral prelude, an accompaniment that seemed more suited to the mood of Wolgast than to the service that was about to commence.

A solitary silver birch, partly uprooted by a slippage of the soil, leaned into the air a few paces down the slope, its ragged foliage hanging like a moth-eaten trophy over a nearly vertical face of the hill. Standing on the brink of the precipice, Wolgast hooked one arm over the trunk, and with his other hand reached across to stroke its papery bark, producing a fluttering sound to which he appeared to listen intently. Back and forth Wolgast's hand moved, becoming quickly more forceful, as if he were stroking the neck of a horse to calm it. And then he drew it back, cupped his fingers and clapped the trunk with such force that the leaves hissed at the impact. Wolgast turned decisively to face Ettlinger, but his face registered something akin to a desperate confusion, as though he had come out of a dream in which he had stood on a hill overlooking a church, with his hand on the bark of a silver birch.

He clambered clumsily over the exposed roots of the tree, and came to stand beside Ettlinger. His eyes sought out the path he would now take, tracing a line from the churchyard gate right up to where they stood. 'Forgive me, August,' he said, still facing ahead. 'I have certain social obligations, but I am not sociable. I should be glad that my life brings me into the company of so many others, however brief that contact might be. I might learn things from their conversation. And look at that beautiful young woman. Merely to gaze upon her should be a delight. But at this moment I am thinking that when she steps into her carriage she will have spoken the last lines she has to speak in the narrative of my life, as will almost everyone else here. Perpetual departure.' He turned and touched Ettlinger lightly on the back of his hand. 'The morbidity of the modern soul,' he laughed, as though repeating a joke that Ettlinger had made.

Wolgast smoothed the rumpled fabric on his waist and thighs, briskly, like a priest settling the sleeve of velvet on a church column for a feast day. 'Augustulus, I must be away,' he said, looking down on the churchyard, where no more than a dozen guests still loitered. He inhaled deeply and composed his face into a condition of perfect expressionlessness. Under the hard sunlight his profile was beautiful and terrible, like a pitiless Apollo dethroned from Olympus, Ettlinger thought.

Through the telescope Ettlinger watched Wolgast descend with strides so long and purposeful that he seemed to be not so much joining the wedding party as intervening in it. Ignoring Magnus Thielemann, who lingered alone on the churchyard path, Wolgast attached himself to the Davringhausens, who had paused in the middle of the church steps. Ettlinger watched him shake the hand of Karl von Davringhausen and bow deeply to his wife, in a manner that suggested an ambassador of the previous century presenting himself at court. Helene too received a bow, but one less extravagant and more supple, suggestive of suavity rather than deference. Having exchanged a sentence with all three, Wolgast turned away from them with a choreographed gracefulness and placed a hand on the shoulder of Christian von Nordau, who was passing behind him. Wolgast passed a remark that made the other man smile unsurely and then, his doubt dissolved by a single sly word from Wolgast, break into open laughter.

With his right hand fanned open on the back of Nordau's coat, Wolgast took a pace back as if to follow Nordau into the church in file, but then went back down to Thielemann, who was taking the opportunity for a final inspection of a granite memorial by the foot of the steps. Fixing the mouths of the two men in the telescope's lens, Ettlinger observed their conversation from afar, and he felt that in observing it he was seeing it in its essence, devoid of the decoration of language. In the barter of gestures he saw the mouth of one man replicate the pursing of the other; a smile exact a smile; a grimace from Thielemann prompt a grimace from Wolgast. Though he could not read the words that the lips were forming, Ettlinger understood what was happening as Wolgast and Thielemann, standing shoulder to shoulder, read the inscription on the memorial. Thielemann made a comment on the text; Wolgast took up the comment, recast it and returned it to its progenitor, polished to a new brightness; and Thielemann nodded in concurrence with the opinion that Wolgast had fashioned from the words of Thielemann, who now smiled at Wolgast, perhaps unaware – certainly less aware than was Ettlinger – of the transaction that Wolgast had carried out. Gratified by the sound sense of Wolgast, Thielemann permitted him to take his arm and escort him up the steps to the door of the church. There Wolgast gave precedence to the tedious Thielemann and, holding the door open for him, cast a look back upon the empty churchyard. A look of bleak exhaustion fell across the face of Wolgast, the adroit flatterer, the exquisite hypocrite, who perhaps turned his face to the hill in the knowledge that Ettlinger would be expecting from him something of this sort.

For an hour Ettlinger laboured at a drawing of a portion of the churchyard wall and the yew that grew beside it. Bells pealed a carillon and the married couple emerged from the church. Marianne leaned against her husband as their families flowed around them. Wolgast came into sight at the rear of the procession. Klaus von Kreisel put his arm around Wolgast's shoulder, and through the glass Ettlinger saw Wolgast shiver and then grin at the poet. The bride lofted a posy over the heads of her bridesmaids. Wolgast, a real demon in a make-believe heaven, cheered with the rest, showing the glint of his teeth. In the margin of his botched drawing, Ettlinger sketched the name of Wolgast, in the style of a mock-Roman lapidary inscription.

41.

Here were the living quarters for the comic actors: a circle of cells arranged around a light-well, where they made and stored the things they needed.

They were not always accommodated here. When the troupe was first formed, towards the middle of the second year, the actors were housed in a more remote section of the compound, with the vintners and furriers. It was soon necessary, however, to move them closer to the emperor's private rooms. The emperor might summon them at any hour of the night, and it was essential that they arrive quickly to catch his temper.

A chain connected the chamberlain's suite with a small bronze bell suspended in the light-well of the comic actors' quarters. At the ringing of this bell they would scamper to perform their entertainment, running through a corridor that was reserved for their use. Here you can trace the line of the actors' corridor. It connected their quarters directly to the emperor's, so that the occupants of the Residence should not witness nor be inconvenienced by their comings and goings. While a servant worked the bell, the chamberlain himself would unlock the triple doors that sealed the anteroom from the corridor. He would be accompanied by a boy whose task it was to light the lanterns by the outermost door; there were just two of these, and they provided the only light in the passage, throwing the palest yellow glow against the actors' doorway, at the far end of the long, high-ceilinged curve. At the trilling of the bell, they would race along the corridor towards the source of the light, propelling before them a cart laden with costumes and devices for their latest play: mirrors, stilts, false doors, paper beaks, bags of crimson powder. High up, at the midway point of the corridor, two windows opened onto a pergola in the inner gardens. From that place several times I saw them hurtle by, their eyes wide and teeth clenched, or chattering their jokes back and forth at each other. Sometimes at night I thought I heard the rumble of their little cart, and their yelps and squeals, diminishing into silence as they neared the room in which the emperor waited, and no one else.

42.

On the longest day of the year Ettlinger worked beyond sunset in Wolgast's library. He was making notes on the house for Wolgast, or rather he was improvising on the theme of Wolgast's house, for the buildings he sketched in the margins of his observations could not have been built on Wolgast's estate. He pictured his villas and belvederes not in a field above Starnbergersee but on a promontory of a Mediterranean bay, with a volcano's faint silhouette in the background. This transformation was in keeping with the deliquescent sky that filled the windows in front of him. Heavy slicks of magenta and peach-pink cloud, their bases daubed with gold by the hidden sun, flowed low above the roofs of Munich, touched only by the tips of the highest church towers. For a while Ettlinger watched the clouds darkening to purple. He watched as the clouds released a moon that was the colour of olive oil. In the first hour of the night the city's horizon was translated into the crenellations and turrets of a fantastic domain.

Ettlinger returned to his table, lit the candles he had set upon the ream of paper, and read again the page on which was described the villa of Tiberius at Capri. He opened the Palladio and copied a floor plan, enjoying the sureness with which, unaided by compass or ruler, he drew the cluster of oval chambers around the central dome. When he looked up from his drawing, he noticed that one room on the far side of the courtyard was now illuminated by a lamp. From his seat he could see nothing but the ceiling; he rose, and saw on the back wall of the room a large many-coloured map, a projection of the globe it seemed. With a start he realised that the yellow object placed close to the bowl of the lamp was in fact Wolgast's face.

Having extinguished the candles so that he would not be seen, Ettlinger went over to the courtyard window. Wolgast's eyes were closed, and his mouth appeared to be fixed in a snarl. Several minutes passed, and his features changed only when the flickering of the lantern's flame made the shadows of his face tremble. But then, as if suddenly aware of Ettlinger's scrutiny, Wolgast turned and opened his eyes, and in the instant of the movement all expression vanished from his mouth. An arm rose into the light and beckoned to Ettlinger slowly, like a lever rising and falling.

Ettlinger crossed the landing outside the library, and followed Wolgast's voice down corridors he had never entered before. The floorboards subsided slightly under Ettlinger's tread, squealing as the wood slipped on the loosened nails. 'This way, Ettlinger, this way, this way,' called Wolgast, in a lifeless tone that brought to Ettlinger's mind the way he had been called to the anatomy room.

The room in which Wolgast sat was as naked as an anchorite's cell. The walls were adorned by nothing except the map that Ettlinger had seen, and for furniture there was but a table and two cane-seated chairs. Wolgast's left hand held open a book which in turn rested on a sheet of paper; half a dozen lines of writing crossed the top half of the page. His right elbow rested on another book, a squat little volume, and in that hand he held a quill. 'Do sit,' said Wolgast. He rolled the shaft of the quill between his thumb and fingers, inspecting the feather by the light of the lantern.

'You are working late,' Wolgast commented, still turning the quill. 'How are your projects proceeding?'

'I was making sketches for the Villa Wolgast,' Ettlinger replied. 'As I call it.'

Wolgast's brows moved upwards by the merest degree, perhaps in gratification.

'I find this time of the day, on days such as this, conducive to my studies,' Ettlinger ventured. 'The light in the library is remarkable. It compels one to be worthy of it.'

Wolgast laughed weakly. 'I had no idea that the sky might have an opinion of us,' he said.

'I meant worthy of the books, of your library,' explained Ettlinger.

'I apologise, August. I understood your point, and I agree. But I am out of sorts.' He placed the quill on top of his writing, and at last looked at Ettlinger. 'My thoughts were of Siegmund Mölck, our late friend, Abbadon.'

'He is dead?' asked Ettlinger. Wolgast made no reply; his gaze turned on his reflection, confronting it as though it were an insolent stranger. Meekly Ettlinger asked what it was that Wolgast was reading. Facing the glass but seeming to see something in the air before it, Wolgast pushed the open book towards him. 'I cannot read it,' Ettlinger told him, for the text was Greek.

'It is Herodotus,' said Wolgast. 'I have always intended to translate the *Histories*,' he went on, remaining within his reverie. 'The episode on that page concerns the barbaric Issedones, a Scythian tribe. The paragraph at the bottom of the page describes the rites of death.' Wolgast blinked, and his focus returned to the glass and then to the book. He placed a finger on the final paragraph. 'The kinsmen of the deceased, it says, sacrifice sheep and mix the meat with the flesh of the dead man, and eat it all but for the head, which is gilded and used as an idol.' He took the smaller book from under his arm, flicked quickly through its pages, and held it open towards Ettlinger. 'This is the same passage,' he said, but the antiquated typeface made it almost as illegible as the Greek to Ettlinger. 'The translation is stilted. It is too literary, too orotund, too cultured.' He glanced down at the lines he had written. 'It is not inaccurate. The translator knows his vocabularies. But it is more German than Greek in spirit.' Wolgast drummed the fingers of his free hand on the table in a rapid flurry. 'You may have it,' he concluded.

Ettlinger took hold of the book but Wolgast's hand did not release it immediately – not, it seemed, out of reluctance, but from forgetfulness.

'Yes, Abbadon,' Wolgast resumed. 'Allow me to tell you about Abbadon,' and he proceeded with a speech that was loquacious in a style that Ettlinger had never heard from him, and so measured and passionless that it sounded like the delivery of an automaton.

'His face, when I entered his chamber,' began Wolgast,

'bore a concussed, an insensible look, as if the realisation that his life was soon to finish had dealt him a physical blow. He lay on a grey pillow which was strewn with long strands of grey hair. On the chair beside the bed was a half-full glass, with a broad ring of salts where the water had evaporated.'

A frown appeared briefly on Wolgast's face, as though he were bemused by his finding something pathetic.

'He declined so swiftly in the evening that the colour drained from his flesh as I watched. It vanished as the sun's glow fades from the sky. His skin gave off the odour not of a man but of an unaired room. He gripped the sheets, turning them over into a rope, as if his grip could prevent the world from withdrawing. In the middle of the night he rallied; he chased names through his memory and called them out. He seemed vastly pleased when at last he ran one to ground. "Margarita . . . Greta . . . Gisela . . . Maria – Magda!" he cried. Then "Johann!" – but in recognition of someone other than myself. He exclaimed my name four times, and looked at me as if I were inanimate. Once or twice he appeared to be trying to recollect how this man came to be beside his bed. Once he seized a pile of letters that he kept beneath his pillow, and shook them like a child waving a flag at a parade.

'For an hour, in the middle of the night, he rested. Expressions of many different kinds – jubilation, dismay, wariness, satisfaction, disgust – formed on his face and vanished straight away, as if he were being visited by memories so fragile that they lived but an instant. Memories so fragile they might not be memories at all. When he awoke he spoke in lucid sentences, but I could discern no connection between them. "I advise against the walk beside the river," he said to me, and nodded his head slowly at his own wisdom. And then – "If that is Wilhelm, please take the money and forward it to the persons concerned. The inspection cannot proceed. It is too great a distance." From what he said it seemed he thought that I was his brother. I do not know if he has ever had a brother.

'When I told him I had to leave, he smiled and whispered to me – "I am stepping into a room full of people I know well." He did indeed appear to be seeing something delightful in the air, but only for a moment. From his throat came a sound like that of the last few ounces of water emptying from an upturned bottle. I thought the end had come. Then he gasped and resumed his breathing, releasing a bitter sigh as if aggrieved still to be in his own company.'

Thus Wolgast reached the end of his recitation. His hands were quivering on the arms of the chair. He leaned back and breathed deeply, like someone clearing his seasickness, and teased the sheet of paper from under the book, in readiness to start his work again.

'He died badly,' said Ettlinger in sympathy.

'We all die badly,' replied Wolgast, and he smiled coldly.

Ettlinger took his leave, departing in a state of mind that was mournfully laden, but not so much with thoughts of Abbadon as with the heavy resignation of a man who anticipates a bereavement. When he looked back from the library he saw that Wolgast was writing, with teeth gritted as if he were taking part in a test of strength.

43.

This was where we built the replica of the streets around the palace in which the emperor was born and spent his childhood.

On each side of the principal avenue stood booths of saffron-coloured brick, copies of the shops that lined the equivalent street in the capital. In structure they were uniform: a waist-high counter fronted each one, and at the back, behind the narrow area in which the proprietor stood to conduct his business, there was a room for the storage of goods, though there were no goods in this reconstructed quarter. Set into the low wall on which the counter rested was a panel of beaten lead, bearing a representation of the trade or craft that was followed there. An octagon of neatly segregated discs identified the premises from which the moneylenders worked. The oil merchant's sign bore discs of similar size, but scattered and flattened to represent the fruit of the olive tree. Some shops declared their function with more ostentation: an eye of lapis lazuli for the manufacturer of jewels; a mosaic of a naked goddess on the wall of the booth from which cosmetic oils were sold; a painting of a horse race outside the saddler's.

Midway along the avenue, on its western side, as in the capital, an arch opened onto a rising side-street. Standing at this junction and looking east, one would have seen, at a distance of a hundred paces, the gateway to the marketplace. Our facsimile of that gateway was perfect: the mortar of the masonry was painted blue; the phoenix above the keystone was speckled with rust along its wings and talons; and the cedar planks of the gates were decorated with hexagonal-headed nails. With equal care were the other streets simulated. In one of them, a tunnel-like alleyway of high brick walls and buttresses that spanned the pavement, there was a green-doored house in which members of the emperor's household were sometimes installed, with orders to read aloud a certain text in a certain room. Other houses had no function other than to complete a scene; looking up from the street one saw ceilings through their windows, but the rooms were in fact open to the sea – just as, had one opened the gates of the marketplace, it would have been revealed that beyond them lay nothing but the plain and the distant mountains.

At the foot of such a street of depthless houses stood a warehouse. Its façade was marked by smoke stains, and in the hall of the lower storey there were blemishes on the marble floor, like patches of mould. They were coins, fused into the stone by fire, in replication of the coins that were melted during the conflagration that destroyed the capital a century before the emperor's birth. The emperor visited this building frequently, and his visit was always attended by the same courtiers, playing always the same roles. As the emperor picked at the molten coins with his thumbnail, a woman with hair that matched the auburn hair of the emperor's mother passed by outside, walking on the farther pavement so that nothing of her but her hair could be seen from where the emperor crouched. He would continue to pick at the coins, chipping at their crust of verdigris, and a girl of eight years of age would begin to talk in the street to a silent boy who played her twin brother; her voice had a distinctive pitch, rising at the conclusion of each utterance as if in perpetual interrogation. When the girl and boy moved away the emperor left the building. At the moment he crossed the threshold a man brushed past him; the man had a tattoo of a porpoise on his right forearm, and the middle finger was missing from that hand.

This scene was enacted in the mid-afternoon of autumn days on which a morning fog persisted right through to noon. On autumn days that began with a clear frigid sun, then brought before midday a warm breeze and slow, low-lying clouds, a child might be induced to cry as the emperor passed below a window that had a border of peach-coloured paint. A certain quality of sunset – the sun spilling like a broken yolk across a dish of purple cloud, and the air bringing a chill in sporadic gusts – sometimes prompted the order for a lyre to be strummed tunelessly somewhere behind the furrier's shop. Five children would scuffle on the lip of the fountain in the middle of the nearest crossroads, and run in circles round the emperor, smacking their palms on the furrier's counter.

Some spring afternoons, when a brief light rain had ceased and the rays of the young sun were raising a delicate steam from the earth, we were required to strew the soil with lemon rinds and crush them into the ground. When these preparations were done, the emperor would walk the length of the street, turn at the milestone before the wall that closed the vista, and stop before the spice-seller's shop on his return. Opposite, a dilapidated dwelling showed a piece of the ocean through its ruined doorway and walls. Some minutes later, an old woman emerged from the shop to tend her long grey hair with an ivory comb, closing her eyes as she did so, in order that the sunlight might apply its balm to every part of her face. She smiled to herself, and opened her eyes to see the emperor, to whom she gave a smile of the same sweetness as her own thoughts had elicited, as if he were a product of those thoughts. We would see the emperor's chest rise and fall rapidly as he struggled with himself. His gaze moved slowly along his shadow, and then leapt to the sea, where it rested a while before returning to the shadow his body cast across the pelleted soil. The old woman went back into the spice-seller's shop; the emperor knelt, sat upon his heels, and rested his hands on the chest of his shrunken double, as if trying to press him under the undulating, sea-coloured earth.

44.

A dissatisfaction as onerous as the July heat had settled upon him that morning. The house was quiet, the street beyond was lifeless, and Ettlinger's presentiment of failure took on the character of something shameful, as if the silence in which he sat were that of the watchful judges of his life. And later, when he came to recast his life in dramatic form, it was in this scene, this morose solitude in the vetiver-scented library of Johann Friedrich von Wolgast, that he was to place the commencement of his catastrophe.

Heaped before him in a slurry of scraps were the products of the week, a scatter of jottings for a patron whose mind was as changeable as an infant's. Having rejected the Gothic temple for something in the style of the Tower of the Winds, Anton Erwin Herterich had in the space of a week reverted to his preference for a medieval plan, the latest whim for

Ettlinger to translate into stone. With a slow wipe of a forearm, he spread the sketches across the table: a lancet window; a trefoil; a rose window; an arcade of squat columns; a list of biblical scenes for the capitals' carvings; a detail of a moulding from Ulm, perhaps misremembered. He imagined the limestone base that was waiting to receive his building; he saw tatters of paper blown across it, and ivy weaving its net over the stone. Recalling the thrill with which he had read of his commission, he blushed at his credulousness. Meshing his fingers behind his head he scanned the walls of Wolgast's library, and the lustre of it, the glow of the gilt-embossed spines and the golden wires that criss-crossed them, was like the glow of a treasure that would remain always barred from him. He reproved himself for his lethargy, and returned to it with visions of a life as the functionary of weak-willed masters.

From this torpor he was rescued by Wolgast's messenger, an unknown young man who entered the room with the obsequiousness of an official sent to bring a pitied prisoner to the courtroom. For a moment Ettlinger thought the servant might have come to take him to another anatomy, a possibility which, through the miasma of his dejection, appeared less terrible than it should have done. He doubted, however, that Wolgast would employ an intermediary for such a summons, and as soon as the request for his attendance was spoken he knew that he would again be going to the study in which he had first talked to Wolgast.

Wolgast was seated at the small table, where he invited Ettlinger to again take the place he had occupied during that remote conversation. 'Perhaps some water to drink?' he asked, and there was a jauntiness in his address which instilled a foreboding in Ettlinger.

'Thank you,' he replied, directing his reply to the servant, who, at a nod from Wolgast, withdrew with a backwards pace.

'It is a pity to labour indoors on such a day,' said Wolgast, dislodging from his brow a droplet of sweat. From the sleeve of his grass-green satin jacket the complex pleats of a long white cuff protruded. The collar of the shirt, held close to his skin by the high buttoned collar of the jacket, was turning grey with dampness. 'But I admire your diligence. It is a quality that distinguishes you, I suspect, from your literary friends. One of the qualities.' He smiled at Ettlinger as his right hand withdrew from the drawer of the table a crumpled piece of linen, which he pressed once, lightly, to his scar, and then replaced.

'They have many qualities that I lack,' Ettlinger responded.

'I am sure they do,' said Wolgast. 'I am sure they are fine young people. Certainly they are remarkably courteous. Indeed, I think it is a mark of their courtesy that they have not asked me to absent myself from their meetings.'

Ettlinger made a gesture of demurral, which Wolgast ignored.

'They made a good show of enjoying my little stories. Perhaps they did enjoy them. Yet I think they disapprove of me. I think they take what they see as my frivolity as a reproof of their seriousness.' A fly ticked against the inside of the windowpane, missing again and again the crack by which the window was open; Wolgast watched it batter the glass for a few seconds, uninterested in such a manner as to suggest that this was an incident created solely to secure his attention. 'And in that they would be right,' he continued. 'I have no patience with Klostermann and his rhapsodic history lessons. All that agony and afflatus. I find it wearisome.' He showed his teeth in a pained smile.

Ettlinger fleetingly felt that it was he rather than his friend who was being ridiculed.

'The Klostermanns of this world would prefer me to play the parlour Ossian. It is a role I could adopt without much difficulty. It is a role anyone could adopt without much difficulty.' He looked at the windowsill, where the fly, expiring, fizzed on the painted wood. 'Bereft I am!' Wolgast exclaimed. 'Bereft, for Wolgast is the last of his race! Arise, ye winds of winter and blow our woes to heaven! Rise ye torrents, and bear our grief away! O moon show thy face! Beneficent calm of night descend; bring us rest at the end of our wanderings!' Thus Wolgast mocked, and yet there was in the fervour of his voice something that belied his mockery and discomfited Ettlinger more than did Wolgast's contempt. In Ettlinger's mind there rose the memory of his father's unaccountable tears, glimpsed through the unlatched door of the summer house, in which his father stood alone on a disc of sunlight.

The servant returned with a silver flagon and a pair of small glass tankards with handles as thin as a baby's fingers. He set the tankard on a circle of lace, to soak up the water that trickled down its belly. Wolgast filled the glasses and set Ettlinger's at the table's edge.

'I think that some of them had hoped I might prove

to be a dubious character. But now they suspect that I am dubious in the wrong way. Whereas they delight in eternal vistas and antique heroics, they think my taste is for farces, spooks and trivialities.'

Wolgast drained his glass, refilled it, topped up Ettlinger's glass, and laughed soundlessly. 'And I do like these things, but a delight in frivolity is not necessarily the mark of a trivial mind. You know this, of course,' said Wolgast, and suddenly the tenor of his gaze was changed, as if the table-top had become the surface of a well, beneath which something obscure was moving. 'It is their turn to judge me,' he continued, rising from his chair. He unlocked a lacquered compartment of the bureau, and extracted from it a baton of rolled yellow paper. 'I shall not embarrass or amuse them again. I shall attend the salon of Wolfgang von Klostermann just once more, and it shall be by proxy.'

Resting his fingertips on it as if on a keyboard, he slid the scroll across the table to Ettlinger.

'Your drawings are very accomplished, August,' said Wolgast, with his fingers still on the paper but his eyes trained on Ettlinger. 'But they are modest, mute creations. The likes of Klostermann require noise. They want to hear the trumpetings of the individual. They want something that will transport them. None of your friends, I fear, can comprehend your passion for the well-turned volute, or understand the perfection of unbuilt buildings. There's no such thing as a tempestuous building, and they require tempests.' He tapped the scroll and released it. 'So here you can give them something more virile, if I may so express it. With this, each of us might change his standing.'

Ettlinger picked up the scroll and turned it to inspect the black wax seal of the oak tree and the phoenix. Wolgast gave him a grin such as an actor playing a conspirator might attach to his face. 'I entrust to you my *gran' romanza,*' he said, and rose again. 'I shall return in an hour,' he said, pausing in the doorway. 'I think it fitting that you read it in the room in which it was written. There is no rational reason for this, but the symmetry of it pleases me. We both like symmetry. I think you will be interested in what you are holding.'

Wolgast left, and Ettlinger broke the seal. He swept the crumbled wax into a cone of black splinters, and began to read.

Even in the most bleak and biting January there was an element of charm to the German winters of my boyhood, and in my memory it is the charm that now prevails, a placid charm, as if the pace of life were slowed by the weight of the thick-lying snow. I recall the creamy flows of snow ladled into the valleys, the broad strokes of snow in the mountain passes, the pines transformed into huge candles of snow. Every year, icicles as fat as organ pipes hung from the eaves of the village church, and I recall, as if it were the most exquisite taste, the unique quality of the sunlight in the depths of them. With the most delicious nostalgia I conjure to mind the moment when, cresting the last rise before the village, I would see the orange firelit windows of the mayor's house, which seemed to convey their heat across the intervening space, as if they were live coals suspended in the air in front of my face. One day in particular recurs, with a hunched, well-wrapped figure on the village street, a prowling skater on the river, a sleigh descending the hill to the east, and steam rising from the unsaddled horses outside the mill. I recall thinking that the scene lacked nothing but a signature in its bottom right-hand corner, beside the farrier's shed.

There was nothing to give pleasure in my Russian winter. The wind came across the plains like the screaming of the earth, and so cold was this wind that you could not look into it. Eyelids would freeze and fall away like broken fingernails. The snow never fell as it did in my homeland: it was dashed against my body as if it were shrapnel shattered from the block of ice that the sky had become. Some days it was impossible to ride, for the horses staggered and fell in the storm. And so we strove against the wind heads bowed, hauling the dead weight of our limbs. The snow often obliterated everyone from view, though the next man stood so close that one stumbled into him as one struggled through the drifts. We walked towards a building as a storm gathered its strength, and by the time we reached where it stood, but an hour later, it had disappeared under snow.

On days when the wind receded, the world was presented to us as an expanse of barely ruffled whiteness, a tedious terrain planed flat by blizzards. Our misery, with no object to check it, flowed out to cover everything. Once in a while we might spot a distant village, a black stitch on a vast cotton sail. I recall breaking the ice of a lake for my horse to drink, and in an instant its muzzle froze fast to the surface. I recall the sutler cutting the day's brandy allowance with a saw, and distributing it in nests of straw that were like strips of wood.

After three weeks of retreating we were attacked. Shoulder to shoulder, back to breast we stood, to endure an ordeal that was not so much a fight as a continuation of the storms we had come through, an attrition by fire instead of by snow and ice and wind. The infantry stood up to muskets and cannon for two hours, and so close did they stand that a dead man did not fall unless his neighbour too was hit. Too cold to hold a sword or pull a trigger, many made no attempt at defence, as if the enemy horde were an avalanche that could not be resisted.

By nightfall a thousand lay dead, their bodies churned into the purple-grey slush. A tidemark of horses and men marked the limit of the muskets' range. With a drunken captain I searched for the wounded who might be saved, and all around us were the cries of the dying, gargling their own blood. Standing over one who had just died, we peered at the blood that steamed in his mouth like a simmering volcano.

That night we slept where we could – under carriages, against the flanks of dead horses, under canvas that had become crumpled metal. I lay under the cloaks of four dead Frenchmen and I looked at the stars, and for the only time in my life I felt the darkness of the night sky to be a warm place, and I wished myself adrift in the heavens.

At dawn we buried the dead under snow, and moved on. Westward we marched for three more weeks without a single day's rest, harried by Cossacks as each nightfall came. For hundreds of miles we marched, and such was our tiredness that it seemed we were wading through the endless shallows of the sea. Our exhaustion was so deep that we had no memory of the previous day. Words congealed on the tongue as we tried to utter them. Our limbs were made of solid bone. We crossed our own frontier without our horses, for we had eaten them all.

The foregoing might be taken as some form of explanation, though I do not offer it as such. I simply record what I must record.

Months later, in a different country, with different companions, I found myself standing in a field of rye, amid stalks so high that the enemy could have approached unseen to within a few yards of us. Sometimes I tread a carpet and its yielding brings instantly to mind the spring of the trampled rye, its desiccated rustle and the smell of barns.

My battalion pushed through until we emerged at the edge of a clearing within sight of a long wall of chalky stone. To prevent our gaining the wall's protection, the enemy propelled a cavalry charge against us, halting fifty paces before our line to entice us into wasting fire. They withdrew, regrouped, and charged again, stopping precisely where they had before. This minuet of cavalry and infantry continued for some time, neither side gaining ground, neither inflicting any damage. And then they launched a charge that broke a few paces closer; we responded with a volley, striking one or two riders and giving an urgency to their retreat.

As we knew it would be, their next gallop was a true assault, a furious attack with all lances lowered and swords unsheathed, and cries of rage that made the riders' faces look like those of strangled men. At our first round some horses reared, their bits slathered with foam, and bore off their powerless masters. One lancer, hit in the leg, pulled his mount around and I saw his boot swing free of its stirrup, held to the thigh by a lace of muscle; the head of another was sliced off by a bullet in the same stride as his horse was shot, and the mare's momentum took them both into our midst, where dead rider and dead horse opened a space and then were engulfed. The rest spurred their horses and hacked away to right and left, felling a dozen men in the front of our square. And yet our formation was not breached, and after little more than a minute the survivors of the cavalry brought themselves clear, vaulting the bodies of their stricken comrades.

Before we could regroup, the artillery commenced a mighty bombardment. An explosion lifted a divot of earth with two men upon it, and then came twenty or thirty explosions in roaring unison. The field beneath my feet trembled as if in terror, and the air pressed like thumbs into my ears and eyes. On all sides the wounded screamed. I saw three soldiers who had been maimed by the same cannonball, which had taken away each man's right arm. I hurried towards them, and as I ran, a soldier within bayonet's range of me took the full force of a canister shot. A fragment of his skull blinded a musketeer standing even closer, on my right hand. I looked about me and saw not a single uninjured man. This is not hell, I told myself, for hell is eternal, and this will end before the day's end, for not one of us will live beyond it.

It was with a strange indifference that I heard the retreat. A fellow officer stepped out of a smoke-drift and shouted at me to run. Together we hurtled across the rye fields. I remember the blood welling up through the matted stalks as I sprinted over it.

My comrade and I awoke at the same minute the following morning, under the canopy of a handsome oak. Stiff-limbed we embraced, then set off to scavenge for food, without success. We drew water from a well, and as I drank I experienced a strange exhilaration, as though I were already dead and the day of judgement was at hand.

The second day unfolded in a manner quite unlike the first. We took possession of an area of raised and exposed terrain, a vantage from which we surveyed an infantry who seemed to have little inclination for engagement. We watched an officer ride off and return at great haste, but there was no guessing what news he brought, for still his men rested at the foot of the rise, content to watch us as we watched them. Then, at eleven o'clock, cavalry arrived behind the enemy line, which then suddenly parted to release the charge. There was no feint this time: they rushed at us in a narrow front, and our musketeers had to work at double speed to repel them. But repel them they did. The attack failed, and our casualties were few.

At my ease, I complimented my men on the accuracy and steadfastness of their fire. With one young man I was especially pleased – a Berlin boy by the name of Markus Schiefler. Watching him stolidly reload and take aim, you would think that nothing much was at stake; that he was practising his drill on the parade ground rather than endeavouring to preserve his skin. I took him aside to commend him and we fell into a conversation of sorts. We talked about hunting, and about Berlin. I recall that he had a sister, who was to marry as soon as Markus returned.

Over his shoulder, I saw a man rise onto his knees behind the belly of a horse. As if his intentions had nothing to do with us, I watched him rest the barrel of his rifle on the saddle. I saw a flash of flame and even the bullet in the centre of the flame, like the moon eclipsing the sun. I saw the marksman fall back at the recoil, leaving a smudge of grey smoke where his face had been. In the next instant, unwitting Markus was destroyed.

In one protracted fraction of a second, Markus's eyes sprang wide open and a plume of blood and skin and teeth erupted through a hole that had been his mouth, bespattering my face and chest. The ball, its violence all but dissipated, cut a course across my temple and made me reel, but my injury was slight. I wiped the mess from my eyes, and tripped over the body of Markus. His eyes were those of a good-natured boy who had been startled by a practical joke; the lower half of his face was a more or less circular crater, with mud in its base.

Up to that instant I had played the role expected of me in this war, and I think I had played it well. I had, furthermore, retained a creditable sense of my neutrality throughout the campaign, regardless of the extremities to which we had been consigned. I was but one of the numberless vehicles of the history of nations, and my thinking self, my identity, was in abeyance, as it were, until such time as I should be permitted to resume my own private history. I believed that my side was in the right, but was conscious that the operations of chance might have placed me in the opposing ranks, and that in all likelihood I would then have been of the same opinion.

But I had been fond of young Markus, and I was now, for the first time, affronted. An insult had been offered, and I would have revenge. And it seemed evident to me, as I wiped my wound, that I was not after all to be tallied among the dead at the close of this day. I was possessed by the notion, by the fancy, that I had been marked by Death as its delegate. Death had marked me with his bloody hand, and through his power I would create a terror that would spread over all the field.

Enraged, exalted, I strode forward, my scimitar raised like the flaming sword of Saint Michael. But I think that, as I pushed aside the men who stood around the corpse of Markus, as I marched towards the shambles of the dead and dying, my fury departed from me, as if it were striding ahead of me. There was no question of my turning back. Yet a coldness had settled upon my soul. Quite dispassionately I foresaw that I was about to remake myself, and I regained the exhilaration that my fury had given me. I regained it in the thought that by this imminent action, this half-willed spasm of my body, I would recast my whole life. I would make myself monstrous.

The first man I came across lay behind the horse that had given protection to the one who had killed Markus. I looked at him, and said to myself that there was some sort of justice in this, though I knew there was none. Pinioned by his broken leg, he raised a hand, perhaps in surrender, and I chopped the arm clean through, and then his neck. I took a lance from the feeble hands of a rider whose body had drained to the colour of rag paper and I stuck him with it. He made a hiss like the punctured bladder of a bagpipe. I saw a marksman taking aim at me, some twenty paces off; I sprinted at him, running straight along his line of fire, and I dashed my blade through his teeth. I found a wounded bombardier slithering beneath the carriage of a gun and I slaughtered him too. Close by, a man was weeping for his slain horse, a beautiful bay. His expression, as I stood over him with my executioner's blade, was that of a person to whom the greatest conceivable calamity had already happened, and I spared him.

At this moment I heard my name in the air, but it meant nothing more to me than the sound of cannonfire.

In a ditch I discovered a drummer boy, who raised the instrument above his head and whimpered as I made ready to dispatch him. Though I saw three men advancing with swords drawn, I did not pause, but put the boy down with a scything stroke. And then somebody grappled my arm. I turned and saw him. Or rather, my eyes received the image of him, as they might receive the image of an unfamiliar room upon waking in the house of an acquaintance. I whirled my sword at him, and slashed him across the neck. He knelt slowly, as if to pray. I struck him again, but before I dealt him this second blow I had seen that he was one of my own. As my arm came down I was hearing words that he might have been speaking before he accosted me. I heard him remonstrating with me. He had been telling me to stop; now he was pleading with me to stop. I struck him a third time and knocked the life from him.

The three men stood aghast at this exemplar of terror, as motionless as I stood over the body of the comrade I had killed. At some infinitesimal point in what had just been enacted I had achieved a condition beyond any happiness: I had almost ceased to exist. Now my senses returned to me in a deluge. A giddiness flooded over me. The things that surrounded me – the trees, the hills, the clouds – were rushing from me with a pounding noise. I was looking down on the body as if we two were alone atop a needle of rock. I planted my blade beside the neck of my compatriot, and turned to face the three foreigners, offering them my unshielded breast. But they saw in my surrender the defiance of a Satan, and they too fled from me.

The man with whom I had rested under the oak came up slowly, gasping as if he had run for miles. He placed two fingers on each of his eyelids, pressing the tears out of them. Quelling my nausea as easily as if it were a half-formed thought, I extracted my sword from the soil, balanced it tip-downward on the chest of the soldier I had murdered, and skewered him to the earth. My companion was sobbing convulsively, rubbing his hands up and down his ribcage and chewing at the air. I took his hands and closed them on the pommel of my sword, and left him.

I strolled through the abattoir I had made. When a bullet ripped a patch of earth onto which I was about to tread, I passed on carelessly, as though it were nothing more than a mole breaking the surface. Though the leaves were not moving, I walked in the noise of a ferocious wind. Inside my skull a ceaseless gale had supplanted my thoughts.

I walked until I came to a farm building which our troops had occupied. The last of the twilight was leaking from the sky. Far away, huge blooms of smoke were blending into the clouds, rubbing out the horizon. On the portion of the battlefield that I could see from the gate, men of both sides were looting the dead, and killing the wounded to rob them. I watched the scene and saw it as an event that was also a vision, such as are visited upon the vicious in the stained glass of ancient churches. In the opposite direction the sun sank without radiance, like a coin under muddy water. It began to rain, raising from the earth the stink of market day, the smells of vegetable rot and meat on the turn.

Wounded men lay in every room of the farmhouse, and I slept among them, between two who had been abandoned to the will of God. That night's dreams were not true dreams. They were but recapitulations of the preceding hours, and so vivid were they that I awoke in disarray. Was I Wolgast, who had just dreamed he was a monster, or was I a monster who was now dreaming he was Wolgast? The soldier to my right was dead, and the soldier to my left was dead. In the night someone had folded a sheet over each of them. Someone had looked down on me as I slept. How had my face looked in the night? Had I taken on a face more apt to the man of whom I had dreamed?

It was a fine dawn, an apocalyptic and banal dawn. The sun, seeping over the horizon, was refracted by the smoke of a hundred fires into ribbons of violet and marigold, interspersed between runnels of bright new lead. To the west, clouds that seemed to have been assembled from gargantuan clods of filthy clay squatted on the skyline. To the north stood a house blown down to low walls like an animal pen; beside it was a barn reduced to timbers of quilted charcoal. Wisps of smoke rose from the beams like spectral weeds. I absorbed it all as if it were my last experience of an innocent world, and then I recalled myself to reality.

I took a horse and set out to retrace my retreat of the previous night, taking as my one true landmark a wrecked cart that I knew I had ridden past. Descending the gradient beyond it, I spied a man lying in a field some two hundred paces distant, as if lounging in the rays of an imaginary noonday sun. The curve of the hill soon hid him from me, but I pushed through the scrub to where I thought he must be, and suddenly I was upon him. He lay in a circle of blackened grass, under a halo of flies. He looked as if a plough had been driven over him, opening a furrow from his crotch to his throat. Scorched clothing was strewn about like fruit rind. I leant over his face; it was repulsively easeful, and there was something in the set of his mouth that made me think I was looking at my reflection. Seeing myself where he lay, I tried recall an incident, any incident, from my life as it had been but a year earlier. A dance came to mind, and an exchange of glances, but so weak was the force of the memory that it was as though I were hearing of an episode from someone else's life. I imagined myself a month hence, standing before the house in which I passed my boyhood. I was looking at a stage on which people had once played people who were happy.

I returned to the farmhouse. An artillery-man sat in the frame of a window, holding to his chest a pewter flask. 'A very good morning to you, sir,' he said in greeting, as though he were a shopkeeper and I the day's first customer. Echoing his cheeriness I bade him good morning in return. These were the first words I had spoken since my conversation with Markus. They were the last I was to speak for a month or more.

I rode south until clear of our lines and the enemy's, then wheeled east. I kept going until I arrived at the town in which I was born. I entered at night and before morning I had departed. Eventually I arrived in Munich, and by the time I arrived I was ready to begin my new life as Johann Friedrich von Wolgast.

Ettlinger tried to picture Wolgast at work at the bureau, but could picture him only as he had first seen him in this house, motionless as a dead man at the end of a long corridor. Uneasily, he looked around the room. Opposite the tile-oven hung a watercolour portrait which Ettlinger had not noticed before. Only after a minute's study did he recognise the young man with chestnut hair as Wolgast. He stood to look more closely at the face, and detected there a suggestion of awkwardness under inspection that was more appropriate to his own disposition than to Wolgast's. Mounted on the wall opposite was a cast of a face in plaster. A scar across the temple marked it as Wolgast, but the prim mouth and reposeful eyelids made it no closer a semblance of the living man than was the portrait. He returned to the picture, hoping to find a date somewhere on it; there was none.

Ettlinger was considering the consequences of leaving before Wolgast could return, when he heard the squeal and chortle of Wolgast's shoes on the waxed floorboards outside the room.

Wolgast leaned against the bureau, extending a hand to take back the manuscript.

'Is it true?' Ettlinger asked, expecting evasion.

'Do you think I would have expended such effort in writing a piece of make-believe?' he asked with an acidic tone. 'Yes, it is true.' Wolgast sat down. His steady gaze was presented to Ettlinger but there was no purpose to it, as if its object were a thing he had seen every day and no longer looked at.

'I do not know – ' Ettlinger began.

The skin around Wolgast's eyes became creased in concentration, but the focus of his eyes did not change. He placed his elbows on the table's surface and lodged his thumbs beneath his chin, it seemed in mimicry of attentiveness.

'You have placed me in a position, a position of some – ' Ettlinger faltered, his gaze tracing the whorls of the table's grain.

'Yes, I have,' said Wolgast, but he was listening to something other than Ettlinger's voice. 'We appear to have nothing more to say today, Augustulus. Do as you will.'

45.

This circle marks the rim of the dancers' theatre.

The dancers danced in the darkness, on nights when the moon was new or old. Four hours after sunset, servants left the Residence to soak with oil the rocks that flanked the route to the theatre. Returning, they touched torches to the oil to light the path. We watched the flames approach us, and in silence we followed the curve of fire towards the distant mark that was the uppermost circle of the theatre's seating. At the brink of the pit we looked down into the inverted cone of the building, where the stage of sand-strewn brick, sunk a man's height below the lowest ring, revealed itself slowly and ambiguously, like the surface of the water of a well in which there might be no water.

Cautiously we descended the tiers, feeling our way down the uneven steps. Each of us sought a place out of sight of his fellows, for the experience of the dance was in essence a solitary one, albeit an episode of solitude in society. Except for the sporadic screech of a nightbird, there was no sound but the soft clap of sandals and the faintest low note of breath inhaled and exhaled as we waited for the dancers to enter by their invisible tunnel. A rasp of feet on sand would make us aware that the dancers had come onto the stage. It was a moment like a hunter's vigil, when the unseen quarry disturbs the cover of its lair. The rasping might become a rhythm or the random noise of a crowd in motion. One would make out denser zones of darkness, movements of black air, as the dance took its mysterious shape, but how many bodies were below us on the stage was a question that could never be resolved. Half-blind we watched the lethargic struggling of shadows and the frenzied conflict of ghosts. There, it seemed, was a figure trying to throw off another as though it were a cloak; there one discerned an embrace, or a figure falling from the cradle of another's arms, or a salute or a wave of valediction. There was a shape that was perhaps the undercurve of a breast, or perhaps a shoulder. Something swung back and forth in the way that Cassandane's hair would swing, and two bodies appeared to couple; we heard the smack of skin on skin and the whisper of loose-fitting gowns. A vertical form became horizontal, as if felled by an assassin's knife. Intermittent sighs went up from the audience, but nobody spoke, not even the emperor, who was said to attend every performance, dressed in the cloak of a functionary.

There was no subject to the dances, nor was it known for certain by whom they were devised or danced. Erotic and tedious, the obscure nocturnal spectacle eased our drowsy minds into and out of sleep. Once I dreamed that I sat in the midst of a parliament of mutes, grinding my teeth on gritty little balls of material that I knew to be words. Another time I was striding slowly, effortfully across a plain, through air that resisted me like water. I received a kiss in an empty room and found myself alone in a desert that sweltered when the sun went down. Sometimes I dreamed of the theatre in which I was sleeping. Waking, I could not tell at first if the stars I saw were shining in the sky or on the skin of my eyelids. I strained my hearing against the night, uncertain if the dancers had departed.

Our bodies numbed, we shuffled back along the avenue of hot stones. Veils of guttering flame were wrapped over some of them, and the fragrance of burnt oil rose all around us. We sleepwalked back towards the Residence, guided by the lanterns that glowed in scattered windows like little moons. The pinnacles and towers of the Residence looked as insubstantial as grounded clouds. I walked towards them, and for a moment it felt as if they were nothing more than a phantasm born of my weariness, and my memories were merely day-dreams.

46.

Often, in the weeks that followed his reading of Wolgast's confession, Ettlinger would enter the library to find Wolgast reading at a lectern positioned close to the armillary sphere. Wolgast might come over to the table to learn his intentions for that afternoon, but they exchanged no pleasantries such as one might expect to pass between two men in such circumstances, and nothing was said when the time came for Ettlinger's departure. Ettlinger would take his coat, tidy the books that he was leaving on the table for the next period of study, and exit from the library with a silent salute for Wolgast, precisely as he had entered. Their conduct towards each other was like that of a favoured student and a faculty member in the library of a college.

The traffic on the street was sparse at all times, and the atmosphere of Wolgast's library was rarely disturbed by sounds from outside the house. At four o'clock one Friday in late July, however, Ettlinger's concentration was disrupted by the racket of wheels, a carter's shout and the snort of a dray-horse beneath the windows. A whip-crack was heard, but the cart did not move off. With the air of a man ceasing his day's work, Wolgast shut the book he had been reading and bore it back to its shelf. That done, he went to a window and cast a quick look down at the street, as if to verify a supposition. Passing Ettlinger's table he said: 'I shall not return today. You may stay as late as you wish this evening.'

The manner of Wolgast's departure compelled Ettlinger to look out from the window at which Wolgast had stood. He saw an open-sided cart, to which a pyramid of barrels was lashed. On the tail of the cart, on a coconut mat, sat an obese and elderly man with a shiny moist scalp. His chin was sunk into the collar of a frayed grey garment of indeterminate type, and he seemed to be directing a continuous complaint against his own feet. His words were in fact directed at the younger man who had stationed himself in the mouth of the alleyway that joined the street opposite Wolgast's door. Wrapped, despite the heat, in what appeared to be a greatcoat that had been stripped of its soldier's insignia, the latter character leaned in a ladder-like posture with his feet together a pace from the wall, his back and legs locked straight, and his shoulders flat to the bricks. He shrugged and spat in the pauses of the other's monologue, and turned to squint at the windows of Wolgast's residence, where, to judge from the length of time he stared in Ettlinger's direction, he saw nobody. In his right hand he held a horsewhip which he cracked against the bricks, twice in quick succession.

Ettlinger then saw Wolgast emerge from the house and stride over to the younger man, who quickly smoothed his hair with the swipe of a hand. The exchange that followed was suggestive of some form of bartering, albeit between a pedlar who was not eager to sell and a customer whose distaste for the seller made him a reluctant buyer. A mime ensued of opened and closed hands, of denials and skyward glances. At one point Wolgast became vehement, exposing his clenched teeth and raising a level finger to the man's face, as though he were about to jab it into his eye. The other crossed his hands on his breast, pleaded with Wolgast to withdraw, and traced a circuitous line along the mortar-courses of the wall. This demonstration appeased Wolgast somewhat, though he continued to question the man for a while longer. An expletive from the man seated on the cart seemed to hasten the conclusion of the transaction. The younger man vaulted onto the cart, took his seat on top of the barrels and lifted the reins. He turned to say something to Wolgast, but already Wolgast had walked off down the alleyway.

A few days later, Ettlinger, alone in the library, was worrying over the problem of how he might tell Wolgast that he had not spoken to anyone of his confession, and never would. He was pondering the reasons for his discretion when a commotion arose directly below the window. He saw three men, all of them wearing berets that shadowed their faces, shouldering a trunk from the back of a shabby carriage. The burden having been placed on the ground, one of the men disappeared into the house; the other two raised the trunk by the rails that were fixed to its sides. A few minutes later, Ettlinger watched them mount the carriage again, and realised from the way the driver crouched on his seat that he was the younger of the pair he had seen previously from where he was now standing. And the way in which the man on the rear seat huddled his cloak about him was strongly reminiscent of his older colleague.

On the Friday of that same week, at eight o'clock,

Ettlinger was at the door of the library, admiring the bust of Alexander that Wolgast had recently set above the cornice. From the bust his gaze slid upwards to the landing of the upper floor, where he saw, through the balustrade, a trunk with a brass rail riveted to its side. Possessing no conscious intention, Ettlinger ascended, padding up the stairs with a burglar's tread.

He sat on the uppermost step, listening, hearing nothing but the knock of his heart. The trunk's lock had been left unengaged. He reached through the balusters to ease it open, but at the first movement of the lid its hinges emitted a squeal that to Ettlinger's ears was as piercing as the cry of a trapped rat. Ettlinger held his breath, as if afraid in any way to prevent the restitution of silence throughout the house. He lowered the lid of the trunk, inserting the hook into its slot so slowly that the trembling of his hand made the lock's brass plates chatter against each other for a second. The resurgent silence had the quality of an atmosphere under raised pressure; through it, in a quiet crescendo, returned the percussion of his pulse.

And then, from the depths of the dark corridor, came Wolgast's voice, mockingly sweet. '"There once was a prince who was afraid of nothing,"' he called, making of 'nothing' a sound that was loaded with malevolent glee.

Ettlinger, still seated, slid onto the step below, gripping a baluster as one might grab a spar on a pitching boat. His tongue seemed to detect the taste of its own blood. He shut his eyes tightly, and in this mimicry of a terrified child he briefly found belief in the fiction that Wolgast's call was a reaction to something other than his misdemeanour.

But the silence was a gravid interval, like a lull between claps of thunder. Wolgast counted his heartbeats, and on the twenty-eighth all hope of escape was eradicated by Wolgast's voice, reciting – '"And one day he came to a giant's house, and as he looked around the yard his eye fell on the giant's playthings."' The taunt of it compelled Ettlinger to rise. His arms outspread to stroke the walls of the unlit corridor, he neared the rectangle of lamplight that drew the door at its terminus. Again he entered the dreadful room.

On the ceramic table lay a young woman. Wolgast was straightening her limbs, pressing on a knee with one hand, tugging at a wrist with the other. A fig-coloured bruise marked the side of her neck. Wolgast lifted what appeared to be a ribbon of weed from the inside of her thigh and flicked it from his fingers onto the floor. At last he looked up, and smiled at Ettlinger. 'Why so bewildered, my boy?' he asked with what seemed frank curiosity as to Ettlinger's state of mind.

Wolgast's face was the only thing in the room that possessed any clarity; Ettlinger found himself unable to speak.

'Come now, August,' he said, 'you have already passed your initiation. And besides, you have enjoyed similar scenes before. The vehicle, if I may so term it, is crude, but the tenor is by no means new. Think of us as the cousins of your artists and their decorous moralities – the shepherds crouching before the tomb in a sylvan landscape; the mouse in the foreground of the party; the fruit, the sundial, the broken lute, and all that paraphernalia.'

'Who is she?' Ettlinger asked wanly.

'Ethics forbid the disclosure of her name,' replied Wolgast, raising a reprimanding finger before turning up his hands as though to disavow responsibility for this constraint. 'You may, however, know the gist of her story. It might turn out to be a romantic tragedy.' Wolgast braced his arms on the table and pityingly regarded the faces of the dead girl and Ettlinger. 'A few evenings ago her father went to her room to bring her downstairs to supper. She was seated at her escritoire, with her head pillowed on her arms. The noise of the door did not rouse her from her sleep. Her father placed a hand on her cheek and found it cold. Perhaps her heart had simply failed. It happens, even with the young and beautiful. But her father heard rumours of a liaison between his daughter and some peripatetic Polish roué, and suspected a different explanation. He believes that his girl became ensnared by love.'

From a shelf behind the table Wolgast took a square of muslin and a bottle of water; he doused the muslin and wiped the corpse's torso and neck. 'She took poison, perhaps, on losing her lover to a rival, or was poisoned in some devious way by a rival who had been bested by her. In his grief the poor man will give credence to any plot, however Shakespearian. He fears the scandal that would arise should a doctor examine his daughter and confirm what he suspects.' Wolgast stoppered the bottle and discarded the soiled cloth on the floor. 'But of course he also finds intolerable the idea that he might pass the rest of his life in uncertainty. He may well have revenge in mind as well, I suppose. Whatever his motives, he has asked for my assistance in unravelling the tale, and in the names of science and truth, I have donated my services.'

Wolgast slid a hand under the cadaver's head and turned it so that the face was presented to Ettlinger. The eyelids were slightly opened, revealing a crescent of eyeball like greasy glass. Ettlinger sealed his mouth and nostrils with a hand and bent to look more closely. The irises were the colour of damp coal-ash. The mouth, drawn into a simper by the first inroads of decay, revealed a tongue that resembled a globule of yellow fat.

'You should stay, August. You also may learn something from my procedure.' He resettled the head in the wooden bracket by which it was held. Ettlinger did not withdraw.

'This job used to be the preserve of barbers, you know,' said Wolgast, rinsing his hands in a bowl by the corpse's ankles. 'The anatomist would recite the ancient books to his pupils while a barber cut apart the body to reveal the harmonious system that the texts described. The texts were often wrong, but the harmony of theory took precedence over the empirical shambles. If what was described was not seen, the failing was the specimen's.'

Having dried his hands, Wolgast ran a fingertip from the corpse's shoulder to its knee, as someone might stroke the lid of a piano before sitting down to play. 'Sophistry extracted from anatomy the proofs of a grand design. One might demonstrate the divinely constructed perfection of the human body thus' – and with this Wolgast hit the corpse lightly, with bent knuckles, across the cheekbones, brow and nose. 'See how well the bones of the skull protect the eyes,' he declaimed. 'Eyes which, moreover, have providentially been positioned in such a way as to permit the bearer to get the maximum benefit from them, for their altitude makes the fullest possible use of the body's extent. In this species the eyes are like the watchman in his tower. Creatures consigned to a lowlier posting on the great ladder of creation, such as the dog or the hog, are obliged to make the best of an arrangement that places their eyeballs at the same height as their hips. What clearer proof could there be of God's practical-mindedness and of the elevated role assigned by Him to His uniquely hairless biped?'

Seeming to grow weary in mid-phrase of his own jocularity, Wolgast turned away to rummage among the miscellaneous implements scattered along the shelf on which the water stood. He lifted a stick of charcoal and prodded its tip into the corpse's midriff, in the peak of the arch of its ribcage.

'This is where we shall find the significant parts,' he continued, and proceeded to inscribe on the oyster-coloured skin a diagram of the internal organs, mapping carefully and rapidly the lungs, the heart, the stomach, the liver.

Ettlinger watched the progress of the charcoal as it traced the involutions of the bowel and the symmetries of the reproductive tract, pushing up wrinkles of skin like wavelets flaring from the prow of a boat, leaving a wake of black dust. So intent was he on following its course that he did not notice the movement of Wolgast's other hand, which suddenly closed on Ettlinger's right wrist and forced his palm onto the girl's right breast. It was soft, cold and inelastic, like a hemisphere of goat's cheese, and its touch produced in Ettlinger a revulsion that made him gasp as at the shock of freezing water.

Wolgast laughed, and gently pushed Ettlinger back from the table.

'What will he tell them?' was all Ettlinger could think to say.

'Who tell whom?' asked Wolgast, now swabbing off most of the charcoal with a freshly saturated cloth.

'The father. What will he tell the priest, the rest of the family?'

'He will invent something,' Wolgast blithely assured him. 'You would be surprised how creative people can be in a crisis, and how easily a rich man can acquire accomplices. This is not a difficult case.'

Wolgast took up a knife with a twin-faced blade and held the instrument upright before the dead girl's face, as if showing a flower to an invalid. '*"Tu trembles, carcasse; mais si tu savais où je vais te mener tout à l'heure, tu tremblerais bien davantage."* Wonderful words.' He stared into the lantern above the table, miming the last phrase twice.

In an instant Wolgast commenced the dissection. Pressing the point of the blade at the rim of the navel, he made a circular incision with one rotation of his wrist. Satisfied with this beginning, Wolgast extracted the blade and repositioned it on the sternum, from where, with the firm and steady pressure of his whole arm, he pulled the knife down the torso till the cut met the ring around the navel. A little blood and some cloudy water oozed from the parted skin, and flowed quickly to the waist. A third incision cut down to a point just above the vulva, then two transverse cuts, quartering the body. Wolgast turned back four flaps of skin, working a blunt knife under the surface to prise them from the underlying fabric. The flaps came free with the sound of paper peeled from a wall.

From the bloody structure he had thus exposed, Wolgast ripped frayed tissues of membrane and veins, and dropped them into a box at his feet. He removed long strips of muscle and discarded them; others he severed but left connected, fastidiously pinning them back with finger-length skewers. He cut through the wall of the belly, segmented it and excised a pouch of fatty meat. As if displaying a captured pennant he held it aloft, perusing its weave of arteries and veins and the attached length of colon, before casting it into a cherrywood barrel which he dragged nearer with his foot.

Wolgast sawed through the sternum with a saw shaped like a quarter-moon, and the force he applied to the dissection became yet stronger. So violent was his sawing that his action made the corpse's arm move back and forth, as if it were feeling the cool enamel. Ettlinger felt a knotting in his gullet; his eyelids became cold.

Pausing to replace the blunted blade, Wolgast suddenly asked – 'Now what do you think of this story? Last week I was browsing in my library – I think you were there too – and I came across the story of a man who had been wounded in a siege. It happened in the sixteenth century. At Hesdin, I think it was. It does not matter.' Wolgast bore down on the bone again, glowering at its resistance. At the crack of the sundered chest he stopped, set down the crescent saw, and equipped himself with a diminutive steel hammer, a chisel and a straight-bladed saw that had a mother-of-pearl handle. He set to work making a passage through the ribs, and resumed his tale. 'The injuries inflicted on this soldier were so severe that in order to prevent his immediate death it was necessary for the physicians to remove what remained of his spleen. His comrades then waited for the decline that was inevitable after such surgery. But the doctors' prognosis was mistaken, for the wounded soldier lived for many years more, and outlived several of those who had left the siege unscathed. My book does not record how his recovery was received, but I should imagine it caused great consternation. What did his survival do for the notion of the perfection of the Lord's masterwork? Was it decided that superfluity was a divine prerogative? Did they convince themselves that the very redundancy of the organ was the hallmark of the supreme manufacturer?'

Wolgast was dragging a curved knife through the cartilages between the ribs. Like a gardener wrestling with deep-rooted weeds he twisted the recalcitrant bones from the chest and tucked them under the corpse's flank. With a triumphant expression he inspected the sticks of rib spread along the table and wiped his brow, leaving a smear of stale blood across his skin and a tint of fecal colour in his hair.

'God, my God,' he whispered, as if commencing a solitary prayer. He gazed into the chest's cavity through the riven ribcage. 'What made this chaos live? And, of more immediate concern,' he continued, 'what made it die?' A stuttering intake of breath seemed to indicate that he was battling against an impulse to weep, but the breath was released in a quick deflation and his face took on the look of one who had arrived, with some sorrow, at a conclusion that could no longer be postponed. 'A ruptured aneurysm, I believe.' Wolgast smiled and shook his head. 'An aneurysm, beyond question.' He gestured Ettlinger to approach. 'Do take a look, August,' he said impatiently. 'I am affording you an opportunity given to few young men outside the military and medical professions.'

Ettlinger remained rooted to the spot, gulping like a man who has struggled against the current to the bank of a river. From where he stood he could see a slimy gobbet protruding above the surface of the blood. The air had begun to stink of the slaughterhouse and to taste of mucus.

Using a pair of shears not unlike the sort used in wool sheds, Wolgast chopped through thick tubings to free the heart, and lifted it to his face. 'In all my years of anatomical investigation I have as yet seen nothing that I have not already seen in the pages of my books. But perhaps I am not looking as clearly as I like to believe I am.' He took a pair of scissors to open the heart, and he cradled the bisected organ in his hands, like a rose-head.

'Andreas Vesalius, to use the Latinate title under which Wessels of Brussels plied his trade, would perhaps have gone on to deduce the blood's circulation had he but heeded the incontrovertible evidence of his eyesight. His forerunners insisted that blood passed through this septum. But this partition is not porous.' Pinching the indicated piece of muscle, Wolgast lifted the split heart from his hand and laid it aside. 'In the course of an illustrious career in Padua's university and in service to the

Habsburgs, he would have dissected numerous hearts, hundreds I should imagine. He made short shrift of the notion, then still believed by some, that the heart possesses an armature of bone. But he should have gone farther. Time and time again he prodded at this septum with horse-hairs to locate the tiny conduits by which the blood was supposed to pass. He admitted that he could find none, but shied from concluding that there were none to be found. In order that the theory could live, he thought of his success as failure.' Wolgast put a compassionate expression onto his face, and let it fall quickly away.

The anatomy proceeded rapidly, and to no purpose that Ettlinger could discern. With a soup ladle Wolgast baled the blood from the body, emptying the product of each trawl into an iron pail. He snipped through hidden fibres in the recesses of the chest to extract the lungs and liver, and deposited them in the cherrywood barrel. A spongy organ was hoisted from the blood – 'The problematical spleen,' Wolgast announced, before letting it drop onto the lungs. With his hands he scooped out the intestines; they slipped like eels through his fingers and into the barrel. He flopped a misshapen disc of flaccid maroon flesh from palm to palm. 'Behold the kidney,' he said, and patted the organ as if in commendation of its service.

With steel probes and needles and long-handled knives Wolgast lifted and segregated the knots of blood vessels and nerves at the root of the neck. Lowering his face so far that it brushed the corpse's shoulder, he speared a gland with a pipette and drained its peaty fluid into a jar. He held the jar up to the lantern. 'One cannot but ask, is this all that the soul amounts to?' Wolgast ruminated. 'Are our thoughts no more than the bubblings of these chemicals?' At the sound of rain on the blacked-out skylight Wolgast looked upward. 'Our magnificent glooms and ecstasies,' he went on, his eyes directed at the blackened glass. 'Are they nothing but the weather of the body?'

Wolgast peered again into the scoured thorax, and then into the tub of innards. 'By what means does this mess acquire the capacity to think of itself as a mess?' he asked, glancing at Ettlinger in such a way that Ettlinger thought for a moment that an answer was required of him.

Wolgast raised the barrel and tipped the slurry back into the hull of the corpse. He crammed the rags of muscle back in, and the segments of bone, and closed the huge incisions with broad stitches of hemp that pulled the skin into hideous fat seams. At the sight of this last metamorphosis of the dead girl into a doll of flesh, Ettlinger's nausea overcame him. He vomited through his fingers onto the floor.

When Ettlinger raised his head he saw that Wolgast had come round to his side of the table. In his eyes Ettlinger observed a look of apology, which gave way instantly to amusement, and then to regret. Wolgast placed an arm across his shoulders and led him out into the corridor.

'I still have not finished. Think about how you came to see this, August,' he said sternly, and went back into his room.

47.

This quadrangle, attached to the south-western wall of the compound by a corridor of stockades, was the stable of the emperor's horses. No animals were ever more devotedly treated. Three weavers and a dozen seamstresses were employed to make nothing but their caparisons. The metalwork for their bridles was manufactured not at the forge but by a silversmith. The finest hides were sent to the adjoining tannery, where they were stitched into saddles as supple as gloves. Cherry and maple trees were planted for shade in the stable yard. The stable had its own well, its own pasture, its own mill.

The barbarians destroyed the stable before the siege began. We heard whinnying that we mistook at first for metal scraped on metal, and then saw a meander of smoke against the midnight sky. Fires had been lit in all the stalls. Flames nibbled at the doors of the stalls like rats on their haunches. The horses battered their hooves against the stable walls in a maddened tattoo, a din so loud that we could not hear what we were shouting to each other. I rushed to the well in the centre of the yard. Its spindle and handle had been smashed. I looked down the shaft, and saw not water but four bloodied scalps. A stallion charged through the men who were running into the yard; another burst through the gate of its stall and galloped through the stand of cherry trees, its mane a streak of flame. A third, spurred by the pain of its burns, danced across the yard, its back arching in spasms, and dashed itself into the broken gate, piercing its chest on a stave.

The emperor ordered that the stables should be left to burn and had a stool set on the roof of the atrium so that he could watch the destruction. The smoke stung tears from his eyes, while the flames cast playful shadows around his mouth, making his lips seem to twitch as if he were asleep and dreaming.

Flames as big as cypress trees waved on the naked beams; whirlwinds of smoke spiralled between them, bearing spangles of glowing wood. A surge of flame flung up a thousand crimson points which but a second later disappeared, like luminescent insects disappearing into the hive of the night. Incandescent flakes the size of a man's hand swivelled out of the sky. One of them landed beside me, and I watched it turn grey as it cooled. Picking it up, I discovered that it was a fragment of a picture from the gallery of the equerry's quarters. It showed a horse's eye, once as bright as the eyes of the living creature, now as dull as a sliver of slate. Artabanus took it from me and handed it to the emperor. There came the sound of a wall collapsing onto an earthen floor, a sound like a vast sigh of exhaustion. The emperor himself sighed and placed the charred piece of painting on the ground. Smiling at the blaze, he rubbed his foot on the scrap of ash, as if it were a prophecy to be dismissed.

The following day the emperor's poet read a threnody for those who had died. 'The darkness, which wipes the globe each day, has gathered them up,' he began. The biers were laid side by side in the atrium, under a tent of perfumed white cotton. We circled them thrice in procession as the poet spoke on; a tambourine and a single-stringed lyre kept dolorous accompaniment to his recitation. 'Through memory we shall exalt them,' he concluded, and at this another musician took up his flute to play a tune that echoed the rhythms of the poet's peroration and then protracted them, transmuting his speech into an elegy in which we might find our consolation. The music ceased, and our ceremonial was almost ended. To the sound of martial drums we bore the dead from the Residence and placed their bandaged bodies upon a pyre. 'Thus we cleanse their bodies of their wounds,' the poet declared, as we sprinkled the aromatic spices and oils around the base of the pyre. 'Thus the flesh becomes fire and fire becomes air. Thus are their spirits released.' Above us, so high that each was nothing but a single folded wing, a troop of black birds drew careless circles on the sky.

That night I climbed to the summit of this hill, from which one can see the lights of both the Residence and the port. A wind blew in bursts that were like the gaspings of the mountains, and the brittle leaves of the oak trees, agitated by the gusts, raised a maleficent whisper behind me. Clouds as slim and quick as ermines raced across the moon, which shone with a light that was of a new intensity, as if the planet had shed a skin. Though the wind grew colder and stronger with each wave, I wrapped my cloak about my body and regarded the brilliant deserts of the moon. They were lit so brightly I could feel the texture of the lunar earth. I could see the gradients of its dunes. And as I traversed that heatless landscape, a spirit of triumphant desolation descended upon me. It seemed to me that I beheld the image of future time, that I foresaw my extinction in those plains of frozen sand, those craters of grey and ragged ice. Anointed by perfect hopelessness, I stared into the light until the moon burned itself from my eyes.

It was then that I heard a sound beneath the noise of the wind. It was a sound like the rumble of casks in a hull, but it continued without pause, becoming neither louder nor quieter, and I knew that what I heard was the hooves of horses on the plain to the north. I looked down at the silent Residence, the city of the dead with its walls as white as the moon, as white as paper.

48.

Though nothing came of his repeated suggestion that Klostermann convene another session, Ettlinger had no doubt that before long there would come an occasion to advance his friendship with Helene von Davringhausen.

In the weeks immediately following the Kreisel wedding he saw her three times while walking through the centre of the city: once outside the Theatinerkirche, in conversation with an elderly man he did not recognise; the second time by the Karlstor, where she took a bouquet of flowers from a young woman who was seated in a phaeton; and then in a carriage, alone, on a street by the Münzhof. His feeling that circumstances were converging to his benefit became yet more persuasive when, in the middle of June, he encountered Helene, Maximilian and their father on Königsplatz. The conversation was brief and the father's demeanour far from welcoming, but it was clear to Ettlinger that this very aloofness was proof that he was seen to have a claim to Helene's affections. Moreover, from Helene's eyes it seemed evident that she wished him to perceive her displeasure at the impoliteness of his reception, and that their private hour at the Davringhausen house had been of no little significance. Ettlinger walked away in good spirits, and turned to watch Helene leave the square. She walked between her father and brother as though she were alone, and to Ettlinger it was as if her beauty were a criticism of the world.

Their next meeting, late one evening on the steps of the Nationaltheater, was less satisfactory, occurring as it did soon after the death of Siegmund Mölck. Confused at finding no effect of the bereavement in Helene's face, Ettlinger directed his remarks on the play to Maximilian rather than to his sister, and though he suspected that a more subtle and practised suitor might act in just this way as a tactic to secure his victory, he knew that in this instance he was squandering the minutes he had been granted with her. Nonetheless, Helene hinted, as she took her brother's arm, that another party might soon take place at their house, and that it would not be presumptuous for Ettlinger to assume that he would be among the guests.

Eight days later occurred the incident through which Ettlinger most closely approached happiness. It was some time between three o'clock and a quarter past the hour. He had crossed the Isar and was walking north, towards the Praterinsel. In the instant that he realised that the two people standing side by side, leaning on the parapet opposite the island, were Helene and Maximilian, Maximilian waved to him. He greeted Ettlinger with an exceptionally effusive handshake, the vigour of which appeared in some way to annoy his sister. Maximilian named a nearby vintner's he was intending to visit, as he had heard that some superb Burgundies had recently been delivered there.

'Will you come with us?' he asked.

'I shall wait for you here,' said Helene to her brother. Shielding her eyes from the sun, she turned to look down on the river and added – 'I prefer watching geese to haggling over bottles.'

'I cannot leave you here on your own,' Maximilian remonstrated.

'In that case, don't leave me on my own,' she replied wearily, gazing at the water. 'I'm sure you can conduct your transactions without August's assistance.'

Maximilian looked at Ettlinger as if accusing him of provoking her to this stubbornness. 'It would be better if you accompanied us. From the shop I shall be going to the market,' he said to Helene's back.

'It would be better if I did not,' she replied definitively. 'From the shop you can come back here. It's not far. You said so yourself.'

Maximilian strode off, every blow of his heels making manifest his annoyance at being thwarted.

It was perhaps the hottest day of the summer, and there was no shade where they stood. The sunlight raised glints of red and gold in the darkness of her hair; it glowed on her fingers and on the soft declivity of her cheek. Unabashed by his presence, she placed a hand palm outwards over her eyes and lifted her face into the heat of the sun. Ettlinger saw the fine hairs on her neck, curled over like the eddies of a breeze made visible.

'How is your work proceeding?' she asked him, still masking her eyes, and he told her, as succinctly as he could. She made a cowl of her hands to look at him. 'I am glad it goes so well,' she said. He moved to her side and at the same instant they turned to look across at the island. They talked for a while about things that were of no concern – her brother's fondness for costly wines, the infant Gotthard's digestion, the abundance of her father's garden. 'Do you remember that joke about the trees speaking German? Well, my father speaks the language of the vegetable kingdom,' she said. 'Whose joke was that? Not yours?' she added, and after she had spoken her lips made a small movement, as if shaping a word that had passed unuttered.

A skiff appeared on the river, rowed by two children: a red-haired boy of about twelve and a slightly younger girl, also red-headed. Helene followed the little boat until it was out of sight, craning her neck over the parapet to watch it go. Ettlinger saw her mouth form a smile, but when she looked up there were tears in her eyes. Slowly, as if in resignation, she turned her face to him, and he was bewildered to see that the expression in her eyes was not one of sadness but of affliction. She was not making an appeal to him, but there was in her look something that told him he was implicated in whatever it was that she was suffering. Her hands rested on the stone, one lying inertly on top of the other. Ettlinger moved to take them; she lifted her upper hand and placed it on his wrist. To kiss her seemed the only act that would not be inappropriate, and he would have kissed her had he not first looked along the pavement and seen Maximilian, who was perhaps too distant to observe Ettlinger's action unambiguously but close enough to negate his impulse.

This moment's timidity impelled Ettlinger to rashness. When, in the last week of July, he heard through Klostermann that Maximilian had gone abroad with his brother and father on business of some sort, he at once set out for the Davringhausen house. He did not return to his lodgings to change into his best suit of clothes, but simply left the café with Klostermann, shook his hand as if nothing out of the ordinary were in his mind, and commenced his walk westward.

He reached the house in the first hour of the afternoon. From a hidden vantage in the lane, crouched beside the ditch, he saw the family's groom appear from the back of the building and stop by the door, where he scratched his head and stared into the sky in an attitude of puzzlement that seemed more dramatic than genuine. Seconds later, two servants emerged from the house and engaged the groom in a conversation which was conducted with plentiful head-shakings and prayerful gesturings. The atmosphere of falsity unsettled Ettlinger. It was as if the scene were being staged in response to his surveillance. He knelt on the bank, his feet on the floor of the ditch, and from there, through the branches of a wilted shrub, he saw Helene. She was sitting on a swing which hung from the garden's oak tree.

Remembering that a wicket gave access to the garden from the lane, Ettlinger ran past the gateway and along the hedgerow. He quickly found the entrance he sought, and there composed himself to approach her in a manner that was purposeful but not impetuous. Linking his hands at his back, he moved across the garden with his gaze directed respectfully at the ground until he heard his name.

'August,' she remarked rather than exclaimed, and put down the board on which she had been drawing. Remaining seated on the swing, she greeted him as if his arrival were in no way remarkable, and proceeded to talk to him as if they were again at a party, in the midst of many guests.

'My father made this for me when I was three years old,' she said, and looked up along the ropes. 'Perhaps this is where my character was formed.' From her tone it seemed that the notion had just occurred to her, and she was not certain how seriously to consider it. 'Swinging back and forth, back and forth, back and forth,' she sang softly, making the seat sway.

'I hope you have not taken offence,' Ettlinger began. 'Twice a week I take a long walk,' he said, his thoughts stumbling. Helene squinted at him, seeming to wonder why he had taken the trouble to make this statement. 'What were you drawing?' he asked, staying two paces away from her, and upright as a guardsman.

She lifted the board and showed him the sketch that was pinned to it. A genderless figure sat before a screen of yarns, with bobbins clustered like udders above one knee; the left hand was easing out threads amid a contraption of rollers and ropes as complicated as the riggings of a ship. 'A gift for Karl's wife,' she explained. 'It's very clever, don't you think? So like me. I'll make an embroidery of it.' She tossed the board back onto the grass. 'It's the Gobelins factory. I find Gobelins especially disgusting, don't you?' she asked with a vehemence that Ettlinger could not comprehend. With a small kick she set the swing in motion again, and then she smiled at him in a way that suggested commiseration, as if they were both enduring the same disappointment.

'I do,' he said, and Helene's smile subsided.

A consciousness of encumbrance troubled Ettlinger,

a state of mind for which Wolgast was chiefly to blame. He wished that he could disburden himself of what he had seen and heard and read; it was imperative that Helene remain unaware of what he was protecting her from, and yet he wished she might know that she was being protected. Fleetingly, he pictured himself and Helene as they would appear from the lane, enacting a scene of bucolic courtship. Then he heard himself ask: 'What do you know of Wolgast?'

Helene appeared puzzled by the question, but uninterested in it. 'Less than you do, I should think,' she replied. 'He has been a soldier, I know that. And he was once a physician, so Maximilian tells me. An insatiable collector of books, a veritable sage, my brother says. But then he is not the most astute of judges.'

The dismissiveness with which she pronounced the final phrase gave Ettlinger the impression that he was held in some way responsible for Maximilian's shortcomings. 'I think your brother is somewhat in awe of Wolgast,' he said, 'but I would not condemn him for that.' His words were laden with implications, but Helene heard none of them.

'I should feel sorry for my brothers,' she mused, as if she had no audience. 'They are required to justify everything they do, while I enjoy the liberty that comes from an excess of leisure.' She gave Ettlinger a quizzical glance and grasped the ropes of the swing. 'They are on their way to Turin. Turin silks are the best, I believe,' she said, in the voice of someone reciting a children's rhyme. She stood up and turned away from him to walk out of the shade of the oak.

Ettlinger followed her, their feet rustling the dried grass in unison. At a bush of pink roses she stopped and cupped a flower's head in her hand. Ettlinger said her name, and she covered her face suddenly, catching her breath in an effort to stop her tears.

He stepped beside her. With her hands still over her face, she lowered her head onto his shoulder and wept silently. Resting one hand lightly on her hair, without speaking Ettlinger consoled her, but for what he did not know. So they stood for some time, until the noise of a carriage on the lane broke Ettlinger's tormented idyll.

'My father returns,' she said, and gently she pushed herself from him.

'I had heard he was not here,' protested Ettlinger.

She gave him a look that did nothing but exempt her from his misunderstanding, and gestured him towards the gate. He took a hand, kissed it and departed.

That very afternoon Ettlinger bought for Helene a silver brooch in the form of an owl – the symbol of Athena, he explained in the note he tucked into its case. He dispatched it the following day, and returned to his lodgings to await her reply. Nothing had come by nightfall; no letter came on the following day, nor on any subsequent day.

On the thirteenth of August, Wolfgang von Klostermann received a letter from Maximilian von Davringhausen. 'I must tell you that reasons of honour make it impossible for me to frequent your society in future,' he wrote. 'Our sister is no longer our sister.' He reported that Helene, of her own accord, had followed them to Turin. 'There she made the acquaintance of a negligible count, a Neapolitan, a dissolute wretch whose name I cannot bear to write. She has become his wife, and travelled south with him, to the pestilential city of his birth. Our father is adamant that her name shall be removed from the family's annals. Our mother weeps all day,' read Ettlinger for the fifth time, too distraught to hand the letter back to Klostermann. 'Believe me,' Maximilian concluded, 'the hours I spent with you and Martin and August and Leopold were a great amusement to me. I can only regret that my memories of them will be for ever tainted by the shame our sister has brought upon us.'

49.

Ettlinger shivers in the shadow of the narrow alleyway behind the harbourmaster's house, and turns into the sunlight of the cobbled path that winds up past the fishermen's quarter and through the olive groves to the church of St George. A burgeoning honeysuckle overspreads the wall of a garden close to the foot of the path, in a place where the whitewashed plaster of the enclosing houses redoubles the sun's heat. Swags of honeysuckle hang from a trellis surmounting the entrance to the garden, snagging the cast-iron prongs of the gate. A bee ambles in and out of a pendulous mass, falls out of it, attaches itself again, falls out again, pestering the flowers relentlessly. For a minute or so Ettlinger watches the bee at close range, observing the dust of pollen on its fur, the tentative probings of the mechanisms of its mouth, the frenzy of its wings, blurred into a little ball of black gas. The insect burrows into the depths of the foliage, and Ettlinger raises his willow staff to part the leaves, disclosing the blooms along which the bee is working. He presses a hand into the plant, inviting the creature to alight on his glistening skin.

He then realises that he is being watched through the bars of the gate by a man who is seated on the side of an overturned barrel in the middle of the garden. With a hand placed on each side of his face and his elbows propped on his knees, the man is watching with patient, doleful curiosity. Ettlinger smiles at him, and the man slowly closes his eyes, as if falling asleep. In the gesture of someone releasing himself from a problem, he moves his hands away and turns the palms outward, towards Ettlinger. Gouts of blood, lifted from the sores that corrode his cheeks, make stigmata on his palms. He opens his mouth and blood drips from his teeth. Revolted and ashamed, Ettlinger steps away from the gate. Immobile as a statue of Christ, his hands raised in a gesture of absolution, the diseased man watches Ettlinger as he bows and retreats without turning, in the manner of a courtier withdrawing from the presence of the king.

Ettlinger ascends the path to the terrace around St George's church, where he seats himself on the bench set into the south wall, beside the water trough that has been fashioned from a salvaged lintel. With the tip of his staff he traces the date carved freely below the spout, scraping a crust of lichen from the cross-stroke of the 7. Parallel to the railing on the terrace's edge a bank of tangerine clouds is turning carmine along its base while its upper edges dissolve. Ettlinger obscures the clouds with a hand that trembles like an old man's. There comes to mind his conversation with Wolgast in the church of St Johann-Nepomuk, and the flourish of Wolgast's hand as he gestured at the plasterwork angels. In the body of the clouds he discerns a colour he has seen only once before, and that was in the furrow of Wolgast's scar, the texture of which, it now appears to Ettlinger, resembled closely the microscopically veined wings of a bee.

He rocks his head against the wall. Sweat edges across his scalp and his hand quakes on the staff. Anxiously he scans the terrace and the olive groves as though he were a captain suspicious of an ambush. His skin shrinks onto his bones. Ettlinger closes his eyes and tries to distract himself with the never quite definite shapes that pulse and judder across the field of his eyelids. He recalls a book from Wolgast's secret library, and sees a woodcut of a naked man. Flasks adhere to the flesh of his limbs and torso. Fungus-like tumours are growing from his armpits and groin. Ettlinger's memory retrieves some part of the text around the illustration: a reddening of the eyes and tongue; violent coughing, then vomiting; the intolerableness of the contact of cloth; an intolerable sensation of heat; an unassuagable thirst. A man might be healthy one day and dead the next. He tries to remember when his illness began, and fails. The bench seems to move slightly.

A crescendo of voices rises inside the church, which Ettlinger had assumed to be empty at this hour. The crescendo falls to a drone of basses, a platform of sound onto which leaps a single tenor voice, singing an extended and seemingly extemporised melody. A bellow of full-throated basses subsides into a murmur, and is succeeded by a chorus of all the men. In unison the children and women respond, the higher voices piercing as pipes, the lower making a heavily-laden cadence. It is a mordant sound, a sound of sweet mournfulness, an expression of exultation within a condition of suffering. And then a final chorus vibrates the wall of the church, a chorus of every voice, a chorus in which Ettlinger hears the people expelling their woe in the act of voicing it. In the ensuing silence, Ettlinger savours a sorrow that is delicious, the pathos of his exile raised to a higher power.

The church door scrapes the grit of the threshold, and the congregation emerges. There are fewer people than Ettlinger had anticipated from their singing, and most of them are elderly couples, the women and men alike dressed completely in black. The old people depart arm in arm without speaking, their heads lowered, as if obeying a custom that has been followed for decades. Two fair-haired young women, sisters certainly, linger close to the water trough, and there receive the compliments of a burly young man who has a tattoo of a serpent or dolphin across one wrist. They are joined briefly by the priest, who similarly commends the bashful sisters, then dips a piece of cloth in the water and uses it to wipe a mark from his door. The sisters walk away along a track that rises into the field behind the church; the tattooed youth observes them, longingly perhaps, and makes a comment to the priest that prompts from the latter a sympathetic shrug of bafflement. The young man takes the cobbled path down through the olive groves. The priest turns to follow his descent, and strokes his long, string-like beard; the beard is mostly grey, though he can be no more than thirty years old.

Advancing to the edge of the terrace, the priest surveys the sea. Ettlinger closes his eyes and tries to imagine what the other man sees, the ocean as a symbol of his immeasurable God. Involuntarily, Ettlinger lets out a sigh, and when he opens his eyes again the priest is kneeling before him.

'You are not well?' he asks, or so his gesture suggests.

Ettlinger shakes his head. The movement seems to scour the bones of his neck against each other.

'Ill?' the priest seems to ask, circling Ettlinger's wrist with his hand.

'Is there a plague?' Ettlinger asks in German, in French, then in Latin.

'One man is dead,' the priest replies in Latin. His tone is such that he might be reporting the fulfilment of a divine instruction.

'One man?'

'One man, and one boy.' The priest rubs his hands together, as if to wipe the matter away. 'For how many days have you been like this?'

'A week,' Ettlinger lies.

The priest smiles, and his smile is that of a man whose mind is on something far away. 'Do not be worried, then,' he says, then adds something in his own tongue, a remark of which Ettlinger comprehends nothing. The priest goes back into his church, after scuffing away the dust trapped between the door and its sill.

Ettlinger raises himself from the bench, and a cold wave seems to dissolve the substance of his flesh as it passes over his body. The sea is the colour of old blood. There are two boats close to the headland, sailing away from the harbour. Their sails are like flat patches of saffron on the water. The darkness will close over them before they reach the island midway between the port and the horizon. 'The third part of the creatures which were in the sea, and had life, died,' Ettlinger recites inwardly. 'The third part of the ships were destroyed . . . the third part of the waters became wormwood . . . the third part of the sun was smitten, and the third part of the moon, and the third part of the stars.'

50.

The last true conversation between Ettlinger and Wolgast took place two weeks after Ettlinger heard of the elopement of Helene von Davringhausen.

Munich was intolerable to him during those weeks. Hour after hour he lay in his room, his eyes open but registering little more than that the path of light across the plaster was not where it had been when last he noticed where it was. Unshaven and with his sweat-stained clothing awry, he went out to buy bread and apples, his only sustenance. Discarded cores rotted on the floor below the unopened window, turning as dark as the colour of the boards on which they lay, filling the room with a sweetly fecund stink. At night he might take a walk, patrolling the darkened city through heat that was as constant as his unhappiness. His mind contained nothing but his memories of Helene, which he suffered as if his consciousness were a penance imposed upon him.

On the ninth or tenth day he spent a morning on the briefest of letters, a note for Anton Erwin Herterich, seeking permission to come out to the site. An invitation arrived the following afternoon. 'It would be my pleasure to see you here on Saturday,' wrote Herterich. 'In your previous letter you mentioned a drawing, a scheme for the façade,' read the postscript. 'I should be most grateful if you could bring it with you.'

Ettlinger had left the drawing in Wolgast's library. He went there on the Friday, in the middle of the day, hoping that Wolgast would be at his meal. Wolgast was reading at the lectern when Ettlinger entered, and it was apparent he was surprised by Ettlinger's arrival.

'I have a meeting with Herterich,' Ettlinger explained. 'He has asked me to take this.' He lifted the portfolio from the desk.

Wolgast smiled and nodded, and there was a tenderness in his movement that reminded Ettlinger strongly of their visit to Siegmund Mölck, and touched him unsettlingly.

'I apologise for my absence,' Ettlinger continued. 'I should have written to you. That was unmannerly of me.'

'Not at all, August,' replied Wolgast, gently turning a page of his book as he spoke. 'You are to treat my library as yours. When you decide that your studies here are finished, then I expect you to inform me of your departure. Temporary absences are no great matter.' Wolgast returned to his book, and took a lens from his pocket to inspect a detail. 'I take it you would rather I did not accompany you?'

'My company would not be enjoyable,' said Ettlinger, tucking the portfolio under his arm.

'Yes, I can see that,' Wolgast observed affectionately. 'When is this conference to take place?'

'Tomorrow,' said Ettlinger. 'Tomorrow afternoon, at three o'clock.'

'Come here at one,' Wolgast told him. 'My phaeton will be at your disposal, with one of my staff. I shall not expect to see you then, nor when you return.'

The man to whom Wolgast assigned the task of driving Ettlinger could not have been more to Ettlinger's liking. Aged about sixty, with cheeks reddened by broken veins and forearms that bulged like skittles, Benedikt Hempel was polite without subservience, and taciturn in a way that bespoke strength of character rather than gracelessness. He conveyed to Ettlinger the best wishes of his master, confirmed their destination, and thereafter they exchanged barely a word, a situation that seemed as agreeable to Hempel as it was to Ettlinger, for throughout their journey he maintained the alert expression of a man for whom the cobalt sky and the changing vistas of the road were as stimulating as any picture gallery. And something of his pleasure transmitted itself to Ettlinger, who found himself sorry to leave the company of the formidable Hempel when the phaeton came to a stop.

Up on the limestone platform, Herterich was waving his arms as a survivor of a wreck might hail a distant boat from his raft. He was wearing a capacious white linen shirt and moleskin trousers, and when Ettlinger stepped onto the foundations Herterich was surveying the land with his hands on his hips, striking what he perhaps thought was a buccaneering kind of pose.

'We have made a good start, you see!' declared Herterich, stamping his boots on the slabs, as if rehearsing the steps of a country dance. 'Fine stone, very fine stone, excellent stone,' he insisted as he jigged.

'Perhaps we should leave it as it is, a civilised patch on the face of nature,' Ettlinger remarked. 'A traveller might mistake it for ruin that has been stripped down to its base.' He was struck by the thought that Wolgast might have ventriloquised his words.

Herterich gave Ettlinger an uncertain look, then a brittle smile. 'It is a fine sight already,' he concurred. 'But just imagine how fine it will be, if this is how well we have made the parts that no one will see. Come with me,' he said, and he led Ettlinger round to the lee of the hill.

There, under an awning of thin canvas, a quartet of stonemasons sat on three-legged stools, chiselling at stones that were raised to waist height on wooden pillars. Herterich introduced the oldest of the four, Johann Zeiller, to the architect – 'my architect', as he called him – and commandeered a conversation that would have been far freer had he withdrawn from it. While the young landowner expatiated on the good fortune that had attended his search for craftsmen who embodied the German tradition, Ettlinger's attention wandered to the youngest of the crew, a sharp-faced youth who was scowling at the capital at which he worked. 'You say that there should be no more difficulties at the quarry?' Herterich asked of the mason, from whose reply it was clear that this was a question he had already answered. The young man bent behind the stone to throw a furtive look in

Ettlinger's direction, and winced at being observed in the act. Ettlinger excused himself from Herterich's company and went over to the spy.

'You think you might know me, don't you?' said the young mason before Ettlinger could say anything. 'I know you,' he said. 'And I think you are now remembering where it was you saw me.'

As the last phrase was spoken Ettlinger did indeed recall him, though he had experienced no sense of familiarity until the young mason had begun to speak. He saw him in a tabard, emerging from shadow with Wolgast's hand at his collar.

'I can assure you that your honour is not in any way compromised in associating with me,' he went on, addressing Ettlinger in a manner that seemed more appropriate to the place in which they had first met than to their current circumstances. 'I have never done a dishonourable thing in my life. I never have. I couldn't,' he insisted, his speech becoming more natural as it became likelier that Ettlinger would not rebuff him. 'My name is Paul Schäfer. This is what I do. I did work for the Kreisels, but as a mason, not as a servant. That was a job for one night. The painters and gilders did the same. One night's work, two days' pay.' He chipped a flake from his side of the capital. 'I did what I was paid for, and I did nothing wrong.'

'I believe you,' said Ettlinger.

'I am employed here,' Schäfer continued. 'That's proof enough of my innocence, isn't it? I have a skill, but it wouldn't get me the work if I were a villain.' He set his mallet to the chisel again, as if satisfied that his words had clinched his case.

The stone on which Schäfer was working was blank

on every side except the one he faced. Ettlinger went round to inspect his handiwork, and saw that he was cutting a scar into the face of a figure that was hanging by its neck from a noose. A money-bag was hitched to the rope, and the figure's feet almost touched the windlass by which a demon was unravelling his bowels.

'This is very good,' said Ettlinger.

'A day's work,' replied Schäfer with some pride.

'Very quick.'

'And versatile too,' said Schäfer, not bragging but rather with the forthrightness of someone who has but one brief opportunity to account for himself. 'Whatever style you would like, I can do it,' he went on. 'Egyptian, Roman, Florentine, I can do them all. Not Bernini. I can't do Bernini. Nobody can do Bernini. But the others – it's not hard. Wait a moment and I'll show you.' From the jumbled fragments around his feet he took a rough ball of pale stone and wedged it underneath the capital. Without the slightest hesitation he began gouging lines into the stone, tapping the head of a fine steel point with such speed it was as though the mallet were no heavier than a lady's fan. His head weaved back and forth like a fighter dodging punches, coming close to blow dust from a groove, falling back to gauge the accuracy of the whole. After five minutes he raised the capital and handed to Ettlinger the finished carving, a perfect replica of a lock of hair.

'I am astonished,' declared Ettlinger. He shook the sculptor's hand, which was as rough as the stone itself.

Schäfer retrieved his work, and swirled a fingertip around the curls he had fashioned. 'With stone of this colour I prefer to cut deep and fine, like this,' he explained. 'The dust gathers in the valleys. It looks sharper as it gets older. Time underlines the details. Perhaps you've seen how this happens?' he suggested, and answered with an affirmative smile the question that Ettlinger's consternation put to him.

'He pays me very well,' continued Schäfer, rolling his shoulders to ease the suppleness back into his muscles. 'The girl has left Munich, I believe. The following day she was nowhere to be seen. Well paid for her trouble, I should think.'

At this point Herterich called 'August, here, August!' so excitedly that Ettlinger thought he might just have unearthed a treasure trove. There was, however, nothing of any importance in what Herterich had to say. His talk with Zeiller had quelled his unwarranted anxieties about the quality of the stone they had been sent from the quarry. Now there were items relating to schedules and payment to discuss. Ettlinger discussed them for an hour, knowing that a week thence he would receive a letter from Herterich revising every clause of their agreement.

His business concluded, Ettlinger trudged down the hill to the waiting phaeton, feeling like a man giving himself up for arrest. He asked Benedikt Hempel to take him to the street in which he lodged rather than return him to Wolgast's residence, and to thank his master for his generosity, and to advise him that in the immediate future his visits might be less frequent than they had become of late.

51.

The house of Anysis was here, adjacent to the emperor's own quarters, for the design of the emperor's tomb was the project to which most of the architect's time was devoted.

Within six months of our landing he presented the first and most extravagant of his schemes, a necropolis to be hewn into the rock of the southermost mountain. This tomb was so large that it would be visible from the sea's horizon. Sleeping lions of ten times their natural size would recline in shallow caves cut into the base of the mountain, at the feet of the colossal figure of Xerxes. Fissures of cliffs formed the folds of his gown; his belt was a stream flowing athwart the slope; his crown was a stand of cypresses; his beard a tumult of mossy boulders. In one palm he held a lake, in the other a temple. The tombs of the emperor's officers were arrayed about the cliff like enamelled medallions on the arms of a throne.

After that came the tomb that was to stand at the top of the Valley of the Sun, on a shelf of scree below the pass, in the middle of a stand of massive pines. Engineers were to create a dam on the approach to the tomb, and the waters of the new lake would be dyed black, so that it would resemble a circular fragment of the sky, held in a bowl of stone. The tomb itself took the form of a pyramid of travertine, with the emperor's name carved into its east-facing slope, and it was to be guarded by marble sentinels, six of them. Positioned between the trunks of the innermost trees, behind saplings of bronze, they stood in attitudes suggestive of extreme vigilance and wonderstruck discovery, as of explorers happening upon a lost marvel of the world.

Another plan was for a tomb in which the emperor would be accompanied by the men who fell in his service at Urmia. Set atop a small mound on the highest point of an escarpment, a large cube of black granite marked the place of the emperor's burial. Approaching the tomb, one saw nothing but the granite cube set against the sky; the greater part of the memorial was revealed only at the mound, which looked down on a forest of pines that covered the scarp. Set within each pine's trunk was a small bronze plate, cast with a single word: not a name, but in each instance the same word – 'Here'.

Anysis pleased the emperor greatly with the Tomb of the Elements. The emperor's name and the years of his birth and decease would be carved on a slab of stone from the green quarry. This slab would form an island in the middle of a square water-filled basin, in the sides of which were concealed spouts that spilled oil onto the surface of the water. The oil blazed finely on the version of the tomb that was constructed a short distance outside the perimeter of the Residence. We rehearsed the emperor's funeral around it, processing through the gates of the Residence at midday, in the train of a catafalque draped with gold cloth. We remained bowed by the graveside until nightfall, listening to the orations of Artabanus, watched by the emperor from the walls of the compound.

It became a monthly custom for us to gather in the architect's quarters to hear his latest scheme. Soon after the dismantling of the Tomb of the Elements, Anysis showed us his sketches for the Shaft Tomb. In a high and sunless corner of the surrounding terrain a shaft was to be drilled deep into the earth, deeper than any of our wells, and the emperor's bronze coffin was to be placed on the floor of it. There would be no parapet to this seemingly infinite pit, but around its edge would be placed a circle of marble mourners, their heads lowered and arms folded. A refinement of this plan was then presented by Anysis. It was the most austere of all his conceptions. Instead of statuary there would be a simple ring of slate around the lip of the shaft, which would be sunk at such an angle that only when the sun was at its highest on the day of the emperor's birth would one be able to see the bronze lid at the bottom.

In the ruins of the architect's quarters I found traces of a building of which nothing had ever been revealed by Anysis. It was a tower, like a chimney of brick but with a cap of gold. There were perhaps a dozen drawings of this splendid roof, which was to be constructed from a cone of gilded cedarwood. On the exterior of the tower were listed the titles of the emperor: Lieutenant of the Sun, Master of the Three Deserts, Lord of the Three Oceans, Potentate of the Mountains, and so on to the fiftieth term. Under the conical roof, suspended by eight iron chains, was the gold sarcophagus in which the emperor's body was to be preserved. It encased another of bronze, which in turn encased a cask of iron, within which a cask of lead covered the wooden coffin in which the body of the emperor reposed. One hundred feet of air lay between the sarcophagus and the stone floor of the windowless tower. Three sentences were to be carved into the bricks of the interior, in a spiral of script that ended in the shadows of the tower's summit, where the cone of cedarwood sat upon the brick. The light of a dozen torches would make the underside of the golden sarcophagus shimmer like a pool of wine, but would not suffice to illuminate the full text of the inscription.

'I did reign many years in victory and in peace, beloved

of my subjects, dreaded by my enemies, and respected by my allies,' the inscription began. 'Riches and honours, power and pleasure, all have waited on my call. In this situation I have diligently numbered the days' – and here the darkness would begin to make the words ambiguous – 'of pure and genuine happiness which have fallen to my lot,' – and this is the last word that could even be guessed at – 'and their number is ten.'

52.

Ettlinger did not know his destination until his walk brought him to the asylum's door, and he had no purpose in mind when he pulled the bell-chain. He rang it three times, and at the sound of the bell he recalled that Wolgast had done the same. It occurred to him, with the force of a friend's accusation, that he was observing a superstition, or making some kind of pilgrimage.

'I am an acquaintance of Johann Friedrich von Wolgast,' said Ettlinger to the doorman, 'and formerly an acquaintance of a resident at this address. It was with Johann Friedrich von Wolgast that I came here previously, in December of last year. I believe that you were the custodian then.' The doorman regarded Ettlinger with mild impatience. 'Would it be possible to talk to the director of the establishment? I shall be brief. I have but a few questions I should like to put to him,' Ettlinger went on, hoping that in the course of his speech he might lure from his mind some plausible reason for his presence.

'It would be concerning what exactly, sir?'

'Concerning the former resident of whom I spoke. Herr Mölck. His name was Siegmund Michael Mölck. My name is August Ettlinger.'

He was conducted to a small waiting-room in which there were no chairs and no decoration save for the thin layer of whitewash that had been applied to the blistered plaster. The doorman's lugubrious tread dwindled into the silence of the building, and almost at once rose out of it again. With the reluctance of a man obliged to act against his judgement, he invited Ettlinger to follow.

The director's office was a long, narrow and high-ceilinged room, like a partitioned segment of corridor. It overlooked the garden, and felt as damp as the air outside. Its walls and ceiling were blotched with yellow smoke stains, and the flaking grey paint of the half-open shutters matched the tone of the ill-formed sky, on which the clouds lay like swabs of grey linen on an unwashed floor. The director, Herr Catel, advanced from behind his desk as if he believed Ettlinger had been sent on a mission to alleviate the ghastliness of his day, and knew that such an enterprise was futile. His cuffs were creased and grey at the peak of each fold. His eyes were the colour of gutter water but his handshake was that of a man in panic. Ettlinger could feel the dejectedness of Herr Catel and his office beginning to infiltrate his soul, and countered its dispiriting action with a boldness which ordinarily would have embarrassed him.

'I thank you for permitting me this interview, Herr Catel,' he commenced, setting the offered chair in a position farther back from the director's desk. 'I shall not detain you long.' Herr Catel nodded, as if he were hearing a piece of unhappy news that was not unexpected. 'As you may have been informed, it is in connection with one of your residents, now deceased, that I am here. The one known as Abbadon.'

'Siegmund Mölck.'

'Precisely, Siegmund Mölck,' said Ettlinger, surprised to find that he was grateful to hear the name confirmed. 'I believe he died here, in June?'

Herr Catel turned sharply in his chair, preparing to reach for one of the ledgers on the shelves behind him, then thinking better of it. 'Yes,' he replied, and seemed to leave his sentence unfinished, as if wary of where it might lead him.

'Might I know where he is interred?' asked Ettlinger, and he felt a blush appear on his cheeks, caused by his relief at having happened upon the justification for his visit.

'Of course. He is here,' said Herr Catel, gesturing vaguely towards the window. 'We have a small cemetery,' he explained, for his visitor appeared puzzled by his information.

'Not with the Davringhausens?'

Herr Catel's face twitched, as though he were digesting something unpalatable. 'He is here. In our cemetery. We have a plot of consecrated land.'

'The Davringhausens wanted him buried here?' Ettlinger persisted.

'The Davringhausens?' queried the director.

'His family,' stated Ettlinger curtly, suddenly conscious of the sound of his own breathing.

'Siegmund Mölck had no family,' Herr Catel replied. 'No family at all,' he repeated, drawing himself up in his seat, as though revivified by the mystery of which he had become an agent.

Aware that he was about to blunder out of a place in which he had been secure, Ettlinger enquired – 'How then did he come to be in your charge?'

'He was brought here by Johann Friedrich von Wolgast,' the director answered. 'Ten years ago, more or less. He was very distressed, violently distressed.' For a moment, Herr Catel contemplated the sky and the imponderable misrule of Abbadon's soul. 'I was reluctant to admit him, but his guardian had the means, and he was most persuasive. Siegmund Mölck had long been mad, Wolgast told us, and his father had been mad as well. A nephew took care of Siegmund for a few years, then abandoned him to Wolgast, who was no more than a friend of the mother. She had fled to Mannheim, so Wolgast said. There was no hope of restoring Mölck's reason. I think we made his life tolerable. Do you wish to see the grave?'

Emptied of motivation, Ettlinger allowed the director to lead him out into the garden, past the tree where he and Abbadon and Wolgast had sat, and through a dilapidated gate into an overgrown acre of meadow grass. After a minute's searching, Herr Catel pressed aside a clump with his foot to disclose a little grey wooden cross with the text 'S. M. Mölck' inscribed along the arms. Already it was splitting along its grain. Though he had no wish to stay longer, Ettlinger did not disagree when Herr Catel suggested he should not leave before seeing the chamber that had been Abbadon's. The room was now bare, but for the bed and the empty frame of the *Transfiguration*, which was now propped against it. 'Wolgast visited Siegmund every week, and every holy day,' Herr Catel stated, and he seemed humbled by the diligent care that he was reporting. 'He provided for all his necessary expenses and more besides. He used to take him on drives through the forests, in his carriage. The only thing that would certainly calm Siegmund Mölck was the company of Wolgast. Sometimes they would say nothing to each other. They could sit for hours together, like mute brothers. And sometimes Mölck would talk to Wolgast long after he had left. I found it most touching,' the director admitted, and sniffed away tears that were not there.

'Did he leave anything?' asked Ettlinger.

'These are all his effects,' replied Herr Catel, pulling from under the bed a narrow lidless box of thin board. 'Perhaps Wolgast will be taking them? He paid us for the service of interment, but since then we have heard nothing from him.'

'I shall find out what he intends,' said Ettlinger. He lifted from the box a dirty felt cap, a few mildewed letters, a coverless Bible and a sword. The blade of the sword was encrusted with rust along half its length from the tip; embossed on the pommel was a small phoenix, raising its wings amid the branches of an oak tree.

53.

He was reconciled to never knowing for certain what had happened at the party given by Konrad von Laun, but it was necessary for Ettlinger to find out why Wolgast had lied about Abbadon. Yet in his misery at

Helene's absence he could not summon the resolution to exact an explanation. He could not apply himself to a problem that was but an adjunct of something far greater and perhaps for ever insoluble. But then, six days after his conversation with Herr Catel, Ettlinger was brought a message from Wolgast.

'Your books are wearing a pall of dust, August. I shall allow them to lie undisturbed, for they have become your memorial. Every day I read for an hour or two in my library, and I am always conscious of the company of a disembodied presence. I sympathise with your antipathy for society. You will find no company at my house. Today I leave the city to inspect a property in the region of Ingolstadt. It is an ugly little dwelling, I am told, shoddily constructed and decorated in a most execrable style. There are pagodas on the walls and dragons on the ceilings. But its estate is a superb piece of land, within sight of the Danube. One day you might build another house for me there – unless I have been misinformed, the position is perfect. I can already see the colonnades framing the view of the valley. But you must resume your studies. One little chapel on a Bavarian hillock will not suffice to make your name, however accomplished its design. You were ambitious. You must sustain that ambition, and it will sustain you. We have so little time, August. Yesterday I looked about me as I stood beside your desk, and the thought came to me that I will die without so much as opening most of my books. And I imagined a sort of prophecy. I imagined those books that I shall consult falling from the shelves onto the floor. I saw this paltry pile of books, presenting me with the synopsis of my remaining years. To you it must seem that your days are too long, but what I say is true – our time is brief. Return to your work, August. That is what our descendants will judge you by, not the quality of your suffering. For ten days my house is yours. My staff have been instructed to attend you.'

Two days later, Ettlinger returned to Wolgast's house, where the footman's silent greeting seemed imbued with a lofty satisfaction that his master's persuasion had prevailed over foolhardiness. In the library his papers were lying exactly where he had abandoned them. He removed the uppermost sheet, revealing a triangle of brighter whiteness in the corner of the sheet underneath. He read the pencilled notes in the margin of the paragraph he had last written, and could not conceive how he had intended to proceed.

A different servant, a man whom Ettlinger had never seen before, brought a dish of cold meats to his desk on the stroke of one o'clock, by which time Ettlinger had made no progress at all. As Wolgast had sensed the presence of Ettlinger in the library, so Ettlinger felt as if he were constantly subject to Wolgast's ghostly invigilation, a scrutiny that was more oppressive than that of the actual man, for his presence was now in every part of the room. And twice in the course of the morning the ghost had become almost corporeal, first startling Ettlinger with the sound of Wolgast's aggressive footfall, then making his heart flutter at what might have been the quick scrape of a bow across the strings of a violin.

In the afternoon Ettlinger applied himself to the translation of a passage from some arcane Latin treatise, and in this otiose labour he succeeded in holding the spectre of Wolgast at bay. The following day he began by pacing the length of the library five or six times, as if measuring a field for a sport, and found that this ritual served to diminish his anxiety. He worked for several hours on his villa for Wolgast, drawing a prospect of the main façade against a forest of oaks, sketching fireplaces for the principal rooms, modifying the floorplan of the wings. He commenced a design for a hunting lodge in a rustic style, with columns like knotty timbers and windows surrounded by stone creepers.

On the fourth day he was asked if he would care to take for his midday meal a portion of a stew that the cook had prepared for the staff. Ettlinger accepted, and the stew was served at the customary time, but not in the library. Bearing the dish before him on a silver tray as broad as a shield, the servant conducted Ettlinger to a chamber across the corridor from the study in which Wolgast and Ettlinger had twice conversed. The room was dark, for there was but one window and most of it was covered by thickly swagged curtains of maroon silk. The furniture was draped with the same fabric, except for a wicker-seated chair and a folding table, set close to the door beneath a badly preserved painting of some mythological scene. A weak, sweet, damp perfume rose from the fabric of the silk, as if incense had been burned in the room many weeks before. As the servant arranged his cutlery, Ettlinger perused the painting. Through the muddy varnish he could see that a satyr or a faun was being lashed to a tree by others of his tribe, under the direction of a figure in a toga, whose feet rested on what might have been a knife, or a flute.

It was not until he had finished eating that Ettlinger realised that the door by which he had entered the room was not its only door. There was another in the shadows behind him, partly hidden by a length of silk which was caught on something that protruded from the middle of the door. The object was a doorknocker, a strange enough thing to find inside a room, but stranger still was the form of it. Instead of the customary boss or nail, the door-mounted part was a naked female figure made of iron, with her back flat to the wood and her knees pulled up to her chest. In place of a hammer or ring there was an iron satyr, whose horns, entangled with the tresses of the woman, formed part of the hinge. Ettlinger lifted the satyr, and its penis slid out from the vulva. He released the figure, and the pair coupled with a hollow clank. The impact nudged the door ajar.

Ettlinger pushed, and the door touched something that prevented it from being opened by much more than a hand's span. He squeezed through the gap, and came up against a naked man of sleek white plaster. Removing the cloak that had been thrown over the head of the figure, Ettlinger discovered the expressionless face of a handsome youth, and a crown of plaster laurel leaves. From the crook of the right arm he removed a pair of breeches and from the hand Wolgast's peony-patterned jacket, thereby uncovering the lyre of Apollo. The lyre was extended towards a room that resembled the ransacked office of a book trader. Every surface, even the base of the statue, was laden with books. Stacks of books had toppled across the floor; books were splayed spine-upwards on top of slews of unbound volumes; in the far corner rose a curving pile that was almost as tall as Ettlinger. Below the farther window and under the low table in the middle of the room were books that seemed to have been hurled there; their leaves stood half-erect like the wings of dead birds.

It seemed impossible that there could be any order to this room, and yet the harshly used books that were scattered across the plinth of Apollo all pertained to the same subject. Translations of Avicenna and Rhazes formed the upper layer; underneath them Ettlinger found the *Apology and Treatise* of Ambroise Paré and Hermann Boerhaave's *Institutiones Medicae*; at the bottom, underneath the nine volumes of Caladani's *Icones Anatomicae*, lay a book as big as an atlas – the *De Humani Corporis Fabrica* of Andrea Vesalius. Ettlinger crouched to make a lectern of his lap, and opened the Vesalius at an image of a flayed man. A rope was threaded through his jawbone, and the muscle of one calf hung down like the guts from the underside of a slit fish. Mutilated bodies flaunted themselves on page after page, dancing to show off the complicated ply of their skinless backs, gesticulating at landscapes with fingers from which swung pendulums of muscle. Deeper in the book he saw torsos and heads dismantled in stages, limbs stripped down layer by layer to the bone, assortments of glands and tubes and shapeless pieces of tissue. Ettlinger turned back a batch of pages and released them quickly one by one, causing the bodies to reintegrate from their constituent parts. He set the Vesalius aside and picked up a book called *Some Observations on Fevers*. Having read a page, he looked about the room again.

A mirror filled much of the wall between the

windows. Below the mirror was a sconce on which several books had been piled; between them were pressed perhaps a dozen single sheets. Ettlinger went over to the sconce and extracted the loose pages; they were engravings, and the first one he looked at made his mouth as dry as pumice in an instant. The engraver had drawn a young priest, shabbily dressed, looking through a keyhole and kneading himself between his legs. In the background a servant girl dropped a pitcher in surprise. To this scene some alterations had been made in pencil: the priest's face had been adorned with a pair of ovoid spectacles such as Ettlinger often wore, and the Bible protruding from his pocket had been modified by the addition of the name of Vitruvius on its cover. The intention was plain: the voyeur had been made to represent the man now looking at him.

Ettlinger let the print fall, and with trepidation raised the one that had been beneath it. On the stage of a deserted theatre, a number of nuns and soldiers were engaged in an orgy, making use of various trapezes and vaulting horses to achieve their improbable couplings; the one spectator, a drunken general, sat on a costume trunk in the wings, fiddling with the erection that protruded from his unbuttoned breeches. The next illustration continued the theme: it showed a queue of young men, the one at the front ejaculating over the breasts of a pubescent girl, the others each sodomising the one in front of him. Ettlinger dropped all but the last sheet. It depicted a woman supine under a young man who was being penetrated by a dildo brandished by an obese old man who was being sodomised in turn by a figure clad in the habit of a Franciscan friar.

Ettlinger retrieved the engravings, sorted them into the order in which had found them, and turned to leave. As he picked a path back through the books, he noticed a tapestry that hung on the wall opposite the windows. It was as exquisite as the engravings were repulsive. Woven onto a ground of wheaten fabric, threads of infinitely varied colours were worked into a scene as subtle as any painting. From a promontory irradiated by the crimson rays of the setting sun, nymphs clad in lime-green dresses looked down on a fragile golden ship which was approaching the slender passage between two craggy rocks. The crests of the sea and the pasture of the headland were recreated with such skill that Ettlinger was compelled to touch the tapestry's surface. He stroked a strand of turquoise in the sunward curl of a wave, and as he did so the material moved away from him. He laid his palm flat on the sea and pushed, and the tapestry gave way as his arm straightened. Behind it was a recess furnished with a plain wooden bench, a broad shelf that could have been used as a desk, and, above it, a short shelf of books. It was a low-ceilinged alcove like that in which certain artists used to represent the scholarly Saint Jerome, except that one wall was covered in paintings, none larger than a foolscap page.

Ettlinger pinned the tapestry's edge with a block of books, and went up to the nearest of the pictures. In a panelled chamber, through the window of which a full moon was glowing, a naked woman was manacled across a bed, her eyes fixed on a man in a billowing nightshirt, whose right arm was raised to the bolt of the door of the chamber. The painting above it, a canvas no larger than a playing card, portrayed a Carmelite in ecstasy before a crucifix: with one hand she stroked the image of the Redeemer; with the other she rammed a candle into herself. Another showed a woman seated on the edge of a bed, her skirt pulled up over her waist; at her feet a woman knelt, her mouth open greedily and her gaze fixed upon the other's thighs. The alcove contained dozens of lascivious scenes set in boudoirs and convent cells; there was a grotesque Leda, a Pasiphaë, a Priapus; there was an obscene reworking of a Raphael Madonna; and in the highest row, at the back of the alcove, hung a portrait of Josepha Heldt, depicted at a piano with one hand turning the page of her music, the other raising her skirt to stroke the inside of her thigh.

It seemed that all were the work of one painter. The similarities between the sharp-edged folds of the protagonists' clothing, whether it be a seducer's nightshirt or the attire of a goddess or Josepha's skirt, were almost sufficient to identify the pictures as the product of a single hand, but an even stronger characteristic was the way he painted skin. In every picture the artist indulged a penchant for applying tiny highlights of pale pigment to the flesh, little splashes of colour that made the skin look wet. In the picture of Josepha three spots of near-white had been applied to her hip, thigh and ankle, giving her naked leg a shine like lacquer. The legs of Pasiphaë, too, had been dabbed in this way, as had the limbs of the Carmelite.

Peering at the tiny streak of candle-light reflected on the side of the piano at which Josepha sat, Ettlinger happened upon the proof of his deduction. In the space to the side of the keyboard, against the creamy rectangle of a window shutter, there was a monogram, the painter's signature. It resembled a K with its lower diagonal joined at its foot to the foot of the vertical stroke. Ettlinger selected other pictures at random, and eventually found the monogram on each. He discovered it, no larger than the body of an ant, hidden in the plumage of Leda's swan; it was circled by a link in the chain attached to a manacle; it was worked into the pattern of a carpet, the headdress of Mary, the bulrushes beside Diana's bathing pool.

About to step out through the alcove's low arch, he ducked his head and in doing so he noticed a picture he had missed. The unframed canvas was propped against the side of the bench, its painted surface away from him and protected by a piece of muslin. He took it up, slipped the muslin off, and was confronted by a portrait of Helene von Davringhausen. She was lying face down on a wide divan, naked, her legs clasped around a pink satin bolster and her breasts nestled into pink satin cushions. One arm made a cushion for her head; with her free hand she reached out to tickle the head of a black and white lapdog, which sat gazing at her, its thin little tongue protruding slightly. Helene's dishevelled hair tumbled over a bunch of blue-blushed grapes which filled a golden bowl beside the divan; cavorting putti carried torches and harps and garlands around the bowl, while behind the divan, on an ormolu table, leered a garlanded bust of Pan. On the edge of the scene, a bulge in the curtain of the doorway implied the presence of an onlooker. In the shadows at the base of the curtain Ettlinger found the modified K.

Ettlinger placed the painting on top of the bench, carefully, as if it were glass. A clamp was tightening against the bones to the side of his eyes; his shirt had become a cold skin; the painting itself had become a pattern of colours against the pattern of the bench's grain. He was precisely conscious of just one thing – that he was aroused – and the shame he felt in having thus been made complicit in Wolgast's licentiousness caused him to moan. It seemed that a decisive action was required of him, and that he would recognise what that action should be if he were to focus again on what the picture showed. Yet he could not look at it again. Repelled by his own cowardice, enraged by the duplicity to which he knew he had been subjected but could not muster the courage to oppose, he shook with the urge to shred every one of the paintings, to rip apart all the books, to inflict damage upon himself. Ettlinger searched the alcove for a blade, a pen, anything that might serve as an instrument of harm, but even as he raked through the newspapers and pamphlets that littered the lower shelf he knew that he did not want to find anything. He could not deface the portrait of Helene. He could not even stand before it again, perhaps because he feared that his fury would not remain uppermost. He rooted blindly through the sheets of paper heaped on the floor, despising his vacillation.

At last, he thought of something he might do. With no greater passion than that of a man looking for some workaday item he has mislaid, Ettlinger detached the paintings from the wall one by one, scrupulously setting each level on its hook again once he had turned it in his hands and inspected its reverse. On two or three he found a title, on one he found the words 'Wolgast, no. 7 of 20', and finally, on the back of the painting of the Carmelite, he read a label attached by the man who had framed it, W. S. Durst. A vein of grey mould underlined the address; the street was perhaps an hour's walk away.

Having checked that he had left no evidence of his intrusion, Ettlinger made his way out of the building, taking care to avoid confrontation with any member of Wolgast's staff. Bare-headed under a rain that made him feel both shriven and implacable, he crossed the centre of the city without glancing once to left or right, as if his mission might evaporate at the slightest distraction. Not far from the river he heard a church clock strike some portion of an hour, but did not trouble himself to ascertain which hour it was. Somewhere behind the Rathaus a passing carriage sprayed a fan of filthy water over him, soaking his coat and throwing grit into his eyes, but it was a mere tribulation, a weightless addition to his burden of insults. Each stride seemed to push his determination yet more firmly into his soul, to take him nearer to a place in which his misery would be annihilated. And yet it was a determination that had no definite goal. In some way he would vent his revulsion and anger, and from that release, perhaps, would be born his retribution.

The picture-framer's shop occupied a corner of a residential street. Dusk was approaching, and a lamp had been lit in the window above the stunted easel that bore the cartouche of Durst's name. It was the only light on the street, a circumstance that Ettlinger perceived as a confirmation that matters were following the course they had to follow. Wiping the rainwater from his hair, he looked at the paintings that flanked the advertisement for the business. To one side there was a dark and Spanish-looking Crucifixion, encased in a thick gilded frame; on the other, similarly encased, was a portrait of a government official, flaunting a decoration on his distended chest. Set at an angle from these, by the door, there was a landscape. It was a meadow at daybreak, with a spire and the sails of a windmill in the distance, and in the foreground a flock tended by two shepherdesses. The smock of one shepherdess was lifted to reveal a calf that glistened as if she had just stepped from a stream; in the centre, superimposed on a hawthorn bush, was the monogram that Ettlinger sought.

A little brass bell danced on the end of a spring attached to the door, and the framer came out of his workshop. A man of sixty or seventy years of age, he had a reddened nose so broad and protuberant that it was more a snout than a nose, and red-lidded, widely-spaced eyes, which blinked in the manner of a nocturnal creature forced out into the daylight.

'Are you the proprietor?' asked Ettlinger.

'I am,' Durst replied firmly, as if rebutting an invidious suggestion. His fingers opened and closed on the square ebony frame he was holding.

'I am not a customer,' Ettlinger stated. Durst nodded as if this were of no relevance to the present situation. 'I wish to establish the identity of the artist who painted this landscape,' Ettlinger went on. He took a step back towards the door and pointed backwards at the picture, as if indicating a miscreant to its mother.

'Karl Lizius,' said Durst, his eyes directed at his hands as they tested the joints of the frame.

Keeping his voice low, fighting an impulse to shout, Ettlinger continued. 'I believe he is also responsible for certain indecent pictures, several indecent pictures, which I believe were framed on these premises, at the commission of one Johann Friedrich von Wolgast.' Durst laid the frame flat on the counter and blinked in Ettlinger's direction, but made no reply. 'The pictures are all marked thus,' Ettlinger explained, tracing the monogram in air. 'As this landscape is marked.'

'Your argument is incontrovertible,' Durst conceded.

'You know the pictures of which I speak?'

'Oh yes,' said Durst. He picked up the frame again, shuffled into the workshop with it, and came back with a pad of paper and a pencil, on which he appeared to be making notes that had nothing to do with Ettlinger's questions. 'Yes, I know them. They are by Lizius,' he went on. 'It is a lucrative line of work for him. He has a gift for it. Many clients.' His tone was so lifeless that he might have been identifying the species of certain animals from Ettlinger's description of their markings.

'Is he in Munich?' Ettlinger demanded.

'He is not far from Munich.'

'May I know where he lives?'

'Yes, you may know where he lives,' Durst replied, like a man wearied by a child's guessing game. He placed the pad on the counter, wrote the location of Lizius's studio below the column of numbers he had been adding up, and tore it off. He folded the strip and pressed it into Ettlinger's hand like a beggar's coin.

'I thank you,' said Ettlinger.

Durst gave his visitor an exhausted wave of farewell, and bolted the door as soon as Ettlinger's coat was clear of it.

Ettlinger lingered briefly in the light from the shop. He gazed into the twilight of the empty street, as if into the void of the hours ahead, and could not explain to himself how his resolve had left him.

54.

This declivity is where the athletic games were held.

At noon the athletes entered the arena. In single file and in step, they emerged below the daïs on which sat the emperor, one or sometimes more of his wives and Darius. A rosewater fountain sprinkled a bed of fragrant herbs beside their bench; a stone canopy, inset with mosaic sunbursts, shaded them from the sun.

The games lasted one afternoon and consisted always of the same sports, in the same sequence. The javelin throwers would begin the entertainment, followed by the weightlifters. We had two jumping competitions, separated by the wrestling bouts; the high jump was the prelude to the two foot-races – the short and the long – with which the games concluded.

The narrative of Shapur, whose race lasted three hours, was completed even before the athlete had been conducted back to his quarters, such was the eloquence it inspired in the scribes. 'It was at the midpoint of the second hour,' its concluding page began, 'that the contest began to assume its definition. Pace by pace the runners moved away from the weakest of the number, who ventured a mighty effort to reduce his disadvantage but succeeded only in increasing it, as relentlessly his fellows strode on to accomplish his elimination. The moment of his collapse imparted new momentum to the others, who sustained their unity for two laps more, before the price of their exertion was exacted. It was as if the hand of God were teasing apart a necklace strung with their bodies. One by one the runners fell away from the pack, each man grimacing at the foretaste of defeat as the space appeared between him and the man who was leaving him behind.

Three athletes ran into the third hour: Battus, Shapur and Bahram. None seemed aware of his rivals, though shoulder to shoulder they sped around the track, their sweat flowing from one man's hand onto another's arm. In unison their feet rose and fell, in unison as perfect as horses in their traces, even as the sun beat down on their heads with hammerblows. Twenty times these three passed the starting line together, brothers of the agon, deaf to the exhortations of their compatriots. From the tiers a continuous cry of acclamation accompanied their endeavours, a cry that reached its zenith when at length Battus succumbed, tumbling into the sand with outspread arms, taking the earth into his lifeless embrace. Shapur and Bahram strove onward, bearing down on victory as if racing towards a foe whose destruction they had sought for years. Bahram vied with Shapur lap after lap, and it seemed they would run into the night however hard their hearts beat at their ribs. A silence came upon the spectators, in reverence for the surpassing feat to which they were bearing witness. There was nothing to be heard but the squeak of the runners' feet on the dampened sand.

Neither from their rhythmic gait nor from their resolute eyes was there any telling what the outcome could be, but suddenly Bahram fell, so suddenly that it might have been a tripwire that brought him down. Shapur, the champion, ran on to the marble line.'

I remember hearing this panegyric. It was read by Artabanus, once at the Residence, and once at the commencement of the subsequent games. I remember too the sight of Shapur continuing his race alone, not realising that the contest was now over. I remember him staring so wildly he seemed to be trying to drink the air into his body through the tissues of his eyes, while his arms beat feebly across his belly. I remember the vacancy of his gaze as he looked down on the prostrate body of Bahram, and then, his head twitching as if he had been stung twice on his cheek, the successive registering of two thoughts: that he was now alone on the track, and that Bahram was dead.

As with all the victors, Shapur's effigy was soon created and placed on the spine of stone that occupied the middle of the track. Had he stood beside the figure that commemorated him, he would not have known that he was looking upon the image of himself. The deep-set eyes bore a partial likeness to him, as did the thin lips, albeit less so. But there was nothing of his posture in the figure that stood upon the inscription of his name, nor of his broad hips, his jagged lower ribs, his attenuated calves. His statue stood next to that of Zeimal, who could raise three times his own weight; Zeimal was transformed into a man but a hand's span shorter than Shapur, though in life he was no taller than Shapur had been at the age of ten.

The sculptors obeyed their rules of fidelity, but it was not to mere appearance that they were faithful. 'We are memorialists, not literalists,' as one of their number once remarked. Though the proportions and features of their sculptures were derived from their studies of the athletes, the figures by which they made tribute to the heroes of the games bore close resemblance to none except the magnificent Tubal, who in the second games of the fourth year hurled the javelin so far that its spearhead shattered against a stone bench in the second tier of the stadium. Each face the sculptors carved was divided into equal thirds by the brow and the base of the nose; the forearm of every statue was the same dimension as the width of the chest; the height of the entire body, from the soles of its feet to the crown of its head, was calculated as the eighth multiple of the height of the head. These perfect lineaments were the work of many sculptors, whose dexterity imbued these ideal forms with the vitality of the victors. One artist did nothing but carve the veins of the neck and arms; seeing his work, one could not resist running a finger along the hard blunt ridge that surmounted each bicep. Another sculpted the genitals in a manner that made them seem invulnerable as clenched fists. A third was expert in the plated muscles of the chest and the convexities of the calf and buttocks; his son was unsurpassed in the way he could impart tension to the shoulder blades and tendons.

Often I would walk through the tunnel at dawn to inspect the phalanx of marble victors. A week before the siege began, I stood in the stadium and placed a hand on Shapur's arm, and felt the sweat on the glossy stone.

Shapur never saw his effigy nor heard his victory recounted. No athlete ever did, and no champion ever won twice. On the day of the games, the winners were certain of receiving nothing more than a laurel crown, tossed by Darius onto the ground beside their feet. Sometimes, as on the occasion of Shapur's race, the emperor would remove a ring from his finger and discard it on the sand, whence it would be raised by the attendant charged with the coronation of the victor, his immediate aid, and his preparation for exile.

I was among the party entrusted with the escort of Shapur on the day that followed the games in which his fame was secured. We left the Residence in the depth of night, so that the departure, observed by few, should have as little of the quality of expulsion as was possible. A cart festooned with laurel and drawn by white oxen took us to the harbour, where the preparation of the boat had already begun. The loading was in progress when we arrived on the wharf; I recall an iron brazier that burned by the capstans, lighting the turquoise glaze on the façade of the southern gate of the harbour, throwing shadows up from the ram's head keystones. A casket of gold coins was tucked into the prow, amid flagons of water and crates holding more food than would be necessary for even the most ill-starred voyage. A chest of fine cloth was carried on board, along with the panegyric of Shapur, copied onto leaves of parchment that were sewn with gold thread and sealed with a disc of gold leaf. A chart to assist his navigation was the last item to be placed in the vessel.

Twenty men of the emperor's bodyguard stood immobile on the quayside, ten on each side of the steps. They kept their backs to the water, and did not once look at Shapur, not even when we let out the chain and the boat moved into the current.

55.

His eyes directed at the map-like stain on the ceiling

above his bed, Ettlinger brought to mind the room to which he had been led on the preceding day. He raised the memory of it like a thing that lay decomposing in the grave of his mind. He looked again at the enigmatic painting above the fireplace; he noticed again the second door; he saw the disarray of the room beyond the door. He hesitated, conscious of the suffering that would ensue were he to proceed. He closed his eyes, as if he might thereby abort the vision that now was forming.

Betrayed and diminished, he lay enveloped in the foul atmosphere of the day that had brought him to this condition. He rose from his bed and began to dress, and while he busied himself with buttons and laces he saw a glimmering body he knew to be Helene's. From his pocket he drew the strip of paper that Durst had given him, and three times he read aloud the address that it bore, for the sound of his voice brought some relief. Yet Ettlinger left his lodgings not in the hope that liberation would come of this visit, but in the certainty that it would seal into the present the calamity of the past. As he trudged along the muddied pavements and the lanes to the village in which Lizius worked, he gave no thought to what he was doing, other than to tell himself that he was answering a summons that could not be avoided.

Shortly before noon he arrived at the house, a dilapidated two-storey dwelling flanked by a seed supplier's and an inn. The shutters were askew and stripes of rust ran from their pivots down the plaster. On a wicker chair beside the bottom-floor window dozed a red-bearded old man, with a sheepskin rug over his upper body and a somnolent hunting dog stretched across his feet. Man and dog looked up as Ettlinger approached, and gave him the same slow perusal, as if determining to which species the intruder might belong.

Ettlinger asked where he could find the artist Karl Lizius, a question which was considered in silence for a minute, then seemed to be adjudged reasonable, if inconvenient. The old man levered himself upright, and beckoned Ettlinger to get behind him. The dog roused itself and pushed into the space between the two men, and the trio ascended to the attic storey, by a staircase that had worm-holes in every step. Without knocking, the leader of the party threw open the door at the head of the stairs, disclosing a tall, narrow-shouldered and thin-limbed man at work at an easel, directly underneath a hole in the roof, into which a cracked rectangle of glass had been jammed. The painter wore a large beret of sand-coloured felt, and a jacket of Scottish tweed that restricted his movements more than one would have thought practical. His mouth was ringed with sores, and his hands were excessively pale and disproportionately large, features which confirmed him to Ettlinger as a suspicious character.

The dog circled Ettlinger's legs, sniffed the air in the vicinity of the painter, then padded off to follow his master back to the street.

'My name is Lothar Seidl,' said Ettlinger.

'Karl Lizius,' said the painter, laying his palette on the cabinet beside the easel. Paying no attention to his visitor, he slowly wiped his brush and set it down in the groove below the canvas. It was a painting of a shipwreck, barely begun. He adjusted the arrangement of the pots of pigment and oils on top of the cabinet, and then continued, as if addressing the pots: 'I prefer not to be in company. I don't wish my life to be taken up with incidents. That is why I live where I live.' He turned quickly, as at a sudden disturbance. 'May I ask what you want?' he said. His gaucheness and arrogance were those of a precocious student, though he must have been at least forty years of age.

Ettlinger surveyed the studio before replying. It was much neater than he had expected the pornographer's lair to be. The boards were well-swept and uncluttered; clean rugs covered the settee beside the door; a solid wooden rack the size of a tea crate, positioned squarely against the far wall, held upright what appeared to be a collection of drawings and prints; a plain white cotton curtain suspended from an iron rod partitioned the room so precisely that Ettlinger could see nothing of what lay on its other side. 'I should like to discuss your work,' he said.

Lizius looked askance at his shipwreck, and seemed satisfied by his morning's progress. 'I can undertake no commissions at present,' he replied.

'I am not offering one,' Ettlinger informed him.

The painter scowled and indicated that Ettlinger might seat himself on the settee. He removed his beret and hung it on the easel's spar; his hair had the appearance of dirty strands of raw cotton, and covered incompletely the higher reaches of his scalp.

'Yesterday I saw a picture in the shop of W. S. Durst,' Ettlinger began, remaining on his feet. 'It was by you – a meadow, a church, a windmill.'

'He's asking too much,' said Lizius ruefully. 'How much is he asking?'

'I don't know,' said Ettlinger. 'I did not ask. It did not interest me.'

Offended and suspicious, Lizius dropped onto the settee and pulled a cushion to his midriff.

'It was something else that brought me there,' Ettlinger went on.

'Something of mine?' asked Lizius.

'Yes, something of yours.'

'I didn't think Durst had anything else,' said Lizius, raising his eyes to the skylight in an effort to remember.

'He does not, as far as I am aware.' Ettlinger took time to clear his throat, for there was some recompense to be had from the unease he saw created by this preamble. 'Yesterday I was also in the home of Johann Friedrich von Wolgast, and there I saw some quite different specimens of your art.' His anger could no longer be dissembled; his voice became that of a prosecutor. 'I should like to know the circumstances in which you made them.'

Lizius lifted his hair from under his collar and patted it against his neck. There was something familiar in the gesture, and in the next instant it at last occurred to Ettlinger that this was the portraitist, the face painter, whom Wolgast had pointed out amid the wedding party. Lizius placed his cupped hands over his nose and mouth, and inhaled noisily. For a moment Ettlinger wished that Lizius had turned out to be a more robust character, a man who might have thrown him out of his studio for making such a demand.

'I was asked to make them,' said Lizius at last, jutting out his lower lip like an incriminated child.

'When was this?'

'Within the last year. No, eighteen months. About eighteen months.'

'All at once? Was it one commission?'

'No, five or six.'

'And whose idea were they? Who thought of the subjects? Was it you? Was it Wolgast? Who was it?' asked Ettlinger flatly, marshalling behind these pointless questions the courage for the questions that might bring him to the last corner of his labyrinth.

'I couldn't say. I don't remember every instance. Chiefly Wolgast, I should think. He is the more inventive of us,' Lizius told him, his nonchalance only partly covering his irritation and his fear.

'There is one picture in particular I want you to tell me about,' Ettlinger continued. 'And I shall insist that you tell me everything I need to know about it.' He turned his back on the painter, and described the picture of the young woman and the lapdog, listing the characteristics of it soberly and evenly, as if he were giving evidence of an affray. 'You do know the picture I am describing?'

Lizius blushed and apologised for being unable to recall it with any clarity. 'I have done a lot of work in that style for Wolgast and other gentlemen,' he explained, feigning unhappiness at this abuse of his talents. Whether the sneer in his voice was intended as a comment on Wolgast or on him, Ettlinger could not tell. 'I have lived in this room for five years, longer even, and in that time I have painted so many things. Hundreds of them. And I am no more attached to them than my neighbour is to his customers. They pass through the village and are forgotten. My paintings leave this room and I forget them. I have to forget them,' he said disconsolately.

'No, no, no,' said Ettlinger without expression. 'That will not do.' Staring into his eyes he bent over the painter and clamped a hand upon his knee. Lizius frowned at the clenching hand. 'I am certain you can recall this painting. It is a quite memorable creation. Think again.' Ettlinger released his restraint, straightened, and walked over to the easel. The charcoal frame of a broken hull lay in the middle of frilly waves and glassy rocks, to which three mariners – no more than outlines of arms – were clinging. A smear of blue above the wreck was the only colour. 'You seem to be versatile,' Ettlinger commented. 'Are there any subjects you do not paint?'

'Religious subjects,' replied Lizius. 'I cannot do religious subjects.'

'That is not quite true, is it?' responded Ettlinger in a dark voice. 'You paint religious subjects if they can be made obscene, don't you?' Ettlinger inspected the twists of colour on the palette, to make a pause in his absurd bullying. He lifted a sable brush from the rack, and peered at Lizius over it, as if it were a gun sight. 'You do remember the painting, don't you? You must have been pleased with the way you did the figures on that vase. You wouldn't forget that, surely?' He pointed the handle of the brush at Lizius. 'When was it painted?' he demanded, slashing the air with the brush. 'Where did you paint it?'

Lizius crimped his brows and bit his lower lip, pretending to strain at the work of recreating the picture in his memory. It was an unconvincing performance, a performance so unconvincing that it could only have been intended as a provocation.

Foreseeing a violent crisis and doubtful that any resolution would come of it, Ettlinger moved to the collection of prints and began to browse through them. He alighted upon an etching of Lizius, depicted with one hand upon his forehead, his eyes narrowed myopically.

'You do portraits,' Ettlinger remarked, pinching a corner of the sheet and lifting it slightly to show the artist what he had found.

'Rarely,' said Lizius, giving the picture no more than a glance. 'There are many better portraitists. That is why I do that sort of work. I am not very talented,' he explained, smiling wryly at his feet.

Infuriated by this specious humility, Ettlinger leafed rapidly through the sheets in the rack. At a Flemish-style interior he stopped, though there was nothing in the pastiche that interested him. His gaze skipped across the chequerboard patterning of the tiles, as if the alternating squares of black and white were a coded instruction to him. In the corner of his vision Lizius squirmed, squeezing the cushion against his belly.

Nothing was to be lost by prolonging the silence. Ettlinger turned the prints, endeavouring to transmit, by his studied indifference, the threat of an imminent and decisive action. A picture of the Bamberg rider passed by, followed by a misty portrait of a boy, a quivering horse in a storm, a pert serving girl leaning out of a window to hear the serenade of a lutenist clad in doublet and particoloured hose. Next was a portrait of Helene von Davringhausen. About her shoulders was wrapped a shawl of Turkish pattern, an exoticism enhanced by a thick rope of pearls that slackly encircled her neck, and an elaborate headdress from which hung pearls as big as snowberries. Ettlinger raised the portrait to oppose his face, and noted to the side of each pupil the curved reflection of a skylight, its panes and woodwork drawn by Lizius with fussy exactitude, as though the eyes were a jeweller's design. On the back of the sheet two dates were written, one above the other, with another pair of numbers below them.

'What do these signify?' Ettlinger asked.

Lizius leaned forward to read the figures, though there was no need to do so. 'Date of painting; date of engraving; number of prints made; number of specific print,' he replied. He presented to Ettlinger a smile that suggested a belief that he might, by this information, have brought their encounter to a conclusion satisfactory to both.

'This woman,' continued Ettlinger, 'is the same person as the woman in the painting I have asked you about.' He held the print at arm's length, covering the figure of Lizius. 'We should now desist from the affectation of forgetfulness, and address this straightforward question: was this picture' – he shook the paper as if trying to dislodge something from it – 'painted at the same time as the one that is our subject? And when you have answered that question, you will tell me the circumstances in which it was made.'

Lizius hunched his shoulders and raised his meshed hands towards Ettlinger in a supplicating cringe. 'You are asking me to betray the confidence of my most generous client,' he murmured.

'Your most generous client would do the same, I can assure you of that,' Ettlinger airily replied. He stooped to lay the print face-up on the floor, like a tribute on a tomb, then sauntered back to the easel. He took up a brush, reversed it, and drilled its handle through the canvas.

At his back, Lizius made a whimpering sound. Ettlinger stirred the handle, opening in the sky a hole as broad as his thumb.

'Please!' Lizius cried, and sprang to his feet. He looked down on the portrait, and nudged it with the tip of his shoe. 'This came later,' he said. 'It was painted here; she sat where I am standing.' With a spread of his arms he indicated exactly where the chair had been placed. 'It was not painted for Wolgast. Her father commissioned it, but it was unfinished when she left, and he would not pay for it.' Lizius glanced at Ettlinger, vainly hoping to find sympathy for this hardship. 'Wolgast paid for it,' he went on. 'He paid for it to be engraved, and he bought several copies. He had the painting sent to her. He paid me to take it to her myself,' Lizius said, gaining a measure of defiance in the retailing of Wolgast's munificence. 'I travelled in a style that I shall never enjoy again.'

'You met her there?' Ettlinger asked, and as he spoke he felt that Lizius had become in some way a conduit to Helene's residence in exile. Addressing this man by whom he was connected to the place where she was, he allowed himself to imagine that she might know that at this moment he was speaking of her.

'No,' Lizius replied. 'She would not see me.'

'Where does she live?' pursued Ettlinger. 'Is her house by the sea?'

Lizius put on an expression of operatic bafflement.

Ettlinger urged a response, for in the lull her presence ebbed quickly away. 'Is it not by the bay? Where does she live?'

'What bay might that be?' asked Lizius.

'Naples, of course,' said Ettlinger, and at this Lizius let out a loud, mirthless laugh.

Instantly Lizius raised his hands in apology. 'She is somewhat nearer than Naples. Will you allow me?' he asked, and withdrew behind the curtain before Ettlinger could understand for what his permission was sought. Lizius returned with a ledger. 'This is the record of my business,' he told Ettlinger. Enfeebled by dreadful anticipation, Ettlinger listened as Lizius explained the arrangement of his book, in which every transaction was listed. 'With this, you have no need of me,' Lizius concluded. He opened the ledger at a random page and offered it to Ettlinger, who took it on his open palms and stared at the columns of ink as a wild man might stare at a Bible. Treading slowly backwards, Lizius retreated to the door and there turned to hurtle down the stairs. The hammering of his feet ceased; the timber of the outside door screeched against the threshold; Ettlinger turned to the page on which were detailed the dealings of the previous year.

Halfway down the left page, alongside the name and address of Johann Friedrich von Wolgast, was written *The Bath of Diana*, with the painting's price and a date. Opposite, a *Convent Scene* was accounted for, and a *Conception of the Minotaur*, both billed to Wolgast. Overleaf, in the current year, the juvenile handwriting of Lizius catalogued a *Prisoners' Debauch*, acquired in March by Johann Friedrich von Wolgast.

Three lines below it was inscribed *A Portrait of Helene von Davringhausen*, and again Wolgast's name and a fee, but then Helene's name repeated, and the name of a street in Nürnberg, and a date but recently passed.

His mind received the text as if the whole line were a title; he read it aloud, and it sounded in his ears like a line from a meaningless rhyme. He repeated it again and again, and at last he came to acknowledge what it meant: it meant that she was near, and that the duplicities to which he had been subjected were infinite. Ettlinger moved a trembling finger back and forth slowly above the page, as if the line of writing were the back of a beautiful, venomous reptile. He stood on the bare floor of the studio, under the dilute light of a dreary midday sky, and thought of himself as someone whose actions had been written for him; for a moment he even believed that this was a true image of his life, and found fleeting comfort in the notion.

From his pocket he scooped some coins, which he placed on the floor to replace the portrait. He rolled the engraving and gripped it as a pilgrim might grip the shinbone relic of a saint, though he knew that what he held was but a piece of wreckage.

The village street was empty. Lizius and the old man were in conversation beside the churchyard wall, with the dog asleep between them. Far away, in a meadow that filled the space between the houses opposite, a quartet of cows lay in a field, in a sequestered place of unchanging climate, as in a painting by Cuyp.

56.

This was the main gate of the Residence. Recessed into its granite frame were six slender columns of the mottled-green marble, each of them fluted delicately and irregularly as bark, so that they resembled the trunks of mineral trees. Within a niche above the lintel crouched a lion made of porphyry and as large as an ox. The statue's eyes were balls of jade and its fangs were horns of ivory; the ivory claws of its forepaws pierced the scales of a bronze serpent, the mouth of which disgorged rainwater from the gutters of the gate. The doors were constructed of planks of the palest oak, three layers of them, held together by iron clamps that were embossed with the crest of Xerxes. Two thick timbers of oak, each sawn smooth and gilded on every face, served as the bolts of the gate. It was here that our defences were breached. It was here that the history of the Residence ended.

Three days after the blaze that destroyed the stables, in the middle of the day, we first saw the barbarian horde. Rain was falling, but it was a rain so fine that it was upheld by the breeze between the clouds and the earth, so that it seemed the substance of the atmosphere had become a light water. Peering through the opaque air, a watchman on the northern wall observed the horsemen descend from a ridge beyond the mouth of the Valley of the Sun. We followed his direction and discerned what one might have taken for a mudslide flowing down the flank of the hill and pooling on the plain. We watched a troop detach itself from the army and ride towards us. They were still too far off for us to count them when they stopped. The knot of riders became a line of horsemen that extended parallel to the wall from which we watched.

They stood motionless in the mist, a company of revenants in judgement of us. We never saw them depart: the sun declined and the air grew thicker, and covered the horsemen from our sight.

We send out a scout. He returned at dawn, and in the monotonous voice of one who knows his speech to be superfluous, he described the barbarians' camp. They were of the same race as the sacrificed warrior. They were of lowly stature and had long flaxen hair, and the muscles of their arms and legs were thick and heavy, the men and women alike. Their clothes were made of hides and fleeces, as were the tents of their camp. There was nothing to distinguish any tent from any other, and nothing to signify the rank of any save one man, who was marked from the rest by the spirals of gold that bound his upper arms and by the manner in which the others addressed him, with their faces turned to the ground. This chieftain held council on a floor of skins laid around a fire in a clearing among their tents. As they talked they drank milk from leather pouches and ate flesh that was not cooked but merely singed by the flames. Others were sharpening blades or tending their horses. Their assault would certainly be soon. They were perhaps two hundred in number, and seemed to possess no fewer horses.

In the darkness of the following night the barbarians moved their camp unobserved, and at first light the siege commenced with an avalanche of horses from the hill above the stadium. Their women rode alongside the men, and all bore bows and quivers of stout little darts, and had small round shields strapped to their arms. They carried no standard, but instead flew pennants of horses' tails from shoots of bamboo. They made no war-cry, yet their silence was more fearsome than any noise could have been, and their faces were the faces of hangmen.

But the calamity was not to happen that day. After the fifth charge the barbarians regrouped and pitched their camp just beyond our arrows' range, as if to proclaim their contempt of us by their proximity. While the sound of stone hammers chattered amid the rising tents, pairs of men made forays to retrieve their dead from beneath the walls of the Residence, undeterred by the arrows our archers shot at them. With their bare hands, like foraging boars, they scraped at the grass, throwing up divots of black soil. In the failing light we saw them press the dead men into the slots they had scoured. The graves rippled the field like the undulations of an estuary.

Returning from the upland pastures, a gang of boys drove a pair of cattle that had been ours. The animals were slaughtered with axes before our eyes, and their quarters spitted above the fire. Sprawled on muddy fleeces, the barbarians looked back at us over their shoulders as they gnawed at the bones, as if to make certain that we still existed.

That night Amestris killed herself with a poison she found in the house of the scholars; she was discovered by one of their number, curled beneath a blanket beside the furnace in the alchemists' chamber, smiling as if in joy at awaking beside her lover. The architect Anysis took a compass from his study, walked to the Court of the Fountains, sat down in the water of one of the marble basins, and stabbed the veins of his wrist. We found Artaÿnte in a chamber adjacent to the atrium, attired in her golden gown and ruby necklaces, with a belt of rubies about her neck, and wearing her golden sandals, the tips of which touched lightly the tiles of the floor, as if her body had been frozen in the air as she sprang into flight.

Darius was drunk before the first siege was over, and he was drunk all the next day. It was he who first stated that the emperor had fled, a rumour that was soon reported as fact throughout the Residence. But at twilight we received an order to assemble in the courtyard before the atrium, and there Xerxes himself appeared, preceded by torch-bearers and a retinue of swordsmen, all of them cloaked in scarlet silk. In their wake followed a line of girls and boys bearing gold flagons of wine and platters of figs and pomegranates and thrushes. A throne was set for him under the central arch of the atrium. We sat as commanded by the chamberlain, leaving a square of open space in the middle of the courtyard.

'Our last meal,' was all the emperor said. As the children passed among us with the wine and food, perfuming the air with the balsam of jasmine with which their skin was oiled, the comic actors ran into our midst. They performed for us a strange and lengthy masque, a play intended perhaps to fortify us with the strength of the delirious. One part of it was a battle between apes and spirits; another was some sort of foolish idyll, with the actors gibbering to the moon and cooing to each other as they lolled on the ground; in another they did nothing but stare at us winsomely, like statues enamoured by their makers. My heart was beating strenuously as I watched. The actors kept hiding their faces from Xerxes to wipe the tears from their eyes.

The second siege commenced in the hour after sunrise and was over before the sun reached its zenith. In a single body they charged, and not one adult remained in the camp. Most were on foot and ran behind the broken ranks of horsemen, who had roped between their saddles the trunks of trees, with which they rammed the doors of the gate at full gallop, splintering the wood with every blow. Before the riders could pull their horses clear the horde flung themselves at the doors, crouching under the bellies of the animals to hack at the wood with their knives and axes. Like a whirlpool the savages milled around the gate, tumbling over each other to hammer down the gate. With arms linked they made a chain of their own bodies and beat at the doors in unison, grunting with each impact. We scalded them with water and pelted them with stones. We doused them with burning oil, with liquids from the alchemists' stills and from the tanneries, and still they flailed at the gate, as impervious to pain as insects. The hinges cracked and they redoubled their efforts, pounding with such force that their shoulders bled.

There was scarcely a single arrow or javelin remaining in our arsenal when the doors split apart. The massacre began.

Some fought their way to death. Many fled across the courtyard and were run down and lanced like game. I saw a barbarian woman impale a maidservant with a sword and then impale her child on the body of its mother. I saw Artabanus and his family bow to the invaders and kneel before them. His wife, his son, his two daughters and then Artabanus himself were cut like stalks of corn by the horseman to whom they had surrendered. Their executioner whipped his horse and hauled on its reins, making it leap again and again on the spot, threshing their bodies under its hooves. The barbarians rode their horses into the Residence and along its marble corridors; I heard shrieks from the heart of the building, and howling that did not sound like anything human.

I cowered under a yoke in a corner of the courtyard, just

here. The corpses of two foundrymen made a barricade for me. I lay flat beneath the beam, my face level with the feet of the barbarians as they stamped back and forth. I remember that their feet were like the shells of tortoises, and I remember looking up through the yoke and seeing a piece of muscle that was glued to the brick by a scab of blood. It was then that I saw the emperor. He was no more than thirty paces from where I hid, in the gateway to the path that led to the Paradise. He was sitting astride his favourite horse, running its embroidered reins through his fingers as he watched his people die. His brow and eyes denoted anguish yet he was smiling, and to me it seemed as if he were observing something he had already imagined in every detail, something that he had once willed and then recanted. Exhaustedly, in a gesture of abdication, he dismounted and draped his cape over the saddle. He turned his back on the courtyard and ascended the path, not so much fleeing to the Paradise as withdrawing to it.

The chieftain of the barbarians, his face painted with blood and his sword upraised like a torch, pursued the emperor on foot, bellowing as if in agony. I crawled from my place unnoticed and ran after them, for there was nowhere else to go. I ran headlong down the paths of the Paradise. I ran past the walls of jasper, from which rivulets of clear water still trickled. I dashed along an avenue of cypress and under a quince bower, swatting aside the shrivelled fruits. At the farthest corner of the gardens, on the edge of the largest lawns, I turned. I scanned every approach; certain that I was alone, I rested where I stood. The outer wall of the Residence gleamed through the foliage to my right. I walked towards it, and felt for the first and last time the lawns of the Paradise underneath my feet. I heard the music of the clay flutes that hung in the vines.

I pushed through a screen of myrtle and came to the foot of the wall. Close by was a water conduit, attached firmly to the stones. I climbed the conduit to the top of the wall, where I looked back for a final sight of the Residence. I thought I saw the emperor's silver breastplate glinting at an angle of the labyrinth. From somewhere beyond burst a cry compounded of the voices of the slaughterers and slaughtered. Closing my eyes, I let my body fall into the water of the moat.

57.

This is what happened to August Ettlinger in Nürnberg, in the third week of October in the year 1826.

Having obtained no answer when he rang the bell, Ettlinger took up his station beside the fountain opposite the house that Helene had rented. For perhaps a quarter of an hour he waited, and then he saw a young woman approaching. She was carrying a wicker basket laden with vegetables, and a short distance from the house she stopped to shift the basket from one hand to the other. Ettlinger knew immediately who she was. With the clarity of a memory that was but hours old, he saw her standing behind Johann Friedrich von Wolgast, with the dark avenue of sphinxes in the background. The strangeness of her presence in this street, Ettlinger told himself, was that there seemed nothing at all strange in it.

She stopped once more at the door, to take a key from the pleats of her skirt. A tremble in her hands told Ettlinger she knew him. He crossed the street and asked directly, without introducing himself: 'May I see her?'

'I shall ask, sir,' she replied, and eased the door open just wide enough to allow her to pass into the hallway. Once inside, she gave him a long, anxious look, as if to verify that he did indeed wish her to convey his message, then closed the door on him gently.

Ettlinger remained on the step, with his back to the door in the stance of a truculent porter. He waited for a long time, brooding on his abandonment, repeatedly emptying his mind to repel the intuition that he was trammelled by a plot he would be wise not to unravel. His mood was not, however, one of morose dejection, as it had been so frequently in the preceding weeks. The excitement engendered by his proximity to Helene revealed to him a capacity for desperate action: as he awaited her answer he glimpsed himself berating her wildly, and felt that he might be moving towards the brink of such a rage, though he had no notion of what its consequence might be.

The latch squealed at his back. 'She cannot see you,' he was told solicitously, through the narrow gap between the door and jamb.

Ettlinger felt tears brimming in his eyes. 'What is your name?' he asked.

'Frieda, sir. Frieda Scheffler.'

He nodded several times, making himself calm. 'My name is August Ettlinger. You must pardon my indiscretion,' he continued, 'but I think you know why I feel obliged to be indiscreet.' He looked at Frieda Scheffler in a way that was intended to impress upon her that they were in effect joined by an oath. 'What happened on that evening, the one at which we were both present?' he asked, and was instantly ashamed of his question. His shame was worsened by the ferocity of her response.

'Sir, you know what happened,' she said, and her look changed from anger at his disrespect to contempt for his stupidity.

'I am sorry,' he said pleadingly. 'I apologise.' Frieda's feet shuffled in the doorway; she put a hand on the door. 'No, please,' he said.

'I have to go, sir,' she said.

Ettlinger charged his voice with the determination that the thought of Wolgast and Lizius raised in him. 'If you would be so kind as to inform your mistress that I shall not move from this spot until she consents to see me,' he told her. 'And you may add that I promise to leave this city once she has seen me, and not return.'

A few minutes later he entered the house, experiencing as he crossed the threshold the sensation of stepping onto an unmoored vessel.

Helene received him in a small, comfortably furnished room which overlooked the street. She was dressed in the French style of some three decades past: her plain white dress was gathered tightly by a blue band under her breast, and her arms were bare. She was seated on a white satin-covered sofa, with a book lying on a cushion beside her. When he came into the room she did not rise but simply indicated that he might occupy the chair alongside the fireplace, in which a huge vase of roses had been placed. An ormolu clock on the mantelpiece showed an hour that was long past. 'I have asked Frieda to bring tea for us,' were the first words she spoke, as if he were a neighbour who had just happened to call on her in the middle of the day.

Frieda set the tray on a card table, and Helene asked her to leave the door ajar, a request by which Ettlinger felt more slighted than he had been by any of Wolgast's taunts. While Helene attended to the cups, there was some desultory talk of the decoration of her room, and of his journey from Munich. She lifted the silver pot, and Ettlinger saw small dimples on the back of her hand that he had not noticed before. And then, in the manner of someone concluding rather than commencing a conversation, she said: 'I assume that I am the reason for your being in Nürnberg.'

'You are. You are the sole reason.'

'There are many better ones.'

'I beg to differ.'

'And how did you discover where I am living?' she asked after a pause. She looked through the doorway, as though seeking someone who might walk in on them.

'Lizius,' he replied. 'I found Lizius. He told me where you were.'

Helene sipped her tea as she considered the information he had given her. Replacing the cup on its saucer, she exhaled slowly through her barely parted lips and turned her gaze on the flowers. It seemed she had decided that she should not concern herself with the tale of Lizius. More than that, it seemed from the languid lowering and raising of her eyelids that she might have decided no longer to concern herself with him.

A door clattered shut in an adjacent room, a sound

that alerted Ettlinger to the silence he had let fall. He was on the point of hinting that he had seen the paintings, but instead remarked, avoiding any maudlin nuance: 'I do not understand.'

She frowned, perhaps in sympathy, but she said nothing.

'The last time I saw you – '

'You were a friend. I was unhappy,' she interrupted, and it was clear that she deemed this sufficient explanation.

'And now?'

'And now I am not so unhappy.' Helene rested a hand on the book, a gesture that to Ettlinger signified the closure of the question.

Striving to counter the momentum of his hopelessness, Ettlinger pressed a thin smile and asked: 'Do you know the story your brother put about?'

'No. Tell me,' she replied with flaccid curiosity.

'He told Wolfgang von Klostermann that you had gone to Naples.' Ettlinger contrived a laugh, but it elicited none from Helene.

'It would have been Naples, of all cities,' she commented, in a tone of unmitigated derision.

'So there is no Italian husband?'

'I had an Italian husband?' she responded, and now she laughed.

'A dissolute Neapolitan,' Ettlinger confirmed.

'There is no Italian husband,' she replied, but there was no reassurance to her words. 'Of course there is not,' she went on. 'There is no husband of any kind.' Absently she turned the cover of the book, revealing to Ettlinger the bookplate of a phoenix in an oak tree. Observing his reaction, she said to him: 'You did not think I taught myself from my father's books, did you? The finest library in the city, as I think you yourself remarked on more than one occasion.'

'I did,' murmured Ettlinger, though at that moment nothing in his memory was accessible. His pulse tapped at his breastbone, as if goading him.

The bell rang. Helene went over to the window and gazed down at the street. The shadow darkened under the fabric of her dress, and Ettlinger knew in that instant that the worst thing he could imagine would prove to be true.

When she turned, her eyes were chastising him for his distress. The air in the room became the air of a cemetery. Ettlinger leaned forward to pick up the book; he opened it on his knees, stroked the bookplate, and looked at Helene questioningly. She replied simply – 'Yes.'

Ettlinger tensed the muscles of his face, making a mask of his flesh.

'There is nothing more to be said,' Helene stated sadly, as she seated herself on the sofa again.

'No,' said Ettlinger, but then continued – 'I understand your mistake. I think I too have been in thrall to him.'

'I am in thrall to nobody. I did not make a mistake,' said Helene with quiet vehemence, and Ettlinger realised that there never had been any possibility that she might love him. Against the suddenly loud ticking of the clock she told him she was content. 'I intend to live here with no one else but my son or daughter, and Frieda, if she will stay. I shall educate the child myself.'

'Do you need money? Does he send you money?'

asked Ettlinger. He needed two breaths to utter the questions.

'He does not. I have what I want of Wolgast.' Helene closed all the books on the table; their conversation was drawing to its close. 'Do not worry about my well-being. I am sorry I can do nothing to ensure yours. I shall become a tutor. I have my freedom here. I have what I want.' She sighed, and the sigh was not for herself. 'August, you should leave now,' she said.

The shocking tenderness with which she pronounced his name forced his gaze to the floor. Unable to look at her again, Ettlinger stood up, bowed to Helene and blindly departed. Descending the stairs of her house he was in the sunlit gardens of Nymphenburg. He saw a flock of birds and an avenue of trees, and heard her voice sounding slowly the syllables of his name. At the door, Frieda Scheffler brushed some dust from the shoulder of his coat before passing it to him. He thanked her and kissed her on her cheek, then walked away briskly, as if to accost someone he had just seen at the end of the street.

58.

Every shutter was open, but no servant came when Ettlinger arrived at the door of Wolgast's house for the last time. A dozen blows he struck upon the door, and nobody answered. In exasperation he seized the handle and turned it; the door opened. In the hallway he called out loudly, but nobody responded. He walked along the corridor, and every room he passed was open and unoccupied. In one he saw a padlocked trunk, and a footman's coat folded on a chair alongside it.

At the head of the stairs he became aware of the powerful perfume of vetiver. The doors to the library were ajar. Ettlinger pushed them apart, knocking an unstoppered bottle that lay in a pool of clear fluid on the parquet. Other bottles littered the floor, as did pages of print – ripped, so it seemed, from the books that had been thrown in heaps against the walls. Wolgast was seated at the table that had been Ettlinger's. He was wearing the blue velvet frock coat and buff waistcoat he had often affected before. Pinned to his chest were three decorations: a cross, a golden disc and a bronze sprig of oak. Some thirty or forty books were stacked in front of him, and he appeared to be arranging them into three sloping piles.

'I have something here for you,' said Wolgast, busying himself with the books. 'Sit down,' he commanded.

Ettlinger, so replete with fury and self-pity that he could not speak, remained standing.

Intent on the disposition of his books, Wolgast appeared not to notice. 'You must tell me what you think of this,' he resumed, at last looking up, but merely glancing at Ettlinger in the way one might glance at the stranger who is about to take the adjacent seat in a theatre. 'It is my sublime building, my museum of the sublime, of the grandiose, the heroic, the terrible,' he explained, reciting the adjectives as if by rote.

Ettlinger remained silent, thinking of nothing but the maintenance of his stony appearance.

'This is my plan. This would be the entrance,' Wolgast explained. 'Upon entering, the visitor pauses in this vestibule, dumbstruck by the immensity and majesty of it, as surely as by the sight of the Jungfrau.' He brought the edge of his hand down on the table in a chopping motion. 'The walls rise the full height of the building. Here, at the other end of the vestibule, stands a line of columns. Once through this colonnade you are confronted by a gargantuan staircase. It rises to meet the ceiling at the far end of the building. Each step is sixty feet wide, eight feet high, sixteen feet deep. You ascend by another staircase that slices through the gigantic stairs.' He dragged his finger up an incline of books, dislodging the volume on the top. 'On each side of this huge staircase is another of similar size, abutting the central one but running the opposite way, as you see, from the base of the rear wall to the top of the front. Each of these is cut by steps for the use of the visitors, and the three gigantic staircases have one step in common.' Wolgast laid a forearm across the flights of books, skewing them out of alignment. 'The interior of my museum, Wolgast's museum of the sublime, thus comprises just three flights of steps. They are ambiguous, in that they lead nowhere, but in form they are perfect. From the summits of the staircases you look back down a cascade of right-angles. The entrance is a geometrical ravine.' Wolgast paused, relishing his own utterance. 'Statues might adorn each step, gigantic figures of gods and immortals: Alexander, Caesar, Hector, Belisarius, the whole heroic cabal. On the walls we hang fantasies of the sort with which we habitually thrill ourselves: sea-storms, cavernous forests, rook-haunted ruins smothered in ivy, vast churches amid pines and snow, mad bards, orgiastic tyrants.' Narrowing his eyes lewdly, Wolgast gazed on an imagined bacchanal. 'We might display August Ettlinger's plans for a sublime city. I see a church with a dome one thousand feet high. There is a city gate, a library, a palace of justice, a stadium, an arch, a hall of assemblies, a temple of nature. Above all this, however, arrayed on the three highest tiers, triangulating the museum, is the celebration of warfare – the culmination of the project, its very *raison d'être*. Weapons shining like silver tableware, uniforms more colourful than any clown's apparel, dioramas of the battle of Issus, the glorious action at Thermopylae, the wounding of the museum's benefactor, Johann Friedrich von Wolgast,' – and here Wolgast stopped, for Ettlinger was leaning over the table and rearranging the books into three straight stacks.

'I have no interest in this,' said Ettlinger, in a voice that quavered. 'You know. You know,' he repeated, feeling his composure break. Looking away from Wolgast, he calmly stated – 'You have lied.'

'"You have lied,"' quoted Wolgast. 'I have lied. I shall not argue with you. Indubitably this is so. We have all lied. I see no matter for discussion.' He selected a book from the middle of the middle pile and perused its spine as if intrigued by the title.

Ettlinger removed the book from Wolgast's hand and let it fall to the floor. Glancing first at the book and then at Ettlinger, Wolgast looked helpless and saddened, like a boy rebuked by its parent for an unknown misdemeanour. Only then did it become obvious to Ettlinger that Wolgast was drunk.

'Siegmund Mölck. Why did you lie about him?' demanded Ettlinger.

'It is so vulgar to boast of one's philanthropy,' countered Wolgast, with patrician facetiousness.

'But he was in no way associated with that family,' Ettlinger responded.

A deep perplexity contorted Wolgast's brow and mouth.

'The Davringhausen family,' Ettlinger clarified needlessly. He felt his throat constrict at the word, and then came a sense of his unpreparedness, of his having arrived too soon at the moment of crisis.

'Your wan infatuation might benefit, I thought, from the introduction of an element of the tragic,' Wolgast continued, toying with the cruciform medal. 'My invention did imbue your lady with a certain nobility, did it not? It gave you pleasure, did it not?' He unpinned the medal and tossed it across the floor; it chinked against one of the overturned bottles. 'So easily impressed, August. So,' – his fingers made moulding movements in the air – 'so eager to be impressed.' Commiseratingly he placed his left hand on Ettlinger's, and Ettlinger pulled his arm away as if from a brand. 'For instance,' continued Wolgast, 'all that nonsense with the poisoned girl and her suspicious, grieving father. My supportive medical colleagues. A fiction, a transparent and tawdry fiction. But you were so willing to believe it.'

'I was not,' snapped Ettlinger, 'and did not.'

'Oh? In that case please accept my apology. My mistake,' drawled Wolgast. 'Let us say then that it sufficed, no more than that. I am content if my lies are sufficient to the day. I make things up to make the world more to my liking. To amuse myself and my audiences. You and your priggish young colleagues were once or twice quite taken with my tales.' His gaze wandered indifferently across the ceiling, advertising the factitiousness of his reasoning.

'Why Helene?' Ettlinger asked. As he spoke he detected a tang of salt in his nostrils.

'Why Helene what?' mocked Wolgast, blinking rapidly.

'I have seen her. I have seen the paintings – your paintings, the pictures made by that mercenary.'

Wolgast shifted in his seat so as to confront Ettlinger squarely. He scratched his scalp and brushed his hair flat with a palm. 'Lizius?'

'Lizius.'

'I congratulate you,' said Wolgast, examining Ettlinger's face with judicial thoroughness. 'You have worked quickly. I am proud of you.' A yawn made his lips quiver, and he ground the knuckles of his forefingers against his eyelids. 'Yes, I congratulate you,' repeated Wolgast, making the sentence sound like a challenge.

'So, why?' Ettlinger insisted, grasping the corners of the table and making it shake.

Untouched by Ettlinger's anger, Wolgast casually surveyed the bookshelves to his left, then those to his right. His gaze meandered back and forth from section to section, as though he had been asked to wait there for someone in whom he had scarcely any interest. Ettlinger swept an arm across the table, sending most of the books to the floor. 'One might say it was a project,' Wolgast was thus prompted into saying. 'Another means of maintaining an interest in the world. I asked myself if it might be possible to attract this remarkable woman.' He lifted his hands from his lap and looked up through the space between them in an attitude of veneration. 'It proved possible,' he added, and gave himself an interval of salacious recollection.

Ettlinger straightened and held his jaw with one hand as though to silence himself.

Wolgast continued, still smiling at his open palm as if at a mirror – 'And that dismayed me. In this instance I should have preferred to fail.' Fingertip to fingertip, his hands formed a cage of arches on the table-top. 'This I attribute to an intermittent craving for the metaphysical, a craving of which I have striven to rid myself, in vain.' His fingers sprang apart, and trembled for a moment, tense as guy-ropes.

'And having achieved – ' Ettlinger began, but could not finish his question.

'Having achieved the seduction – is that what you were trying to say? Well, let us express it thus to spare your feelings. Having achieved the seduction, I found that my love expired, just like a flame slammed out, so – ' and Wolgast smacked the back of a hand in cheerful demonstration. 'It is too often like this. You are familiar with the feeling of self-loathing of the post-climactic male? Perhaps not. Well, what I suffer from is an omniverous loathing, swiftly succeeded, almost instantaneously succeeded, by a consciousness, a knowledge, of utter emptiness,' said Wolgast, sighing at the sorrow of it. 'I struggled on for a while, passionately impersonating myself, but she is a percipient young woman.'

Gulping as if in a suffocating gas, Ettlinger stepped

back from the table. A looseness spread through his body, slackening the ligaments of his limbs; everything within his vision quaked slightly – everything except the seated figure of Wolgast, who was stroking the velvet of his sleeves, caressing his own arm repeatedly as though in appreciation of his attire.

'And then, of course, calamity,' Wolgast muttered. 'The unwanted heir. There were arguments, scenes of great discord. And in the end I saw that the outcome was not without its poetry. I had created a child for whom I would be an unknown figure. I would be the mysterious progenitor, a focus of hatred and terror perhaps. A veritable deity. This affair might be my apotheosis,' Wolgast cried, his eyes wide in exultation.

'What you have done is unforgivable,' Ettlinger pronounced, glaring into Wolgast's vacant eyes. 'You lie so thoroughly one would think that the truth had once scalded your tongue. You are a scandal. A violation of nature. An abomination.'

'"Mystery, Babylon the great, the father of harlots and abominations of the earth,"' replied Wolgast, as if correcting an error in Ettlinger's speech. He laughed, and his laugh became instantly a facial spasm that expelled a dash of oatmeal-coloured vomit from the corner of his mouth, spattering his cuff. Wolgast looked down and murmured, 'You are an idiot, Ettlinger. This is all nonsense, you know. What I have just said is nonsense.'

Wolgast sat upright in his chair, sniffed, and crossed his arms tightly across his chest. Speaking clearly, evenly, as if by will he had cast aside his inebriation, he told Ettlinger: 'It is what you expect of me. It is in character. The notion suddenly appeared in my mind, and I gave voice to it because it was fitting.' Wolgast insulted Ettlinger with a simpleton's smile. 'She is comely,' he wheedled at him. 'Have you ever seen a face, a body more beautiful?' He turned his face towards the window above Ettlinger's head, tightening his eyelids against the light. In the trough of his scar the flow of blood made the fragile skin move like the husk of a chrysalis. 'The flesh is all there is, and that is enough,' he told the room in a devotional whisper. His lips formed the words with the self-satisfaction of a wine connoisseur.

'One two, one two, one two,' chanted Wolgast in ridicule as Ettlinger strode across the library to the place behind the door where the épée hung. Ettlinger wrenched the sword from its hook and returned to Wolgast's side, holding the blade upright as if in salute.

'Oh, I am redeemed,' exclaimed Wolgast, placing an effeminate hand upon the medals on his breast. 'Amfortas is redeemed by wee Parsifal and his magic spear.'

Ettlinger placed the point of the blade on Wolgast's cravat, and worked aside the fabric to reveal the skin. 'You put the spear to the scar, not to the throat,' Wolgast told him, folding his arms again. 'The never-healing wound of Amfortas.'

'No,' replied Ettlinger, 'this is right.' He touched the blade to Wolgast's throat and turned it slightly. The point twisted the skin but did not break it.

The pupils of Wolgast's eyes were pulsing and he smiled in a way that seemed ecstatic. Quickly he brought his hands together in his lap and shook them as if in excitement. '"How good it feels to be so determined,"' he sang out, in a prancing, precious tone. At this he raised his right hand, placed the pad of his thumb against the blade, and wiped it swiftly along its edge. A rivulet of blood descended the blade, filling the scrolls of the manufacturer's legend, and dripped onto Wolgast's thigh. Wolgast regarded the stain with a flicker of his eyes, as a nervous guest might look at the crumbs he has dropped into his lap from the table of his punctilious host. '"Mourn then nature, for your son and friend and lover is at his end,"' quoted Wolgast, and for a moment he closed his eyes, peacefully as a man in solitary thought.

Then his eyelids sprang open like fledglings' beaks, and he looked at Ettlinger more intensely than he had ever looked at him before. Fierce contempt was all there was in the beginning of it, but within seconds an inflexion of his gaze occurred, a look that seemed imploring, into which was mingled, momentarily, an expression of voluptuous surrender. Leaning on the pommel, Ettlinger pushed the swordblade through Wolgast's throat.

There was no cry from Wolgast but instead a sound like the in-stroke of a bellows, and then a pop as the blade punctured the leather of the chair. Wolgast's eyes swelled as if in fury rather than in pain. His body bucked in the chair, and his hands flew up to grasp the blade as Ettlinger drew it out. The wound released a spurt of blood, like a mouth spitting a foul-tasting liquid.

Ettlinger ran from the room. He pressed his back to the closed door of the library. Behind him, Wolgast let out a noise that was more a bull's roar than a voice; he roared again, and a third time, and there seemed to be no word within the noise he made. Wood splintered and books clattered, and again Wolgast cried out, but this time he shrieked, as if an object of crushing weight had struck him. Ettlinger heard glass crack, and that was the final sound.

Warily Ettlinger opened the door. Wolgast had fallen on the lectern at which he had used to read, and toppled it onto the windowsill. His right arm had been pushed through the pane; his left was tangled in the struts of the lectern, and in his left hand he grasped the two medals he had torn from his jacket. Ettlinger bent over the body. The wound that he had inflicted had become wider and irregular, and the fingers of Wolgast's right hand were covered in blood. There appeared in Ettlinger's mind the gash in Christ's side and the probing fingers of Thomas, and then he saw that Wolgast was not yet dead. His mouth was moving like the mouth of a landed fish, breathing blooms of moisture onto the broken pane. Ettlinger knelt beside the dying man. Wolgast's eyes were directed at the sky; they were closing drowsily, but pulled back once, as far as they would go, as if he had just understood that this sky, with its clouds slipping from view like melting snow from a roof, was to be the last thing he would see. Blown by the breeze from the courtyard, the eyelashes stirred slightly. A breath, brief and shallow, escaped the unmoving lips; it was like the sound someone might make on completing satisfactorily a testing piece of work. A drop of water split on the bridge of Wolgast's nose. It was then that Ettlinger realised he was weeping.

He pulled the body onto the floor and righted the lectern. He sat below the window, his legs bridging the track of blood, his feet touching Wolgast's shoulder.

Five o'clock struck, and he could not think what he should do; it was dark before he rose. He ascended the silent stairs and passed down the corridor to the anatomy room. On the white table he laid out the saws and knives, the cleavers and hammers that he found in the cabinets. Listlessly he lifted them one by one, and tried to picture himself on the muddy banks of the Isar, consigning the limbs of Wolgast to the water. He went back into the library, where he lifted from the shelves some of the books he had studied there. Two hours after the murder, Ettlinger left the house of Johann Friedrich von Wolgast, carrying the books and a miscellany of papers from the room in which they had first conversed. By ten o'clock he had negotiated the purchase of the horse that was to carry him south from Munich that night.

59.

Through the gaps between his fingers Ettlinger looks down on the pages that are pressed onto his desk by his elbows. The book, formerly lodged in Wolgast's library, is an album of the buildings of Munich. On the left-hand page is an engraving of the Residenz, on the right a view of the palace's Schatzkammer. He has written nothing in the past hour, and has not been looking at the picture for almost as long, though it was for the book that he left his writing. His eyes follow the intricate lines of the pictures as if they were the meaningless cross-hatchings on the skin of his hands. His gaze drifts, seeing nothing but the traces of the burin. He becomes conscious of a low moaning sound in the room, and then realises that it comes from his own throat, and that his face, lying heavily on his palms, has taken on a grimace of a man in despair. In the next moment a profound unhappiness, the misery of the prisoner who has been sundered from his home for ever, drenches him. It is as if a mask of dejection had extruded its own muscle and blood, pushing its fibres, root-like, into those of his body.

He rises and pulls open the door. The sky lies on the island and its waters like an iron lid, and there is no telling how far the day has waned. The finches in the olive tree are not singing, a sign that a storm is imminent. The horizon of the sludge-like sea is tethered loosely to the clouds by threads of falling rain. A sigh passes over the land and the olive trembles in a breeze that scurries a few patches of sandy earth. Announced by the flat clang of its bell, a goat appears on a hillock close to the path that leads to the ruins. It stands its ground and grinds its jaws and stares at Ettlinger with eyes that are not those of a living animal. Overpowered by futility, he picks up a stone and throws it. The goat springs back at the crack of the stone against the bare rock, then slowly walks away. The finches scuffle among the leaves of the olive tree. There is not a single sail on the sea.

Ettlinger slumbers at his desk, his head on his arms and his arms crossed over his manuscripts. He is roused by the clatter of logs dislodged from the woodpile. It is night now and the storm has arrived. The wind is howling as if in exclamation at its own strength. Water slaps the ground under the eaves; it is seeping through the planks of the walls. He opens the door for an instant and sees the moon flash under the slanting rain. He places a hand in the cascade that falls across the doorway, and wipes his brow with the water.

As if instructed by the heroic protestations of the heavens he resumes the story of his exile. Crouching under the candle's flame he writes: 'The murderer's passage of the Alps, so terrifying in prospect, proved less difficult than the leaving of Munich. Within one week he was in a foreign land.' In search of the continuation he looks up from the page, and the flickering light shows him the portrait of Helene. He cannot write another word of the narrative, but it is essential that he write, for despondency will follow the cessation of his work as surely as the extinction of the candle will admit the darkness. Ettlinger takes up another piece of paper and writes: 'My dear Wolfgang.' Again his attention leaves the page. He decides that this night shall be his last in this room.

60.

Here, on the eastern coast, is where the lagoon was created.

One afternoon, on the cusp of summer and autumn, the emperor led a train of courtiers down to this bay, where the arc of the cliffs and the slope of the sea bed combined to shepherd the water onto the shore in wide, low ripples. He commanded us to remain where he had stopped us, and set off alone along the sand. He walked with his shoulders hunched and his head lowered, as if concentrating on the impression of his feet on the humid sand. At the farthest point of the bay, where a buttress of pitted black rock ran far into the sea, the emperor turned to his right and, brushing the rock with his fingertips, walked down to the water's edge. Standing on a spot where his feet were dabbed by the froth of the spent waves, he crooked his neck to face inland and appeared to be listening to the sea, as he would listen to the whispering of a petitioner. Once or twice he looked across the bay, shielding his eyes from the hazy sun. Beyond the thin parabolas of the surf, beyond the seal-coloured swells of the open water, the remote mountains of the mainland appeared not as a body of land but as the thickened meniscus of the sea.

A wall of boulders was soon joined to the wall of black rock, forming a barrier that was perfect but for the narrow channel by which the tides were allowed to replenish the waters of the new lagoon. In the lee of the natural rock we raised the belvedere, a squat cylindrical building, scarcely taller than a man seated upon another's shoulders. A roofless structure, it contained nothing but a wooden ladder and a circular wooden bench affixed just below the level of the parapet. Here the emperor passed many days.

In the shadow of the belvedere all reflections were obliterated from the water's surface, opening a view to the floor of the captive sea. Through the pellucid liquid moved fish like splinters of precious stone or supple blades of steel. One saw featureless creatures that resembled pieces of floating fat, some of them adorned with fringes of pink tendrils. Pleated weeds, erect like purple fans, waved in a slow breeze of water. Around their roots scuttled crabs with roseate shells and others that were the colour of kelp. Animals created in the likeness of animated stones shifted under the sand, raising a spume of ochre ink.

Ceaselessly through day and night the sea clapped against the outward face of the barricade, but rarely did it cause anything but the slightest disturbance within. The winds that chopped the surface of the sea into chunks of obsidian barely perturbed the surface of the lagoon. Through every season its placidity was constant, as was the perfume of its air. The lagoon's own atmosphere possessed a savour of sweet salinity, like that of the oil of the finest olives.

The route of my flight brought me here, many days after the siege. Under the blank sky of winter, the lagoon was a pool of black wax; I paused on the brink of the water and recalled the lagoon as it was in the light of the naked sun, shining like a plate of new brass. I looked at the ruin of the belvedere, and saw on the seawall below it a growth of purple moss. The moss was revealed, as I walked out along the wall, to be the sodden cloak of Darius. The boy lay on the floor of the lagoon, a stone crammed into his mouth and a spear through his belly. In one eye socket an anemone winked onto its food; thick green fronds were entwined around the peeled femurs, and a section of bared skull was scabbed with limpets. I saw an eel flicker through a hole in the flesh above the hip, nudging loose a bread-coloured piece of tissue, which drifted away, chased by a shoal of tiny silver fish.

I heaped some fragments of the belvedere to make a bench, and on this I sat, and looked out across the sea. The day was almost over, and the shadow of the land lay upon the gulf, making of it a pavement of battered iron. Behind me the slothful clouds were coming apart on the ridgelines of the distant mountains. I imagined the end of Xerxes.

The Residence is aflame, and all its occupants are slain

or have fled. The emperor watches the horsemen as they prance through the rubble, stirring the dead with their lances. Flaxen-haired men emerge from the atrium: one holds a tourmaline ewer, another a pair of silver candlesticks, a third bears a golden head and wears a crown encrusted with jewels of coloured glass. Through a breach in the wall of the Court of the Fountains, the emperor sees an archer carrying a block of ice as if it were a casket of ransom money.

Xerxes departs, to ascend the track that follows the Valley of the Sun. In a leather sack he carries the regalia in which, many years ago, he was crowned: the jasper rings, the mace, the filigree crown, the scapular of damask, the voluminous cape of purple silk, stitched with small pearls.

The barbarians send riders across the mountains. They search every valley, every cave. They burn all the vessels in the harbour and sift the wreckage of the Residence. For a month fruitlessly they roam the plains, and at last they gallop away, having never found the emperor.

I pictured a golden throne set upon the summit of a mountain. Around it I saw drifts of small grey stones, shattered by centuries of nightly frost and noonday heat. I imagined the apotheosis of Xerxes. I saw the crown slipped askew on his skull, the creases of his cape sprinkled with tiny bones. I could hear the wind whistling in his ribs and teeth. I could see him grinning at the rising sun.

61.

August Ettlinger began his return to Germany on the twenty-eighth of June 1827.

The first stage of the voyage was to have taken him

to Gibraltar on board the vessel of a timber merchant, but five days out, suffering a resurgence of his fever, he was put ashore in Malta. He passed a month in dusty Rabat, tended by a young Dutch woman who had come to the island of St Paul in the last months of her novitiate, and there, in her airless hovel of a cell, had lost her vocation. Nursing was now her calling, and it had brought her the devotion of a husband whose life she had preserved after he had fallen from the roof of her convent while replacing its tiles. Berthe prepared milky poultices for the traveller, and Dom laid them on his brow with the gravity of a man placing votive offerings on the altar of a God who had never failed him.

In his last week on the island Ettlinger made notes at the temples of Tarxien and drew sketches of a pregnant goddess with hips as broad as his bed. In the subterranean chambers at Paola he extinguished the candle he was carrying and murmured the name of Johann Friedrich von Wolgast into a niche in the walls. The words reverberated through the cave and soaked away into the rock. The following morning, in the silent main square of Rabat, he shook Berthe's hand and embraced her husband in farewell; she rubbed the tears from his cheek with maternal vigour, and pushed him lightly towards the waiting cart.

It took but half a day to find a berth at Valletta, whence he made a placid crossing to Marseille. There he disembarked and soon transferred to a boat bound for Lisbon, where for a week he was broiled in a room right under the eaves of a hotel that no breeze ever seemed to reach. From Lisbon he escaped to Bordeaux, a swift and tranquil sailing until the day the port came into view, whereupon the Atlantic, as if in a contrary humour, began to frisk and roll. The wind changed its direction with every hour, and the harbour came no closer. Nesting amid coils of rope in the stern of the ship, he suffered a seasickness so acute he feared it was the beginning of another fever.

When at last he disembarked he took a room for a month in the first hotel he happened upon, the Garonne. There he fell in with a fellow guest, an Irish wine dealer from London by the name of James O'Connor, who had interests in a local vineyard. An accommodating and easy companion, O'Connor was of equable temperament and medium stature, thoroughly unremarkable in appearance but for one feature – his right eyebrow was fixed in a steep arch, as though his extraordinary good fortune in making so much money from an occupation that afforded him so much enjoyment had left him perpetually quizzical about the mechanisms of fate. He spoke German that was more than acceptable, and more proficient than Ettlinger's English, though his manner of speaking it was strange, for he had a habit of rushing at the end of his sentences like a tightrope-walker dashing to the safety of his platform. On some thirty consecutive evenings they ate their supper together, shared a bottle of wine, strolled along the harbourside, all the while conversing in a manner that maintained a relaxed familiarity without once requiring Ettlinger to reveal anything of any significance concerning himself. Easing him into the future, setting him adrift from his history, the friendship with the gregarious O'Connor seemed at times a proof of divine ministration. It was with a sense of gratitude that Ettlinger left Bordeaux in the second week of October, on board a London-bound vessel leased by one of O'Connor's numerous associates.

After a few days in expensive and cramped lodgings in the St James's area of the British capital, Ettlinger abandoned the centre of the city and took a room in Greenwich, close to the river and within sight of the observatory. He made enquiries as to where he might procure the services of a clerk to transcribe into copperplate script a German text that was in his possession. An acquaintance of his landlord directed him to a lawyer's office behind the grim church of St Alfege, and there he commissioned Mr Horace Turner, son of Mr Theobold Turner and his wife Cornelia Turner, née Hoerle, to make a copy of his manuscript. A week later, the immaculate object was ready; Ettlinger sat in the adjacent cubicle as Horace, for no extra charge, applied to a topsheet of crisp white paper the single word 'Xerxes', in a hand that evoked straining sails and ropes.

Before wrapping the copy, Ettlinger composed a letter to accompany it.

My dear Wolfgang,
Should you have any use for this, please use it. Any phrases you might like to employ, feel free to plunder them. I have no more claim to these pages than a dead man has on his bones. Take this as my apology for my perfunctory contributions to our gatherings, which I frequently recall with affection, even though we were often ridiculous. Should you find these fragments

and scenes absurd, throw them onto a fire without a second thought. I want to be rid of them, as I wish to rid myself once and for all of Johann Friedrich von Wolgast. I am sure there are other reasons for sending my little word-building to you. Perhaps I hope it is an appropriate way of rounding off the story of our friendship. If I have failed, forgive me. I have been a dilettante in everything I have done, but for one decisive act, and my love of Helene von Davringhausen.

Since the afternoon I first saw her, in the garden at Nymphenburg, there has not been a day on which I have not recalled her face as it appeared that afternoon, turned into the sun, looking over the water, away from me. She no more knew the profundity of my devotion to her than did you or any of our friends, but I am certain she detected at once that there was a flimsiness to my character. She found my seriousness too much a matter of will, too strained and too consistent, and her judgement of me was just. I hope that she will be happy, and that you too will enjoy success. I shall return to my homeland before this year is out, but I shall not return to Munich nor to any place near the city in which the matter of my life was determined. Is this cowardice? I should like to think not. Rather it is pride, for I regard myself as an innocent man.

Might this confession make you despise me, if you do not do so already? I regret many things, but I do not regret the murder of Wolgast, neither do I regret seeking refuge. Helene is entitled to pronounce sentence upon me, but the law is not. I recall that on one occasion, a rare occasion, I took issue with Wolgast, and rebutted him with the words – 'Only the law can give us freedom.' Now I find myself at odds with myself, and in agreement with Wolgast. At this moment I can hear your voice. You are telling me that I have become a sophist. It gives me great joy to imagine the sound of your voice, and great pain to think that I shall only ever hear it now in the attenuated tones of memory.

Within the hour the manuscript was dispatched. The following year, a literary magazine in Zürich published Wolfgang von Klostermann's *The Ruins of Persepolis*, a 'poetic vision in prose', in which pieces of his erstwhile friend's manuscript were embedded, without acknowledgement.

Ettlinger stayed for almost a year in London, earning a modest income by providing translations for scholars, lawyers and merchants. For a while he also gave tuition in history and art to the daughters of a Greenwich man who had become rich through the manufacture of bricks, and was now investing much of his capital in the refinement of the manners and education of his family. When it became clear to Ettlinger that he was being assessed by the father as a potential addition to that family, he made his plans to move on from London. One November morning he stepped onto a Deptford barge in a sea-mist so dense that nothing of the city, not even the pavement on which his baggage was being stacked, was visible from the deck. The next solid ground he saw was a wharf at Hamburg.

Seeking obscurity, he settled in a town in the province of that great city. There, assuming the name of Lothar Seidl once again, he invented for himself a previous life as an itinerant printer. He became the orphan of a Potsdam-born military engineer who had given his life in the Prussian war of liberation; his mother had not survived his birth; he now had no family, and it pained him to discuss his origins and the brief lives of his parents. He had left his native country for France, where he had worked for several years in a Bordeaux printshop. The skills he had acquired there had enabled him to travel widely, and he spoke fondly of his years in Munich and, in particular, London, where a certain Mr O'Connor had treated him with a kindness he would never forget.

Lothar Seidl gained employment first as an underling in the workshop of a printer of naval charts and plans. While inking plates and hanging paper he carefully observed every process from engraving to publication, and thereby acquired a theoretical knowledge of the things he was supposed to have mastered long before. It was a knowledge he was never required to prove. His next position was as an archivist at the town hall, an undemanding post at which he remained for two years.

Then, three years after his return to Germany, the peregrination of August Ettlinger came to its conclusion when he moved to Hamburg itself. There he became the librarian of a wealthy, unambitious and febrile clergyman, a bibliophile and amateur scholar of architecture who was delighted to find in Seidl an assistant whose unassuming manner camouflaged a knowledge of the noblest art that almost equalled his own. Licensed to spend a sum far in excess of his own salary on the acquisition of fine books, Seidl passed his days happily in the company of booksellers, auctioneers and the executors of estates, or at his desk in the cosy cork-lined library. Precisely one year after taking up this appointment, Seidl married Eva Eichner, the only daughter of a local brewer. It was an affectionate marriage, and it produced four children – Heinz-Friedrich, Gottfried, Wilhelm (who lived but a short time beyond his fourth birthday) and Elisabeth.

August Ettlinger returned to Munich once, in October of 1858. His employer had died in 1856, and had left him one half of the proceeds from the dispersal of his library, with which 'the indefatigable and most trustworthy Lothar Seidl' was charged. Despite its financial necessity, it was with heavy reluctance that Seidl organised the sale of the books he had so diligently purchased and catalogued, and though the sum that he received from it was substantial, the contentment it brought him was brief. Within twenty months he was in mourning for Eva. Her decease made the occupation of his own house an agony to him. Alone in the silent rooms, he heard the echo of her breathing in their quietness. The objects Ettlinger and his wife had used each day suddenly seemed alien, almost hostile in their inertness, as if only through her touch could they regain their utility. Hour after hour Ettlinger stroked the clothing she would never wear again.

Not knowing what else to do, he eventually journeyed to Munich, where he found a room overlooking the Englischer Garten. The first day established a routine from which he was never to deviate during the fortnight he spent in the city. At eight o'clock he took breakfast at his hotel; at nine he set off on a long walk in the Englischer Garten, then returned for lunch in the hotel; in the afternoon, after a nap, he walked into the centre of the city, meandering without purpose but always passing the Isartor, the Viktualienmarkt and the Residenz, a building transfigured since his youth. He would punctuate his afternoon ramble with a cup of coffee at four o'clock, then wander for a couple of hours and be back in his room by seven. He ate at nine, read for an hour, and slept soundly. He felt no attachment to anything he saw, nor even revisited the street in which he had lived. Gazing coldly at a street-corner where once he and Wolfgang Klostermann had found a torn love letter discarded in the mud, he gained a bleak satisfaction in the insensibility that his grief conferred upon him.

At 3.20 p.m. on the fourteenth of October, on Marienplatz, August Ettlinger saw Helene von Davringhausen again. It was the style of her stride, at once graceful and suggestive of dauntlessness, that made him single her out from the other strollers. His attention thus caught, all the singular details of her form appeared to him again, unchanged. The ermine collar of her coat pushed up the coils of her hair, and the sheen of those coils and the angle of her head were exactly what he had seen at Nymphenburg, the first time he had set eyes on her. He shivered at the recollection of the indifference with which those dark eyes had looked at him, and yet the late sunlight on Marienplatz seemed to take on something of the jubilance of that bright afternoon, and he felt again the proximity of a new and different life. And then it came to him, with the same slow-dawning dejection as he experienced each morning as the contours of his hotel room solidified out of sleep, that some three decades had passed since then. The woman at whom he was looking was Helene's daughter. The grey-haired woman walking silently beside her, with her arms crossed and her head lowered, as if to deflect the attention of any bypassers, was Helene herself.

Ettlinger followed them to a market stall. He watched Helene break off a crumb of marzipan and taste it, and though the skin about her mouth now bore the lines of age, they were still the lips that had blown the dust from her palm as her brothers approached. Ettlinger looked back to the daughter, and found nothing of Wolgast in her features. He stood at the neighbouring stall, balancing a wooden mannequin on his palm, looking over its head at Helene. In his memory he turned his back on the room in which Wolgast was playing dementedly, and followed Helene. He saw that she was wearing, on the lapel of her coat, the silver owl he had given her. There rose before him the possibility that her wearing of this gift betokened the gravest error of his life. Had he stayed in Nürnberg for longer, had he spoken to her more directly, had he been more courageous, what might have happened? Guiltily he suppressed the thought, and fixed his eyes on the toy in his hand.

So intently did he stare at it that he did not hear the stallkeeper's question as anything more than a noise until it was repeated. 'Will you be buying it, sir?' he was asked. Helene's daughter, standing next to the stallkeeper, was looking at him with curiosity, as if he were a strangely attired tourist from abroad. Her mother, falling in with her daughter's gaze, turned to face Ettlinger. Their eyes met. Helene looked steadily at him, and nothing in her expression gave the slightest sign that she knew who he was. Her daughter slipped a hand into the crook of her elbow, and they walked away, in the direction of Marienplatz.

The next day Ettlinger left Munich, never to return. The rest of his life he devoted to the cultivation of forgetfulness and to the austere study of Bavaria's rococo architecture, a discipline he adopted principally because the subject aroused in him no passion at all. In 1872 he published a monograph on the church of Vierzehnheiligen, to some applause from his fellow scholars.

August Ettlinger died in February of 1875. He was buried beside his wife, but in his will he requested that his heart be placed in the cemetery at Ettal, a place with which he had 'ancestral connections'. None of his family could understand this clause, but ample funds had been bequeathed for its execution, and so the heart was removed from the body, and sealed inside an urn of porphyry. Of his children, only Elisabeth attended the ceremony in Ettal; both Heinz-Friedrich and Gottfried had taken offence at their father's withdrawal from their society in his bereavement, and were adamant that their filial duty had been fully honoured by their attendance at the interment in Hamburg. While Elisabeth travelled south to Bavaria, they remained at home, dividing the inheritance according to the instructions of the will.

On the day that Elisabeth had intended to depart from Ettal, she received a letter from her brothers. In their opening sentence they warned that its contents were 'shocking', that they were of the opinion that their father had posthumously disgraced them, that his modesty, his probity, his simplicity, were now as nothing. Papers had been discovered in a chest in the attic of the house in which they had been raised. It had been hidden beneath piles of the clothing they had worn as children. There were dozens of drawings in the chest: one of them was a defaced picture of a woman; there were two factory scenes; the rest were plans and elevations of buildings. Underneath these they found some tattered medical books and a crudely sketched map of an unnamed island. Right at the bottom of the chest, inside a neatly folded old frock coat, were discovered two mildewed manuscripts, both in their father's hand. One of these was the draft of, or notes for, some sort of exotic fantasy to which he would appear to have given the title 'Xerxes'. The other was a disjointed narrative concerning one August Ettlinger, the murderer of a certain Johann Friedrich von Wolgast, a dissipated and violent nobleman with whom Ettlinger had once been closely associated in Munich.

Why had Elisabeth been dispatched to Ettal? Had their father once known a character called August Ettlinger, a man to whom he was so attached that he had composed a memoir of him and stored souvenirs of his life? Of course not. There was only one tenable explanation. Lothar Seidl and August Ettlinger were the same person. Their father had been a liar and a murderer. To verify this inescapable conclusion, they required their sister to investigate the circumstances detailed in a lengthy addendum to their letter, in which they detailed the salient incidents in the narrative.

An unwilling accessory to slander, Elisabeth gave

a month to her brothers' mission. She found that a man by the name of Johann Friedrich von Wolgast had indeed lived in Munich earlier in the century. He had disappeared some fifty years ago; at exactly the same time a young architect by the name of August Ettlinger, described by a magistrate to whom she spoke as the protégé of Wolgast, had also disappeared. This Ettlinger had written to a friend, a member of the Klostermann family, confessing that he had killed Wolgast. Nothing more had ever been heard of him; it was believed that he had settled in England, and had become a seaman. A beautiful woman of the Davringhausen family was in some manner implicated in the story, but Elisabeth continued her enquiries no farther. What she had heard was enough to convince Heinz-Friedrich and Gottfried that their supposition was unassailable, and to allow them to dissociate themselves absolutely from their father, while allowing her to maintain the notion that the tangle of circumstances might permit some other resolution.

Seventy kilometres south of Munich, between Oberammergau and Garmisch, stands the Benedictine abbey of Ettal. The abbey was established in April of 1330, during the reign of Emperor Louis of Bavaria, but the complex that one sees today is of a much later date, for in 1744 a fire gutted the church, ruined its conventual buildings and obliterated the foundation's great library. Abbot Benedict Pacher raised funds from the families who had benefited from the education offered by the famous Ettal school, and from the pilgrims who came to Ettal to make obeisance to the abbey's miraculous statue of the Virgin. Under the supervision of the architect Joseph Schmuzer the abbey was rebuilt to a grandiose baroque design derived from the Roman church of Sant'Agnese in Agone. By the time of August Ettlinger's birth, the frescoed and stucco-laden church was receiving as many as seventy thousand pilgrims each year, but in 1822, following the secularisation of the abbey and its school, much of the complex was demolished. It is probable that it was some time in the last two decades of that century that the small basalt square marking the burial place of the heart of Lothar Seidl was lost. On the thirty-sixth page of a ledger in the abbey's archive one may verify that Seidl's burial took place at Ettal some seventy-five years after the christening of August Lorenz Albrecht Ettlinger, an event inscribed on the twenty-eighth page of the same ledger, six lines from the top.

The documentary record of the Gothic chapel designed by August Ettlinger is more tenuous than the record of his life. A letter written in May of 1837 by a certain Norbert von Reitzenstein contains a brief account of an 'ersatz church' which he ridicules as his 'great-uncle's folly' and the 'orphan of the pedantic Ettlinger'. From this letter it would appear that in 1837 some work was still required to finish the building, but ambiguities of phrasing make it impossible to ascertain exactly how far from completion it was. A page of the diary of Alphonse Minguet, a Parisian architect who, in 1908, undertook what he called his 'Bavarian pilgrimage', evokes a 'small ruin' that bears certain similarities to the structure mentioned by Reitzenstein. In particular, his observations on the carvings of the capitals and his celebration of the view from the chapel make it likely that he and Reitzenstein were describing the same chapel. Minguet's diary places the ruin on a hill between Munich and Freising, but it is not known exactly where it stood, for not so much as a stone of Ettlinger's solitary building has ever been discovered.

From the window of the room in which this book has been written I can see a bus carrying a party of tourists away from the abbey of Ettal. The tyres, glossy as anthracite, hiss upon the road; the engine heaves with the change of gear on the incline, and the bus is gone, leaving a silence from which emerges the whisper of rain. The air bears the vivifying fragrance of chlorophyll. Spills of rainwater are running down the patchwork bark of the plane tree below my window, giving it the appearance of a laminated map; droplets fall from the luminous leaves onto the saturated, closely mown grass. To the west, little clouds are moulting from the closest hill. The sun has just stamped a golden seal onto the pasture on the side of a distant mountain. From the shadows of the room behind me comes the voice of Fritz Wunderlich. He is singing the first aria of Handel's *Xerxes*, in which the king of Persia extols the paradisal shade of his favourite plane tree.

THE BIOGRAPHY OF THOMAS LANG

Jonathan Buckley

Elusive, arrogant, volatile, a genius certainly, Thomas Lang became the most admired classical pianist of his generation before he died mysteriously, probably by his own hand. Bit by bit, in volleys of letters between his would-be biographer and Lang's brother Christopher, his life is pieced together and the real Thomas Lang emerges.

'A multilayered and captivating book.'
DAILY TELEGRAPH

FICTION £6.99 1 85702 802 3